TOMORROW'S DEAD
THE JULIA POE VAMPIRE CHRONICLES

CELIS T. RONO

Cover Designed and Illustrated by Tariq Raheem http://www.tariqart.net

This book is a work of fiction. Any resemblance to actual events or persons, living or dead, is entirely coincidental.

"Tomorrow's Dead: The Julia Poe Vampire Chronicles," by Celis T. Rono. ISBN 978-1-62137-179-3 (Softcover) 978-1-62137-180-9 (eBook). Third printing.

Dedicated to Elvie Hawk and
Simon Garcia Kim

PROLOGUE

JUDGMENT AT NUREMBERG OR get-out-of-jail-free card? Such was the dilemma facing Kaleb Sainvire's skeleton crew of the resistance. The Gray Armageddon had choked the world and left only a few survivors, and powerful undead ancients edged out of hiding to reign for nearly 20 years. They herded and marked humans as cattle, drugged them with toxic bites, and harvested blood to feed the vampire population.

A year after permanently killing master vampires and removing despots from their lofty thrones, Kaleb Sainvire and his allies were left to mop up the mess in Los Angeles. Option one – kill vampires and the human leeches that committed crimes against humanity. Option two – pardon them. His main goal was to get Plasmacore, a manufactured blood alternative, in the hands of vampires in major cities around the country so they could release human cattle from captivity. This wasn't going to happen if he slaughtered vampires in his own city. Neither did he want to be a Mussolini or a Mao, butchering their own countrymen to supposedly disinfect the city.

Sainvire was well aware of history. Even though he was an American from Chicago, in the 1930s he had fought against the fascists in the Spanish Civil War in the 1930s. Stupidly he thought he could fight against Franco's regime, and for his effort a Spanish whore turned him into a vampire.

These days all he could think of was how to restore order and end violence without resorting to iron-fisted or Machiavellian tactics. And of course there was Julia Poe, whom he hadn't seen in months. An important figure in the release of cattle, she'd firmly decided to stay on Catalina Island and avoid returning to Downtown Los Angeles, a place of unrelenting nightmares for her. Because of Sainvire's impossible schedule he couldn't visit the only woman he'd ever loved. In his mind Poe didn't want to have anything to do with him, or perhaps the bullet she had received from master vampire Quillon Trench pierced not only her chest but her confidence. The small superhero, as many called her, was broken. The woman who was as responsible for the obliteration of the ancients and master vampires that had ruled the city with viciousness was a shell of her former indomitable self.

Sainvire sat in his spartan office at the old Biltmore Hotel in Downtown Los Angeles. He had dropped the trappings of extravagance of the vampires of old who lived in the best buildings. He conjured her face, marred with a five-inch scar that only added to her mystique. She was the most beautiful woman to him. He had never loved anyone so stridently, yet his work with Plasmacore and the cause always won out.

Sainvire ran fingers through his black hair and sighed. All he desired in life was to be alone with Poe and enjoy the smell of her, the taste of her. He wanted to take her away from the slime of politics and live with her and hold her close until old age took her away from him. Perhaps then he could end his own life.

He hoped for James Maclemar to persuade her to leave the island that shielded her fears. Even love for another man would have been better than her isolation and fear of the world.

CHAPTER 1

UNDULATING WINDS COURSED ALONG unrelenting rain that beat down on the inhabitants of the 22-mile-long, 8-mile-wide Santa Catalina Island. One human, a terrier, bison, and indigenous animals of the wild variety currently occupied the rocky land mass, once a favorite Southern California getaway.

The one human in three layers of thermal underwear, wool sweater, Dickies pants, rain slicker, and Wellington boots sat on the stump of an ironwood tree, watching a half-dozen bison munching on grass, not at all affected by the downpour. Windswept island oak and torrey pines camouflaged her small frame. She inhaled the tang of the ocean mixed with the clean scent of rain. Her dog, Penny, kept dry under an open umbrella and waited patiently for her friend to scrap the sightseeing and slink inside their dry cabin.

The young woman named Julia Poe observed the majestic creature 20 feet from where she sat and shuddered in wonder. No matter how many times she watched the non-native bison, her awe never seemed to subside. She had lived most of her life in a basement bunker, and nature was a marvel to her.

A movie production had brought the animals to the island in the 1920s, and they never left. They'd become tourist attractions, but the tourists had been unaware of the slow extermination of the majestic beasts as they crowded out native island species. Poe's shivering was incidental to the sight of a baby calf nudged by her mother to eat more grass. The scene reminded her of Piper, her goddaughter, and she felt a pang of guilt. She'd promised Megan, the child's mother, that she would look after Piper after her death. Instead she accepted a solitary life. She failed in her duties like she had failed in many things.

"I told you to stay home, Pen," she said in a husky voice unbefitting her youth. "You know shivering like that is an easy way to pump up the guilt." She glanced at the miserable-looking dog and sighed. Her one true companion was getting on in age. Penny had slowed down, and her hearing hadn't been the same. The dog's sense of smell remained strong, however, as proven by her tracking skills when it came to island foxes and mule deer.

There was nothing she wouldn't do for her dog. The thought of Penny's waning days always brought tears to her eyes. *I don't know what I'd do without you, old pal.*

Poe had hiked the hills and camped the length of the island the past year and a half, hoping to find solace from plagued memories that still fueled nightmares. Nature soothed some of her cares, and she stayed outdoors as much as possible. However, sometimes the silence bothered her. There was a time when the voices of Sister Ann, her parents, and Goss, whether real or imaginary, would enter her mind and advise her where to aim her gun or what to do next. They had all left her head, never to be heard from again, when Trench enslaved and tortured her. She knew then that she was on her own.

"Let's go then, Pen. I'm pretty damn cold myself." As she reached under the umbrella to pet her dog, Penny emitted guttural noises only a tongueless dog could make. The girl had heard the twigs snap, too. Someone was on her island. She reached under her rain jacket and pulled out a Blackhawk .45 Colt just moments before a looming presence appeared a few yards behind them near the oak trees. Without thinking, she fired six shots in succession in the direction of the enemy. The bison scampered away from the unnatural blast of bullets. Poe was as startled by the booming sounds. It had been a while since she'd fired a weapon.

"What the—! Sharren, don't shoot! It's me, James." The man's accented voice sounded like a croak. The large man was hiding behind a young oak that barely covered half of his body.

"Oh shit. I'm so sorry!" cried the girl.

"Dammit, Poe! You don't wait to know who's around? You just shoot them dead?"

"I'm really sorry," Poe said, her voice nearly breaking. Maclemar was a dear and loyal friend, and if Poe had killed him, she never would've forgiven herself. The tall man wearing blue rain slickers approached her. "It's fine, Poe. Next time look first." He didn't like the defeat in her voice and the shame in her brown eyes.

Visibly shaken, Poe, the one-time feared Public Enemy Number Two, allowed James Maclemar to take her trembling hand. Without saying a word, the two humans and Penny climbed a hill to Poe's cabin. The vacation home was a small wooden cottage with two rooms, a bathroom, and a tiny kitchen. Poe could've chosen a more spacious home, but she wanted to be near the docking area to see the comings and goings on her island.

James Maclemar switched on the lights in the cabin, but they didn't turn on. "Must be a short," he said mostly to himself. He helped Poe with her raincoat and hung it on the door peg. He slid out of his, clapped his hands, and rubbed them for warmth. The cottage was arctic. No piled logs could be found on the porch, and Maclemar had no choice but to stomp on an old rocking chair until he had an armful of wood. He crossed the room, piled pieces of the rocking chair into the fireplace, and lit them.

"Give it 10 minutes, love, and we'll get you warm and toasty." Looking shamefaced, Poe still stood by the door. "Ah, Poe, no need to look like that, or I'm going to drown you in a barrel of ale with the kittens." He held out his arms, and she went to him reluctantly. The feel of her friend's strong arms reminded her how long she'd been without his company. Three months and six days.

Maclemar was the only one who made the effort to see her at all. Not even Kaleb Sainvire had visited her since he left the island 18 months ago.

"You're lucky I'm not a sure shot anymore," she said, her voice extremely still.

"You told me so last time I was here. I didn't believe it. Saying you're the best shot in our shoddy world would be an understatement."

"Not anymore. I've lost the one questionable talent I had. I fired six rounds, and I should've plugged you good. But I missed."

"You sound sorry you didn't make Swiss cheese out of me," he said. He ran his hand lightly over her back.

"You're my only friend now. Why would I want to turn you into cheese?"

"Ah, sharren. You have many friends, but now they're busy laying down the foundation for a better city which includes vampires and humans alike. That's not a simple feat." Maclemar nicknamed Poe "sharren" for in Welsh it meant a woman who thought she was tough.

"Yeah, well they got stuff to do. So do I. I hope you're not here to convince me to go back with you again," she grunted. She pulled away from his embrace and kicked off her Wellingtons. Penny was already sitting on her hunches by the fire.

"Why don't we talk about it after dinner, eh? I brought seaweed, shellfish, and goodies for my famous seafood porridge. Take a hot bath while I prepare the best meal you've had since last time I was here." He ran his hand in his dark, buzzed hair as his deep green eyes followed Poe's every movement.

Poe smiled for the first time. "Must be a stiff decree from Sainvire to send you all the way here in rainy season. He'll get the usual no from me." She cut Maclemar off before he opened his mouth. "I haven't had hot water in two months. No electricity. I'm going to have to heat up some water on the grill outside."

Maclemar seethed with anger directed at himself. Poe had been living without heat or electricity since he'd left, and her rough lifestyle made him feel like a heel. "I'll take care of it, sweetheart." He grabbed a tool box from under the kitchen sink and put on his rain slicker.

Maclemar, an exceptional mechanic and repairman, went outside to have a go at the generator. "Poor girl," he whispered to himself. Pain suddenly inflamed his entire body. The woman he loved had turned into a fearful hermit. She'd been so magnificent once, destroying Revenents and vampires with her eyes closed. There hadn't been anyone like her with her fierce fighting skills and tenacious love for her friends. He recalled the girl running through an ocean of Revenents, non-sentient walking dead that could reform broken bones to repeatedly attack, to rescue Michelle and him. Without pause for her safety, Poe had tried to reach the farmhouse where the last of the fighters holed up to protect Megan who was dying from childbirth. Trench's henchmen outnumbered her friends.

Her legend had grown on the mainland. She had rescued hundreds of cattle and protected revolutionaries fighting against Trench, master vampires, and Vampire Council members who had been angling to keeping human slavery alive for their bloated self-interests. The city needed Poe. A symbol of hope. Sainvire had asked him to deliver a letter and convince Poe that she was needed back Downtown.

"No matter how much she refuses, you've got to get her back to L.A.," instructed Kaleb Sainvire before Maclemar left. The vampire's hair had grown to the nape of his neck and stubbles freckled his face. The man responsible for distributing Plasmacore was neck-deep trying to keep Downtown and its residents afloat without a return to violence.

"I'll try my best, Kaleb," said Maclemar.

Sainvire's gray eyes bore into his green ones. "Don't try, my friend. You have to do it. I don't care if you have to hogtie her in your boat."

Maclemar didn't envy Sainvire's task. Being an idealist could kill a vampire.

———————

Clutter spread over the kitchen sink and dining table. Maclemar petted Penny's bloated stomach on the floor while gazing up at an equally satiated Poe. Maclemar hadn't seen anyone gulp down food like that in a long time. The girl took down three bowls of his seafood porridge, and he felt good about himself. He was feeling remorseful for being away for so long. He tried to visit once a month, but his duties had absorbed his time for weeks on end.

He studied Poe. The indomitable girl he knew was no more. In her place was a woman unsure which steps to take next. Julia Poe was one of the most attractive women he'd ever met, not only because of her unusual beauty stemming from a multiethnic background of Scot-Irish, Japanese, Mexican, and Filipino. Her grit was near palpable however much she claimed to have lost her fighting prowess. She was tough and caring despite her pleas for a solitary existence.

The five-inch scar on her face and the multitude of cuts, whip marks, and bullet holes in her body gave her the right to live as she wished. She'd done so much for what was left of humanity, and she earned bitter little in return. The diminutive Poe stood a little over five-foot-three but seemed so much larger because of what she'd accomplished by the young age of 26.

"Er, Poe. I must apologize for not visiting sooner," he said. He ran his eyes over Poe's damp waist-length black hair. The girl always tied her hair in a ponytail. If it weren't for the fact that Poe was drying her hair by the fire, he'd never have seen the rare sight. "I've been indisposed." The muscular man of over six feet in height looked uncomfortable.

"You don't need to apologize to me, Maclemar," said Poe. She rubbed her stomach like a pregnant woman expecting a kick from little feet. A man that could cook like Maclemar would make a young woman giddy-toed someday.

"Yes, I do. The thought of you here by yourself without heat in the middle of winter freezes my heart. I should've checked the electricity and the—"

"I've been alone most of my life, mister. Don't get all dramatic." She'd fended for herself since age eight in vampire-infested Downtown Los Angeles until Sister Ann and Goss took her under their wings and taught her how to defend herself.

"I'm not being dramatic. You know how I feel about you," he said uncomfortably.

"Yeah, well I don't think I can handle a relationship with a man or vampire ever again. Anyway, what's so important in the mainland?" Poe changed the subject.

"Sainvire asked me to start a school for the children of victims we found in blood farm nurseries. Unbelievably there are over 200 of them from toddlers to 12-year-olds. I started a curriculum in the autumn. I have to say I love my job."

"I can see you as a teacher," said Poe. Her dimples showed, and Maclemar couldn't help but grin. "Plus, all those American Lit books you've read ought to come in handy."

"Yes. They should," he said. The Welshman had been working on a degree in American Literature when the Gray Armageddon poisoned most of humanity. He rose from the floor and reached into his pack by the fireplace. He took out a letter in a plain white envelope. In a broadcaster voice he said, "This is the moment you've been waiting for, love."

"Ah. I thought you were on my side, Caveman." Poe reached for the letter and shook her head. The envelope wasn't sealed and had the word "Julia" written on it with masculine old-fashioned script. Poe unfurled the letter and read to herself:

Dear Julia,

I hope you are in good health. I often think about you. I understand how that must sound since I haven't come and visited you since we evacuated the island. I would like to say, however, that my feelings for you haven't changed. Circumstance has a knack for keeping me away from your side.

Calm confusion is the tone in Downtown. We are finding ways to bring vampires and ex-cattle to support certain causes. Our mission is to persuade cities around the neighboring states to free blood slaves and utilize Plasmacore as the main food source. The other (more difficult) goal is for the living and dead to get along. For now, Plasmacore in lieu of blood is accepted and surprisingly rather enjoyed for its benefits like being able to stay in the sun and the gift of strength. To humans, having vampires strengthened and out 24 hours a day is a nightmare naturally. A faction of ex-cattle is organizing to convert themselves into vampires so they can protect humans from undead predators. They will be the new police force if they have their way. I haven't decided whether this is a good idea or not. In any case, humans have started paying vampires to turn them into the undead.

On to positive news. Our campaign to lure vampires from other cities is coming to fruition. The deal is for them to bring at least three humans or children in exchange for Los Angeles citizenship and a decent place to stay.

Morales started a hospital at the Biltmore Hotel where most of the old timers are living, including me. He's also training volunteers to care for wounds, infections, rotten teeth, and what have you of every willing human Downtown. You know how Morales is. He's still T-Doc to everyone. He and Joseph (with help from Habib and Passionada) devote much time to raising little Piper despite their harrowing jobs. Joseph (who says hello by the way) is in charge of distributing Plasmacore and propaganda leaflets to other cities with Rufus who flies him everywhere. Michelle is in charge of security, and even hard-edged vamps fear her. They consider her your protégé.

I'm sure Maclemar can fill you in if you have any questions about our friends. For now I must ask you to keep an open mind.

We get an exodus of both vampires and humans to our city expecting a new, safer life. Because of nearly two decades of heinous vampire acts, trust is of course close to non-existent on the human side. You have become almost a legendary symbol for the humans, a Joan of Arc. You've never been bitten or turned into a blood slave. You have destroyed the most powerful vampires and freed hundreds of human cattle. We need someone like you to help keep the people calm while we organize the city into a safer, habitable, more productive place.

We need your expertise to forge a new world where Piper can be safe and prejudice is curtailed by respect and understanding. I know, dear Julia, that you think I'm nothing but a sentimentalist and a follower of lost causes. Perhaps you're right, but these are strange days. If we could fix things now and make it better for the next ten years, then all the suffering and sacrifice would be worth it.

Please consider my request. I am out of ideas. I want the powder keg to be stoppered. I believe you can help me.

With much love,
Kaleb

Poe crumpled the letter and threw it in the fireplace. Temporary solace came to her when the fire consumed the thin pieces of paper. Kaleb was asking too much of her. Didn't she deserve to be left alone after all she'd done? She simply wanted to stay on the island and watch bison for the rest of her life. Was that too much to ask?

"You know what's in the letter?" she asked a pensive Maclemar.

"Yes. He asked me to read it."

"Well it's a bullshit long-winded letter, my friend. I deserve this retirement."

"Lots of people deserve peace, Poe," he said quietly.

"Well I was fodder for Trench and his vampire pals after my back was whipped. They fed on my blood like caviar. That ought to be payment enough."

"My flesh was cut and my blood drunk," answered Maclemar. He became human sushi when vampires found out they could partake of his blood without turning the Welshman into catatonic blood cattle.

Poe banged on the wooden table with her fist. "What is this, a goddamn competition? I was sexually tortured then shot in the heart for fuck's sake!"

"No one's questioning that, love. We just need help on the mainland. Badly."

"Forget it. Downtown is a bad memory. My parents, brother, sister, Goss, and Sister Ann all died there. I was mistreated. I hate that miserable place!" she spat. "In any case it would be stupid to suddenly make an appearance when I can't shoot worth shit and I'm afraid of everyone. Of being abducted again. And how dare Sainvire bring Piper into the picture? The son of a bitch knows I feel guilty enough for neglecting her."

Maclemar kneeled in front of Poe's chair and took her hand. "If you don't want to go, you don't have to."

"But you'll think badly of me," she said, her brown eyes studying his emerald ones.

"Never," he said.   He kissed her hands. Whatever you do, I'll always be proud of you. You're my best friend and the person I love the most in this fuckall world."

———

She heard Maclemar lightly snoring in the next room.   After putting the world's ills on her shoulders once more, Sainvire had wrecked her sense of peace.   How could she go back when people knew what happened to her in Quillon Trench's hands? She may have killed Trench, but not before he had debilitated her with the worst form of humiliation.

Penny snorted in her sleep, and Poe combed her coarse firecracker fur.   The dog must have been about 15 or 16 years old. She didn't really know. *Maybe I should go back Downtown just to be near Morales in case Penny gets sick.* She slapped her forehead for even thinking about returning.   *I don't owe anyone anything!* Carefully she lifted the blanket and snuck out of bed in her Keroppi pajamas.   Barefoot, Poe padded into Maclemar's room.

Her friend's left arm draped off the bed. He was shirtless. For the briefest moment Poe felt desire, but it was quickly quelled by unpleasant memories. She slid in bed with Maclemar and used his extended arm as a pillow. She hugged him under the blanket and thought about how she couldn't live without him.

"Hey, Caveman," she said out loud, shaking him when he wouldn't budge. The man was a heavy sleeper. She had nearly been picked apart by Revenents because Maclemar was too busy snoring below the deck of his boat. "Wake up!"

Confused and disoriented, Maclemar's eyes opened wide. "Huh? What?"

"I need to talk to you, James," said Poe, plucking a chest hair near his nipple.

"Ouch!" he yelled. "Then talk!"

"Geez, you're not even grateful that I'm sharing your bed."

Maclemar realized this was so and smiled his approval. "Come to think of it, I'm very grateful." He kissed her forehead.

"Don't pester me. I just can't sleep, and I want to be held tonight."

"Fine with me, love," he said in half-brogue. He laid his big hand on her flat belly.

Poe scratched the hairs on his chest distractedly. He smelled salty like the sea. The man was mad about boating, and she knew that if she'd asked him to stay with her on the island, he would. Of course he'd regret it eventually for forsaking all those children who needed educating.

"What should I do?"

Maclemar sighed. "I can't answer that for you, love. It wouldn't be fair to you or me."

Knowing her friend was right, Poe remained silent. The choice had to be hers alone. "Sorry for putting pressure on you, bub, but I'm feeling like shit right now." Before he could say something, Poe continued. "My confidence is gone, James. I have the shakes, and the thought of being around vampires scares the shit out of me. The way I see it, Kaleb wants me to be a propaganda piece. The human to his vampire. And to tell you the truth I haven't quite got the Queen Elizabeth wave down. I'm not ready for my close-up."

Maclemar hugged her closer. "We'll all be there for you. You won't be standing alone on the throne. We want this new society to succeed."

Poe's throaty laugh aroused Maclemar more than a little. "You've given your opinion quite clearly, my friend. You want me to be a showpiece, too."

"That's not—" Before he could say another word, Poe laid her cheek on his chest. "No matter, chum. All's good. I'm not going because it doesn't feel right."

"Then you should stay on the island, and I promise to visit every weekend," he said with a light voice. Poe knew how hard it was for Maclemar to appear cheerful.

"I love you, Maclemar."

"I love you, too, sharren."

Poe listened to Maclemar's heartbeat all night long. Even his shallow breathing couldn't lull her to sleep.

CHAPTER 2

MACLEMAR BOLTED UPRIGHT. SLEEP left his state of mind damn quickly. He reached for the six-shooter on his bedstand and quickly slid his feet into his New Balance shoes. In his dark-blue boxers he scurried outside the cabin.

"Poe," he said with fear. The woman who had held him all night was not in bed. "Be alright, please."

Thunderous gunshots continued to disturb the silence of the morning. He realized somebody must have followed him to the island, and he stupidly led the culprit to the one woman he needed to keep alive.

His heart dropped when he saw Poe crouching on the ground as if in pain. Maclemar clutched his gun as he stiffly tried to spot the enemy.

"Oh. Hey, Maclemar," said Poe. She was bent over, picking up bullets from the moist ground. She'd been refilling magazines when she clumsily spilled bullets. "Sorry about the noise. I couldn't wait for you to wake up."

Maclemar lowered his gun while breathing erratically. "You fired the shots! I could kill you for nearly giving me a stroke! What the hell are you doing?"

"I should ask you that," she said with a snort. "You're in your underwear, and it's cold."

"I thought you were getting murdered," he said. Maclemar was feeling the bite of island winter weather.

"In a way I was. Take a look at my target." She gestured to the full-size poster of Arnold Schwarzenegger appearing fierce in *Commando* stapled on a chunky tree and frowned. Out of two rounds she'd managed to shoot the lower edges of the poster. Not one hit.

"Ah, sharren. You just need to work on your aim," he said encouragingly. "I myself couldn't shoot worth shite, but I worked on it. Now I'm a little better than before."

Poe squinted at Maclemar's Dirty Harry gun and shook her head. "What did I tell you about heavy, antiquated six-shooters like that, Maclemar? That gun is hella slow to load, and it's gonna get me killed if you're going to be my bodyguard. I swear, between you and Morales—"

"This gun is tops. And Morales did give it to me. Don't you start that again," he said with a shudder. "Now about the bodyguard remark, does this mean you're coming back with me?"

"If you don't mind a useless girl who lost her spirit and would probably never sleep with you," she said in all seriousness.

"Fine with that, sweetheart," he shrugged. "As long as there's 'probably' then there's hope.

Now mosey on back to the cottage before my only asset freezes over and falls off."

"Right. Plus I'm going to need you to chop my hair off. Can't look fierce with long, girly hair."

CHAPTER 3

MACLEMAR WANTED TO LIE down and die during the grueling session cutting Poe's thick hair to a more manageable shoulder length.

"I can't believe you had me desecrate your beautiful hair," he said. He brushed away hair trimmings from her neck.

"It's only hair. It'll grow back," she grunted. She couldn't help her insecure mind and a moment later asked, "Do I look awful?"

"Nope. You look snappy, but I'd gotten used to your lustrous hair." The way Maclemar gave his answer earned him a punch in the gut.

"Ouch! What do you care anyway? You're going to pull your hair into a ponytail after I finish brushing." And indeed, Poe took a hair band from her wrist and tied up her hair.

"I'm ready to go now," said Poe. She got up from the chair and pinched Maclemar's cheek. "Gracias." She stuffed another pair of sweater in her pack and slung it over a shoulder.

"Sure you're not forgetting anything?"

"Only my sanity."

A metal barrel crashed through the bay windows of the cabin, causing all three inhabitants to jump out of their skin. Penny began running in circles like a mad dog. Poe reached for the pair of Blackhawks in her shoulder holster, and Maclemar fished in his jacket for his six-shooter.

"Hell on earth! I think I was followed, sharren," whispered Maclemar.

"Well that's not your fault." Poe resheathed one of her guns and went through the closet in the hall. She picked up an angular machete she'd forged in one of her pathetic attempts at swordsmithing.

She checked her wrist knives and exhaled a breath just in time for a Molotov cocktail to splatter the west wall.

Maclemar grabbed Penny and kicked open the back door to the mini-garden. "C'mon, Poe! The cabin's burning!" Poe didn't have to be told twice and secured her pack on her shoulder while blinking the smoke from her eyes. She followed Maclemar outside, and both coughed from the acrid smoke.

They hovered three feet in the air.

A rather chubby undead in green plaid under a medieval-looking tunic with a red cross on the front stared Poe down. Her companion, a haggard brunette with thinning hair and the same type of gray tunic sized her up.

"Sally and Bette," hissed Maclemar. "What the hell?"

Sally, the big-boned grunge Generation X-er spoke clearly so there would be no mistaking her motive. "She stays on this island or she dies."

Bette smiled and said, "This morning we saw she can't shoot worth shit. She's no match for us."

Maclemar put Penny down. "Your politics are Downtown," he snarled at the two sun-immune vamps. "You have no jurisdiction on this island."

"There's only the two of you," said Bette, swiping her thin hair back. "And an old dog that's dying as we speak." She laughed as if she'd told a joke to die for.

Poe who had been silent narrowed her eyes. "Don't talk about my dog that way. Tell them how sensitive I am about Penny, Maclemar."

The Welshman stared at Poe, who seemed the perfect model of concentration, and shrugged off his fear. "She's bloody sensitive when it comes to her dog, ladies. Don't make her angrier than she is right now. He watched Penny, her sinewy body taut as she stood bravely by Poe.

"Or else she's going to shoot us and miss?" said Sally. Bette joined her in laughing at Maclemar's words.

Poe spun her .45 with her index finger like Clint Eastwood in The Man with No Name Trilogy. The muzzle pointed at Bette when the spinning ended. The vampire was as shocked as her companion. "Let's find out, why don't we?" said Poe, too calmly acting the cowboy.

"You're a fraud, Julia Poe," Bette said and flew at Poe. The ex-vampire executioner shot at the undead who suddenly hovered above. She missed. A raging Bette pried her gun from her fingers and threw it to the ground. She lifted Poe by the back of her neck. "Your shooting days are over, and we know this now."

Poe turned from the visage of the angry vampire. "Could you quit talking that close? Your breath kills."

Bette eked out her dissatisfaction and prepared to hurl Poe to the trees. But Poe took her by surprise, seizing the vampire's neck, burying her garlic-oiled wrist knife in her throat, and cutting open her neck like the lid of a can of beans. Poe fell from the air with a thud but quickly rolled to her feet before Bette's dead body could flatten her.

"Next!" she said as Sally's eyes became slits.

"You shit! I'll kill you for this," Sally said as she looked at her friend's lacerated neck.

Poe walked to her pack and unearthed her crappy sword, slick with garlic oil, one of the few things vampires were allergic to. "Let's go then." Penny suddenly ran toward the vampire while Maclemar raised his pistol.

Sally hissed at the goofy weapon and Poe's pathetic friends and lunged at the girl. Like a boomerang, Poe hurled the machete at Sally before dog or bullet could beat her to it. The triangle-tipped sword slashed at the heavy vampire's right thigh. The vamp, an undead for less than a year, screamed and pulled at the weapon. Once it was dislodged and dropped, Sally took to the air, wailing like a banshee.

"Those guys aren't L.A. vampires, are they?" asked Poe tightly. "They were pure amateur league." She patted Penny on the head.

"In a sense, they are," answered Maclemar. "They're ex-blood cattle who chose to become vampires. They call themselves Tunics."

"And they don't want me on the mainland because?"

"Because you can show friendship between vampires and humans is possible." Maclemar hugged Poe and kissed her on the head. "I thought you said you couldn't hit anything anymore?"

Poe grinned. "I said I was a worthless shot, but my knife skills and Bruce Lee moves are still a-ok."

———

After a choppy voyage on a retooled Chameleon, Maclemar secured the lovingly maintained boat to the San Pedro dock. He led Poe and Penny to the four-story parking structure where his carefully restored 1985 Ducati 600 TL was tucked away.

"What in the world, Maclemar!" complained Poe boisterously. "How the hell are the three of us plus my giant backpack going to fit on your antique motorcycle?"

Maclemar cleared his throat. "I left Penny out of the equation, but she can sit up here with me. I won't go so fast."

Poe wore a black hooded waterproof coat which cut made her look taller and slimmer. Beneath she had on a plain black American Apparel t-shirt, snug black jeans, and high-top Converse shoes. To Maclemar, Poe looked like a fresh-faced teenager not quite ready to face the real world.

"If you drop her, I swear, I'll snap your neck," she said in a frustrated voice. "She's my prized friend, you know."

"Aye. I know, sweetheart. That's why I would never do anything to the pooch." He watched Poe fiddle with her wrist knives and secure her guns in the shoulder holsters hidden by her coat. The bent machete hung from her bulky backpack. The engine sprang to life like a brand new motorcycle. "Hand Penny to me." The dog whimpered when Poe deposited her on Maclemar's lap. "Now, Penny, be still, won't you? I promise not to let anything happen to you."

"Pen, stay put, okay?" ordered Poe. She kissed the mutt on the head and climbed to the back of Maclemar, and her travel backpack containing her only possessions weighed on her shoulders.

The little hairs on the back of her neck warned her that something was wrong. She shivered as she scanned the garage that was chiefly in the shadows. *You're imagining things, Julia Poe*, she chided herself. *You haven't been to L.A. in over a year, and you're all nerves. You've got to cool it.*

Maclemar revved the engine. Without realizing what she was doing, Poe tapped the Welshman's shoulder. He had parked in the middle of the half-full garage of two-decade-old cars. He turned his head to the right, and Poe whispered, "We're not alone." The moment she mentioned her fears, the Ducati's engine fizzled and expired. Silence enveloped the garage.

The sudden clang of metal cages opening and closing from three different nooks of the concrete parking facility spurred Poe from her stupor. Dogs. She scanned the first emaciated dog heading toward them. "Take Penny. Climb up the storage shed in the middle of the garage," she ordered Maclemar. The metal storage container was over six feet high, and she doubted the dogs of various states of starvation could reach the top. They came silently with not even a bark. Poe realized later that their vocal cords had been tampered with to keep them silent. She counted 15 dogs, all selected for their larger size.

"I don't think I can hit any of them," said Poe, backing away when a balding husky with a limp boldly approached her. "Try shooting the ones close to you, alright?"

"Okay, but you should come up here. It's safer," said Maclemar.

Before she could answer her friend, three dogs sprung, and she fired her Colt as a warning. When they didn't take flight from the thunderous noise, Poe backed up and swung her machete to the nearest abused dog that intended to eat her and her friends. Maclemar fired his useless Magnum, and Poe prayed that he'd hit at least a few of them.

Poe blasted the balding husky with a blue eye and a brown one but missed, hitting its ear instead. "Fucking A, Poe," she cursed. "Two feet and you miss?" Again she relied on her ugly machete and beheaded two more salivating dogs, but at this point she was surrounded by dogs unafraid of gunfire. She hacked at the ballsy ones that dared invade her space. Then she noticed it. She figured out that the poor starved dogs had blood in their ears. Somebody had punctured their eardrums so they wouldn't be able to hear. The dogs were meant for her.

Poe tried shooting with her left hand, but she found more success hacking with the homemade weapon in her right hand. So far she'd killed at least 10.

Behind her a German Shepard whose ribs protruded like a barbecue grill nipped at her coat. Poe cursed like a barmaid. She was distracted from the four dogs she was fighting in front of her. Suddenly a flash of white ran past her and confronted the much larger German Shepard. Penny the spitfire attacked the weaker dog's throat fervently. Penny was well fed and exercised daily, and though old she still had some umph in her.

Maclemar reloaded his heavy gun and shot to kill. His aim was better than Poe remembered. Growling in her quiet way, Penny attacked any dog that went near Poe.

"Don't overdo it, Pen. Only six left," said Poe. A Doberman in better shape than the others leapt at Poe. The aggressor bit her wrist as she tried to protect her face. Poe raised her left arm and shot the dog in the mouth. She was furious at the inhumanity of the person who had starved, debarked, and deafened these dogs. "I'm gonna get you, you son of a bitch!" Poe yelled in the parking garage, her words echoing. "You hurt and starved these dogs, I'll fucking crucify you!"

She allowed the last of the dogs to move in and shot them in the face until the final German Shepard fell to its death. Poe scanned the desecrated bodies lying dead in the garage and felt rage she hadn't experienced since Quillon Trench.

"You okay, love?" asked Maclemar who was suddenly beside her.

"Yeah."

"You got bit. Better have Morales give you rabies shots," he said worriedly.

"I've already been needle-poked. I'll be fine. Besides, my coat is pretty thick.

Maclemar inspected his motorcycle and learned the enemy had siphoned petrol from his motorcycle. "The bastards left us without gas so the poor dogs could eat us."

Poe's full lips became a line. She inspected the garage while Maclemar siphoned gasoline from a luxury sedan. Penny followed her like a bodyguard, turning her head from side to side and sniffing at the air. Behind a blue van she came across the first cage where a third of the dogs had been starved and abused. She soon found the other two cages in the nooks of the garage. Poe wanted to cry. *I left my island for this carnage?*

Maclemar hollered for them to get back. The Ducati was ready.

Surprisingly Penny sat still like a trooper in front of Maclemar, who drove 20 miles an hour, swerving left and right to avoid collision with stranded automobiles. He took the Harbor

Freeway for a smoother ride. Trench had begun a project to clear freeways before Poe shot him dead, and the improvement may have been the best accomplishment in his miserable life as a vampire. Poe, on the other hand, was more accustomed to Vespa scooters than motorcycles which made her want to urinate on the leather seats. She hugged Maclemar's waist like her life depended on it.

The sight of the Downtown cityscape from the freeway made her heart beat faster. The jungle she condemned as a grave place of suffering looked gorgeous even with a slight drizzle of rain. Buildings stood proudly for her eyes to view. Dread tightly held her heart, but hope and the promise of a new direction excited her. She was going to see Piper, Michelle, and other lifelong friends.

Her musings were cut short when a large motorhome parked horizontally across the freeway blocked Maclemar's ride. "Poe, get your guns ready," he barked, slowing the bike down as he drove around the vehicle. Poe reached for her Blackhawk and said, "Please be careful with Penny."

"I will, love. There's a flare gun in my jacket pocket. I want you to point toward Downtown."

Poe took the gun with her left hand and fired. The girl was ambidextrous and had been viciously accurate in her prime.

Maclemar stopped the motorcycle and lifted Penny to the ground. Above them were three vampires who landed softly in front of them. *I thought I killed most of the flying vamps*, Poe thought. The door to the camper opened and another three stepped out. The six vampires, four women and two men, each wore a drab gray tunic with a 10-inch red cross emblazoned on the front. *What is this, the Crusades?*

"Are you Julia Poe?" asked a startlingly thin platinum blonde with a hungry expression. She was one of the three that could fly.

"Yeah, that's me," answered Poe. Her .45 lay against her thigh. "You guys in search of the Holy Grail or something?"

"Only you, Julia Poe," said a hefty black vampire that was hiding out in the camper.

Poe's mind was surprisingly clear after defeating Sally and Bette on the island. She didn't feel any fear. *The old me would've been proud*, she thought. "So what's up?"

"You need to come with us," said the blonde.

"And if I don't? Will you send some more starved dogs after me?"

"Don't know what you're talking about, but we will be forced to take you and Maclemar against your will."

Maclemar scoffed. "Don't worry, sharren. These are the new self-proclaimed vampire police I was telling you about. They're a bunch of bullies, but they won't harm a human hair."

"I guess it's a different rule on my island, eh? I'm fair game," said Poe while locking eyes with every single one.

Poe took a gamble. She looked down at mute Penny standing protectively next to her leg.

"Listen. I don't know who you are, and I don't know anything about your Kool-Aid cult because I've been out of the city for over a year. But since you seem to know about me, I'll assume you know my reputation. I've killed hundreds of vampires," she lied. "I've rescued as many human cattle. And I don't like being intimidated by you or abused dogs. Either you get out of our way or I'm gonna have to destroy you like I smote Bette and Sally."

The blonde and the black woman who seemed to be the leader among the six looked at each other. "Sally reported you can't shoot straight. I'm afraid we're going to have to ask you to come with us."

"Wow, this conversation is like a flushing toilet. The dirty whirlpool never stops going around and around. I'm not going anywhere unless you tell me what you have in mind for me."

"We're taking you to Perla," the black woman answered.

"Perla? The scientist who invented Plasmacore, Perla? My friend, Perla?"

The woman nodded.

Poe frowned. Perla was once her tutor and Maple's sweetheart. Her invention broke the blood dependency for vampires. Last time she saw Perla was in Gilroy, catatonic from a vampire bite and nursed by the mallet-armed Maple who was her life partner. Poe turned to Maclemar.

"Long story short, Perla went nuts after she woke up from her year-long coma, and she's now head of the new vampire police. She's recruiting ex-blood slaves to become vampires themselves to protect humans against city undead and outside forces who want to harm the new order of things. And they want to punish ODs or old city vampires for their crimes against humanity and execute human leeches that served master vampires."

"Man. I missed so much in so little time," Poe said and shook her head. She holstered her weapon and rubbed her shoulder. "Ladies and gents, I will certainly meet with my friend, Perla. But not now. I'm tired, cold, and hungry."

Since Poe had sheathed her weapon, the tense look in the vampires' eyes dissipated. A speck in the sky arrested their attention, however. "It's Sainvire," one of them said.

Poe swallowed whatever spit was left in her mouth and gulped nervously. The vampire soft-landed next to Poe and Maclemar. "Problem here, Melanie?"

The blonde shook her head. "Just saying hello to the conquering hero."

"That's big of you," said Sainvire with reserved friendliness. His gray eyes hardly blinked as they surveyed the sight before him. "I believe you should be going now."

"Can we come for you tomorrow?" asked the black vampire.

"Sure. Maybe after lunch?" said Poe with a nod. "And your name is?"

"Becca," said the vampire.

Poe bent down to scratch the ears of a tense Penny. "Don't worry, Pen. They won't hurt us. I'm Perla's friend. Well, Becca and Melanie, I'll see you both tomorrow. And I hope you understand I don't like being a passenger on the back of a flying vampire. A car would be nice."

She turned to Sainvire after the vampire police drove away. It had been over a year since she'd seen him. She hadn't forgotten the misshapen shoulder, the scarred upper lip, and the intense gray eyes that seemed to penetrate her thoughts. She'd never loved a man or vampire like she loved Kaleb Sainvire, but he chose saving people over loving her.

"Hey, you," she said with forced cheer. "What's up?"

"Oh, you know, bickering vamps, demanding humans, confused halfdead, a crazy city, and screaming babies with red hair."

"As idealistic as ever, I see. Light-the-fire Sainvire. Same old same old," said Poe a little less cheerily. She gazed at Maclemar who was pretending to inspect his Ducati. "As you can see, I'm here as requested. Your letter and Maclemar pretty much clued me in about Downtown madness. I figure I'll stay two months. Then I'm off to my buffalo herd. Deal?"

"Deal," said Sainvire in his deep gravelly voice. "Thank you."

"One thing," said Poe. "Could you fly Penny to where I'm supposed to live? I don't trust Maclemar to keep her splat-free."

"Of course," he said, reaching for the mutt who remembered the vampire. He tucked the 24-pound dog in his black trench coat and nodded. "Did you want to fly with us?"

"No, sir. I'm riding with Maclemar here. See you in a minute."

She watched Sainvire levitate into the air and shoot up to the sky. The vampire looked haggard. He always tried to fix things, and his selflessness cost him plenty. Poe tucked her coat under her seat and embraced Maclemar's waist. She closed her eyes as the Ducati accelerated to blinding speed and dreadfully destabilized her bladder.

———————

The Biltmore, one of L.A.'s oldest and most ornate hotels, was an historic landmark smack in the middle of Downtown across from Pershing Square. Early Academy Award ceremonies were held in the Crystal Room, one of the several grand ballrooms of the Beaux Arts hotel. The distinguished 11-story building housed close to 700 rooms, enough to accommodate Sainvire's people who wanted to stay close to the master vampire.

Since the revolutionaries peacefully took over city management, the Biltmore had served as a hospital, nursery, school, meeting space, artillery factory, library, gym, and 24-hour cafeteria since vampire and human shifts varied throughout the day.

Taking in the grandeur, Poe climbed half of an elegant stairway. Maclemar led her down a marbled hallway where gilded cherubs festooned the ceiling. The splendor of the hotel was almost lost to her after curious onlookers whispered their disappointment. Wherever she'd walk, people and vampires alike would gawk like she was a giant talking insect. Snippets of "I didn't expect her to be so small" and "tiny" bothered her for in her mind she was five-foot-eight like her mother and not a malnourished shrimp. And how people bantered around the words "scarred face" made her grit her precisely flossed teeth.

She had lived a solitary life after most of humankind, including her family, perished in the Gray Armageddon. Poe wasn't used to the gossip or the looks of judgment.

"Jesus, Mary, and Joseph, Welshman! You dragged me back for this?"

"Don't worry about them, love," said Maclemar. The man sounded harsh and grumpy. "Some people are just ungrateful and ignorant."

"That's alright," Poe lied, swallowing bitterly. "How can I stand up to an out-of-control legend that magnifies my past adventures?"

He hugged her briefly and kissed her forehead, second nature to Maclemar. "You're growing up, little one. The real flesh and blood Poe is a damn superhero, and everyone who encounters you knows it."

Ed, a five-foot tall halfdead who could juggle a bulldozer with his pinky was waiting for them. "Poe! Welcome back!"

"Ed! You look so good in a tie," said Poe as she embraced the strongest person she'd ever met.

"Thanks. I hate it," he said, tugging uncomfortably at his blue checkered tie. "They're expecting you in there." He opened the door for her, and Poe had to blink her eyes twice to register the familiar faces in the hall illuminated by giant chandeliers. The biggest was Passionada, a tremendous woman hovering over six feet tall in her yellow heels. She was carrying a crying baby with teeth sprouting all over the place.

"Hey, honey! You look great! This little bundle of tears is your goddaughter." The woman thrust the ornery child into Poe's arms. The vampire executioner's eyes bulged, holding the baby at arm's length. She'd never in her life carried a baby, and she was terrified. Instead of wailing even harder, the redhead girl with light-brown eyes stared at Poe curiously.

"Maclemar, help me," said Poe.

"You're doing fine, love. Just bring the babe closer to your chest."

Poe was greeted by a bevy of old friends like Maple, Habib, Rufus, John Danby, Kawana, and even the ever annoying Romulo Gutierrez. Because of the baby she couldn't say her proper hellos. Joseph walked up to her and kissed her cheek. He squeezed her shoulder and said, "Isn't my little bundle of joy purty?"

"Sure," said Poe, her nose breaking into a sweat in the cold hall. She spied bowlegged Sam Morales enter the hall. The T-Doc – short for Temporary Doctor as the others fondly called him – was all smiles. "Julia Poe, my favorite person next to my daughter, Piper!" He kissed her ear, the one that was missing an earlobe. He wiped the dots of moisture on top of her nose for which Poe was grateful. Morales and Joseph were Piper's fathers, but they were far from lovers. Morales had donated his sperm to Megan, the vampire Joseph's wife, and they produced a baby together. When Megan died, the two friends decided to band together for the sake of the little girl.

"Guys, I think I'm gonna drop her," said Poe tensely. The redhead girl kept saying, "Cayot, yuck!" over and over and was biting at Poe's nerves. The baby meant carrot but couldn't pronounce the r's. Everyone in the hall was enjoying Poe's discomfort so much that they refused to take Piper off her hands. Sainvire, who was tucked away by the velvet curtains, chuckled his last laugh and wound his way toward Poe. He swept the baby in his arms and kissed the rolls of fat on the child's neck. Piper squealed like a tiny hag and began kissing Sainvire back with her saliva-sodden mouth.

Poe's relief was cut short when she spotted Jenna, one of the most important leaders of the resistance and Sainvire's ex. Her heart dropped to pathetic level, and she didn't appreciate it one bit. The woman waved at her with a smile and Poe did the same. Perhaps they could be friends after all.

Sainvire looped the baby's plump leg behind his neck until she was resting comfortably on his shoulders. "Well, Poe. I'm sure you know most everybody here. We're grateful that you could come."

Poe hailed her welcome committee to settle down when hooting and clapping invaded her fragile sensibilities. She was tired, overwhelmed, and somewhat seasick. The crowd was too cheerful for her hermit ways. "Thanks, guys. Good to see you all again. I'm sure we'll have a chance to chat soon. Cute baby, that Piper," she added. "Scary, too."

"You'll get used to her," said Joseph with his usual laidback grin. His ponytail was still ever present. "She stopped crying when you held her. That means she likes her godmother."

Poe smiled timidly. "That's what I'm afraid of." Again, people laughed. *Why are these people so giddy?* "Well I kinda know why I'm here. To be a poster girl. A PR person or an ambassador of sorts. I get it. I'm yours for the next two months. Then I'm going back home to my island."

Poe's to-the-point speech sobered the mood. She cleared her throat. "I already have an appointment with the tunic-crusader vamps tomorrow, so I have to go to sleep pretty early. If someone can show me to my room, I'd appreciate it."

No one spoke for a few uncomfortable seconds. Only Piper's baby gibberish echoed in the roomy hall. "I'll walk you to your room, Julia," volunteered Sainvire, breaking the silence.

"What about dinner?" asked Habib, an Iranian American who was the head chef of the Biltmore. "I prepared your favorite vegetarian dishes." Poe had impressed the man by gobbling down his concoctions years back, and he forever loved the little warrior.

Poe reddened. "Sure, Habib. Maybe I can come down in an hour. I'm feeling a little weird right now."

"Sure. Poe. Sure."

"Thanks, Habib," she said, hugging the cook with bushy eyebrows. She followed up with a kiss. Before she could make for the door, Maple asked, "Are you ill, Poe?"

Poe shook her head. "Nah, just seasick. Hey, do you have some time to talk tonight, Maple?"

Maple, who had been turned when she was 50 years old, nodded in her quiet way.

To Poe's surprise, Maclemar didn't follow. Sainvire pressed the button on the gilded elevator and waited for the door to open. Piper pulled at Sainvire's neck-length hair and screeched, "Kaleb! Kaleb! Kaleb!"

Poe was relieved when the door opened and Sainvire punched the button for the seventh floor. "Very classy, this place," said Poe for having nothing important to say.

"Yes. I used it as my offices years ago if you remember."

"Yup. That I do. I contemplated blowing it up with you in it."

They turned right at the hall and approached Room 702. Sainvire unlocked the door and held it open for Poe. Penny's throaty whimper and wagging tail greeted her. Poe couldn't help it; she got down on her knees and hugged her loyal friend. Penny's was the only familiar face she cared about at that point. "Good girl, Penny Pen! I love you, doggy!"

Poe was startled when young Piper walked with drunken legs toward her dog. Penny's tail stopped wagging, but she stood her ground. The girl tapped Penny's head and said, "Good dog."

The weary traveler smiled a genuine smile for the first time since coming Downtown. "That kid talks funny. Must've learned it from you."

"Unfortunately, yes." Sainvire nodded in defeat. "That's why no one listens to me. I think I may have to borrow Piper's high-pitched screams to get everyone's attention."

Poe shrugged. "That's what you get for being a saint, mister."

Sainvire took a step for a better view of Poe's upturned face. "I never wanted to be a saint. Hell, I'm not even religious."

"Just like I never wanted to be a superhero. And I'm no longer one if you haven't heard yet. Lost my cape and can't shoot straight anymore. A disgrace, really." She looked around the spacious room that very much resembled a hotel suite. "Wow. It's like I'm on vacation from my perfect island."

"Sorry for taking you away from Catalina, Poe. I'm simply desperate right now." Sainvire's gray eyes looked so pained that Poe had to turn away. "Every faction needs to be convinced that they're an important part of the equation, and we all have to come together if this new society is going to succeed."

Poe narrowed her eyes. "Listen. I'm here, okay? I don't need to be convinced how dire the situation is. Everything is life and death with you. That's why you're so damn unhappy. I'm sorry that getting this city back on its feet is your burden, but really, Kaleb, you can just walk away. It's that easy." The words from her mouth surprised Poe. The vampire who owned her heart could've chosen her instead of political intrigue. They could've been living the life in a mountain hideaway. Anywhere away from conflict.

Sainvire touched her face with the back of his hand, savoring the softness of her skin, and traced the angled five-inch scar with his index finger. "All the time I think about starting over. But I can't. The thought of you on your island would be the only light in my dark tunnel, Poe. I think about you to keep hope alive in my chest. I love you more than anything, and I feel like a damn heel for choosing you last all the time."

"How do you think I feel?" said Poe, laughing bitterly and turning away from his touch. "By the time you can pencil me in your daily planner, I'll be 70 and sagging. But you know what? Doesn't matter. After what Trench did to me, the thought of a relationship makes me retch. No matter how much I love you, the feel of your cold dead flesh would probably make my skin crawl." She was being nasty, but she didn't care.

"It's probably for the best then," the master vampire coolly said. "Maclemar will probably have a better chance of thawing your heart since his flesh isn't cold or dead."

"Maybe," said Poe, turning catty. "At least he never forgot me. He visited me and comforted me during the hardest moments of my life. For that he deserves my love and my loyalty."

Sainvire gently took Poe's face in his hands and kissed her lips that seemed to have parted on their own. The two kissed deeply with the unmistakable sadness of an opportunity lost forever. The lovers had only shared one night of pleasure together and had since been separated by circumstances beyond their control. Poe cleared her throat when the kiss ended. "Your hair has grown, and you have stubble. You look like a serial killer."

"Thanks, sweet Julia. You're looking marvelous yourself," said the vampire, amused. "Straight talker to the last, eh?"

"Learned it from Sister Ann, you know." She brushed his dark hair with her fingers. "I'll always love you, Kaleb, but my days of waiting for you are over."

Sainvire kissed the top of her head. He and Maclemar were similar in many ways. "I know, my love. I don't expect you to wait around. Be happy with Maclemar. He's a good man."

Poe hugged Sainvire's waist and fought back tears but failed. "Why do you have to be so goddamned good all the time? I love you so much that I wanted to die from want of seeing you. And don't pass me on to Maclemar again. You make me feel cheap."

All the vampire could do was apologize, and all Poe could do was resent him for being so damn altruistic.

Because Poe had become deliberate in her actions, her youthful clumsiness and filthy mouth lessened noticeably. No longer was she easily provoked (unless her dog was involved), nor was she quick to inflict pain for a slight. Habib watched the young woman eating his creation with aplomb in contrast to the engulfing way Poe had dined years back like there was no tomorrow. She forked hummus, grilled eggplant, and mushroom spaghetti in her mouth like a proper lady. She also didn't pay heed to the gawking eyes and whispering mouths in the 24-hour cafeteria.

"Here, Pen," she whispered to Penny who sat guardedly by her leg. She placed a plate of deboned chicken on the floor. Animals weren't normally allowed in the cafeteria, but Habib made an exception for Poe's companion who refused to leave her side.

"So how did you say you got all this food?" asked Poe to a lively Habib.

"The Christian farmers in the Valley have an agreement with Sainvire. These vampires throughout history declined human blood and settled with drinking animal blood. They supplied human cattle with food for master vampires, but they were against enslavement in general. Toiling the fields to feed humanity was their calling. With the new arrangements, these vampires are happy to send over the best meat, fruit, and vegetables to restore strength to poor humans," explained Habib. "Sainvire sends them vats of Plasmacore, of course. They also have an agreement allowing rehabilitation of certain humans at the farms."

"Good for everyone," Poe mumbled, popping a slice of papaya in her mouth. "And what about the Los Angelenos? How do they fare with the new government?"

"There's no government yet," said Habib, scratching his balding head. "That's the problem. City vampires are hated by both humans and revolutionary vampires. Everyone hates human leeches who stooged for vampires in the olden days. Many admire Sainvire, but more than a few prefer he gives up his ad hoc power. What will happen when Sainvire steps down without a replacement? Chaos, my friend. In any case, some things are in decay and some are up and up."

"I haven't been outside. I don't know how things are."

"We usually have quiet all around except when ODs are murdered."

Poe put her fork down. "What's an OD again?"

Habib pushed a glass of freshly squeezed orange juice to her. "That's what we call Old Dead who participated in the enslavement of humans."

Poe thought about the vampires wearing tunics with crosses and narrowed her eyes. They must be the new dead behind the murders. Before she could ask any more questions, a scream ricocheted in the 600-strong cafeteria. From habit, Poe unsheathed her gun and stood up quickly. The metal folding chair she had been sitting on clanged to the floor.

A woman with wild, curly hair ran toward her, belting out the squeakiest of screams. Poe hardly recognized her friend wearing a tight-fitting pink tank top and low-rise mini-skirt. A wide-eyed girl behind the hysterical woman was carrying her coat.

"Poe! I can't believe it! Finally you're here," Michelle cried. "I missed you so much!" The pretty hazel-eyed woman with a belly button piercing hugged Poe after she resheathed her gun.

Poe grinned and clapped Michelle's powerful back. It was apparent that Michelle had been working out. "I missed you, too, Michelle! Good to see you."

"I can't wait to tell you all the shit that's been happening in DT. Everything's so fucked!"

Poe nodded. "Yes. Habib and Maclemar have been telling me a little."

Michelle slapped Habib's back. He didn't seem to appreciate the abrasive gesture. Before Michelle could say more, Poe walked over to the little girl of about 10 holding Michelle's large coat like a tiny servant. "Is that you, Percy?"

"Hi, Poe," said the girl with brown hair and solemn eyes. "You remember me?"

Poe took Michelle's coat from the girl's arm and draped it over a seat. She pinched the girl lightly on the cheek. Percy smiled, transforming her naturally mournful eyes, and embraced Poe tightly. "I knew you'd come back. We missed you so much!"

"I missed you, too." Poe had rescued the girl from the clutches of baby vamps inside the Metro tunnels, and Percy had suffered from hero worship ever since. "You're still looking out for Chops?"

"Yes. She's waiting outside the cafeteria. Habib won't let her in here," Percy said, whispering the last bit in case the chef could hear her.

"Thanks for dinner, Habib! C'mon, Michelle. I want to see old Chops."

When Poe last saw Chops, she was a pint-size piglet. Now the animal was near four feet long and weighed about as much as she. "Holy shit! What in the world have you been feeding her?"

"Habib's cafeteria scraps," answered Percy. "She's pretty cute, isn't she?"

"Sure is. I think Penny recognizes her." They watched Penny sniff the rotund animal with interest.

"They're pals again," said Michelle. The two animals did indeed seem like old friends after a couple of smell tests.

"Where do you keep her?"

"In my room. She's my friend just like Penny is yours."

Poe kissed the girl fondly on the cheek. "You're a good kid, Percy. And I'm glad I'm back." For the first time since returning Downtown, Poe felt a glimmer of hope. She didn't know what it was about Percy, but she was drawn to the girl. Perhaps her youth and having to deal with bullshit vampire politics at age 10 made the difference. Percy reminded Poe of herself, and she vowed to clear up the wrongs and teach Percy the skills she knew before leaving for Catalina.

Michelle walked Poe and her dog to the fifteenth floor to Maple's suite. "She's been working like a mad hatter to clean Downtown, keep the peace, and teach useful skills to lost souls. You know she used to be a mechanic, right?" Poe nodded. "But you know she's bummed about Perla. She doesn't show it, of course. You know how she is."

Poe frowned at the athletic girl she'd trained in Muay Thai at the farm in Gilroy and asked, "What the hell happened? They were so in love. I mean, Perla had Sainvire turn Maple into a vampire after the Gray Armageddon."

"I didn't know that," said Michelle.

"Not many do, so keep it under your hat."

"You can count on me, boss. Here's her room. Good luck." The young women hugged, and Michelle couldn't help but ask, "Is true you can't shoot?"

"Unfortunately, yes." Poe turned away from her friend who looked crestfallen and walked briskly away. Feeling depleted, Poe knocked on Maple's door. An oversized man wearing a polka dot sweater opened the door and swung at her with a Phillips screwdriver.

Her body responded automatically by deflecting the man's punch with her left arm and hitting him in the throat. To keep the man down, Poe kicked his left leg under him and shoved his face on the floor. Within those seconds one of her wrist knives had unfolded.

"Stop! Poe, for the love of God, he's one of us." Maple kneeled in front of the man and removed Poe's grip on his head by prying away her fingers one by protesting one. The vampire killer heard sobbing from the man, and Maple cradled his head. "What the hell are you thinking?"

The girl glanced up at the Y-vein circulating dead liquid through her lined forehead. She was more than a bit annoyed. "He attacked me. You saw, right?"

"Yes, but he's special," said Maple with care, wiping the tears from the big toothy man with the bottom of her shirt.

"Yeah, special in the head," said Poe disbelievingly. Just as the words left her mouth, she noticed the man's slack mouth and childlike gaze.

"Julia Poe! We will not start labeling people in this new society of ours. You should be ashamed!" She helped the 40-year-old with a 10-year-old's mind to his feet and sent him on his way. "Thank you for replacing the wall plates, Jonah. You did a good job. Tomorrow we'll work on changing light bulbs."

"Okay, Maple. But your friend's no good. I was just funning," said the big man with resentment, wiping his wet face. "I don't like you, you witch!"

"Well she's new here, love. Now go on." Poe's anger waned. She was trying to defend herself, but it was wrong to call people names. Her parents would've been up in arms at what she had said. The old ignorant, filth-mouth Julia Poe hadn't been eradicated after all.

Maple, wearing a purple shirt and brown corduroy pants, embraced the small vampire killer who had shaken the old order with her sheer fortitude. "Welcome, Poe. Let's forget all that with Jonah. You don't know how glad we are that you're back."

Poe sat on the neatly made bed facing Maple, thinking about the intellectually disabled man she'd just downed and shook him out of her head. "I don't really know how much I can change things around here, Maple. I nearly killed a friendly a minute ago. In many ways, I'm still broken by Trench, and I've lost my balance." She rarely spoke about her three-month imprisonment with Quillon Trench, a master vampire that liked to play games, torture, and humiliate.

"I know it was hell, Poe. I'm so sorry about what happened to you. But if you only knew what your presence means in this city."

"Do people really care?"

"You've been here less than 24 hours, and the crime rate has already crashed," said Maple. She leaned to pat Penny, who was sitting on the carpet and looking as though she was participating in the conversation. "Everyone fears you. ODs, newly formed vamps, humans, and halfdead respect you. You represent destruction and in many ways, hope. You've rescued most of the people in this city, and they have your complete loyalty. Vampires know you only kill when you need to. Even locked up leeches who raped and tortured blood slaves are waiting and hoping you'll speak up for them."

"That's a tall order for someone who's been out of the picture," the girl proclaimed, swatting the beads of sweat from her nose that had been bothering her since Jonah.

"You're telling me," said Maple with a sigh.

"What do they plan to do with the leeches?" asked Poe. She despised the men and women who had worked for vampires in exchange for their lives and a steady stream of narcotics. They cared for their human cattle while the undead slept, impregnated comatose women who'd been raped multiple times, and harvested blood.

"The Tunics want to execute them. Sainvire is looking for a way to avoid vendetta killing. He reminds us that almost everyone was guilty of one thing or another and that if we want the new society to survive, we must learn to tolerate the intolerable."

"Idealistic as ever, that man," grumbled Poe. "But what about Perla? How come she's the leader of the Tunics?"

Maple reached for Penny and lifted her to the bed. "She woke up once we got to Los Angeles. She hardly spoke to me. Just stared into the ceiling when she wasn't writing in her journal. One day she said I was filth and decided to leave me. She moved to one of the loft buildings on Spring Street. I was told later that she paid a vampire to turn her into an undead. Ever since then she's been recruiting ex-cattle to become vampires. They want to protect what's left of humanity and eliminate leeches and ODs who've harvested and drunk blood from humans. The Tunics are now 90-strong and growing. Many join because sleeping on cots for years left a lot of people weak with anemia and bone ailments. They're hoping to feel strong again."

"What does she want from me?"

Maple continued to massage Penny behind the ear. "She wants you to be one of them."

Poe swallowed wrong and began coughing. *Me a vampire?* "No way!"

CHAPTER 4

JOSEPH PLAYFULLY TUGGED HER ponytail as she was about to spoon fruity oatmeal into her mouth. Poe considered the Filipino undead with an eternally amused face a brother. The vampire was Sainvire's best friend and one of the speediest vamps now living in DT.

"Hey, you freak!" she complained half-heartedly. "I could've spilled my only nice shirt. Not wise to look puked on for my first diplomatic mission." She wore a black button-up shirt with white ruffle lapels tucked in fitted gray slacks and black high-top Converse.

"Oh my. Forgive me, ambassador. I almost destroyed the mariachi-slash-slacker outfit that would save the City of Angels today," grinned Joseph. "By the way, Kaleb thinks I ought to come with you just in case the Tunics hold you down, puncture your head, and spit blood in your brain to make you an instant vampire."

"They wouldn't dare because if I do turn vamp, I'd annihilate them all. Plus I'd probably have awesome dead powers like flight, superhearing, and sun-immunity for starters."

"You've thought about this before, haven't you?"

"Not to be conceited, but yes," said Poe in all seriousness. "I'm such a fear-inducing human, so they say, that naturally I'd have more super abilities than even Sainvire."

Morales sat down next to Poe and placed Piper on her lap. He didn't know whether his friend was pulling his leg. Poe had never been known for her sense of humor.

"You think so? In my professional opinion you'd be a Picasso vampire mess."

Poe gave him an ugly face and took a deep breath. She said crossly with a half-smile, "Maybe. But I did sound like a dick. Most likely I'd end up being a halfdead or something."

"Listen to our Poe, Joe," said Morales. "She can keep her trigger-finger off her gun and join in a joke. Our girl's growing up."

Poe pursed her lips and concentrated on the heavy child on her lap. She decided to change the subject. "She kinda looks like Megan because of the red hair, but the resemblance stops at that. This kid looks like a mixture of the two of you. Weird looking."

Both Joseph and Morales pinched her sides until her eyes watered. "Okay, okay. I was just kidding. She's a good looking baby. My goddaughter. The baby I'm supposed to protect. Sorry I haven't been around, Piper."

"But bless it, now you're here," said Morales. His teeth were brighter than she'd remembered. The handsome ex-realtor turned bombmaker, mechanic, and doctor draped his arm about her shoulders.

"For two months."

"That's something at least."

Poe didn't take up Joseph's offer to accompany her. She was strapped with two .45 Colts in her shoulder holster, wrist knives which she could still throw with precision, and a machete slung on her waist. She was feeling pretty confident like a pirate. She vowed to clean the mess for Percy, Piper, and especially Sainvire so he could finally abscond with her.

A green Jeep Wrangler pulled up in front of the well guarded hotel where Poe stood waiting in her dark coat. She'd been watching day vamps concentrate on protecting the building from possible intruders. Penny was waiting patiently by her side. The day was grim and cold, and suddenly she lost her poise. A man with the boniest face she'd ever seen, almost like a Revenent, opened the back door for her. *These Tunic vamps look really dead and horribly nasty to the eye. They must've been turned on their sick bed.*

The car braked at the Alexandria Hotel which was ridiculously close to the Biltmore. Poe let herself out. The hotel, festooned with terra cotta griffins, had once been impressive, but time and abandonment gave the place a dank, blighted look. The driver escorted her to the bar on the ground floor that used to be known as the Down and Out. Inside were a bevy of sallow-faced vamps looking wearily at Poe. She sat at the bar and accepted a flat orange soda from an androgynous bartender. *Like I'm gonna drink poison.* As an extra courtesy, they placed a bowl of water for Penny.

Three ex-cattle and three vampires joined her at the bar counter. Apparently they knew of her for two vamps licked their lips like lizards, and one of them said, "You're next, sweet thing."

Like a dream, Poe watched as the vampires punctured holes in the humans' skulls using primitive tools – a Phillips-head screwdriver, a siding scraper, and a ball point pen. The vampires who didn't look too healthy themselves bit their tongues with their incisors that grew over an inch and spit their blood in the head holes they had formed. Poe wanted to throw up.

"You next, sexy?" said the bigger of the three vampires. "We need you in our group."

"Fuck off," said Poe. She stared at the emaciated ex-cattle writhing on the floor as they transmuted into vampires. "I'll never become a vampire!" She turned her gaze at the interesting billiard tables and pinball machines.

As if the three vampires had one mind, they pinned Poe down where she sat and laughed. "We'll take it into our own hands then," said the vampire called Larry. The bartender held up his hand and said, "I want no part in this, man. Perla's not going to be happy."

"You snooze you lose," said the vampire holding her left arm in a vise. Even with her JKD moves she was too entangled to move. *I knew I should've sat in the booth!* Penny tried biting ankles but the vampires didn't seem to feel anything.

The third vampire not touching her person chose the siding scraper from the medieval set of tools. He was about to tap her skull with the bloody instrument when Poe went limp, limp enough that even the two vampires had a hard time holding her up. She tugged at her left arm, flicked her wrist knife, and aimed at the vampires' thighs and kneecaps, harming all three of them enough to let her go. She got to her feet and slashed their faces like she was the wind herself. When she hurt one, she hurt them all the same way, slicing off noses, ears, and lacerating cheeks. Her captors covered their faces with their arms and begged for no more.

Perla was 15 minutes late. When she entered the Down and Out, she witnessed Poe's wrath. The leader of the Tunics screamed her anger, stopping the vampires and Poe in their tracks. Only the soon-to-be-former-humans struggling on the filthy tile floor broke the silence.

"What's the meaning of this?" she seethed.

"She started slashing us, ma'am," said Larry. He held what was left of his nose.

"These three tried to turn me into a bloodsucker," Poe said with viperous tongue.

"Get out!" said Perla. The three, including their spawn, left the bar. She turned to her friend. "I'm sorry, Poe. I was in the warehouse district rooting out a sadistic vampire called Syrus. He raped and mangled women for fun.

"Did you get him?"

"No."

"Your den is disgusting. I shouldn't have been asked to see you here."

"My people are good. I'm sorry those three had minds of their own."

"It's good to have minds of your own. I think that's what you're forgetting. Are you commanding some kind of cult?"

"I'm not a cult leader, Poe."

"Then you sure have gross people making poison Kool-Aid for you." Despite her anger at nearly getting turned, Poe stood up and hugged her middle-aged friend who looked more like a soccer mom than a vampire with revenge on her mind. "Last time I saw you was in a trailer in Gilroy," said Poe. "Maple faithfully dressed you in your favorite pajamas." The vampire was in love with pajama patterns. "I picked you some apples."

"Thanks, Poe, but I don't remember since I was attacked by a vampire and I lost a year of my life." Perla sounded bitter.

"Yeah. Sorry about that. At least our side won."

Perla laughed. "Criminals and rapists are running around free. Leeches are protected by prison bars because Sainvire is too bleeding-heart to approve capital punishment. Blood sucking vampires still live their privileged lives. That's not winning, Poe."

"At least it's better than before. The blood farms are gone. Kids are going to school. Vampires are only drinking Plasmacore. Things might not be perfect, but at least it's improving. Give it time. It's only been a year and a half."

"You really are a cheerleader for Sainvire, aren't you?" jeered Perla. "You haven't been here. You don't have any idea."

Suddenly defensive, Poe shifted in her seat. "You've known me a long time, Perla. I don't do anything lightly, so I don't appreciate you calling me a cheerleader. You're the one with an army of dumbass cheerleaders like the heftiest ex-cattle I've ever seen behind you."

Perla turned her head to see Sally glaring at Poe. "Sally, go away."

"She and one of your goons tried to off me. She probably starved dogs to eat me and my friends. I assume it was on your order."

"I never wanted you hurt, Poe," said Perla sincerely. "I just didn't want you to leave the island. Sally and Bette went too far."

"Yeah. You never know about bitter ex-cattle. You never know if they're following your vengeful example or acting on their own. No matter. They're your cheer squad, and whatever they do reflects on you." Poe stared hard at Perla. "I love you, Perla. You and Maple taught me many things, and you've protected me from harm. I'll always think of your wisdom and brainpower. You're the goddess creator of Plasmacore. The vampire I see before me confuses me. As a scientist and preserver of life, I can hardly believe you've become the Gestapo, wanting to hunt down everyone for incineration. I won't be a part of it."

Perla looked whiter than her bloodless face. "Do not compare me to a Nazi, little girl! I only want to clean up this city and erase nightmares for the good people enslaved in their prime."

"Like the Nazis."

"If you say that again, Poe, I'll—" Perla ran a hand through her short salt and pepper hair.

"You'll what?"

"You're family to me, Poe. I would never hurt you."

Poe nodded. She knew Perla's statement as truth. "What do you want from me?"

Perla held Poe's calloused warm hand. "I want you to join us. We need someone charismatic like you."

"You want to turn me into a vampire? Are you kidding? You want me to join these walking skeletons who tried to do away with me five minutes ago?"

"You'd be a potent undead, Poe. You're the most powerful human I've ever met, and as a vampire you'll be unstoppable. Have they told you about the San Diego undead? They want to crush our city because it's inciting havoc in San Diego and other realms. San Francisco is also wary of us and won't stand for a fledgling democracy. We need to unite our own people and defend ourselves against slavers."

"Maybe you should start by giving everyone a second chance. Maybe that'll unite the city."

"How naive you are, Poe. It's not easy to forgive criminals. We've got to crush them and start over with a clean slate. We need a trial."

She squeezed Poe's hand a little too hard. Perla didn't know her own vampiric strength. "You'd be a first-rate leader for the Tunics and a powerful dead."

Poe glanced down at Penny whose tail had stopped wagging a long time ago. "I want to grow old and die a human death, Perla. I don't want to turn for you or anyone so I can be a Downtown dictator."

"So you're siding with Sainvire?" asked Perla with disgust.

"Nope. I plan on doing research on my own, and I'll see what improvements I can recommend at the next town meeting. I hear there's a session in a few weeks." Poe whistled to get her dog's attention and stood up. "Don't worry, Perla. I still think highly of you despite the fact that your girl Sally tried to kill me and torture poor dogs. I'll have a fair analysis come next meeting. No need to call the driver. I'll have a look around my old haunts on my own, thanks."

Downtown was a difficult monster. The streets were clean and orderly, traffic flowed smoothly, and crews were slowly restoring damaged buildings like Sainvire's old headquarters at the Los Angeles Central Library, which had been bombed four years back. Julia Poe walked Spring Street and eyed the lofts that were now occupied by ex-cattle awake from a decade-long stupor. Those staring from the windows waved timidly at her and Penny. Apparently her wanted poster face that had been plastered all over the city turned her into one of the most recognizable faces on planet Earth.

Poe waved back, her cheeks dimpling. She beckoned some people to come down to the street and speak to her.

"How do you like your place?" she asked a toothless woman of uncertain age. "I like it. It's so spacious. I feel like I'm ripping somebody off."

Poe smiled. "Whatever luxury you get, you deserve. How can the city help you more?"

"T-Doc's been training some stronger ex-cattle and vamps to give Shiatsu massage. I get worked on twice a week. I think it's the best thing to come out of this tragedy, and I believe Dr. Morales is a fine soul."

"He's got vision," piped a 40ish man with cataract eyes. "He cures the body and heals the spirit. Getting a massage, even from a trained vampire, is alright by me. It's their turn to kiss our butts."

Most of the people had positive things to say about Morales and his holistic approach to health. T-Doc had taken up psychological counseling and had been training volunteers to help traumatized humans. Some despised all vampires with the exception of Sainvire and Joseph. Their presence provided confidence and protection to the unhinged.

"What about the Tunics?" Poe asked a bartender at a local bar. Folks had begun brewing beer and distilling spirits again. "What's the word?"

"Well, Ms. Poe, that's a conundrum of a question," said the man who resembled Mr. Burns from The Simpsons as he wiped the bar.

"Please call me Poe or Julia," she said. Poe pretended to take a sip of beer. She hated the taste of alcohol. "What's the conundrum?"

"We like vampires who want the human population to bounce back, the ones who helped free us. The Tunics don't fit. They hate vampires, but they want to be vampires, so-called knightly vampires. They want revenge, and they want to protect humans. They sound like lunatics. Imagine turning yourself into a vampire just to have power for vengeance or to restore your weak body. Walking skeletons protecting my fat ass does something to my liver."

"Yeah, but they swear to protect humans first," said a pretty woman who had aged before her time. "San Diego vamps are after us and are bent to destroy Downtown. Then there's San Francisco. We need the Tunics." Only Maple had mentioned the San Diego threat to Poe. She was surprised the imminent danger was common knowledge. Apparently a kamikaze pilot from San Diego had flown a Cessna filled with explosives with the aim to destroy the Downtown hub. Fortunately an informant notified Joseph, and he alerted Sainvire. Flying dead intercepted the aircraft, directed it east toward San Bernardino, and let it exact its damage there.

Poe went to two more human pubs and three vampire bars and was surprised at the welcome she received. She'd never spoken to so many people and vampires in all her life.

"Of course we're afraid of the Tunics," a bearded OD said. "They look like the grave, and they're paranoid. We harvested blood because that was our main food source. There's nothing sexy about blood. It's just food. If you ask most vampires they'd say they prefer to drink Plasmacore because it protects them from the sun. And our humanity never left some of us. We have eyes. We didn't like to see human cattle connected to transfusion tubes."

"Then why didn't you do anything?" asked Poe who had always been curious about the lack of revolt from city vampires.

"We were afraid of the Council and the master vampires we worked under. Simple as that. If you ask questions, you lose your head."

"So you'd do differently if the San Diego folks try to enslave the human race again?"

"With Sainvire at the helm, I'd back him up. But unfortunately we're now considered Old Dead, and the Tunics want to off us."

Leeches and Old Dead, thought Poe. *What a dilemma.*

Poe and Penny walked to City Hall where Michelle's team imprisoned the human leeches. To her surprise, a large crowd had started to form, following Poe's every move. She pumped some them with questions to get the lay of the land.

Tunic guards blocked her way into the 27-story white building. "I'm here to see the prisoners," said Poe, already assuming a diplomatic role of sorts.

"I'm sorry, Ms. Poe, but I can't let you in," said a female vamp with an inordinate amount of facial hair.

"Who's in charge?"

"We're not supposed to let you in," said the Tunic.

"That's not what I asked," said Poe. Someone from the crowd yelled, "The Tunics are in charge during the day and Sainvire's people at night."

Poe nodded and pushed her way inside the metal door. The hairy vamp tried to stop her, but Poe's unique voice halted her. "You touch me, I'll cut off your head. Now show me to the lock-up."

The Tunic nodded to her male counterpart, and he beckoned Poe to follow him down the hall to the holding area. The prisoners looked ill fed and miserable. Medieval chains and wrist braces had been drilled on the walls. Fresh and old blood adorned the white cells. At least two prisoners hung just high enough for their toes to touch the ground by fetters from the ceiling. From what she saw, the leeches were roughed up during the day and patched up at night. Poe knew they were the dirtiest kind of human beings. They had raped, tortured, and only their consciences knew what else.

"Hiya, fellas," said Poe cheerily. "I'm Julia Poe, and I'd like to know how you're enjoying this establishment.

———————

The crowd, people and vampires alike, stayed with Poe until she reached the Biltmore Hotel. She turned to the different factions of the Downtown community and said, "Nice to spend the afternoon with all of you. If you have any ideas about improving your city, let me or Sainvire know, alright?" When the hordes didn't move from their positions, Poe's nose twitched. She was tired of her entourage.

"Go home now and eat something," she ordered. At once the crowd dispersed.

Poe heard clapping as she and her dog entered the building. Maclemar was leaning against a portico with his arms folded and a grin on his face. Sainvire stood next to him, trying not to smile but failing entirely. Several humans and vampires milled around the lobby area but Michelle was the first to shatter the silence with her whooping.

"Poe! One day and you've got a marching band behind you," said the sexy femme fatale.

Poe motioned for Percy to come to her. She laid a loving hand on the girl's shoulder. "Wanna have dinner with me? I'm super hungry."

"I was waiting for you," she said. Poe noticed the girl's short pants and scratched her head. "Got any plans tomorrow, Percy?" The girl shook her head. "Tomorrow I'm taking you to the fashion district and we'll get you some clothes, alright?"

"Alright, Poe. You with us, Michelle?"

"Can't. I'm head of security now. I'll get you a car, though."

"Thanks, but I think I'm going to need a truck."

"You serious?" asked a puzzled Michelle.

"Very. Read somewhere that clothes makes people feel better about themselves. Saw a lot of oversized clothes on really thin people today."

Sainvire walked toward the three. "Can I talk to you before you head to the cafeteria?"

"Sure." She turned to her friends, "Meet you guys there." They passed Maclemar, and she frowned at his wink. They walked to the offices behind the halls. Separate bathroom aside, Sainvire's office was one of the smallest and most private.

"You know what you've done, right?" he asked. He didn't sit down, and Poe leaned on an antique redwood desk. She'd forgotten how tall the vampire was. He practically loomed over her.

"No. What?" Poe was suddenly confused and nervous.

"You just had a parade full of ex-cattle, Old Dead, and custodians talk to you and even follow you to the hotel." Sainvire smiled. "We've been trying to have a discussion with these separate groups but have failed. And look at you, going to the beer halls of both humans and vampires."

"You've been spying on me," accused Poe, tilting her head up and narrowing her eyes.

"I'd never let my one love face danger alone," said Sainvire. His gray eyes looked silver.

"Don't get too excited. I hardly did anything. But I'm committed to making a change." Her heart pounded. How she missed the vampire's intelligent and compassionate eyes and angled features. She had the urge to run her fingers through his thick black hair but stopped herself. Instead Poe smiled and stood on tiptoes. "Can I kiss you, Kaleb?"

"Please do," he said quietly. The two softly locked lips. Both were still uncertain about their directions in life.

"I wish we could sleep together again just because we've only made love once," uttered Poe in a pained voice. Her overture surprised herself.

"Three times," he corrected. "In one day. Four years ago."

Poe burst out laughing at the memory. Sainvire walked her to the cafeteria and joined her for dinner. He drank a tumbler full of the clear liquid known as Plasmacore, and for the first time in a long time he enjoyed the company of his friends.

Before the week was out, Poe had organized clothes drives, enlisted former seamstresses and tailors to open boutiques and clothes alteration shops, recruited men and women to start beauty salons, and convinced a vampire and human to start a pub together. The latter was by far the easiest to convince since Bob Chang, a vampire, and Faith Hurt, a human, were best of friends. They called their new establishment Glowdown.

The farmers helped them set up the bar while ex-cattle and vampires touched up an old German pub on Main Street. By Friday, three clothes shops, four beauty salons, two barbershops, and a pub had been cleaned and opened for business on Main and Spring Streets.

One of Poe's proudest moments was opening wig fitting facilities for she and Percy had discovered two warehouses full of pretty hair that was sure to boost ex-cattle egos. A number of ex-slaves had suffered hair loss, a cause of depression and tattered self-esteem among other things.

By the following week people with a lot of time on their hands had approached Poe to secure jobs to cure their boredom and sense of alienation. Poe set up interviews with Morales for those interested in learning counseling or healing arts. Surprisingly over 50 applicants came forward. Maclemar welcomed candidates interested in working with children. Many women who'd been impregnated while drugged and had their babies taken away volunteered as nurses and child care providers. With the eager help of human and vampire volunteers, Maclemar had more time on his hands for his core responsibilities.

Willing vamps and stronger ex-cattle who showed promise were taken in by Michelle's team for physical training to become Downtown security. For the older folks who still had lucid minds, Sainvire invited their help in planning political strategies and teaching the older children games with a special emphasis on chess.

Poe, on her part, began teaching Jeet Kune Do and Muay Thai to those interested in muscle development and bone strengthening therapy. By the third week her class had become so popular that she moved it outdoors to Pershing Square with almost 100 humans and a spattering of day vamps attending.

For those unable to leave their beds, Poe arranged for Sainvire's vampires to read to them and help them with bathing. She also made delivering food to the elderly much easier by putting Meals on Wheels into operation. Habib and his large staff packed three meals of fresh food for the debilitated. She preferred ODs for this job so they could see their lasting damage and perhaps volunteer to serve their former victims on an ongoing basis.

Poe didn't set out to be a reformer. She planned activities and programs because she thought the community would be stronger if everyone worked together. She had the knack for convincing people and vampires to try something they normally would never do. "If you don't like it, you can kick me. I won't kick you back," she'd say. Her ability to remember every face and name like a gamemaster served her well. In all, she'd met over 600 Downtown residents by her fifth week in the city.

If she weren't a household name before, Julia Poe was now unforgettable in her superstar achievements. She was well regarded because of her sincerity and ability to listen. Her martial arts classes drew a hundred people, but her audience was double that. She taught with strong will, and it showed with every kick and punch which lessened the fears of ex-victims.

In short, Julia Poe became an icon whether she wanted the tag or not.

CHAPTER 5

THE LAST THURSDAY OF the month was an important community event held at the Biltmore's grand ballroom. Poe was expected to give the recommendations she had promised, and her nerves were jangled. She never thought of herself as a public speaker, and she could never forget she had once stuttered. She spent most of the morning trying to mentally sort her plans. Percy looped her arm around Poe's elbow while they walked to the park for martial arts lessons. The two had been inseparable. Penny and Chops trailed behind them, both creatures swaying their behinds like a couple of drunken women.

Percy had become like a little sister to Poe. She'd never loved anyone like she did Percy in the five weeks she'd been in the city. Not even Piper's cute baby antics could steal her heart away from the little girl with sorrowful eyes. She was resolved to ask the girl to live with her on Catalina. The prospect of having a friend in the isolated island heartened her.

The students were already situated in their rows of 12 while the observers sat on benches and fences. She knew she'd never get used to the spectacle of teaching. She motioned for the Judo Club as they used to call themselves in Gilroy and approved of their black outfits and red waist sashes to differentiate themselves from the crowd. Five older men, ex-boxers, coaches, and athletes participated from the club, helping Poe with teaching basic defense stances to the near-impossible number of students.

"Morning, class," she said loudly to accommodate the hard of hearing. She removed her coat and shoulder holster and tossed them on the grass. The machete lay glistening on the ground. She slipped off her wrist knives and flung them on her coat. The class was divided into five groups to make it easier to hear and be seen. "It's a beautiful sunny California day! Let's do our 10-minute warm up. Percy and the Judo Club, do your thing."

Poe was dressed in a black t-shirt and black Adidas jogging pants. The scars on her arms and face showed clearer in the daylight. She bent down to double-knot her Converse, an old tick she could never get rid of, and was startled when people began to scream and scramble away from the green.

An enormous Paul Bunyan standing at six-foot-eight pushed the crowd of students out of his way. She'd never seen the muscular bearded man with fuming eyes before, and her nose twitched. His red flannel shirt made Poe wonder whether the man had an axe behind his back.

"How can I help you, mister?" Poe asked as he finally reached her. Her neck ached already from looking up at the man.

"All this karate bullshit and stories about you kicking vampire ass and humans bigger than you makes me real angry. Well here I am. Do your worse so I can show what a fraud you are. You're nothing but Sainvire's bitch."

Poe's nostrils flared. *Fuck me sideways*, she thought, trying to curb her filth mouth at least out loud. The big dummy disparaged her in front of her class, and she had no choice but to fight. "You're a dick, and I'm gonna kick your head in. I'm nobody's stooge, and truth be told, I don't even want to get embroiled in Downtown politics."

A dirty fighter, Poe rained a volley of punches into Bunyan's kidneys until the old calluses on her fists began boiling. She kicked him in the groin three times. Not a sound escaped from his lips. Her eyes traveled to his and discovered his serene countenance. The man was a halfdead who hadn't quite turned into a vampire but arrived at some vampiric powers.

"You're a halfdead!" Poe cried. "Foul."

"Go on. Beat me up. I won't touch you. I want to show these folks here that you're no superhero."

Poe sighed and began slugging the man as viciously as she could, even punching him in the neck and kicking him without reservation on his sides. The halfdead clutched at his throat but didn't alter his quiet stance.

"You tired yet, girl? Can you see she's only a puny human? She's a propaganda piece doctored by Sainvire. See how weak Julia Poe is," he said in a deep voice. That was when she noticed a tiny white cross on the man's sleeve. He was a Tunic.

The audience cringed and yelled at Poe to give up before the halfdead unleashed his punishment. The reaction angered Poe even more.

"With Jeet Kune Do, you can do anything. Even the dirtiest tricks," shouted Poe and jumped on the halfdead's back. An arm wrapped around the man's neck as if to choke, and the giant man laughed.

"What? You're gonna choke me to death? You want a piggy ride, vampire killer?"

"Actually," said Poe breathing heavily. "I'm interested in your nose. With her index finger and middle finger, she invaded his nostrils and yanked back until the flesh ripped up to his eyelids. The big man finally cried out and shook Poe from his back. The girl broke her fall by rolling on the grass. Part of his face was still in her hand. She tossed it to the crowd who stepped back as if the bubonic plague exploded from a rotten rodent.

The halfdead was on his knees and covering his face with his hand. He could feel the shell of his nose, and he cursed like an Alaskan fisherman. He stood up and lunged at her but she slipped through his legs. She kicked the back of his knees until the man fell on the grass. Poe approached him and said out loud. "Whatever you need to survive, do it," she lectured as if still in teaching mode. Without batting an eyelash, Poe brought her Converse to the back of Bunyan's head over and over again until his neck cracked and his head exploded.

"Class dismissed," Poe said, facing the shocked students. She bent down and slid knives on her wrists in case there were more of them.

"What the—" said an instructor named John Kang. "Look out, Poe!"

Three flying vampires wearing ski masks descended on the lawn. From what she could tell, two men and a woman came to disrupt her already scattershot class.

"Class is not quite over. Go home, Julia Poe, or we'll kill you. You are weakening Downtown," the woman with a grim voice said.

Déjà vu, thought Poe. Only this time the vamps were carrying pistols aimed at her. "If you're going to kill me then you could at least show your face, lady," Poe said harshly.

"I would but we're instructed not to," answered the woman wearing faded blue jeans.

Poe flicked her eyes on her guns and the machete. The visitors were five feet away, but they seemed farther because of their agile flying. She had two knives at her disposal, and she was hoping to down two of them long enough to retrieve her other weapons. "Well I'm not leaving. I still have three more weeks, so why don't you start killing me already?"

"Sure. My pleasure."

Percy's heavy breathing behind her snapped Poe out of her own anger. "Hold up. There's a kid behind me." Poe turned to look at Percy. "Go

sit by John Kang. I don't want you getting hurt."
The crowd stayed to watch. "Okay, go," said Poe.

The three vampires looked at each other
holding their guns, apparently not used to fighting
anyone. Poe didn't wait for them to make up their
minds. She unsheathed the knife at her left and let
it fly to the woman's heart. The vampire quietly
tumbled to the ground clutching her chest. Poe
hurled her other wrist knife at the taller of the two
male vampires. She grunted when the knife hit the
man's throat. She quickly rolled on the ground
and picked up her machete. The last vampire fired
four shots at Poe but missed emphatically as she
zig zagged and kept low. As the vampire
launched into the sky, Poe sprung and took hold of
the creature's leg.

"Not so fast, assbrick!" The vampire was no
Sainvire. He couldn't carry passengers or fight.
She lifted her machete and began hacking away at
the man's hip. He screamed at the burning pain
the garlic oil brought on. Poe's feet touched grass
as the vampire sank lower to the ground. Once he
was down Poe kicked his leg from under him and
pushed his chest to the ground. Forgetting her
audience, Poe brought her malformed weapon
down on the vampire's neck. Sounds of quick
inhalation and disgust filled the air.

Poe quickly leapt to the other vamp she'd hurt
with a knife to the throat. She straddled him as
she removed his hood and extracted the knife just
below his Adam's apple. "Percy, get their masks
off will you?" The vampire underneath her legs
was coughing violently.

"Any of you recognize these vamps?" asked Poe.

The bolder humans crept closer to the bodies and shook their heads. Even Percy shook her head. "I've never seen them before."

"You think they're Tunics?"

"I don't know. Maybe."

Within minutes, Michelle's red Hummer followed by Jeep Wranglers thundered down the street. They skidded to a stop in front of the crowded park, nearly extinguishing a shaken woman. Sainvire's spy must've run for help.

She asked Michelle the same question. "They're dressed like nerds, and they're cadaverous. They're probably Tunics. I'll bring throat boy over to City Hall and maybe interrogate him somehow. Make him write out his statement." She smirked at her humor. "By the way, five leeches were arrested along with Syrus about an hour ago. He's the Flesh Tailor among his many names, according to the Tunics. He liked to stitch cattle together and burn them with chemicals. Hope they all get what they deserve."

Poe glowered at her friend. "You're head of security. How can you say that about your prisoner?"

"Hey, they're leeches. Leeches rape, remember? Half the kids at the nursery are their spawn. They friggin' raped me, too," Michelle said matter-of-factly. "I disagree with Sainvire on this matter. I think they all ought to be executed instead of feeding them good quality food the rest of their days."

Poe gritted her teeth. "You have anything to do with them getting taken?"

Michelle looked at Poe with disgust. "I'm security. I'm no turncoat for nobody. If I'd seen the culprits, I would've capped their asses. You're my friend, so I'm going to pretend I didn't hear accusation in your voice."

The muscular young woman motioned for the bodies to be lifted onto a Jeep and boarded her own Hummer.

Poe realized she was shaking.

"Get back into position," ordered Poe. She wouldn't take no for an answer. "We're going to have our lesson today or bust." Slowly the humans formed lines. Poe turned to John Kang, the leader of the Judo Club. "I'm gonna take off. Can you teach this class today?"

"Sure. No problem, Poe."

"Everyone. John Kang and the Judo Club will run through grappling techniques. I got somewhere to go, but I want you all to pay attention. Strengthen your body. These folks," Poe nodded at John Kang, "are great teachers. If you stick with them, you'll get your strength and confidence back."

Poe turned her back to the class. She quickly donned her shoulder holster and coat and began jogging away from the park.

"Poe. I'm going with you," said Percy, running alongside the vampire killer.

"Probably not a good idea. I'm talking to vamps with deadly attitude."

"Don't care," Percy said. She was looking up at Poe with determination.

"Fine, kid," Poe smiled then looked behind her shoulder. Penny and Chops were running right behind them. "Keep an eye on the animals, alright?"

"Okay."

They reached the Alexandria in a couple minutes. That was one thing she loved about Downtown – nearly every corner could be walked if you knew the grid. "Alright, Percy. You need to stay out here." Poe weighed the machete in her right hand. "No," said Percy. "I'm coming along." With her chin in the air, Percy marched inside the Down and Out followed by animals.

"Damn kid," cursed Poe. The bar windows had been tarred to keep sunlight from crisping standard-issue vampires. The billiard tables were occupied by skinny, malnourished folks who moved with unnatural speed. Poe and Percy watched similarly emaciated vampires casually puncture the skulls of three humans sitting on bar stools. The undead stared at Poe while they bit their tongues. Like motor oil, blood leaked from their mouths and dripped in the holes to the humans' brains. The humans fell on the ground a few seconds later and suffered grotesque convulsions. *First stage of becoming a vampire*, thought Poe. *Good luck with that.*

Poe laid a hand on the girl's shoulder as they spotted Perla sitting in a red vinyl booth with

Sally. "Keep behind me, Perce. I'm not relenting this time."

The girl nodded. Recognizing Sally as an enemy, Penny made a throaty growl.

"What can we do for you, Julia Poe?" asked Sally sarcastically. Her smug look withered when Poe brought down her warped machete on the table, cracking wood.

"I've come to report that the three clumsy dead you sent to kill me are really dead or dying as we speak. And your Paul Bunyan halfdead disciple is pulped."

Perla frowned with concern, setting down her mug of Plasmacore. "It can't be. We don't do things like that here."

"Sure about that, Perla? Sally and her ugly friend tried to off me on my island. You had nothing to do with that?"

"They were sent to convey a message, that's all," said Perla, narrowing her eyes at Sally. "Whatever you think of our group, you know that I could never hurt you nor order anyone to kill you."

Poe's dimples appeared as she pondered Perla's answer. She knew in her gut that Perla wasn't capable of hurting her. No matter what had been said and done, Perla was still protective of Poe.

"I believe you, Perla. But somebody sent mercenaries after me." She bore her large brown eyes at Sally. "You have an inkling, Sally, of who that could be? A Brawny Man that had a white cross on his sleeve? Three flying vamps? For some odd reason you guys have a knack for flying."

Sally sat up straight and hissed. "The halfdead acted on his own, but I haven't done anything behind Perla's back. She's the leader of the Tunics." Again Poe believed the vampire, but she couldn't resist bumping Sally's mug of Plasmacore with the edge of her machete. The clear liquid spilled all over the front of Sally's jeans. She grinned as the vampire scrambled for some napkins.

"Oops," said Poe in feigned surprise.

"You bitch!"

"Thank you, ma'am," Poe bowed, smiling. "I believe you, Perla, because I know from our brief history together you're basically a good person. I believe Sally, too. But if you tell me you have nothing to do with the nabbing of five leeches and a Nazi vamp known as Syrus you were hunting weeks ago, then I'd say you are lying."

Perla's pale face turned even more pallid. She was not resistant to the sun. "That will be everyone's business tonight, Julia. These issues will be resolved at the assembly. Other than that, I have nothing more to say to you."

"Fair enough," said Poe. "I'm not Tunic police. I'm not security like Michelle. Can't wait to see what little drama you'll be conjuring up tonight. In the meantime, my parting words to you are to leave me the fuck alone or I will blow up your goddamn building. Then you really will be down and out."

When they left the hotel bar, Sainvire was waiting for them. He was leaning against a street sign, his hands crossed against his chest. He looked like he was cold despite the warm coat and the fact that he was dead.

"Percy, can you take the animals home? I need to speak to Poe alone."

"Yes, sir," the girl answered in her 10-year-old child's voice. "C'mon guys." She lightly slapped Penny's rear end when the dog wouldn't budge. When the crew rounded off 6th Street toward home, Sainvire scooped Poe into his arms and flew in the air.

"What the hell! Put me down, Sainvire," Poe gritted. "What's wrong with you?"

"You've been taking too many risks in my opinion," he said steadily. He headed for the Central Library and lowered both of them through the roof hole that used to be topped with a tiled pyramid. The once-impressive landmark had been Sainvire's home until the Council desecrated it. "And this isn't your fault."

He lowered her to the marble floor of the children's wing. They walked silently to his old bedroom that used to contain impressive Art Deco furniture but now only contained a mattress and a thick blanket on the ground. *This must be his fortress of solitude.*

"This is the first incident, Kaleb. I'm surprised nothing more has happened to me," said Poe, throwing the ugly machete on the floor.

"Did you make that thing yourself?" asked Sainvire, his eyes staring at the malformed sword.

"Yeah."

"Figures," he said. He laughed without mirth. "As long as it works then it's fine by me." He took a step toward Poe and stared into her eyes. "I'm mucking this up, Poe. I don't want you hurt."

"Too late. I'm going to get hurt all my life. I figured that out a long time ago."

"I don't want you to get harmed on my watch again," he said, tucking a tendril of hair behind her ear. Poe felt heat in her stomach as she stared up at the tall vampire.

"It wasn't your fault what Trench did to me. You thought I was dead."

"I should never have stopped looking. Three months he tortured you," whispered Sainvire in her ear as if ashamed that the world would hear his heinous sins.

Poe brushed her hand across Sainvire's face. She traced the shell-like exterior of his ear. "I killed him, didn't I? And I lived even though he shot me in the heart."

"You're a wonder, Julia Poe. You're wreaking havoc in our city, and I think I like it." He dipped his head lower to be able to kiss the woman he'd cared for most, but Poe turned her head. Honestly she loved Sainvire, but his cold tongue would conjure up bitter memories of Quillon Trench.

"I need to prepare for tonight. Fly me back to the hotel?" she asked, avoiding Sainvire's wise eyes.

"Of course."

The assembly was akin to San Diego Comic-Con in her childhood days. Folks were dressed in their group uniforms like tunics emblazoned with crosses. Farmers with long hair and white linen shirts reminded Poe of the Beatles in their Maharishi kick. The 600-person capacity hall was bursting to accommodate over a thousand guests. The humans who had scarcely participated in past meetings attended in droves. Though Julia Poe would shut down the rumors, humans of all backgrounds came to the assembly to hear the mighty woman promote her ideas on how to improve city conditions. The fight at the park brought the curious for they'd witnessed the fighter Julia Poe and found her to be the real thing.

ODs or Old Dead hated for participating and partaking of slave blood during the reign of terror stood in one corner. When an assembly was called, they were expected to appear and listen silently as the past was rehashed, and they were aware their crimes on display could easily turn the crowd into a lynch mob. That evening, however, the vampire killer was in the room, and she was the same girl they had spoken to in their pubs and homes about city matters. Nothing would change, thought many, but at least they were willing to hear Julia Poe out.

Many rallied around the custodians, usually of ethnic backgrounds. Vampires had considered their blood impure, so they were relegated to cooking and cleaning for human cattle. The custodians removed and carried dead humans to the incinerators. The Downtown-based custodians cared deeply about Poe who had promised to fly them out of Downtown and kept her word. At the assembly they wore red t-shirts to distinguish themselves from the others. Danby, a black man and an ex-attorney, headed the group. He had met Julia Poe in Gilroy a couple years back and thought highly of her.

Only two Ancients remained in the city. These vampires were hundreds of years old, and they looked it. They had unmanicured walrus teeth that grew down to their chins. The Ancients had marble skin and violet eyes and were as strong as five vampires. The male called himself Kilbur while the female referred to herself as Stanza. Both vampires and humans didn't quite know what to do with such horrendous looking beings.

The halfdead contingent wore yellow. These were humans who hadn't quite turned but had the power of a weak vampire and were immune to sunlight. They were politically scattershot by nature. Except for the halfdeads who sided with Sainvire and his cause, they usually said nothing at the assemblies. Rufus, a loyal friend to Sainvire, headed the group. Once a foe of Poe who had yanked off his ear in a "friendly" demonstration, they had patched their differences after Rufus ate Poe's severed earlobe in retribution.

The humans had the greatest turnout of the evening in their green shirts. Many of the women wore make-up and stylish wigs that sparked up their appearance. The usually laconic group, including those recovering from vampire bites with brittle bones and weak constitutions, was bursting with energy and excitement.

The different colored t-shirts were Joseph's idea to distinguish each group from one another. The American Apparel warehouse was in Downtown Los Angeles, and its clothing stock made it easier to accommodate each group with style. Those like Joseph, Morales, Habib, Maclemar, Passionada, and Sainvire who preferred to be apolitical wore regular clothes or suits.

Poe dressed in Kevlar over a black long-sleeve shirt and black jeans. While pacing her messy hotel room, she sheathed her wrist knives. The meticulously furnished room had clothes strung carelessly around the bed and floor. She wasn't usually such a slob, but she couldn't find decent clothes to wear. She looked down and decided she must've double-knotted her Chucks.

A knock sounded, and Poe nearly threw up her dinner. She hadn't memorized her crib sheet because she realized she was bad at committing anything other than names and maps to memory. She opened the door and found a grinning Maclemar wearing a dapper James Bond suit that was fitted nicely over his respectable physique. Downtown Los Angeles once had a suit district, fabric district, and even a bead district, so suits weren't too hard to come by. "Ready, my star?"

"Heck no!" Poe turned back to pick up her shoulder holster holding two Colt .45s. Mumbling angrily, she secured it.

"Ach, sharren. A tornado blasted through your room, did it?"

"Shut it, Maclemar! I'm in dire straits. I can't memorize what I'm supposed to recommend tonight."

"Wing it then. You're good at that." The man began to massage her shoulders.

"Piece of shit. That feels good. Wish you could massage me while I'm at the podium." To which Maclemar said, "Easily done, beauty." Maclemar had become a great friend to her. She was aware of his feelings toward her, and his attention made her feel nice. She'd be going back to Catalina in a few weeks, and he'd be the only person to visit her. "Make sure to use neutral words like folks, beings, community. We want the entire t-shirt rainbow to buy in."

"Good idea. You truly look handsome, Maclemar," she said, tugging his black tie. "Take me out on a date after I get pelted by eggs?"

"It would be my pleasure. We'll eat omelets for dinner. " He walked her down to the hall.

A Tunic who sounded awfully like Sally was speaking. "We're wasting our rations and manpower on leeches that raped us, prepared our blood for vampires, and burned our bodies with their cigarettes and drug paraphernalia. Our platform tonight is to finally set a date of execution for these inhuman bastards." The crowd cheered. Killing leeches was a popular platform.

Poe, who was hiding behind the red velvet curtains, surveyed the crowd before her. Many of the humans, including Michelle who was standing at the other end of the stage, were applauding. Michelle abhorred leeches, and Poe still believed that her friend had helped Sally bust out the prisoners. She sighed, thinking about her lack of speaking skills, and wondered what happened to the five leeches and the vampire that Sally and her Tunics had kidnapped.

Morales, looking dapper as always was the moderator of the evening. He wore a designer suit just like Maclemar. *Only the best for Morales*, Poe thought. "Okay, Sally. You'll have time to talk some more about the execution of leeches if Perla grants you her minutes. In the meantime, it's time to hear from the woman I personally saw shoot down Council members and their minions with an old clunker rifle. For those of you who escaped using the subway tunnels four years ago, you wouldn't have made it without the help and protection of this woman. And how can we forget about the time our friend defeated the city's master vampires, rescued custodians, and laid her life on the line to give us the chance to start over in peace?"

The crowd roared, screaming Poe's name. By the curtains, Poe couldn't harness a smile. "This is like a frikkin' concert with my horrible voice at center stage."

"Good luck, Poe," said Michelle. It was the first time her protégé talked to her since the leeches were kidnapped.

"Thanks, Michelle."

"I'll be down in the crowd to keep an eye if someone wants to harm you."

"Appreciate it." The woman was still cold to her.

Something chilly rested on her hand. Sainvire had done his appear-out-of-nowhere trick. "You okay, Poe?"

"I don't know. My mind's a jumble. I've got a couple of weeks anyhow, and I'm out of here." Poe squeezed his hand. "You know, you're very manipulative, right? Getting me to leave my island. Getting me to speak."

"I don't mean to be. You're just very important to all of us."

"Why don't you marry me then so you can have access to my brainwaves and charisma?" taunted Poe.

Sainvire narrowed his eyes. "Would you consider marrying me?"

Poe shook her head. "Hell no! You'll get me to hawk Plasmacore for you all over the country until I lose my arm, my leg, and my nose."

"You think I'm only using you?"

Poe shrugged. "Yeah. With this politics thing. If you really loved me, you've have left me alone. It must be nice to have someone to puppet around all the time. And the world knows generals make the worst politicians."

She didn't know why she lashed out at Sainvire. Perhaps she'd been thinking about her role in Sainvire's plan. Maybe she was still pissed that he never visited her in Catalina. And maybe she was tired of creatures attempting to murder or threaten her while Sainvire would clap her back and say he was sorry and he loved her.

The pain in Sainvire's eyes nearly made feel her guilty. Fortunately Joseph grabbed her arm and led her to where the curtain was parted.

"Here she is, the Small Giant, the Sureshot Wonder, and our very own hero, Julia Poe!" Poe accepted the podium and frowned at Morales, who sounded like an over-the-top boxing announcer.

The vampire killer lowered the microphone and cleared her throat. She reached inside her right pocket then her left while silence reigned in the hall.

"Shit," she cursed. "Must've dropped my speech." The crowd laughed. *Just what I didn't want to happen.* She looked around the expectant faces and the colorful shirts and shook her head. "I'm no speechmaker anyway. I can do a lot of things, but they don't make much sense these days." She glanced at Morales who smiled kindly at her. His shiny white teeth lifted her spirits.

"I was left alone here in Downtown at age eight. I won't bore you with the details, but everyone I loved was lost. Like most of you at that time, I was on my own. I survived by hiding, killing, and later by stealing cattle with Sister Ann and Goss. They are also gone now. Then I met Sainvire, Joseph, Maple, and Perla." Poe searched for Perla among the Tunics and found her. Their eyes met. "When Morales here says I single-handedly did this and did that, he exaggerates. I couldn't have taken on Trench and the Vampire

Council without the help of vampires, halfdead, and humans. We all did our part, starting with Sainvire asking Perla to come up with a new food source to end the blood bath, to end human slavery," she said in her husky tone. Her ears were red and burning.

Poe looked around the crowd. "Did you know this about Sainvire?" She watched heads turn in the negative. "Sainvire is an idealist. His friends know this. Perla is a gifted scientist who deserves a statue somewhere for creating Plasmacore. If you haven't heard of her, she's the head of the Tunics. She also taught me a little something about guns.

"Maple was as central to the destruction of the reign of vampires. She was human. Dying, actually, from the Gray Armageddon. Then her partner asked Sainvire to turn her. And I'm glad this vampire did because Maple's dignity, clear head, and mallet arms saved a bunch of you sitting here today." Poe purposely omitted Perla's name.

Poe cleared her throat. "Then there's Joseph with his amazing speed who pledged to save humanity along with his friend Sainvire. These two vampires tried to make a difference, and they lost their friends and loved ones in the process. Joseph, he's probably going to kill me for this because he's very private," she said. "He lost his wife, a human. Megan. She was dying from childbirth complications. He asked if he could turn her and allow her to live forever, but Megan declined. Joseph honored his wife's wishes and watched her die a human death."

Poe was disoriented suddenly. She was supposed to only speak about her list, not be a storyteller. "I'm sorry if I seem like I'm going nowhere, but please indulge me with one more person. He is standing here to my right." Looking somber, Morales blinked at her.

"When I first met Sam Morales or T-Doc to all of you, I thought he was a handsome man with a very playful nature. Later I thought he was a pervert who wore too much cologne. And still does, by the way." The crowd guffawed and cheered. "I met him and Megan when they would pick up humans I broke out from Downtown blood banks. They took care of placing these people in real farms in the Central Valley. This guy, a real estate agent, became a ballistics expert, a bombmaker, a dentist, a doctor, and a father. I'm sure he learned even more when I was away."

Her hands shook suddenly. "You see, these are some of the people that helped retake this city. They are vampires, humans, halfdead, and what have you. This goes to show that all humans and undead aren't all bad. My biggest wish is for the people of Los Angeles to pull together and create a Downtown we can all be proud of. Start from scratch. I think we can start by writing up our own stories for our city history. Our stories are all-powerful, and our children will benefit from them. Our Central Library is getting repaired with the help of some of you, so we'll soon have our history intact again. We should do a census just in case you have relatives in other cities, but that's another bale of hay. Anyway, here I go now without my list. I hope I don't forget anything.

"Not only do we need to compile our stories, we need to bring back the free press because we're a democracy. We have the Los Angeles Times building several blocks away, so we should get back in there and get those printing presses rolling.

"T-Doc needs psychologists and other physicians. We have few professionals who can teach counseling classes. His massage therapy seems to be a great hit, and so is the talking kind. I'm sure many of you have some sort of skill to share.

"We need garden projects because growing new things is vital and soothing according to a Martha Stewart Magazine article I came across when I was a kid. The farmers are willing to take farm helpers if people want to get away from the city.

"Churches for some of that old time religion or simply a hall to commune with your friends might be a good idea.

"Movie theater revivals. We have tons of theaters on Broadway and folks sure love to watch movies. I personally watch all sorts of films, so I'm looking forward to that project.

"Very important. We ought to monitor vampire creation. We don't want angry vampires on the loose no matter how righteous they think they are." Poe's words hushed the crowd as they stared where the Tunics sat. Poe eyed Sally then Perla who looked away.

"Clothes drives for children and adults. This means shopping in Santee Alley and the garment district. If you look good you feel good. Seamstresses and tailors out there, teach classes.

"We need to limit our alcohol consumption because it leads to stupidity and violence in our depressed state of mind. Right, Roger?" The crowd laughed. Roger was a known lush who drank at vampire and human watering holes from morning to closing. "You can't turn into Rambo and take on the world with a crossbow. Besides, there's nothing worse than an alcoholic. My uncle was one, and he was punchable."

"We need to mix different folks up. We need a place of entertainment where everyone can enjoy a show. I want to introduce you to Shandra. Where are you?" A redhead dead with a tiny waist and breasts double the size of Jane Mansfield's stood up in her tight leather alligator mini-skirt. The hollering and wolf whistle from both humans and vampires created a ruckus. Shandra had been Trench's favorite stripper, and Poe had been fascinated by her. "Alright, folks, that's enough. Shandra's starting a club where men, women, and vamps can show off their dancing prowess."

Poe hung her head low. "I know I'm forgetting something. Oh well. In any case I believe we should have a council of nine representing the different factions out there. This is how we'll deal with problems and approve measures. Basic line is: we're gonna need to work together because we're a community. I'm just an ignorant girl with no schooling, so don't be too hard on me. Okay. I'm done." Poe ignored the clapping and concentrated on getting down the platform.

Poe received a hug from Morales and shook hands with attendees who shoved themselves in her face. She sat between Maclemar and Percy who was minding Chops and Penny in the seventh row. Penny parked herself next to Poe's leg and was lovingly massaged about the neck. Poe slid her free cold hand in Maclemar's which he squeezed to show support. "I love you, Julia Poe," he whispered in her ear.

The vampire eradicator stared into his jewel eyes and smiled at him.

The girl could barely contain her yawning. Politics bored her. When the different factions stated their points, Poe fought to keep awake. More than once had Maclemar nudged her to life. The only time she perked up was when Sally took the stage once more, taking over Perla's turn.

Poe sat up straight and Penny growled.

"Let me continue my speech," she said. "Whereas Julia Poe would want us to have an entertainment center starring the lewd vampire Shandra as a platform, I'd like to recast your attention to leeches. It's time for them to die!" The Tunics led boisterous shouting.

From behind the curtains, thrown to the stage were six bodies – five emaciated leeches and Syrus, the vampire butcher. Sturdy rope bound the humans' wrists and ankles while the vampire was handcuffed. The sound of shock from the assembly filled the room. Perla along with three other Tunics flanked Sally in support of the measure.

"Sainvire, you have no more say in this matter," Sally hissed. The blonde, grungy vampire's wrath was nearly palpable. "They have no use in our new society. These worms will die tonight."

Poe looked around for Sainvire who leaned against the wall nearest the Tunics. He looked relaxed. Too relaxed. She reached down to pat Penny on the head but felt nothing but air. The dog had disappeared. "Penny?"

On the stage was Penny, baring her fangs at Sally.

"What the hell!" Sally cursed when Penny took a nip at her thick ankle. "Goddamn dog!" She kicked Penny like a football, and Sainvire from the other side of the room whizzed in a blur to catch her.

Poe's ears were on fire, and her eyes teared. Before she knew it, she was standing in the middle aisle and glaring at Sally.

"Oops. Was that your dog?" asked Sally and everyone on the stage, except for Perla, laughed.

Poe tried to still her voice and her shaking hands. "No one kicks my dog," she said crossly. "No one!"

"Well I just did," said Sally smugly. "What are you going to do, shoot me? I heard you can't shoot worth shit! And—"

Before the woman could finish her thought, the twin Colt .45 guns were out of the holsters and

Poe had fired and caught Sally right between the eyes. The surprised audience and shocked Tunics shrieked in fright. The Tunics took to the air, and Poe smiled bitterly. Her left hand shot knee caps while the right aimed for the stomach because the ripped organ hurt vampires like a son of a bitch. Perla's people landed on the stage, screaming in pain from burning garlic-dipped bullets.

Poe ran to the stage and scaled it. She stood face to face with Perla. She'd blotted out the noise in the hall and concentrated on her old friend.

Maple yelled from one of the side benches. "Poe, don't! Leave her be!"

Poe's eyes narrowed. "Oh, I'm not going to harm her, Maple. She was good to me once." Then she turned to Perla. "Isn't that something? She's still trying to protect you after the shitty way you've treated her."

Perla looked away. Poe sheathed one of her guns and picked up the microphone.

"Don't look away, Perla. You're gonna get what you wished for. You're all gonna get what you've come for. Poe walked to the first leech and pointed her gun at his head. The audience in the auditorium screamed. "Hush up! Have any of you really killed before? It's not romantic. It's not like Chuck Norris on a pleasure cruise to some dank tropical country. I wonder if any of you would have the brass to do this." Poe pulled the trigger, and the leech's brain splattered on the curtains. The other leeches tried to scamper away, but they couldn't. They cried and begged Poe for mercy.

"How's that, Perla?" She met the woman's eyes. "Do you feel better?" She located Michelle on the first row with a look of revulsion on her face. "What about you, Michelle? An eye for an eye? Well here's one dedicated to you." Poe fired without looking at the second leech in line. The bullet destroyed his face, leaving a pool of blood.

"That's enough, Poe!" ordered Sainvire who appeared on the stage.

"Leave me alone, Sainvire. You see, I'm not like some people who think you ought to retire and let creatures like the Tunics take over. I think without you, life in this city would be chaotic and brimming with vengeance. What if the San Diego crew comes over like they did this morning as they tried to kill me? You're gonna beg for Sainvire to save your asses, right?"

The vampire crept closer, and Poe dropped him with kneecap shots. He cursed painfully. Poe had shot him in a similar manner four years ago. The girl had a thing about popping knee caps. Sainvire had the gift of quick healing, but he would be down for a few minutes. "Sorry, vampire with the heart of a revolutionary, but I'm not done yet. Poe fired at two heads and watched them drop dead on the stage. The fear in the air translated into another crashing wave of screams.

"Satisfied yet? Two more and your wish will come true. After this, you Tunics can pick on the ODs, then after that vampires in general. Then after that, the humans will cap your asses for being vampires and their unwanted executioners."

Since there was nobody left to get in her way, Poe blasted the human's face and shot the reactionary vampire in the head and heart. "And that, ladies and gentlemen, is how you judge, destroy, and execute the evil in this world from this day forth." Poe stared with fire at Perla who still stood nursing her shock. As she walked down the steps to take Penny from Percy's arms, she looked Michelle over with contempt. She climbed the steps once more to go backstage, passing the anguished and fearful faces of her friends.

CHAPTER 6

ONLY T-DOC WAS ALLOWED in her room. Penny needed medical attention. Poe watched in silence as he bandaged Penny's ribs with care. She was trying hard not to lose it. The full realization of what she'd done sickened her. She was an immoral sociopath, and everyone found out that night. Morales pounded Aspirin into powder and applied it to the dog's tongue. The man was still wearing his snazzy suit, and there she was, sitting on the carpet with her clothes splayed in all directions.

"Two ribs are broken and a few more bruised. Penny's lucky Sainvire caught her or she would've been more severely injured. Give her more smashed up pain relievers every four hours. It's better to let her sleep on the floor. That way there will be less jostling around. I brought a bag of food from Habib, so you can stay here if you don't feel like going downstairs."

"I shouldn't have been asked to come here. Sainvire should've left me alone," she said, her voice breaking.

Morales sat by Poe on the edge of the bed and embraced her. "Darling, what you've done tonight you will feel guilty about for the rest of your life. But set that aside for a moment. You've changed a lot of minds. What you did will prod Downtown in the right direction."

"What the hell have I done but murder five people and a vampire, execution-style? Sure I was mad about Penny, but Sally got on my nerves. I listened to my impulse to kill just to prove a point. I haven't killed all that much lately, Sam. I feel sick."

"I know. I feel for you, but you must see this as something positive. When you left the meeting, your proposed council of nine was voted on and so was the release of leeches in jail. They are to be indentured to ex-cattle for ten years. When their time is up they can be given their own home and a chance for a new life. Michelle came up with that one, actually."

"You guys continued the meeting after I left? That's kinda sick. And I shot Sainvire, too!"

"The bodies on stage represented the anger out there. Knowing they were executed to tone down vengeance for blood and opened people's eyes. No more theatrics. Who could actually do what you've done without throwing up their dinner? Your words about unstoppable hatred skipping to a new group made sense. As for shooting Sainvire, it only proves that you aren't his puppet. You're independent from Downtown politics. And what you said about San Diego shits trying to assassinate you scared the rocks out of a lot of people. Everyone, including ODs, is on board to be battle ready. Though they might not admit it, most creatures prefer this new society over any other in our little world."

"You don't hate me, right?" asked Poe in a small voice. "Even though I'm a monster."

"You're my little Poe. Of course I don't hate you. Without you on this earth, life would be awfully boring. Besides, you need to spend more time with your goddaughter."

"I'm thinking about leaving tomorrow."

"You promised you'd stay for two months. Just my opinion, but you should keep your word." Morales' wise gaze made her nod.

After Morales left, Poe organized her room and ate Tupperware food. She flossed, brushed her teeth, and showered. She needed to wash away her repugnant failings and clean her mind. The look of fear from those leeches tore at her brain no matter what she did. Instead of being stuck in Sainvire's hotel, she wished she was in Catalina watching bison munching on grass. She didn't dare leave her room because she expected blame in people's eyes.

"I'm sorry. Forgive me," she said to the ceiling. She'd killed a lot of different creatures before, but this incident was undoubtedly the worst.

She woke up in a pool of sweat after dreaming about shooting majestic bison in the head. Drinking a glass of water and placing medicine in Penny's mouth, the killer decided she needed to see Maclemar. He lived three doors down on the same floor. Sainvire was a machinating S.O.B.

The hallway smelled of sulfur and old carpet, and the odor made her nose itch. Tip-toeing to Maclemar's door, Poe knocked loudly because her friend was a heavy sleeper. She pounded on the door for over a minute, reddening in the half-lit hallway in fear of being discovered by a disgruntled neighbor. When she was about to give up, Maclemar opened the door with just his boxers and heavy-lidded eyes.

"Poe!" he said with surprise. At once he was awake. "Come in, sharren. Come in."

Without hesitation, Poe stepped inside. The girl was wearing a plain black t-shirt and faded pajama pants. Wordlessly she slid into Maclemar's queen-size bed and covered herself with blankets. Maclemar sighed and followed Poe to bed. He embraced her shivering body while she burrowed her face into his chest.

"Oh, love. I'm so sorry," he said quietly in his Welsh accent. "I shouldn't have brought you here. I feel responsible."

Poe sniffed. Tears began to trickle down her cheeks onto Maclemar's chest. "Don't blame yourself, James. It was me. I'm a bad seed. I killed those poor leeches to prove a point. A stupid point I forgot already. And then there's Penny. I keep thinking she's going to die anytime and leave me alone. When Sally kicked her I thought she killed my dog."

"Morales said Penny's alright. Don't fret now." He kissed her forehead.

"Penny's the only one who'd really die for me and stay at my side no matter what."

Maclemar tightened his embrace. "You're wrong about that, my girl. I'd die for you and stay at your side forever if you ask me to."

Poe wept, sobbing into the arms of a friend who'd proven his loyalty to her over and over again. Perhaps she was a needy person now that Penny was old and weak, but the thought of spending her life with Maclemar didn't seem bad. He was a decent man with many skills and a heart as immense as the London Eye.

She wiped her face and blew her nose with tissue Maclemar handed her when her eyes couldn't eek out any more tears. Hoarsely she asked him, "Can I stay with you for two weeks until I leave this place for the last time?"

Maclemar kissed her small nose. "It would be my pleasure. I promise not to take advantage either." Poe clung to the man she used to refer to as Caveman, sometimes running her hands on his body to feel the scars vampires had given him. *We're similar in so many ways*, she thought. *My body is bullet-ridden and scarred like a 90-year-old Muay Thai warrior.*

"Would you leave Downtown for me?" she asked timidly, sounding unsure.

"I would if I could live on your island with you."

"What about your students?"

"There are plenty of ex-cattle who can take my place," he sighed. "Listen, Poe. I like these people, but I can live without them. But you. I'd do anything for you."

Poe kissed him tentatively on the mouth. "We can live together, but I won't be able to sleep with you for a long while. Trench has broken me in a lot of ways."

"Sweetheart, you don't have to explain. I'll wait until you're ready. And if it never happens, then I'll be a happy man living with you just the same."

She woke up the next morning in the warm embrace of James Maclemar. He'd been studying her face like a Rembrandt painting. "You're staring at my scar, aren't you?" she accused.

"Nope. I'm imagining living the rest of my life with you, and it makes me want to hum the tune from *The Bridge Over the River Kwai*."

"Hey. That's a good movie. William Holden was a looker," she said, smiling up at Maclemar. "I have a big collection of movies in my old underground bunker. Maybe we could take those and a few DVD players with us."

"Whatever you want, my sweet. I'll haul them for you to Mars. No problem."

Poe's eyes narrowed. Sainvire would never think to put her at the top of his agenda. The vampire used her like a cheap politician sporting around his movie star hand wavers to pander to wide-eyed voters. She wasn't going to allow Kaleb Sainvire to use her again. She was done with vampire politics. She was ready for happiness with James Maclemar and to ensure the rest of Penny's days were loving.

Poe spent the next few days avoiding Kaleb Sainvire, and she kept her distance from just about everyone else. Percy had amassed a closet full of skateboards, and the girl had let her borrow a Vision Skateboards model. She needed wheels to do some investigating, and a skateboard would do. Her brother had been a champion skater, and Poe had dabbled in riding a board when she lived in West L.A. and Catalina Island.

Downtown had imprisoned her most of her life and had been a source of pain and suffering, but downhilling and flying over dazzling urban architecture sobered her hate. The city had potential, and she was willing to do what she could until her two weeks were up. She was going to make her own choices, however, and to hell with Sainvire's maneuvering.

Since her attack at the park, Poe had been trying to figure out where the vampires had materialized from. Their arrival just didn't make sense. Poe hopped off the deck in front of a red corrugated metal structure in the heart of the warehouse district. The district used to be the most perilous part of town where human trafficking, murder, and blood gambling occurred, not to mention the plump rats that had multiplied exponentially. In recent months Sainvire brought in a citywide vector control to exterminate vermin, and he'd succeeded in eradicating a good number of the rat population.

Poe knocked on the warehouse door holding a Mark Gonzales deck under her arm. An Ancient covered in dark blankets beckoned her to come inside quickly. She and her companion were vulnerable to sunlight.

"Hi. You're Stanza, right?" asked Poe as the woman flung the blanket to a yellow couch that had the pattern of *The Kiss* by Gustav Klimt. Their home was lovely. It was filled with antique Persian rugs, hip high vases, leafy indoor plants that brought warmth in the home, lots of mismatched chintzes, and a divan that added bohemian flavor.

"Yes. And you're Julia Poe." The slow moving Ancient indicated a sofa for her to sit on. "That's Kilbur over there. You can call him my longtime companion, I suppose." The vampire's skin was near alabaster with maps of varicose veins on her face, neck, and arms. Poe gasped inwardly. If Sainvire chose to live as long as these Ancients, Poe would be completely turned off.

"Hi, Kilbur," she said. She shook the creature's icy hand which looked extra long for the curling yellow nails on the tip of his fingers. The Ancient could crush her hand like a stack of wafer cookies. "Sorry to disturb you both. I just have a couple of questions. Then I'll leave you alone."

"Miss Poe," said Kilbur. "No one ever visits us. Though we are Ancients, we are not truly dead. We enjoy company more than you think. Isn't that right, Stanza?"

Kilbur had only wisps of brown hair left on his skull, and his lady wore a long red wig that brought out the frightening red in her eyes. "Absolutely. We used to be very social, but both humans and vampires steered away from us. I suppose the alternative to dying would be to live and look like us."

"That's too bad. Nothing wrong with multiculturalism. Or multivampirism. That's what I always say. Your kind is always needed in a growing society since you've experienced history firsthand. Well since you're the last Ancients Downtown, I was curious about your fealty to the group trying to glue this town back together."

"Sainvire cleaned the city. Humans are trying to reform into something stronger. I am for a cosmopolitan city for it makes for a better society. I want Downtown to succeed because the alternative has the appeal of a wet dog. I remember how filthy Downtown was with those uncouth rats in charge."

Poe wasn't sure if Kilbur was talking literally about rats or about the Vampire Council, but she kept quiet.

"Yes. I agree with Kilbur," said Stanza. "Some sort of order laced with humanity is the path we must take. Plasmacore has changed our world. It has made most of us stronger. Our desire for human blood lessens as we imbibe the life juice that is Plasmacore. Because of the miracle food, we are more nimble as if our old bones were oiled for better performance. Kilbur and I hope one day to enjoy the warmth of the sun."

"Would you protect Downtown against outside aggressors?" asked Poe, drumming her fingers on her board on her lap.

The two Ancients looked at each other in their colorful robes and turned their gaze to Poe.

"Most certainly, Miss Poe. We like our lives now," said Stanza.

"Call me Poe. Everyone else does. But I'm glad of your answer. I need people to trust, and I'd like to enlist you both for something I need to do."

Kilbur laughed softly. "At last. An adventure. Lead the way, dear child."

She couldn't help it. She smiled at the sunny winter day as she kicked her board to City Hall. The Ancients had entertained her with tales about how they first met, and the two were enjoying themselves so much while taking turns with the details that Poe couldn't find it in her heart to end the visit. Finally after an hour, Poe asked for forgiveness and kissed both vampires goodbye on their cold cheeks simply because her inner voice told her to. The Ancients were tickled by the gesture.

Next stop was with Michelle. Poe was certain Michelle had a hand in releasing the prisoners into the Tunics' hands. She was sure, however, that the fiery head of security realized her folly; otherwise she wouldn't have introduced the indentured resolution to the Los Angeles Council.

She grinded to a halt in front of the metal doors of City Hall and kicked her skateboard into her hands. A dour vampire, the same hairy one that wouldn't let Poe visit the prisoners, opened the door for her. Her face was impassive but not unfriendly.

"Hey," said Poe.

"Hello," the woman said with a nod and a hint of camaraderie in her bearing.

"Is Michelle here?"

The woman provided the chief's location on the second floor. Poe thanked the police woman politely and headed to the big cheese's office. City Hall had been one of Quillon Trench's buildings where he collected beautiful ex-LAPD officers. Being in the building gave her the creeps, but she had no choice but to ask Michelle for a favor.

She found the curly-hair vixen with brawny arms and a tight abdomen leaning over her very masculine black secretary. Michelle was wearing a mini-skirt, sneakers, and a halter top that showcased her belly button piercing. "Poe! What are you doing here?" asked Michelle unsteadily. She was caught by surprise.

"Hey, Michelle. I've come to talk to you if you have the time."

"For you there's always time."

"What can I do you for?" asked Michelle as she lowered herself to a comfortable looking chair with built-in massage functions.

"How many vamps from San Diego have defected to our side of town since Joseph and Rufus started dropping flyers from airplanes?"

Michelle pulled out a ledger from her drawer and studied its contents. "I believe 40 vamps and 120 human cattle have crossed over. Why?"

"Could you do me a favor and ask those vamps to come to one of the conference rooms at the hotel? I know Morales is going to kill me, but bring the humans they rescued. I figure most are still suffering from the vampire venom and are still comatose. Am I right?"

"Yeah. I believe so. But what's this all about, Poe? You need to give me more information than this. That's a big request. Lots of bodies. What time is the meeting supposed to be?"

"Five. The earlier the better because we're going to have to transport some of the humans back to their hospital beds."

"Some of them?"

"Yeah. I'll have to explain later. I might be wrong about this, so I don't want to stir things up too much. Just trust me, Michelle."

Michelle, a tough girl who refused to appear weak, cleared her voice. "I do trust you, Poe. I guess I should've trusted you from day one. I let my rage and prejudice rule my head. I'm going to try to be less emotional and look at the world with fresh eyes because I hold an important position. When you killed those leeches, I felt like I was executing them myself. It didn't feel so good anymore. And I lied to you. I turned a blind eye and allowed the prisoners to be taken."

"I know you did. But now you'll know never need to use your office for murder before a trial. You'll be a better cop this way." Poe reached for Michelle's hand. "You're still a sister to me. Don't think you've let me down. I lost track of all the people I've let down."

"You're a sister to me, too. And what you had to do to show how fucked up we are will haunt me forever. Blame the executions on us, Poe. Don't beat yourself up like you always do."

Poe rose and nodded. "I've done so many terrible things in my life. To help me cope, I'm starting to forget what happened a couple days ago. Do you have any favors left for me?"

"Sure, Poe."

"Teach with the JKD Judo Club one of these days. This way humans and vamps won't be so afraid of cops and the up-and-coming government."

"Will do. Are you really leaving DT?"

"Yup."

As Poe skated by she noticed a few hands waving at her from the windows above. She waved back. At least a few didn't hate her after all. She slid to a stop at the steps of the Biltmore to the amusement of guards and passersby. *What the hell. It's as if none of them saw the murders I committed the other day.*

Her next meet and greet was with Morales and Joseph. She needed to convince them to sign on with her plan. "Absolutely not!" said Morales. "These are sick people, Poe."

Poe looked to Joseph for help. The vampire with the ponytail simply shrugged.

She had to run through her hypothesis for the two men before they reluctantly agreed with her plans. "Poe, if you hurt these poor people, I'll have you locked in Maclemar's room without your dinner." Poe gulped. So much for keeping her new roommate a secret.

"Should we bring Maple in?" asked Joseph. "And I assume Sainvire knows your plans, right?"

"Sure. Let Maple know if she's still talking to me. As for Sainvire, we don't need him. This is my brainchild, and I don't want him doing the puppet thing with me again. I won't let him treat me like a guinea pig. Besides, I'm most likely to cap his knees if I see his dead face. I'm so angry I want to be Robin Hood and spring an arrow through his crotch."

Joseph grimaced then grinned and nodded toward the door. Poe gritted her teeth. *He's standing behind me, isn't he?* She turned toward the master vampire. "Fuck," she said.

"Try not to cap my knees, please. They still sting," said Sainvire. "I heard your plan, and its sound."

Poe threw the evilest look at Joseph who hadn't alerted her that Sainvire had crept up. "Sorry. He's my best friend," said Joseph with a guilty look.

"Gee. Nice to get the stamp of approval from the great and mighty Kaleb Sainvire. I feel humbled indeed."

"That's nice that you feel humbled since you're so preoccupied with weaving stories about men in green shooting arrows at my groin," said Sainvire with amusement. Poe's nostrils flared when Morales and Joseph snickered. "Since I'm the puppet master you so despise, I should leave the room. However, as a newly appointed Guardian of the City, I can't let any potentially dangerous plans that concern the city and the Biltmore unravel without my approval."

"Guardian?" Poe asked with conflagration in her voice. "What the hell is that?"

"Seems like you haven't been keeping up with the news. There's a fledgling government now called the Los Angeles Council. They voted at the assembly two days ago and declared me, Joseph, Jenna, and other vampires and humans who'd fought together as the protectors of the city. The nine Council members are John Danby, a custodian; Maple, a vampire; Rufus, a halfdead; Passionada, a human; Bartholemew Howard, an OD; Esperanza, a custodian; Seth Lime of the farmers; Perla, a Tunic, and Habib, a human and the most famous cook this side of the planet."

"Sainvire's the Commander of the Guardians and Joseph's the Captain," added Morales.

"Very interesting, but all your rules, regulations, and bonehead rankings don't pertain to me. I was brought here to move things along, and that means I can do whatever I want to safeguard this city until my time's up."

"You're to blame, you know?" said Sainvire while lazily crossing his arms. "You have a host of ideas, and your followers snap them up. Now most everyone seems satisfied with their exciting but imperfect government."

Poe tightened her ponytail. "So it's my fault people can't think for themselves? Anyway, you heard my plan. Are you in or are you out?"

"I'm in," said Sainvire in his deep timbre that usually caused Poe's legs to turn spaghetti.

"I have lots of other ideas, too. But I'll discuss them later with the three of you if we pull off tonight's plan."

Beside Poe's shooting prowess, the little warrior was also known as a fierce strategist. Morales, Joseph, and Sainvire wouldn't dare wave away her plans for they could be as valuable as the fate of Downtown.

———

A modest hall in the Biltmore Hotel had been purposely arranged oddly. Twenty sets of three beds bearing ex-cattle were scattered around the room while the vampire escapees from San Diego stood by the foot of the beds. The sleepers and their rescuers had been in the dark until they received an invitation from Sam Morales that afternoon.

The ex-cattle lay in still slumber, their faces thin and their complexion gray. Their blood had been milked for nearly two decades. One bite from a vampire could last an entire year, rendering the victim comatose until the annual follow-up bite. Recovered blood victims reported they had been aware of their surroundings but powerless to move in their stupor. Some had witnessed their own rapes but were unable to scream their horror.

They awoke not recognizing their own faces or their bodies which had deteriorated from lack of movement. Anemia and bone degenerative diseases were daily battles Morales had to confront. Morales was a firm believer in aerial propaganda drops to different cities with ingredients and instructions to make Plasmacore. "Plasmacore can show you the sun. Cattle can only remind you of your guilt," was a slogan he wrote. Another was "Drink Plasmacore. Don't bow to a master vampire to be powerful."

They were horrible slogans, but T-Doc was quietly tickled by them.

He was especially proud of Joseph and Rufus' flying missions. They had sent off thousands of pamphlets to incite vampires from San Diego and San Francisco to leave their cities for Downtown L.A., a friendlier, more rewarding place. All they needed as a ticket were two or three human cattle or children. So far the roomful of ex-cattle proved the ballsy gamble a success.

Maple and Rufus stood by the hall doors while Michelle, in skintight jeans, tank top, and low slung Berettas paced slowly across the aisles trying to avoid looking at the faces of the bony humans on the beds. Unlike many ex-cattle,

Michelle rose to the task and worked on her body and fighting skills. Her initiative was an inspiration to more than a few human slaves hoping to regain their old power.

Joseph, looking tired, sat on a stool and rested his head on the wall. The vampire closed his eyes to take a nap with a non-stop grin on his face. His closest friends had surmised that during such lazy moments, Joseph was dreaming of Megan, his love who had left him alone to his musings.

The San Diego runaways were looking at each other as if wondering what the hell was going on. They answered one another with shrugs. An extremely pale man with freckles and pomegranate red hair cleared his throat. "Er, T-Doc. What are we doing here?"

"Just routine stuff," Morales said in his lab coat. "We need you folks to give us more details about where you found these humans."

Before the redhead could ask another question, the door opened. Poe, followed by two Ancients and Sainvire, walked slowly into the room. The girl's bouncy ponytail gave her a disarmingly childish air. But then again, she wore a black t-shirt that showed off 15 years of fighting scars on her arms and face. The .45s were nowhere on her person. The only armament she wore was the homemade machete that the majority at the hotel seemed to snicker about. The weapon was slung in a scabbard along her left hip.

"Hi, fellas. Sorry we're late," she smiled. She shoved her hand in her olive green army pants and pulled out a rather long syringe. "Before I start, can I ask whether you recognize each other from San Diego or San Francisco? I know each city has about 700 to 1000 inhabitants, so perhaps you've seen each other?"

Many disclosed information along the lines of "I've seen him around but I don't know him." One said, "The different vampire houses didn't really socialize with each other."

Michelle handed out Polaroids of the three vamps that had attacked Poe at her martial arts club. "Recognize these people?"

Charles, the redhead, scratched his vermillion eyebrows. "I know these guys. They work for the House of Runer. Runer is a day vamp that's considered an upperdead. He can fly, run like the wind, and his fists turn into sharp stakes. Scary guy.

"Which house were you in?" asked Michelle, looking the vampire up and down.

"I worked at the city orphanage. I fed babies, washed their butts, and sang to them. When flyers snowed our city in, I picked one up that read, 'Cattle will die soon. Use Plasmacore and be humane again. Bring children and humans. You will have a brand new life in Downtown Los Angeles.'" He looked at the three empty beds behind him.

"You brought five healthy children to us. We're grateful," said Morales.

"Those kids are almost old enough for blood harvest. I would've taken more if I could."

"You recognize these San Diego folks?" She swept a hand to the 18 men and a female vamp.

"Sure.   Victoria worked with me.   She smuggled out four babies and two 10-year-olds. We were talking about stealing a van and heading here."

He pointed at a bearded vampire that held an unlit pipe in his one hand. "That's Jones.   His master chopped off his arm when he asked mercy for the older cattle. Jones only wanted those folks to live the rest of their lives awake and unhassled." Michelle gave Jones a once over. The man carried himself like a physics professor, and his eyes were indeed haunted.

"That's all I know though," the redhead said. "Some houses keep to themselves."

Sainvire nodded and clapped the smaller vampire on the back. "Thank you, Charles. How many babies and children did you look after?"

"I was looking after half of the city's children. Say about 80."

Victoria, a woman who dressed like a schoolmarm, timidly elaborated, "We have 20 infants, 10 toddlers, and the rest are children that range from 5 to 12. The total count would be 123 children."

"Thanks, Victoria," said Poe. "That was a brave thing you did. Now I have to conduct some testing." She uncapped a three-inch syringe. The Ancients walked protectively next to her wherever she and Morales approached each ex-slave. Morales listened to a human's heartbeat while Poe poked a needle under his or her nails.

The tedious experiment continued with no substantiating results. "They say sticking needles under fingernails was one of the most painful torture devices ever invented," said Poe. "But we're not here to torture. Like I said, we're just checking something."

She smiled at an SD runaway vamp dressed like a mannequin. "My. You must be awfully strong to carry these three mountain men on your own." The eyes of the human on the first bunk flickered. "Forget this guy, Morales. He's pretty out of it." Once Morales stepped out of the way, Poe dug the needle into the human's toe nail. Immediately the supposedly comatose man sat up and cursed up a storm, mostly directed at Poe. His bunk mates sat up as well, fear burning in their eyes.

The well dressed vampire hissed, and his fangs elongated into a pretty two inches. "Get up, you leeches!" he ordered and brought out a Glock 22. Before he could point the weapon at anyone, Stanza took hold of the vampire's hand and crushed it with the gun still in his clutches. The vampire squealed like a murdered animal and fellto his knees.

Kilbur lifted all three leeches by the cuff of their gowns. He was fast for an Ancient. *Plasmacore is a hell of a drink*, thought Poe.

The rest was smooth sailing after the initial bust with three more double-agents and their leeches coming forward on their own.

"To those who passed with flying colors, we commend you. And we apologize for putting you through this ordeal. We're proud to have you with us," said Maple, who'd been quiet but alert.

Sainvire, Maple, Joseph, Rufus, Michelle, and Poe met up at the cafeteria an hour later.

"Let's have the three SD vamps chomp down on this for a while. Their every word is being monitored and recorded. Forget about them trying to escape, either. When we told them their guards are the two Ancients that crushed GQ's hand, they were shitting masonry," said Michelle. "We'll find out more in the morning. In the meantime, got any more ideas?"

Poe slurped her pasta, chewed quickly, and swallowed with satisfaction. "As we speak, Maclemar, Morales, and a couple guys are stripping the cars these SD vamps brought."

"Huh?" said Michelle, confused.

"Well I figure that's the best way to destroy our sense of safety – terrorist bullshit. And looking back at past warfare, I think of bombs placed strategically in cars. Could be nothing, so I haven't made a big deal out of it." Poe forked more pasta shells in her mouth. Sainvire grinned.

"Joseph. Mind checking on those guys?"

"Nope. I'm getting tortured myself watching Poe devour my favorite food of all time." He looked at his half-filled glass of Plasmacore and grimaced. He downed the lab-produced blood, winced, and said his adieu.

"I'll join him," said Rufus. "I'm bored."

"Michelle, I need to talk to you about something," said Sainvire.

"Can you wait? I want to know more about this bomb thing and why I wasn't told about it."

"I told Poe to keep it under wraps. Even from you. Now come on." Sainvire not so subtly pointed his jaw at Maple, swirling Plasmacore in her glass. Michelle's eyes widened, finally understanding what Sainvire was getting at. Maple and Poe hadn't spoken since the girl killed Perla's hostages.

Poe wiped her mouth with a napkin and realized the setup. For the life of her, she couldn't think of what to say. The usually taciturn vampire broke the silence. *Thank goodness*, thought Poe.

"You did well tonight," said Maple. We're glad you're here looking out for us. You've grown into a very intelligent, confident woman. I'm very proud of you."

Poe's eyes misted. "I have a lot of faults, too, Maple. I do inhuman things."

"You do things that must be done but the rest of us are too cowardly to do. You and Sainvire have been handling the dirty jobs for us. So I thank you."

"I wasn't going to harm Perla, you know."

"I know that. But I love her so much that I had to protect her as a precaution."

"Have you talked to her?"

"No. She won't leave the Alexandria. People say she's creating an army of bedridden vampires."

"I'm sorry, Maple."

"I'm sorry, too, Poe." The vampire rose and sat next to Poe. She kissed Poe's cheek and the two embraced.

"You guys are my family, Maple. We'll get Perla back somehow."

Maple hugged her even closer but did not say a word.

CHAPTER 7

THE SAN DIEGO LEECHES spilled the beans. The vampires sent by the House of Runer were to observe, and once a month one of the three would drive back to San Diego and report. The leeches' role was to roam during the day, take notes of the humans living in the city, and gauge their health. If they could provide food for another 10 years, then they would be worth retaking.

Poe's hunches, sharpened with age, were correct in assuming that the cars owned by the SD vamps were rigged with explosives. Maclemar and Morales needed help from the diminutive halfdead, Ed, who could push an entire locomotive by hand.

"I don't want to chance it," said Morales. "If I snip the wrong colored wire, my kid will be left with one daddy."

"I understand, my friend," said Maclemar, clapping his friend on the back. "You're the most valuable man Downtown, Doc. As for me, you've been teaching me bombmaking and detonation for over a year now, but my skills are still questionable."

"You're better than others, Maclemar. But I'm not going to chance you. The little one will kick my ass if anything happens to you."

"It's not what you think. We're just roommates to scare off each other's nightmares. She asked me to leave with her in a week."

"And are you?"

"I love her. I'll do anything for Poe."

"And she loves you?" asked Morales with a serene smile on his face.

"She said she does. But I know how she feels about Kaleb. I'll take what I can."

Morales nudged Maclemar on the arm. "You both deserve peace and happiness. Our Poe needs to stop killing. It's gnawing on her soul. After what Trench did to her, Sainvire shouldn't have asked her to leave her island paradise."

"If she hadn't come, this town would still be divided. And don't forget the spies and these cars with explosives."

Ed, an unassuming Central American man with a slight accent, lifted a Volkswagen and walked it to an expansive park behind Chinatown. He came back for the other two cars and left them at the outskirts of town.

The two men and the halfdead made their way back to the Biltmore, ready for some shuteye.

Maclemar shut the door quietly to their room. He kneeled on the floor to pat Penny's head and kissed her on the ear. "You'll be better soon, my pet. Hang in there." The poor dog's middle was bandaged tightly, and he couldn't help but feel pity.

He undressed in the bathroom and showered. Working with explosives wasn't at the top of his list of favorite activities. The ever-present danger gave him the shakes. He preferred fixing cars, buses, airplanes, boilers, and plumbing, or figuring out to how to expand and maintain electricity citywide. But bombs? He'd rather make love to Julia Poe 3,000 times.In Gilroy, Poe had asked him to make love to her, and he happily complied. However, before the two could finish with their commingling, Sainvire interrupted to his painful annoyance. Kaleb Sainvire was a friend, but when it came to Poe, he didn't always know what to do with her. *I know what to do with her. She's my goddess. I'll love her until my dying breath,* he thought dramatically.

He flossed as Poe had insisted despite his pleas that it was against the British code to tend to teeth too often. He brushed his teeth and tongue like Poe had instructed. The little fighter sure had her opinions. Because of the trauma brought on by the Gray Armageddon and fighting vampires, her menses had stopped over a decade ago. Maclemar, if he were honest with himself, would have liked mini-Poes bouncing on his knees, but he would have settled for Julia's love anytime.

Maclemar put on some boxers and slipped inside the sheets. Half-asleep and settling herself into the hollow of his arm, Poe turned to her roommate. "You smell good," she said sleepily. "Any bombs in the cars?"

"Yes. All three. You were right," he said, smelling her fragrant hair. Poe's eyes opened wide, and she leaned on her elbow.

"Are you okay? How about Morales?"

"We're both good. We left the heavy lifting to Ed."

Poe kissed Maclemar's scratchy chin. The man needed to shave at least twice a day. "If something had happened to you, I wouldn't have forgiven myself."

"You talk as if you're in love with me," said Maclemar, kissing her forehead.

"I do love you. I think about you all the time."

"But then there's Sainvire. He was your first love and—"

"I was 22 when I met Sainvire. I'm 26 now. I'm aware of the different layers of love I feel for people like you, Joseph, Morales, and so forth. Sure, I love Sainvire, but he doesn't love me enough to give up his work. And it's important work, mind you. Without him, the city would implode. He's chosen Downtown over me," said Poe with resignation. She curled her fingers into his chest hair, her favorite distraction. "But you, James Maclemar, I love because you love me for me, soot and all. You're willing to die for me and love me until I'm old and wrinkled. And you're willing to live with me in isolation. Are you sure you're ready for that?"

Maclemar grunted. "'Course I am," he said. "Wherever you are is my happiness."

Poe had the urge to cry but hugged her big bear instead. "I love you, James. Always."

She sniffed and sought his generous mouth and kissed Maclemar, her unsure tongue saying hello to his eager one. They kissed for what seemed like minutes until both were in danger of shedding their clothing.

"You're so beautiful, sweetheart," said Maclemar, cupping her breasts then capturing each full mound in his mouth. Poe moaned and the sound excited Maclemar. His finger entered her and found moistness. He massaged her little nub until Poe was groaning.

"Maclemar," she said hoarsely. "I love you so. I'll make you happy. Please."

The Welshman braced himself on his powerful arms and sought her lips. Poe guided him inside of her. All the faces of her past drifted away including Trench who had violated her and Sainvire who had more important things to do than love an inconsequential girl.

Maclemar's length and bigness rode Poe slowly as if afraid she would break. "Faster, James. I'm won't shatter." The man groaned and made love to Poe harder and more intense than he had intended. He held himself until Poe screamed her pleasure.

"I love you, beauty," he said, holding Poe tightly in his arms.

"I love you, James." She truly meant it.

Their friends lined up to shake hands with Julia Poe and James Maclemar as Percy stood excitedly next to them. Joseph winked at her while Morales slapped her behind to the dismay of Maclemar. "I've always wanted to do that, buddy. Now that she's yours, I thought I'd better do it now or never."

Maclemar shook his head, and Poe punched Morales' stomach not too hard. "You take care of Percy," said Joseph. "Make sure to make an intellectual out of her, Maclemar. Poe, you train her into a Van Damme splits expert."

"We'll take good care of her, mate," Maclemar said. Poe hugged Percy. When Poe had asked the girl to live on the island with Maclemar and her, Percy cried in her hands. The 10-year-old had been an orphan as long as she remembered.

Sainvire stood on the lowest step in only a black t-shirt and dark slacks and shook the Welshman's hand. "Take good care of her, James."

"Will do, Kaleb. I know you'll keep watch over these parts."

"I'll try," he said. His light gray eyes found Poe's brown ones. "You take care, Poe. You'll always be a superhero around here. Whenever you decide that Catalina bores you, you always have a home with us."

Poe shook his hand. "Thanks, Sainvire. I'll see you real soon for Christmas."

"Real soon," he repeated.

Ed was waiting next to a truck laden with Poe's DVD and VHS collection from her old bunker. Much of the selection was pornography, and Ed and Maple clamped their mouths shut to keep from laughing. The girl certainly watched everything she got her hands on without prejudice. Penny had a small nook in the back seat where rattling wouldn't disturb her as much, and Chops, all 110 pounds of her, remained in the back with the clothing, tools, paperbacks, and movies.

Michelle ran to the truck. "Shit, I thought I was going to miss your sendoff!" She kissed Poe and Percy on the cheek while she slammed a wet one on Maclemar's very attractive mouth.

Instead of feeling angry, Poe laughed. "He's cute, isn't he?"

"Sure is. He wouldn't sleep with me though I tried several times to entice him."

"He's an idiot," said Poe.

"You said it, sister!" She winked at both at them. "See you real soon."

"Yeah. December," said Maclemar.

While listening to Poe and Percy make plans for a new home on the island, Maclemar drove on the Santa Monica Freeway that had been cleared by Trench. Poe thought about her burnt cabin and lost some of her pep.

They reached the San Pedro Pier and began loading the boat with Poe's belongings, Maclemar's tools, and Percy's small bag. Once the animals were safely boarded, Maclemar revved up his boat, The Chameleon, and beckoned Percy to the helm.

"See that spot there ahead?"

"Yes," answered Percy quietly. "The smudge."

"Head for it. If you need a break, let me know. Okay?"

Percy turned to Poe for her approval. "Go ahead," said Poe. She hugged Maclemar's waist tightly. "He's going to teach us a lot of useful things. Enjoy."

Maclemar kissed Poe's small cold nose and embraced her. "My darling, how much I love you!"

"Mahal kita, mister."

Their first month on Catalina Island was the happiest the three companions had ever been. Poe was especially thankful for the company. In the uninhabited town of Avalon, Percy chose a lovely six-bedroom yellow house with a private boating dock and beach. The child born of a slave mother walked around the first week as if she was in a dream. She lived with two of her favorite people whose laughter rang with the wind as they put the house in order.

She turned away whenever Poe and Maclemar snuck kisses, sometimes feeling bothersome and like a third wheel. But Percy's hero Poe and her partner Maclemar genuinely seemed happy to have her on the island. They gave her first dibs to the room of her choice. She picked the upstairs bedroom overlooking the water for two reasons. The bedroom afforded privacy to the couple whom she'd heard discussing the merits of sleeping downstairs as the best defense against unwanted company. The second reason was the beautiful view her three bay windows afforded her which would surely erase nightmares of evil vampires and long-tongued baby vamps that left her sweating and shivering at night.

The three woke up early to hike, watch bison eating for hours, and track foxes in the mud. Maclemar took his girls fishing and cooked three meals a day with a satisfied smirk on his face. Penny had a long ways to go until her ribs healed, and Chops, who was allowed in the house, granted his feet were wiped clean, munched on all things edible on the island.

One day Maclemar learned that Percy only knew of the year of her birth but not much else. He whipped up sticky toffee pudding while Poe took the girl and Chops hiking in the hills. She was to have a special celebration. When the two companions came home, the house smelled of sweets and seafood spaghetti.

Maclemar came out with the pudding decorated with 10 lit candles and broke into the happy birthday song. Poe sang along, too, in her out-of-tune voice.

"You got to make a wish before you blow the candles, love."

Percy closed her eyes then extinguished the candles in one blow. "I don't understand. I don't know when I was born."

"Well let's just say that starting today, November 8th will be your official birthday. We'll celebrate the date every year, okay?" explained Poe.

Percy hugged her new family and dug in her favorite spaghetti recipe. The sticky toffee pudding was so delicious she almost cried.

"Thanks, guys, for taking me in. You don't know how much this means to me."

Poe and Maclemar kissed her goodnight. "You're our family now," said Maclemar.

"Yeah. You're ours, and we're yours," said Poe.

"I don't feel right sometimes about how happy I am," Poe told Maclemar after they'd made love for a second time that evening. "Our friends are going through perilous days Downtown, but I don't seem to care when I'm here with you. Out of sight, out of mind."

Maclemar tweaked her sweaty nose. The young woman only seemed to sweat on the tip of her nose. "I think of the kids, but I left behind a mighty good flock of teachers before we left. I just hope that Sainvire will succeed in his vision for Los Angeles of people and vampires co-existing without violence."

Poe chewed on her full, many-a-kissed lips and thought of Sainvire. She wished him well but was sure that choosing Maclemar was the best decision she'd ever made. "Yeah. I hope things go well over there. We both remember the days of evil councils and selfish master vampires. It's terrible to think that such archaic rulers are still perpetuating the old ways in other cities."

Maclemar pulled open the drawer next to his bed. "Very scary," he said. "Now I was scouting for equipment at the other houses, and I came across this ring. You don't have to wear it or anything, but I'd like you to have it. I think it's your size." He switched on the light.

Poe took the thin titanium ring without any adornments and smiled. "Are you, like, proposing to me?"

Maclemar kissed her brow. "Well I don't believe in marriage myself, but I'd marry you in a heartbeat." Poe laughed and slid the ring onto her marriage finger. It fit perfectly. "Did you get one for yourself?"

"Well that would be tacky now, wouldn't it?" he snickered. "You have to find one for me to wear if anything."

"Alright, I'll do that."

The following day Poe went foraging from house to house for a plain ring big enough to fit Maclemar's thick finger. She rather liked the dull silver luster of her own ring and was hoping to find something similar for her man. She found large sizes on three different skeletal remains. One was gold which Poe didn't like very much, and the others were silver and a hard gray metal she'd never seen before.

She inhaled the clean tang of the ocean and headed for home. She sniffed the air for Maclemar's excellent stews but could not detect a hint of goodness. The instincts that helped her survive since she was eight years old took hold. Something was wrong here at the cottage. *Vampires. Has to be vampires.* She blinked away her worries, praying to no one in particular. *Please keep my family safe.*

She took out one of the Colt .45s and stuck it behind her back where her windbreaker would hide it better. She realized her decision to stop wearing her wrist knives was stupid. The funny-looking machete hung on a scabbard on her belt, and she groaned. *I wish I had been a better sword-maker. This thing's embarrassing.*

The day was sunny and temperate. She figured the vampires must be sun-immune and damn powerful and their human support well armed and lethal. Her instincts told her that the dead weren't sent by the pitiful Tunics this time.

Poe fiddled with the back door as quietly as possible and headed for the living room where Maclemar and Percy would normally have been. *Too late. Four of them.* Automatic weapons pointed at her. Some vampires had superhearing, of course.

"Search her," ordered a handsome vamp with his platinum hair slicked back with smelly 20-year-old gel.

Poe folded her arms. "If anyone touches me, I will kill every stupid one of you," she proclaimed in all seriousness. "I'll be happy to hand you the gun in my shoulder holster, but that's about it. The machete, I'm keeping."

"How can we trust that you don't carry any more weapons?"

"Because I'm retired and living on this island," she said and shook her head as if the platinum-haired enemy was stupid. Poe looked at Maclemar, and he laid a comforting hand on Percy whose face was white as chalk.

"Take the gun, Paul," said the gel-slicked vamp who was obviously in charge. He had three companions with him, all armed to the goiter and wearing Kevlar vests. Poe opened her jacket and let the man take her gun, butt first.

"What's this about, fellas? The San Diego big-shots send you to kill me?"

Paul, a thin vampire with ambition written on his face, answered, "Not kill exactly but take you back with us and make an example of you."

"Huh?"

"You're the infamous Julia Poe. You give hope where no hope should be given. With you and Sainvire running the show, you're creating chaos on our streets. Plasmacore brews in secret, vampires and halfdead talk about jumping ship because they don't like the established regime. And get this, they're feeling remorse for the blood cows that had been feeding them for nearly two decades," explained Paul. "Having you in San Diego in front of a crowd would destroy all sedition."

"And what is to happen to her in front of the crowd?" asked Maclemar in a steady voice.

"You really shouldn't speak before you're spoken to, Mr. Maclemar," said Platinum. "But since you didn't know the rules, I'll answer your question. Your girlfriend will be publicly flayed, raped, and hanged. As a finale she can expect decapitation to show she's nothing but a short human with a violent hand. Then we're going to fly her remains to San Francisco for our ally, Peter Newbitt. Her body parts will be displayed on stakes until the buzzards leave nothing to be desired."

Maclemar rose out of anger, his fist opening and closing. Angrily he spit, "Dos i ffwcio dy hun y cont."

"And what the hell does that mean, I wonder," said the amused leader.

"It means 'Go fuck yourself, you cunt,'" answered Maclemar. The creature was so fast that Poe missed a thin silver knife leave the intruder's jacket and stab Maclemar twice. Three fingers fell from Maclemar's left hand as they impeded the strike of the knife. Poe's fury rose when Maclemar hit the ground twitching. Percy forgot her fear and tried to stopper Maclemar's chest wounds like a girl with a good head on her shoulders.

Poe reached for the .45 tucked in her back and shot Paul, the closest target, in the head. Platinum rose in the air and disappeared to the second floor. Desperate shots were fired by the other two lackeys as she hid behind a camphor Chinese chest. Poe closed her eyes. *Mom and Dad, Sister Ann and Goss, I want you back.* The moment firing stopped, Poe took to her feet and fired at two couches where the flunkeys were hiding behind. She knew without looking that she'd hit both of them in the face through the frame and cotton of the couch.

At last her killer instinct returned. She imagined shooting the two heads, and without even seeing them, completed her task. She ran to the room expecting Platinum to hover in the hallway. She was right. He pointed his Sig Sauer at her chest. Poe's expression was furious. "My man is bleeding to death, you fucker. I don't..." She shot him in the head twice before the vampire realized that Poe had raised her gun at him. "...have time to dick around."

She ran downstairs where Percy was coolly applying pressure to the wound. "He's still alive, Poe. We got to get him to Morales."

"I know it. Put ice in a Ziploc and place his fingers in it. Then get the carrying contraption Maclemar made for Penny. We need to get him on the boat." How the two small people dragged Maclemar's body to the boat was one for the books. Poe ran back to the house to get Penny and the pig while Percy collected warm clothing for all three of them and comforters for Maclemar.

Poe turned on the engine and punched it, creating a choppy wake. Percy took over and aimed for the big land mass on the horizon. "Be alright, please. We just discovered each other. You can't leave me, James," said Poe as she taped gauze on the bleeding wounds on his back and chest. The blade had penetrated through his back. The vampire killer bit her lip. The knife wound was awfully close to his heart. She shivered thinking about her own gunshot wound a year and a half before.

"Maclemar," she whispered in his ear. "I love you, you crazy Welshman! Remember how you said you'll do anything I say? Well I'm telling you to hold on and live for me. I can't go on without you now. I just can't."

They reached Los Angeles Harbor in San Pedro at three o'clock with Percy nearly colliding with a docked boat. As quickly as they could, they heaved Maclemar's makeshift carrier bed on the truck and hoisted the pig alongside him. Poe stashed Penny, whining, in the back seat.

"You know how to drive a car?" asked Poe.

"No. Sorry."

"Don't worry. It can't be that hard. Take care of him while I drive, will ya, Perce?"

"I will," Percy promised, covering Maclemar with another blanket. "But he's turning purple, Poe."

"It's just the cold," insisted Poe. "That Welshman is tough."

Poe turned on the engine and pulled the gear to drive. She pressed the gas and braked a couple times, jarring the passengers. "Sorry, Penny. Hold on."

She kept her foot on the gas and maintained speeds up to 90 miles per hour on the Harbor Freeway. Steering was difficult because of her urge to turn her head and look at the back of the truck. *Please. Help him. He can't die. Mom, help me. Dad, help me!*

She slowed down the vehicle as they veered to the 6th Street exit in Downtown. There was a concrete barricade and two Jeeps waiting for her. Poe jumped out of the truck and was greeted with AKs, Armalites, and Uzis pointed at her.

"Stop right there! Do you have a password or—"

"Shut the fuck up!" Poe shouted in distress. "Open your eyes. I'm Julia fucking Poe! I got a hurt man in the back of the truck. I need to see Morales, pronto! If you don't get that barrier out of my way, I swear I'm going to destroy you."

They quickly removed the barricade. In one sentence Poe apologized for her threats, thanked the petrified guards, and told them to radio Sainvire and Morales. She floored the gas and ignored the one-way signs. At the Biltmore Hotel she pressed violently on the brake and bounded out. Sainvire had to jump in and shift the gear in park.

Morales and his team carried Maclemar inside the hotel. "Percy, can you take care of Penny and Chops?" he asked. "Take them to Habib's so you can eat."

Poe noticed the blood on Percy's hands and stopped the child. "I love you, Percy. Thanks for being so brave."

"I love you, Poe. Maclemar's going to be alright, and we'll be a family again."

Poe nodded and bit her lower lip. Sainvire embraced her on the steps of the Biltmore where they had just said goodbye a little over a month ago. "Please don't let him die," said Poe.

"Morales and other surgeons will be at hand. They'll do more than their best," he said.

Poe pushed away from the vampire. "Fuck! I forgot these." She took out the Ziploc with three fingers in melted ice water inside. She ran inside the building with her man's fingers. She entered the OR set up in the back of the hotel, but before she could take a second step, a nurse wearing gloves and a surgical mask stopped her. "We need to keep this area clean of germs, Miss Poe. Let me have that bag. We'll reattach them right away. Quick thinking on your part."

"How is he?"

"He's being prepped for an x-ray. Then we'll see where we'll go from there. We're all pulling for Maclemar, Miss Poe. He's a terrific man, and he's in the best of hands."

Poe left the kind nurse more nervous than when she entered. Her bloody hands were shaking, and she felt faint. Before she hit the ground, Sainvire shot over to catch her fall. The vampire had been watching the girl from the end of the hall.

Poe blinked and stared into Sainvire's grays. "What's going on?"

"You fainted."

"No, I didn't. I was just feeling really sick," said Poe. "Where you taking me?"

"My office. You can wash your hands and face and take a nap if you want."

"I'm fine. Really. I should wait outside the operating room."

"Believe me, Poe," said Sainvire as he opened the door to his office. "You need to collect yourself. Clean yourself up."

Poe gaped at the blood on her hands. "Yeah. Wouldn't want James to see me like this."

Sainvire sat her on the toilet lid and left her in peace. He cobbled together the stabbing at the island, but he needed more answers. Poe was too grief-stricken to answer his queries. In all his years the worse he ever felt was when Julia Poe suffered from fiends and heartache. He'd done her so many injustices that he couldn't count them anymore.

When Poe left with Maclemar for the island, Sainvire swallowed the pill and told himself that was the right course of action for the couple. Inside, however, he felt like permanently dying. Their new life together a stab in the heart, the thought of Maclemar touching Poe made him obscenely jealous. Poe was his, and he stupidly thought she felt the same way. There was a time when she would've accompanied him anywhere on earth, but his duties prevented him from leaving with the only woman he'd ever loved.

The fault was completely his. And now that Maclemar, a truly fine man, was down, his heart was breaking for Poe.

———

Poe took a shower in Sainvire's bathroom, scrubbing blood from under her nails with a face towel and a horsehair hairbrush. Her black t-shirt hid the blood stains, and thankfully her green army pants remained untouched. She left the empty office and walked over to the waiting room. Kawana, an old friend, was the only one waiting for Maclemar's results.

"Poe!" said Kawana. She hugged the girl who was the same height.

"Kawana!" Poe embraced her friend for a long time. The beautiful black vampire had been Sainvire's undercover agent under Quillon Trench's nose. Next to Ed she was the second strongest vampire Downtown. "I'm glad you're here. I feel so damn weird right now."

"I know, honey. Maclemar's a great man. He'll pull through."

"Has anyone come out yet? Any news?"

"According to Nurse Amy, he's in surgery. We won't find out for a while. Kaleb actually sent me down to get you. If you want to think of something else other than this tragedy, then maybe you can come to the meeting with me."

"What meeting?" Poe asked.

Kawana looked both ways at the empty hall and whispered in Poe's ears. "We're going to take all the babies from San Diego."

Poe's eyes bulged. She contemplated the balls of such an idea and immediately wanted to listen in on the plans. Besides, San Diego needed to be punished for ruining her life.

The vampire wearing blue workpants and a pullover walked hand in hand with Poe to lend what little support she could give. Kawana had also been there for her during her days captive at Quillon Trench's lair.

They took the elevator to the third floor and headed for a small conference room that could comfortably fit 30 people. Four guards were posted outside the room and upon seeing Poe and Kawana immediately opened the door for them. All eyes turned to them and away from the long table containing enlarged assessor maps and engineering plans of Downtown San Diego.

"Come in, Poe," said Maple as other people and vampires beckoned her inside.

"Thanks. I'm just here to observe," said Poe. She didn't know why, but she walked toward Sainvire and Joseph and insinuated herself between them. Joseph reached for her cold hands and squeezed lightly for support.

To her right stood Sainvire. He was looking down at her. Poe turned away from his disconcerting stare, but she held his freezing hand just because she felt like it. The distraught vampire killer focused her attention on the schematics before her. She'd always been good at reading maps and architectural plans though she only had a third grade education. Her heart was pounding, and she needed to get her mind off Maclemar.

"We land the helicopters on the San Diego Freeway by the airport and await word that the children are outside. Then we'll fly in," said Rufus. The halfdead was responsible for training over four-dozen Downtown residents how to fly helicopters and small planes. Sainvire was positive that Downtown had the most elite flying force in California thanks to Rufus' addiction to flight simulator video games.

"Since we're taking both nurseries plus custodians, we'll need sea backup, and that's where the Tunics come in. Many of them can fly and are resistant to sunlight," said Michelle. For the first time, Poe noticed the faces around her.

Perla was in the room standing next to Maple. "They'll run the yachts after we drop off some kids on the boats. I believe there will be three boats, right Maple?"

"Yes. Three. We can come up with a fourth if you need it."

"We'll hold off on that."

"Wouldn't it take too long to gather the kids, wait for the helicopter, pack them inside, then drop them off the boat?" said Sainvire. "Isn't there an easier way out? Everyone will be exposed in the middle of Downtown San Diego."

"They won't dare shoot us while we have the children," said Michelle.

"That's a big gamble, Michelle," said Sainvire. "Our raid will be during the day. That means sun-immune dead and drug-addicted leeches. Very unstable elements there."

Poe detached her hands from Joseph and Sainvire and began walking around the room studying the plans. Her wet hair smelled of shampoo.

"Most of these guys can't shoot," said Charles Bedo, the redhead escapee from San Diego. He provided detailed locations of the two nurseries. "There are a few more sunblockers than ever since vamps have taken to making Plasmacore on the sly."

"About how many?" asked Poe, staring at the first nursery site on the map.

"I don't know. Maybe 50."

"That's a lot of dead to gamble with, Michelle," said Sainvire. "You know we can't go on this mission unless we have an absolutely error-free plan."

Jenna, who was standing next to Poe, tapped the girl's shoulder. "Hi, Poe."

"Oh hey, Jenna," said Poe a little awkwardly since she was too busy nosing around to bother whose foot she was stepping on. "How are you?" she asked the tall pretty blonde with a pixie hairstyle.

"Good. I was wondering your opinion about the plan so far."

Poe shrugged. "I'm just an observer."

"We'd like to hear what you think, Poe," said Kawana.

Michelle nodded. "You're a megahero, girl. Let's see what you can come up with."

Poe's jaw worked trying to decide if she wanted to interfere or not, but at the same time the plan was so bad she didn't want anyone to get hurt. "Alright. I'll put in my two bits, but you don't have to do as I say.

"We'll listen," said Michelle.

"Okay. A day before you carry out this raid, I would drop flyers saying, 'Is there humanity left in you? Save humans.' And the second one should be something like, 'Custodians, get ready. Freedom is near.' This will screw with their minds."

"There's nowhere in the city we can land our birds without getting jacked," said Rufus.

Poe brushed wet hair from her face. For many it was the first time they'd seen Poe's hair free from a ponytail. "The map here shows you'll have at least six helicopters and two backups. I'd personally position them in front of the Gas and Electric Building where the kids are being held on the first floor. Put one helicopter on Ash Street and another on A Street. As a precaution, I'd land one on the roof. You'll look badass."

"That's crazy. Park them in the middle of the street? They could ruin our birds," said Rufus. "Leeches will shoot at us."

"Not if we catch them off-guard. Instead of transferring the kids to the ship, the helicopters ought to fly them straight home. I think four or five helicopters will carry 120 kids. Now the last two or three helicopters will be used for the custodians. If they read our flyers right, they'll be ready for us. If we need more than two helicopters to take the custodians, then we'll drop them off with Maple on the boats."

"They won't all fit with our team and the kids combined in a helicopter," said Michelle.

"Sure they will. A lot of Perla's Tunics can fly. They can take the kids and place them in the copters and fly back to the boat. The kids are light enough to carry."

"What about our soldiers?" asked Joseph.

"Keep more than half of them on the boat to wait for the custodians," said Poe. She bit her lower lip. "I know the Tunics aren't battle ready, but they can do what they need to do and pull back. Once the other two helicopters with custodians are empty, pick up the soldiers. These guys will deal with firefights. No vampires other than the day vamps will bother us because when the dead are asleep they're truly dead." Poe had kicked sleeping dead and set them on fire, but none of them ever woke up.

"I'll be on the bullhorn scaring the shit out of people on the ground. I have it on good authority that I scare the blue shit out of them over there. That's why they came after us on Catalina." The thought of Maclemar's injuries pained her.

The group members conferred with each other, adjusting some points but mostly agreeing to keep Poe's strategy.

"What a mind you have, Poe," said the redhead. "No wonder the House of Runer is so determined to capture you."

"Is Runer a daywalker?" Poe asked with anger in her voice.

"No, he's not. But he's the most powerful among the four houses in San Diego."

"Good. I'm going to string him up and present him to his people with his skin flayed. Anyone who tries to hurt my family and friends will die by my hand."

"Sounds like you're going with us," said Joseph.

"If you guys don't mind?"

"Hell no," said Michelle, and other voices assented.

As they were walking out the room, Sainvire put his hand on her shoulder. "What about Maclemar? Shouldn't you be with him?"

"I'm no good waiting around. When we get back I'll have the answer about his health one way or another. I have bloodlust, Kaleb. I can taste it in my mouth. I've got to kill Runer for what he did to James."

"I'll be there with you, Poe. Whatever it takes to get the bitter taste of revenge out of your mouth, I'll support you. Just don't lose your head."

Poe kept her gaze level to the vampire's misshapen shoulder. She was afraid to look into his eyes. "I appreciate it, Kaleb." She finally stared into his kind eyes and turned to leave.

CHAPTER 8

AS RUFUS AND JOSEPH flew Cessnas over San Diego urging vampires to humanize themselves once more and for custodians to prepare for flight, Poe lay cold and uncomfortable on the four chairs pushed together to act as her bed. She was shivering in the waiting room from the evening cold at two in the morning. No one had bothered to take her to a room, and she was too proud to ask.

When Sainvire draped his warm coat on her body, Poe nearly fell off her makeshift bed. The vampire had a history of sneaking up on her, and she didn't like it.

"I'm sorry, Poe. Didn't mean to startle you." Poe patted the chair by her head, and the vampire sat down.

Poe rested her head on Sainvire's lap. "I was freezing. I didn't know where else to go."

Sainvire tucked Poe's black hair behind her ears. "You mean no one's assigned you a room?"

"That's okay, really. These chairs are designed for comfort. Look at these contours."

"Yes, if you like bending like an apostrophe," said the vampire.

"Now that I have your coat, I can fall sleep. You can watch over me if you want." What Poe didn't want to admit was her fear of bad news concerning Maclemar.

"We can get you a room right now."

"No. I like it here. If you're busy you can go."

"I'm staying with you, Julia Poe," he said while combing her hair with his fingers. "Go to sleep."

Sainvire stared at Poe's face the entire six hours she slept on the chairs. He caressed her mouth and soft skin and sighed throughout the night. The operation had been going on for 12 hours. The helicopters wouldn't fly to San Diego until noon. With disappointment Sainvire shook Poe awake.

"Wake up, Julia. It's time to get ready." He smiled when Poe, her eyes puffy from sleep, pivoted up quickly in a daze. "You can use my office."

"Any news?"

"Not yet."

"Sorry I was such a bother," she said in her husky voice. "I didn't want to be alone last night."

Sainvire reached for her right cheek and gently caressed it with his thumb. "Don't mention it. That's what friends are for."

An hour later Michelle outfitted Poe with incendiaries and extra gun clips. The leadership decided Poe was to be lowered to the roof of the Gas and Electric building to spot snipers. She was given a long-range rifle and a semi-automatic. She wore her hooded coat and waited for helicopters to land.

"You good, Poe?" asked Maple as they stood outside the hotel steps.

"Yeah. What about you? Aren't you coming?"

"I'm in charge when Sainvire's gone. I'm the Guardian now."

"Sounds pretty cool," said Poe, grinning. "You and Perla okay?"

"We understand each other now. Perla was shaken by what you did that night. She realized that murder wasn't in her sphere. She asked to work with us."

Michelle called her name, beckoning Poe inside the hotel. "What's up, Michelle? Decide to stick me on dish duty?"

Michelle looked odd and didn't smile at her joke. "Poe. Sainvire wants you at the waiting room. Morales is there, too."

Poe's breakfast threatened to escape, so she took a deep breath. She deliberately walked slowly but promptly reached the sitting room anyway. Morales looked fatigued in his white coat. He'd been in surgery for over 15 hours. Sainvire stood next to T-Doc with his hands behind his back.

"Poe," began Morales. "I need to—"

The girl interrupted. "No. No. Don't tell me anything. Anything at all. I'm gonna do this thing in San Diego, and when I come back you can tell me, okay?"

Poe began backing away. "Please, Poe. I need to tell you this," pleaded Morales.

"Don't worry about it. Take a nap. I'll be back tonight alright," Poe said hastily. "I really appreciate you, Sam Morales, for being such a swell guy. I'll see you later." With that, Poe ran outside where Maple stood with Rufus. She really didn't want to know the prognosis. The helicopters were parked in a row outside the hotel on 5th Street. She shoved her shaking hands in the pockets of her coat. As far as she was concerned, Maclemar was in generous health.

A bad report could wait. She didn't need to hear terrible news before the mission. If it was good news then it would be three times the sweeter to hear when she returned. She climbed inside Rufus' bird and prayed she wouldn't vomit her food. *James Maclemar, be alright please. For me. I don't ever want to live alone again.*

She stared at Sainvire's dark head as he sat next to Rufus during the flight. He was staring out the window with a pensive look on his face. His once broken nose marred his profile. Poe never minded such a bent for it made the vampire more human. More approachable. Sainvire was reliable to the end, but never with their personal relationship. Whenever she was in a bind, though, Sainvire had always been around. She imagined him dropping everything for her if she lost

Maclemar, but she knew his obligations would always take precedence.

Anticipating Maclemar's death, she bit her lip, drawing blood. She'd rather have had one Maclemar than a hundred Sainvires. She decided to stay in the city if Maclemar came back in perfect shape. His mischievous green eyes and crooked grin thawed her heart every time. The way he looked at her as if she was the only woman alive for him made her feel special. They shared scars on their bodies and souls that no one else would understand. "I worship everything about your body, beauty," he'd say when she tried to hide the lashing scars on her back. "We came out scarred, but not cowed."

Maclemar wanted children. This she knew even though he'd said nothing of his wish. The way he'd lay his ear on her stomach or kiss her belly made her sad. She never wanted children to be brought to this crazy infernal earth, but for Maclemar, Poe believed she would consider the idea. If only her body had been cooperative.

Sainvire turned his head toward her and beamed. Poe blinked as if surprised. She'd been burning a hole through his head, and the vampire had sensed it. She smiled until her dimples resurfaced. Certainly it was possible to love two men at the same time. If up to her, she would've collected a small harem of her own.

Two minutes before noon, Rufus' chopper landed on the roof. Soon after, two helicopters flanked the Gas and Electric Building. A couple blocks away, the other three choppers edged the second orphanage on Horton Plaza. Poe alighted from the chopper along with the flying Tunics blinking away wind and dust. She didn't follow them down to the orphanage but stayed on the roof and propped up her Barrett M107 rifle. The M107 fired the hugely powerful .50 caliber ammunition that would obliterate anything in its way.

"Be safe, Poe," was all Sainvire said before following the rest into the building.

The first bullet targeting the helicopter on the ground originated from one of the ramshackle buildings next to the orphanage. Poe closed one eye and focused on the telescopic sight. She fired once and heard a distant scream. Movement from the curtains a few feet from the first sniper caught Poe's eye. She pulled the trigger and the movement ceased.

"Here. You might need this," said Rufus. He handed her a megaphone. "Maybe you can let them know that you and Sainvire are here. Scare the living shit out of them."

"Thanks, Rufus." Poe scanned the streets again for any sign of misdoings. The Tunics left the building carrying babies followed by an orderly line of kids, ages ranging from six to thirteen, holding hands. The vampire eradicator lifted up the bullhorn and switched it on.

"Hello. Hello. Is this thing working?"

Rufus yelled, "Yes!" and Poe continued. "Er, this is Julia Poe, your Public Enemy Number Two. We're here to rescue the kids and take home as many Custodians—" Her eye, still focused on the lens detected three men exiting one of the buildings and waving a gun. Poe pulled the trigger three times and downed the men before they could injure anyone.

Poe lifted the megaphone to her lips once more but kept a vigilant watch for more stragglers. "Erm, this is Julia Poe again. I shot those three guys by the way. If you interfere with our helicopters, I will shoot you dead. That's right, I'm a sure shot, and I've killed hundreds. Don't fool with me. I'm here with Kaleb Sainvire, Public Enemy Number One. He can walk in the sun, fly, mangle with his talons, and strike with many other scary powers you don't have. Let us do our job and save these kids. You don't really want to eat them anyway."

She dropped the megaphone and paid attention to the people spilling out on the street. Most of them looked human, but Poe couldn't tell if some were day vamps or leeches. The custodians were easy to spot because they were the non-white folks waving flyers around.

"Custodians, stay on the left hand side. I mean your right hand side. Leeches and sun vamps, stay on the left," Poe ordered. She turned to Rufus and said, "You better get your bird down there. Pick up the custodians only." The halfdead nodded and hopped inside his copter.

Poe's eye, focusing on the scope, was getting disoriented. She observed at least a dozen of Sainvire's people walking the perimeter of the orphanage. The copters that were filled to capacity took off and flew away, leaving Rufus to load up as many custodians as he could pack and fly them to the boats manned by soldiers and Tunics.

The vampire killer grunted when a group of liberated blood slaves obscured her view of the surrounding buildings. Two spare choppers carrying more custodians than Poe had expected lifted from the street. "There's no room for us," said Poe out loud. "We're gonna be stuck here."

Poe forced herself to concentrate on the scope. People of San Diego could probably have cared less that she was Julia Poe. Once they saw her small size they'd laughed their asses off.

The leeches and day vamps who filed into the street suddenly tangled with Sainvire's people. Shots rang.

Breathing deeply, Poe fired first at the day vamps who were out to break bones. She hit two dead and missed two more. Before she could fire on the dead that wore a wifebeater, Sainvire appeared in time for his nails to elongate and decapitate the predator. As fast as vampirely possible, Sainvire went through the line of sun vamps and sliced them like deli meat with his talons.

She concentrated on three leeches busy kicking a soldier down and popped their heads off. She fired until there was no .50 caliber ammunition left. She'd no choice but to join the action on the street. Poe assumed that the children at the orphanage had all been extracted safely. Tossing the sniper rifle in the trees, Poe climbed down a fire escape.

By the time she reached the streets, the widespread fear of Kaleb Sainvire's diamond-sharp talons temporarily restored order. Rufus and another helicopter pilot landed once more to transport another two loads to the boats. In the meantime Poe stood by Sainvire and waited for Michelle and Joseph to join them. The two were in charge of clearing out the second orphanage.

"Faring okay, Poe?" asked Sainvire. The intensity of his eyes showed more broadly in the daylight where anything could go wrong.

"Fine. You heard me on the megaphone?" she asked with a lift of the device. "No one paid attention to me. Not scared of me at all."

"Well I'm scared of you, if that counts."

Poe grinned. "Yeah. That counts double trouble. You mind if I leave you now? I got work to do." Before he could say anything, Julia Poe fled from his sight toward the old courthouse. Sainvire was shorthanded, so he couldn't follow the girl. Vamps and halfdead with serious firepower had come out of the woodwork.

"Julia! Come back here!" he ordered to no avail. It wasn't until 10 minutes later when Michelle, Joseph, and their team arrived that Sainvire was able to leave. "If we're not back in 20 minutes, leave us. We'll find our way home."

"What's going on, Kaleb?" asked Joseph.

"Long story, but the little one wants to make an example of the House of Runer for hurting her man."

In his estimation about 30 leeches had been killed. As for sun vamps, he counted 20. The numbers weren't as high as expected, and the undercount made him tense. In the back of his mind the bastards were looking down at them from innumerous angles. And there was Poe, full of vendetta in a city that wasn't even her own.

The entrances to the courthouse were shut. Poe had no choice but to unpin a grenade and toss it at a doorway. She ran a few feet and hid behind a tree until the explosion destroyed the door. *Let the air clear then go*, she told herself. *Don't get yourself killed over stupid little details*.

Two petrified Mexican American women in their forties stood inside. "Ladies. If you want to go to Los Angeles, then hustle toward the Gas and Electric building right now!" To jar them out of their stupor Poe waved her gun like she was swatting a fly. The women nodded and bounded out the blasted door.

The redhead San Diegan had disclosed that Runer chose the courthouse for his home because he was afraid of heights. He also warned that no less than nine halfdead protected him while he slept. She could hear footsteps upstairs. "Terrified bat shit," said Poe who wasn't all wrong. The halfdead were reluctant to come down after such an explosion. Since Poe couldn't wait anymore, she walked up a staircase to the biggest courtroom and found an Ethan Allen paradise instead of benches and gavels.

In the center slept Runer on a twin bed with Star Wars sheets. The vamp looked like John Travolta in the '70s. Poe pulled the sleeping vampire who had tried to assassinate Maclemar and her until he slid off his bed and banged his head on the cement floor. With the sheet she pulled him toward the front door, but she didn't expect six out of nine halfdeads to have the balls to face her. All six carried handguns.

"Let's end this production, shall we?" said Poe in exasperation. "This loser tried to get me killed, and you bloodfuckers are keeping me from frying him dead."

The men looked at each other, stumped, so Poe shot four of them in succession. "You guys, too?" she asked. Like frightened idiots they threw their guns on the floor and raised their arms.

Poe sighed. Her back was aching from trying to drag the dolt out of the courthouse.

"You four, get this scum outside. He needs to sunbathe," she ordered the frightened halfdeads. They quickly obeyed.

San Diego was a community of 700, but Poe never thought the people could be so senseless and stupid. The men yanked Runer through the charred door and to the courthouse steps. She could already hear him sizzling behind her. She thanked the halfdead for their help and dismissed them. Tired and a little sweaty from the exercise, Poe sat down on a stoop and watched the master vampire crackle. Sainvire found her breathing hard from her task.

"Everything out of your system?" he asked. He sat by her and scooped the sweat from her nose with his index finger.

Poe kicked his long leg. "A lot of things are in my system, mister, but I can't seem to shake them." She looked up as she heard the helicopters flying west to the Pacific. "Shit. Did we miss our ride?"

"Afraid so," said Sainvire. "But no worries. I can still fly us home. With plenty of rest stops in between."

"You have Plasmacore on you, right?" asked Poe as she looked at him sideways. Last time he had carried her away from battle he had nearly perished from garlic-soaked gunshot wounds. He didn't have Plasmacore, and Poe had to search for the concoction. That was when Trench and his people captured her. The three-month period that followed was the most horrible experience in her young life.

Sainvire nodded. He knew what she was thinking. "I carry a large flask with me at all times," he said. He tapped on the breast pocket of his black coat.

A bullet zinged past Poe's ear, dinging a millimeter of cartilage. Sainvire was on his feet in a blink and pulled Poe behind a thick neo-classical column. He snuck his head out quickly and saw a contingent of leech ragamuffins and daywalkers with rifles, shotguns, and pistols. The army of 20 was ready for a fight. These combatants didn't want punishment from their houses for non-action. Although they had been too fearful of the helicopters to take any serious offensive action, capturing or killing Poe and Sainvire would compensate for their earlier cowardice.

"You alright, Poe?" Sainvire asked with concern. "I can smell blood."

"Just a nick. Lucky me." Poe felt a tingling behind her neck like a warning call. She rotated toward the entrance to the courthouse and noticed four halfdead sneaking around to shoot them in the back. They were the ones she had generously let loose. *That's what happens when you're too nice,* she thought grimly. *They stab you in the back.* Poe acted quickly and shot two in the heart and the other two in the face.

"I'll fly above and draw their fire. They're close enough for you to take shots from behind this column."

"Nix the flying. You'll get hit," said Poe, clutching the vampire's lapel. "And are you wearing Kevlar under there? Last time you almost ate it for being stupid enough not to suit up."

Sainvire smiled and kissed her forehead. "I wear a vest whenever there's a raid, my love. Don't worry about me." Poe's legs weakened from the way the vampire looked at her. Her inappropriate feelings ended when a volley of bullets pinged the column she was hiding behind. Without another word Sainvire zoomed into the sky and drew fire. "Good luck, my Sainvire," Poe found herself saying.

With two Blackhawk Colt .45s in her hands, ambidextrous Poe began shooting the halfdead and leeches that raised their guns at Sainvire, splicing faces, necks, and foreheads. She automatically assumed that the enemy wore Kevlar as well, and she didn't want to take any chances. She sprinted out from her cover to the overgrown gardens and accurately shot left and right.

Sainvire landed on the ground with his sharp-as-death nails elongated 12 inches. Poe who'd succeeded in killing leeches paused to look around for more annoyances but found none. Her eyes found Sainvire surrounded by halfdead and sunspots who had a difficult time shooting the vampire because of his speed and hacking ability. A quick-moving fanger rushed at him with a mallet and lost his head with the flick of a nail. When only one halfdead was left, Sainvire retracted his claws. "I'm not going to kill you, man. Stand up."

The halfdead with bleached hair did as he was told. "You tell whoever is next in charge that we're coming for the human slaves soon. If they don't want another disaster on their hands, they'll make it easy for us to evacuate the rest of the humans. You have the recipe for Plasmacore. Start making it. Understand?"

"Yes, sir," answered the petrified creature.

"Another thing. Tell them we know about their collaboration with Peter Nesbitt. If they continue to work with the chief San Francisco vampire, we will decimate your city. Keep yourselves alive and free. Drink Plasmacore and stay out of trouble, alright?" It occurred to Sainvire that he sounded like a commercial.

"Yes, sir. Sainvire, sir."

Sainvire turned and said, "Poe, we have to go."

She was chewing her lower lip in concentration. Peter Nesbitt was her enemy, and now she knew the bastard was allied with San Diego. The son of a bitch had advised Trench to kill her.

"Um, okay. Let's fly now. I'm over this city. Plus you never know who else is lurking around."

Sainvire nodded and cupped his hand behind Poe's neck. "You're right. We can never be too careful. He picked her up from behind her knees and zoomed into the sky. He had instructed Joseph to leave without them. Perhaps it was selfish of him, but he wanted to spend some time with Julia Poe before she was forever lost to him.

"Is it alright to fly lower now?" asked Poe after 30 minutes of flight. The pressure in her ear couldn't be swallowed away even if she did have gum. "I'm freezing to death. It's pretty though. The blue sea and all."

"It's about time for a break anyway." Sainvire was following the coast and had forgotten how the weather could impact a small woman like Poe. As he lowered them carefully to the city of Carlsbad, rain assaulted the earth and lashed at the two revolutionaries. He flew them to the nearest abandoned house and pushed the door open. Poe pulled off her hood and tapped her feet. She'd been wearing her Chucks instead of boots, and her freezing toes were paying the price.

"You hear any pests in the house?" asked Poe. Her teeth were chattering.

"Just rats. No enemy combatants." He removed his coat and draped it over Poe's shoulders.

"Thanks. Sure you don't need it?" she asked facetiously.

"Nope. Your shoes are sopping wet." He kneeled and tried to untie Poe's shoelaces. "I see you're still insane about double-knotting your laces," he said, feeling like a clumsy oaf with his large fingers.

"I can't shake that obsession. But you've got to admit I'm way better now than when we first met. I lost my stutter, and I'm calmer."

Sainvire pulled the Converse from her feet and peeled off her sodden socks. "You've changed a lot, Julia Poe. You've grown into a confident young woman with an intense strategic mind and supernatural aim."

Poe shrugged sadly. She watched Sainvire wipe her feet with an old pillow covering from the couch. "I was pretty broken, you know. I've just started to recover."

"I know. And I'm sorry I had a part in Trench taking you."

"Don't blame yourself. Trench was to blame, and he's dead now. I killed him. Instant therapy for me," she exaggerated. She had stayed in Catalina Island for a year and a half in solitude to escape intrigue and reality.

"Like you said before, I have a knack for blaming myself for everything. Your pain was the hardest. I was glad you and Maclemar found happiness at least."

Poe stared at Sainvire's even hands massaging her chilly feet. "We were really happy. I felt normal for once. There's nothing like someone loving you back. I hope Maclemar is sitting up on his hospital bed asking for me just about now."

"I hope so, too. James is a top-notch human being."

Poe cleared her throat, catching the vampire's gaze. "Are you really glad Maclemar and I are together?"

Sainvire studied Poe's little pale feet for a long time before he could answer her question. "I'm glad for your happiness, and if you were to be with a man, Maclemar is a perfect choice. But you broke my heart. You're the only woman I've ever loved. I imagined us living together and helping the city become more peaceful and self-sufficient. But you've lived with violence most of your life, and you don't deserve any more intrigue. Plus I can never give you children. Even the coldness of my skin is pitiful compared to Maclemar's warm body."

For the first time Poe realized how lonely a life Sainvire had chosen. How agonizing it must have been to see her with another man. But then again, he could've had her anytime. "If you had chosen me, I'd have loved you for the rest of my days."

"I know." He wrapped her feet in the pillow case. "We have good people working with us now. Would you ever consider living with me somewhere? Malibu perhaps. Or the desert?"

She sniffed. "I would. But I have Maclemar now. It's too late. But I do love you still."

A rush of tears burst from her. Maclemar was on his death bed, and she was professing her love for another man. Sainvire was at her side handing her a handkerchief. Poe almost laughed at the old-fashioned cloth. He held her on the dusty couch while she cried her grief away. After the hanky was soaked through and her eyes dry, Poe kissed Sainvire's plump lower lip and cheek.

"I would make love with you at this moment, but if something were to happen to Maclemar, I'd never forgive myself. Or you."

"I understand," he said in his practical voice. "I'll find you some dry socks. We should head home before the storm gets worse."

CHAPTER 9

POE STAYED UNDER THE hot shower to stop her shivering. The melancholy that hovered over her spirit the moment Sainvire let go of her at the hotel threshold nearly debilitated her. She loved two good men, and she wanted to have both of them in her arms.

She was assigned a room, her old one. She hadn't seen Percy, Penny, or Chops since they had brought Maclemar in. *Can't see them now. I'm a mess.* Poe studied her reflection in the bathroom mirror and shuddered. *How can Maclemar and Sainvire think I'm attractive?* The five-inch caterpillar scar that ran diagonally from forehead to cheek was nasty in her opinion. Her ear was mangled, and her eyes looked haunted. *What do you guys see in me?*

Like in a dream, Poe pressed the elevator button to the lobby. "It's now or never," she muttered. "Welshman, you better be okay or else!"

No one waited outside the OR, and she didn't see a white coat anywhere, so she took it upon herself to sneak in the room. Her heart sank when she discovered an empty bed. Her eyes pooled with tears, and she couldn't wipe them soon enough. Someone tapped her shoulder and Poe jumped back in alarm. It was a nurse. Without a mask on, she looked like somebody's kind grandmother.

The woman embraced Poe and placed a comforting arm around the girl. "It's alright to cry, Miss Poe." The woman walked her down the hall to the sectioned areas of the sick ward. Poe looked around and found dozens of children and custodians seated. "These are the people you saved this morning. After a cursory check-up the adults will be assigned their own rooms to live. The children will attend orientation from our own little ones, and they will stay at the children's ward for now."

The nurse stopped before a maze of partitioned hospital beds with discreet sheets between them for privacy. "Here's the bed you want, Miss Poe. I'll leave you now."

Poe shook her head. *What the hell just happened?* She parted the sheet to find Maclemar with three pillows propping him up as he read *A Catcher in the Rye* for the twentieth time. "My beauty!" Maclemar nearly shouted as he tried to sit up. He let out a growl when a bolt of electricity zapped his wounds.

"James, you caveman! You're alive!" cried Poe. Careful not to hurt him, Poe kissed him on the forehead, cheek, and mouth. And once again she started bawling. The last time she was this emotional, Trench was whipping her back every night and spoon-feeding her blood to vampires.

"My sweetheart, I am well thanks to you and Percy bringing me to the doc." He took her trembling hand. "The bloody y cachwr who knifed me missed my heart and lungs. I'll be fine in a few days according to T-Doc. We can go back to Catalina in no time."

Then she blinked twice, thwarting the fantasy she'd just woven. The man in front of her lying in sterile white sheets was as stiff as a mannequin and missing three fingers. He was ashen blue and his jewel eyes were hidden by dead lids. Maclemar was no more. The man who was willing to do anything for her was gone.

She squeezed Maclemar's two-fingered hand as cold as a vampire's. "I'm sorry for being selfish, James. You shouldn't have come back to Catalina. I shouldn't have taken you from your students or the city. Forgive me for not being able to protect you." Poe kissed his purple lips then laughed. "You'll need a shave, Caveman."

Poe dipped a hand in her pocket and procured a dull gray ring and pushed it into his stiff ring finger. "I found a ring for you. I hope you like it." Careful not to touch his bandaged shoulder, Poe pushed off her shoes and got into the small hospital bed. "Read to me, Welshman, until we both fall asleep," she asked of the dead.

"Aye, milady," Maclemar assented in her mind. He scratched his emerging beard and flashed his grand grin.

Wonderful excitement and hope captured the city, especially since 127 infants and children along with over 100 custodians had been rescued. The Los Angeles Council approved Poe's proposal for the display of holiday decorations before Thanksgiving to lift everyone's spirit. Sainvire had unearthed a City of Los Angeles warehouse where Christmas decorations had been locked up and asked a cross-section of the various factions to decorate Pershing Square with angels, snowflakes, and 12-foot-long candy canes. He assigned flying vampires to decorate a hundred-foot plastic Christmas tree with shiny baubles and lights. The Ancients lifted children who fastened glittering décor on the lower branches.

The children had never experienced the bright lights or other Christmas traditions and were confused but in awe. The teachers brought out Christmas books to illuminate questions and focused on love, giving, and sharing. Explaining Santa Claus was a tedious pursuit so movie nights were set up for the children and whomever wanted to brush up on their holiday lingo. *Rudolph the Red Nosed Reindeer*, *A Charlie Brown Christmas*, and miscellaneous other holiday productions saved from the library were played every night until the kids became excited. A few adults with first-rate vocal chords taught Christmas songs to eager children.

Sainvire came up with the idea of a gift exchange between adults and children where the adult could make or find something for the child and the child could draw masterpieces for the adult. Michelle and Percy gathered toys from the Toy District by the truck full in case adults didn't have the cojones to wander off and look for gifts for the little ones.

Broadway, Spring Street, Main Street, and the perpendicular numbered streets were adorned with lights and blinking trumpets. Older kids were allowed to babysit little ones and roam around Pershing Square where Joseph and Jenna were trying to reinstate a skating rink for the children. With cooperation, Downtown Los Angeles began the Christmas season early, and hope was truly in the air.

With the help of Sainvire, Poe and Percy moved into a three-bedroom loft on Spring Street in the heart of a bubbling, revitalized neighborhood. The view of Downtown from their living room was divine, and the girls were extremely satisfied. Everywhere they went, passersby asked Poe to sample foods that hadn't existed in the city for 20 years. Percy happily obliged, but Poe usually declined. She was still in mourning, and the thought of Maclemar missing the festivities made her sick.

Sainvire was as excited as the next, but the lingering problem of Peter Nesbitt haunted him. He'd sent scouts every week to make sure no invasion was forthcoming. Rufus and his air patrol busily trained interested parties to pilot helicopters and airplanes. Cessnas and choppers were retooled in the event of an invasion. Maple and her team took care of armaments, producing explosives and bullets in the warehouse district to buffer against an accidental explosion.

The Tunics helped as needed and tenderly cared for the sick. As a peace offering, Perla had asked forgiveness from Maple who waved away her apology. She also had a long talk with her friend, Kaleb Sainvire, who similarly didn't want to hear open contrition from the woman who invented Plasmacore.

All in all the city was thriving. Even the farmers delighted in being invited to the Christmas festivities. They brought extra treats with each trainload of supplies, carved toys for the children, and made molasses candies and honey sticks.

And then there was Poe. Public Enemy Number Two seemed dazed and floating in a cloud of continuous grief the days after Maclemar was buried in the mausoleum of the Cathedral of our Lady of Angels. The girl had insisted that Maclemar's fingers be stitched on before burial in the crypt next to Gregory Peck. She had a ready smile for Percy and the animals, but it was obvious she wasn't all there. Poe had given Percy her surname and acted the good sister, but when walking alone the vampire hunter was a mess. As hard as Morales and Joseph tried, Poe refused to participate in the early decoration of the city though it was her idea in the first place.

"We need to have some sort of air raid alarm," said Poe to the Los Angeles Council, her only contribution to the meeting. "If Nesbitt invades full force, he could destroy our air strips and planes in one crack."

"How would you do this, Poe?" asked Romulo.

Poe nodded at Sainvire who answered, "There are several civil defense sirens around the city that were never uprooted after the Cold War. Maclemar said before that he and his mechanics could try repairing them, and we could set up a detection system. I think this is a great idea. We can sleep better with raid alarms on our streets."

The Council easily approved the measures as well as the other practical ideas submitted to them by old-timers and newcomers alike like a school house for the children, school buses for emergencies, home placements for children, and an application process for humans and non-humans who wanted to adopt. The hospital was reaching its limits with the catatonic ex-cattle, and Morales had begun to ask city residents to take in a human roommate per household. Surprisingly many took to the task, especially ODs who wanted to make amends.

Within weeks over 20 children had been placed with their new guardians. The more controversial was the granting of guardianship to Kilbur and Stanza who had cultivated a rapport with a 13-year-old girl. The girl named Melinda told the Council that she wanted to live with the Ancients, and she squealed they approved her wish.

Women who had given birth two to four years before they woke from their slumber could choose a baby or toddler without red tape as long as they passed a battery of psychological tests.

Quite a few laws, basically more stringent versions of existing California regulations, were passed regarding child protection. If Downtown residents abused any child or sleeping ex-blood slave, the arm of the law would hunt them down.

Poe attended biweekly Council meetings and was nearly always agreeable with the results. The city was shaping into a wonderful community, and she couldn't imagine being anywhere else. Like the old crew, Sainvire would stand before the committee and introduce ideas for city betterment. She'd watch him with her heart pounding. The vampire was immensely powerful. He could've built an empire to please himself. Instead he stood in line like everyone else to submit ideas. Such humility destroyed her. She was in awe of the man. And her love for him after Maclemar's violent death disgusted her.

Events were proceeding too flawlessly. Something horrendous was bound to happen, and the City Guardians found it in the form of a freckled San Diego vampire escapee by the name of Charles. He was the vamp who divulged the location of the two orphanages to the Guardians. He was now and always had been, according to a woman he worked with in San Diego, a spy for Peter Nesbitt.

"And why do you come forward now?" asked Sainvire in the small conference room on the third floor of the Biltmore. "If you know these things, you must be a spy yourself."

Victoria, a chubby vampire with a calming face nodded. "We're from San Francisco originally. When Nesbitt last visited San Diego in June he left us there and instructed us to try to make our way to Los Angeles by any possible means. When you dropped those flyers, we found our chance."

"Why are you telling us this?" asked Poe. She didn't want trouble. She wanted the children to have a memorable Christmas. In fact she wanted a wonderful Christmas for herself. Maclemar would've wanted it so.

"Nesbitt said you people were demented and rabid rebels and you deserved to be exterminated for stealing cattle. He despised you two especially," she pointed at Poe and Sainvire. "You killed his apprentice, Trench. Since I've been here, I've been impressed by the community you've built. I was rooting for your society because I miss the old world. This whole Christmas thing and the smiling faces of children made me question my loyalty to the ironfisted rule of the San Francisco Council. Most vampires if they were honest with themselves hate milking human blood to survive, but we didn't know there was another way. Whoever talked about Plasmacore in public would've been tortured. Despite that, vampires have started making their own food, Plasmacore, and they feel the difference. Sick blood from cattle starves vampires.

"Believe it or not, there's an underground movement in San Francisco started by ex-hippies to only drink your concoction. I don't know if you've heard, but in Santa Cruz Plasmacore is the only thing they drink now. They call themselves the Core. They nurse liberated humans, bring them back to health, and later fold them into their dissident society when they awake. Their numbers are growing everyday. Peter Nesbitt's threats to his people are eroding these days as human cattle die or are stolen away.

"As for me, I'm telling you about Charles because I want to be part of your city. I'm tired of working for a vampire without any morals. He believes he's above everyone because he came from old blood. Nobody cares. I mean, look at you, Sainvire. You have powers never seen before, and a lowly whore turned you."

"Yes. He's a son of a bitch alright," said Joseph, ribbing his friend who shook his head in offense. "So where's Charles now?"

"Charles meets Nesbitt's people every Thursday at the old Greyhound terminal on 7th and Alameda. He tells them the new rulings your new council passes, especially rulings about the air raid watch. Unlike your camp, only a handful of Nesbitt's people can fly because most of them had been destroyed by Miss Poe two years back. If they're going to fly through the city, they want a quiet affair."

"How many choppers do they have?" asked Michelle, looking fierce in a cleavage-popping top and tight red pants.

"I think about eight or nine. They haven't trained as many flyers as you guys."

"Any guns mounted on them?" pursued the head of security.

"I think all of them have mounted fire power."

"What time are they meeting?" asked Jenna who was carefully doodling on a pad of paper.

"They always meet at eight, but Charles shows up early to scout around first."

Sainvire rose from his chair and said, "We thank you for telling us about this, Victoria. If we confirm what you said, we'll consider you a part of our city because you care enough to stop Nesbitt. However, may I ask you one thing?"

"Of course," said the vampire spy.

"Why did you help us locate the orphanages in San Diego?"

"Charles suggested it so we would be beyond reproach."

"Thank you, Victoria. If you could please excuse us, we need time for discussion."

All eyes were on the awkward vampire as she left the conference room. The meeting participants consisted of Sainvire, Poe, Jenna, Ed, Rufus, Joseph, Maple, Perla, and Danby.

"My instincts may be turned about, but I believe the young lady was telling the truth," said Danby, the ex-custodian.

Jenna sat up and tossed her doodle pad to Rufus. "Feel the same here, John. But I think one of us should leave now to eavesdrop on Charles. You have 15 minutes until contact, Kaleb, so I suggest you skedaddle while we talk some more. Don't do anything to him. We might need him to send false signals."

"Alright. I'm off. Anyone want to come along? I've just had my supper, and I can fly at least two." Every head shook their head with smirks on their faces.

Poe raised her hand like a schoolgirl. "I want to see this jackass in action." She cracked her neck and shoulders in preparation of the flight. "C'mon, Sainvire. Let's jump out the window." And they did.

She'd never experienced anything as exhilarating and frightening as flying with Kaleb Sainvire. Not only did flying make her feel like she was a real superhero, but she got the chance to be truly alone with the extremely busy head of the Guardians of the City. Nothing had pumped her blood since Maclemar left her. He was her anchor. She often slipped into grief coma unless she was working to fight the enemy or keeping close to Kaleb Sainvire. Poe hugged him tighter until her lips brushed his cold neck. She didn't know how it slipped out, but she spoke her thoughts out loud.

"I love you too, Poe," said Sainvire. He kissed the top of her head.

"I didn't mean to say that," she said, guiltily thinking of Maclemar.

"I know. But thank you just the same. And sadly we have to postpone our talk. I see Charles pacing and having a conversation with himself."

Sainvire lowered them onto the flat roof of the Greyhound building, a safe distance from Charles but in range of Sainvire's sensitive ears. Poe was on her stomach watching the pathetic pantomime of the spy. She shivered at the cold breeze that slapped her face. Sainvire, on his side, stared at Poe. "You're so beautiful," he whispered. He reached out to caress her cheek. "If I could reset time, I'd live with you in your old bunker with Penny and your diverse collection of movies."

Poe pinched the vampire's nose and shook her head. "You were an idiot."

"I know it." Sainvire's face turned serious. "I'm really sorry about Maclemar. He was a stellar man. He loved you with his life."

Poe looked away, tears forming in her eyes. She hated people seeing her cry. "I'm sorry, too. I miss him so much. Especially his sense of humor and his cooking."

Sainvire didn't stop looking at Charles, and within moments two men wearing fatigues shook hands with him.

Poe couldn't hear a thing. Her eyes oscillated between Sainvire and the three vampires below. The meeting took no more than ten minutes, and the two watched Charles walk back toward the Downtown center. They went on their way themselves.

"What did they say?"

"They're planning to disrupt our Christmas celebration to lower morale. That's basically it. They can't really hurt the children. They're marked for future blood supply. Our spy only gave the date, but the planning is up to Nesbitt."

"Assholes!" said Poe. Her fury turned to annoyance when Sainvire started laughing. "What's so funny?"

"Nothing. Your anger is something to behold. It energizes you."

"I guess so if it starts a laughing fest!" She tried to turn away in exasperation, but he didn't let her. He rolled her to her back and draped one long leg over her lower body, pinning her. "I want you back, Julia Poe," he said in his gravelly voice. "I want you so badly that I want to gouge my eyes out so I won't see you anymore," he gritted. His lips hovered too closely to her mouth.

Poe looked into his eyes, illuminated by the bright moon. "You've never really had me. You left me to fend for myself after each assignment. I remember our big cattle rescue. You headed on to the Central Valley and left me half-beaten to death to return Downtown and mend on my own. Then after what Trench did to me, you left me in Catalina. You didn't even visit me. You've always chosen your cause, Kaleb. Over me. Maclemar put me first."

"You're right, of course. I despise myself for that. You're the only love I've ever known, and I let you down. I'll try my best to change my ways. Once this city understands they don't really need me, I promise to be with you for keeps."

"I'll be 90 by then. Quit living in fantasyland. Not only that, Maclemar's constantly on my mind. You have no idea how much I miss him."

Sainvire's countenance appeared so sad that Poe felt pity for him. The vampire had shouldered the weight of the world on his misshapen shoulder. Ancients, humans, vampires, and halfdead looked to him for protection. His leadership rebuilt Downtown Los Angeles. Without Sainvire's tenaciousness to free cattle and provide a sense of security, Downtown would never have thrived.

Poe had a personal issue with kissing another man when her partner was recently entombed below the Cathedral of Angels. But then again, she grew up without rules, and her heart told her that she loved two men and she couldn't help herself. She raised her head and kissed Sainvire's mouth, allowing their tongues to reacquaint after all these years. The cold roof dug at her back, but she didn't care. She wanted her vampire, and it had been a long four years.

When their lips parted, Sainvire was silent. "I'll make it up to you, Poe. I love you so much, and I've done you so many wrongs."

Poe shook her head and told him they should go. They flew back to the hotel without saying a word. They entered through the same conference room window where the assembled group had grown. Michelle was standing with Jenna when everyone hushed as they joined the assembly.

Sainvire described what he'd heard and lowered the collective spirit of the room. "Christmas, they say. They want to destroy what we've built."

Jenna looked fierce when she said, "Not gonna happen. Christmas is set. We've got to

figure out how we can foil the Grinch's plans."
No wonder the vampire is a popular leader,
thought Poe.

"How about we formally approve an attack on
San Francisco sometime in December?" said
Michelle. "Chuck can pass the info along. They
wouldn't think of flying their helis our way."

"That's actually a good idea," said Danby.

"I like it. Ballsy enough for you, Jenna?"
asked Joseph.

"It's delicious."

"I think a small group of us should go to San
Francisco and get in contact with the underground.
There's sure to be a bunch of hippies and
insurgents to help us blow up their helicopters and
other transports," said Poe with determination.

The girl's idea met the sound of crickets.
Nobody spoke for a full minute until Morales,
who was able to get away from the sick ward said,
"Brilliant idea, Poe. But you realize it's a suicide
mission?"

Poe looked at her Converse. "Sure. But
Christmas is important, and some of us have more
lives than others," she said. She needed to relieve
her guilt. She needed Christmas to happen.
Maclemar loved Christmas. "I can go by myself.
Maybe you can drop me off as close as you can,
Rufus. I can pretend to be a man with a mustache.
A custodian maybe."

Joseph shook his head. "At home you have a
little girl, a pig, and a dog. And you can't leave
my teething goddaughter!"

Poe bit her lower lip. "Listen. I used to love Christmas. I want everyone to have that feeling again. I know I can do this. I have 20 lives. And if you do lose me, it won't be such a loss. There are tons of you with more important jobs than me."

"That's bullshit, Poe," said Joseph rather angrily. "You're as important as anyone in this town. You symbolize hope, and you have a little niece that I want you see grow up, dammit!"

She'd never seen easygoing Joseph so pissed off before.

Morales picked up where Joseph left off and screamed at her. "I've patched you up one too many times, and I'm tired of it. You're not leaving this city, Julia Poe."

Quiet Maple followed with, "Don't be stupid, Poe. They have at least fifteen hundred residents in San Francisco."

Perla and Michelle further pointed out the foolishness of her idea and implored her to zip up about it. Poe hardly knew Danby, but even he voiced his misgivings. Only Rufus said something positive. "I think she can do it. She's a superhero. I can fly her to the Mission District. Nobody ever goes there. Vamps think it's too ethnic."

The group screamed a collective "shut up" at Rufus who quickly retreated to his corner. Jenna resumed doodling on the notepad. "Like Rufus, I think it's a good idea for a couple of us to infiltrate them like they've infiltrated us. It doesn't necessarily have to be Poe."

Another level of quiet descended. Joseph, who had been eyeing a pensive Sainvire by the window, muttered, "Fuck me." He sighed. "What do you think about all this, Sainvire? You okay for Poe to go to San Francisco dressed like a man with a mustache? Maybe we give her some Coppertone self-tanning lotion to make her pass for a custodian?"

Sainvire lifted his head from the fascinating table stain he was staring at and shrugged. "It's a good idea. But I don't think Poe is the right person for the job."

"And why is that?" asked Rufus.

"She was shot in the chest not even two years ago. And I want her back. I want her safe."

Most in the room groaned. Michelle yelled, "Love is a messy thing!"

Poe covered her face with her hands to hide her embarrassment. "Maclemar passed just six weeks ago, vampire."

"I can wait," said Sainvire without an ounce of shame. "But you will be my priority from now on, Poe. This I swear to everyone here."

Nobody spoke. Awkward only chipped the surface to describe the situation. Many believed Poe was getting what she finally deserved – the attention of the vampire she'd loved for ages.

Poe couldn't take it anymore and punched a hole through the faux wood paneling on the wall. She bit down the sharp pain on her left hand. "Don't swear about anything, Sainvire. I don't trust you. I'm going to San Francisco whether you donkey sacks approve or not."

Poe stormed off, leaving a room full of stunned participants of all brackets.

"Makes sense," said Joseph, leaning his hip against the table. He had a tremendous smile meant for Sainvire. "Let the girl have what she wants or she'll shoot you in the nuts so other women can't have you."

CHAPTER 10

JOSEPH HAD MADE A good point about chemical tanning lotion. Poe and Percy scoured ten Downtown pharmacies in search of the liniment that would make her darker. The past couple of days had been awful. Her friends had taken her aside to lecture about her impulsive and hard-headed character. Joseph and Morales were the worst, actually cursing which they'd never done before. "You little shit," roared Morales. "You got shot in the chest not so long ago. I was crying like a dry dolphin while stitching your chest. Grow up! You're not a superhero like some people claim. You're an impulsive brat that needs to get locked up in the city jail."

"Fucking right," added Joseph. "You alone in San Francisco? What the hell can you accomplish?"

Poe sniffed back a tear and perused the pharmacy shelves with a flashlight. They used to serve delicious Thrifty ice cream at Rite-Aid. Most of the shelves were empty, and she was losing hope.

"Is this it?" asked Percy as she pulled Penny in a Radio Flyer wagon through the empty aisles.

The nearly recovered dog had been languishing at home and whined constantly. Morales said Penny couldn't walk long distances yet because her ribs hadn't healed completely. She was an old dog, and her bones took longer to mend. Chops snorted around the scavenged pharmacy.

"Maybe. Hopefully. I'm tired of this treasure hunt," said Poe. The brand was called Brown Your Bad Self. "Let's get out of here. We're late for our salon appointment." They had planned to walk to a remodeled beauty salon on 6th Street.

"People have been saying you're ready for Sainvire to be your boyfriend," broached Percy nervously.

"Exaggeration. Embellishment," she lied. "Sainvire was my first love. He doesn't have time for me. He takes politics and intrigue over me, and I won't have that again. Anyway, if I took Sainvire seriously, what kind of person would that make me when Maclemar is still warm in the crypt?"

"Everyone knows you loved Sainvire first. And some people are getting religious on you. Some are saying that because you've been spending so much time with the vampire. Gossip makes them feel better. What's a harlot?"

"Percy, I love you, but you can't ask me questions right now because I'm pretty stressed out. I'm going to disappear soon, and I might not be back for a long time. Can you look out for Chops and Penny, and visit Maclemar for me? Tell him he has my heart, okay?"

"Sure. But rumor is they're not gonna allow your flight to happen. You might be doing this for nothing."

"I heard the same garbage, kid. Don't worry about it. I got ideas of my own." Her friends had turned against her and were trying to sabotage her mission.

Percy blinked away the tears in her eyes. "Poe, maybe they're right. I don't think you should go. I think you want to go on this suicide mission on purpose because Downtown isn't enough for you. Me, Penny, and Chops aren't enough for you. You have too much pride to take Sainvire back."

Before Poe could say anything, the girl pulled the Radio Flyer out the cracked glass doors of the drugstore.

Passionada asked Poe to remove her clothing as she slipped on plastic gloves to protect her lovely manicured hands. She lathered Brown Your Bad Self all over Poe who lay rigid on a narrow cot draped with sticky plastic lace. Her salon, aptly named Passionate, was painted peony pink and mint green. By all accounts the colors should've sickened, but instead they fused perfectly to create a peaceful cake-like space. Porcelain poodles, Barbie doll collection, pictures of fairy princesses, and other frou-frou decorations bedecked the salon.

"The brown is supposed to last eight to ten days, Julia dear," said Passionada as she wiped the vestiges of tanning cream off Poe. Once finished the six-foot Amazonian with perfect hair, make-up, and glossed lips tried men's wigs on Poe's head, settling with dark, picked-out hair that looked mighty fine on Poe. She could've been one of the Jackson Five.

"I've always wanted an Afro," Poe confessed excitedly. "It reminds me of my old friend, Goss, who had the baddest Jim Kelly do in the world."

The mustache came next. Passionada placed a Tom Selleck batch of hair on Poe's upper lip, but it didn't quite look right. They decided on bushy facial growth that cascaded down the sides of her mouth. Poe looked like a miniature Superfly.

"I found this exercise waist cincher for your breasts." Passionada stretched the material and wound it around Poe's chest. She Velcroed the material closed, and Poe was instantly boobless. Poe looked at herself in the mirror with the wig, flat chest, mustache, tan, and tinted eyeglasses. She wore a brown turtleneck and black flared pants held up by a snake skin belt with a cobra belt buckle. Passionada had chosen a dark-brown leather jacket that came down to her hip.

"I look so cool!" said Poe as she stared at herself in a full-length mirror. At once she thought about *Black Mama, White Mama*, and other blaxploitation films she had loved growing up in the bunker.

"You look like Arnold Jackson from *Diff'rent Strokes*, mi amor. And who are you supposed to be anyhow?" The beauty expert had been Poe's friend since leaving West Los Angeles, the first forced break in her retirement. The largish woman had clocked her in the head and placed her in Maclemar's boat. Who would have thought that ever since her James died, Poe had been dining at Passionada's house every Friday night?

"I'm a Blaxican," said Poe proudly. "Black and Mexican. I had a cousin who was half and half."

"Dios mio! I hope they don't attack you for looking like a mini-pimp."

"You can still see my scar," said Poe, ignoring Passionada's statement. "What can you do about that, Passionada?" The vampire killer sounded like a churlish child.

Passionada winked at her from the mirror. "Take off your glasses, pretty one. I forgot about this scar blotter I found in Santee Alley." The woman squeezed a tiny amount of brown ooze on her finger and dabbed it on Poe's five-inch scar. After a second application the scar was barely noticeable.

Poe came home satisfied with her new look and was especially thrilled when Percy came in the house and yelled at the strange little man in her living room. "Relax, Perce. It's me, Poe!"

"My God! You nearly gave me a heart attack," said the very adult ten-year-old girl.

"I would have never thought it. You're racist!"

"I'm not racist," cried Percy. "You're just the ugliest man I've ever seen lounging around in our living room!" Percy studied the skinny man disguise and groaned. "You're really going through with this aren't you?"

"Yup." She knew the conspiracy against her plan involved Percy. "Tomorrow night Rufus is going to fly me to the Mission District in San Francisco, and then I'll make my way to the center city by the bicycle I'm bringing with me."

"You'll really leave us just like that."

"Yes. For the greater good. I'll be back for you, Percy."

"Did you ever really love me?" she asked in a pained voice.

"You're like my sister!"

"Why can't you be satisfied? Why do you have to seek danger? What are you trying to prove?"

"I'm trying to stop Peter Nesbitt. He's a fucker. I love you guys, but I gotta keep Christmas alive and Nesbitt everlastingly dead."

Percy went to her bedroom and slammed the door shut. Poe kicked herself for being so selfish. Over the years she'd learned to listen to her heart and instincts. Leaving was the right thing to do. She hung a Do Not Disturb sign outside her bedroom door and prepared her backpack with dozens of clips and as many incendiaries she could get her hands on. In terms of weapons she was only bringing her .45s and wrist knives. She stuffed water and clothing to hide the contents of her bag.

At midnight she snuck out of the loft and biked her way to the Staples Center sports arena where Rufus should be waiting at one o'clock. She'd broadcasted to everyone that she was leaving the following evening to shirk possible sabotage of her trip. Her foresight paid off. Rufus was waiting for her in front of the Lakers home court without any naysayers around. Within minutes they were in the air.

"They're gonna kill me for this," said Rufus.

"Don't I know it," Poe said into the mike. "But think of the kids opening presents while you're beaten black and blue and stuffed in your copter."

"Thanks a lot, you jerk," he said. "You better come back. I agreed to do this because you're a superhero. I mean, holy shit, I used to think I was a superhero until you yanked my ear off."

Poe grinned. He had later eaten her earlobe as payback. "I'm coming back. Five days. Just don't forget to pick me up."

"Will do."

"And lots of people think I'm a scrawny mortal who should stay home and wait for calamity to show up. But that just won't do. The creep has to go."

Percy woke up and noticed a note under her door. It read:

> Percy, I love you. You'll always be my little sister. Think fondly of me until I get back. Less than a week.

The girl cursed stridently, a habit she'd picked up from Poe, then jumped out of bed to put on clothes. She pulled on a sweater draped on a rocking chair and dashed out the door, down to the elevator and out the building. She hurdled over obstacles like shopping carts filled with Christmas ornaments. She made it to the Biltmore Hotel in two minutes flat and with desperation took the elevator to the 12th floor. She was going to kick in door 1207 to show how dire the situation was, but Sainvire opened the door calmly when he heard her pounding feet and graciously let her inside.

"Fucking hell!" shouted Percy. "Poe's gone. She pulled the wool over our eyes and left a day early."

Sainvire's brows furrowed. It seemed like he was struggling with an alligator in the silence of his mind. The vampire's room was spartan, just towers of books on the floor. Not a complete surprise to Percy. The master vampire had always been downtone, humble, and without airs, perhaps reason enough for humans to trust him.

"When do you think she left?" asked the vampire calmly.

"After midnight. I thought I heard the front door closing. But then again I've been so comfortable that I sleep through anything these days. You think Rufus could've flown her?"

"Who else would have the balls?" said the vampire with a sudden violent look in his eyes. "I have to come after her. You realize that, Percy?"

"Yes, of course, Kaleb. You're the only one strong enough to protect her and stupid enough to go. I came here to ask you to look for her. I would go myself, but I have the dog and pig to take care of."

"Of course I'll go. You needn't ask. I love her, too, I'm sure you know." Sainvire walked to the bathroom and removed his black shirt. His misshapen shoulder startled the girl. His body looked hard and well corded. His dark coat covered the vampire's powerful form.

"I know. That's why I came to you first."

To Percy's horror the she watched the vampire pick up an electric shaver and run it through his hair. A completely bald man with flinty gray eyes stared back at her from the mirror. His strong jaw was more pronounced and his eyes stony. The slash on his upper lip between the nose and mouth that Poe rudely referred as a harelip stood pronouncedly on his face. Sainvire had taken shrapnel to the face and shoulder during the Spanish Civil War. "I look damn vicious bald. I don't want to scare Poe into thinking I'm a skinhead."

"Don't worry, she won't be afraid. She'll scare you first with her disguise." She brushed away hair from the vampire's shoulder and neck. "She's brown with a wig and a gigolo mustache. I don't exactly know what look she's going for, but I know you'll be the one offended."

Without asking permission, Percy opened Sainvire's wardrobe and began tossing clothes to the floor until she found what she deemed appropriate. "Black t-shirt, black hoodie, and blue Dickies pants. You'll blend in better than that I'm-a-vampire coat of yours." She tossed the clothes on the bed. When Sainvire didn't move, she raised a fist and said, "Bloody hell! Put on the clothes. Time is running out!" Bloody hell was a curse she had learned from Maclemar. How she loved the words. How she missed the Welshman.

The vampire blinked. Mousy little Percy had grown a spine trying to protect Poe. He was proud of her in so many ways.

Sainvire dutifully removed his clothing in front of Percy who turned her back to him and put on the ones chosen by the angry yet fearful girl. One side of the walnut closet contained an array of guns and knives. Percy chose an Astra A-75 Firefox and a clip belt holster to carry it in. She took all five magazines in the collection and tossed them, along with the gun, on the bed.

"Take those with you. You might have your scary clip-on nails, but sometimes it's faster to shoot when the enemy's more than five feet away."

"Thanks for the lesson," said Sainvire with a grin, sheathing the 9mm into the holster.

"Sorry I'm so rude. My teachers are foul-mouthed and hard-headed," she apologized. "Don't forget your Plasmacore."

"I've got three full flasks in the drawer," answered Sainvire. "And don't worry about rudeness. The past two decades have been beyond rude to all of us."

"Keep hunching so you look like insecure and bored out of your mind. Good. When you do that, your warped shoulder doesn't look so bad."

"Percy, I appreciate your pointers. Now go away and let me get out of here."

"She loves you, you know," said the girl. "More than Maclemar even. Everyone can see that."

The vampire paused for a second and nodded. "I love her, too. I swear I'll never disappoint her again."

The girl nodded. On impulse she got on her toes and hugged the master vampire and kissed his cold cheek. "Save her, Kaleb. She's the only family I have."

Sainvire kissed the girl's forehead and vowed, "I promise. Now get back to Penny and Chops."

Sainvire sought Joseph and explained the dilemma. Joseph, shocked at his friend's baldness, cursed. "You'll need aircraft for that distance. I'm going to airlift you to San Francisco myself, dammit!"

"No. I'll fly myself."

"What do you know about aeronautical maps? And most importantly, can you even fly a helicopter?"

Sainvire shrugged. "Thanks to that Judas, Rufus, I'm a capable choppers and small plane pilot. I'll just follow the coastline north."

"Hmm," muttered Joseph without any faith. Despite himself, he smiled. "I'll hold the fort, brother. Just come back with my insane part-Pinay sister."

Sainvire and Joseph clapped each other's back. The two had been best friends for decades. Sainvire pushed open Joseph's window and flew toward the Santa Monica Freeway, one of the many airstrips around town.

That was when he spotted Rufus chewing gum and polishing his Cessna. Rufus' jaw froze when he noticed the elementally angry bald Sainvire approach him.

"Whoa, hold on there! She asked me to tell you that if you bust me up for flying her, she'll come back and stick a broom handle where lights don't shine." He raised his hands. "Swear she said that."

"Fuck!" said Sainvire who reserved the F-word for extraordinary occasions. "I can't hurt you. Her word is law."

"Don't I know it," said Rufus.

"Better gas her up, Rufus, because you're flying me to the same exact spot you dropped my Poe off to. I expect to be there in 40 minutes or I'll eat your other earlobe."

Scratching his head, Rufus said, "Yes, boss. I thought you'd say something like that." *At least I'm still alive*, he thought.

———

Poe hid out in an abandoned tortilla factory to await morning. In her mind for the twentieth time she reviewed what Victoria had revealed.

"It's known that Plasmacore is heavily produced in the Mission District, Chinatown, and Hunter's Point. But really, most vampires have been making the juice in their own homes."

"What about the rebels? Where do I find them?

"Like I said, they were easygoing vampires before who mostly grew up in the Bay Area. A lot of them attended Berkeley and San Francisco State when they were alive. I believe the underground has grown to over 500 undead around the city. The numbers are growing because of discontent with their watered-down food. Once they taste Plasmacore, energy surges through them, and it makes them feel more satisfied. If they keep up a steady intake, some vamps develop the ability to walk in the sun."

"So that's it? They join the fight because they like the energy boost? That's kind of lame. You don't join a cause for that."

"You're right. Most every vampire has seen a blood farm, and believe me it depresses them. These skinny, bedraggled food sources are unforgettable. Now that most humans are dying from blood diseases and bone degeneration, vampires are ready for another way. Also, they hate the SF Council and master vampires. Their superciliousness and high society Vlad the Impaler shit is a big turnoff. I'll say it again. Almost everyone in San Francisco is laidback and unpretentious unless they're officious."

"About these rebels. How can I contact them?"

"I wouldn't know exactly since I worked for blue bloods, but I guess talking to custodians would help. They're in a tough spot, but they help the movement.

Poe had Victoria circle the San Francisco airstrip on a worn map she had found in the library. "Where's the armory?" she asked.

"I guess it's at City Hall, but I'm not sure."

"Alright. Two years ago a bunch of Hummers and clearing machinery attacked a farm in Gilroy where we were hiding out. Where do they keep them?"

Victoria circled three places in the city. One of them was the Tenderloin. "You better wear thermals and thick socks, Poe. Otherwise you might freeze to death before you get there."

As Poe hugged herself in the tortilleria, she cursed the cold. She'd worn three pairs of socks, two layers of thermals, and her miserable vintage leather coat that provided about as much heat as tepid tea. Her teeth chattered. Sleeping would be out of the question for she was far too glacial and might find herself frozen to death in the morning, so she focused her thoughts on Piper. If she came back to Los Angeles alive, she promised to bond with the child, teach Percy how to shoot, and be more helpful to Sainvire and the Los Angeles Council. And Sainvire staked a claim on her finally. She didn't know whether to shout her happiness or to slap the vampire for being four years late.

She sighed. Poe imagined Sainvire and Maclemar cuddling her in her California Queen mattress. Her mind wandered to Sainvire brushing her hair, Maclemar massaging her feet, and all three of them taking baths together in a heart-shaped bathtub. *Is that too much to ask?* Then she remembered Maclemar's dead body at the hospital and almost retched. She was a sick person.

A rat that must've weighed at least two pounds ran over her foot, and Poe couldn't help but eek out a horrified scream. "Fuck you, rat," she whispered when her heartbeat slowed, expecting vampires to come out and get her. Unless they were daywalkers, the dead walked at night and slept during the day. She heard footsteps two minutes later. Poe reached inside her coat and tapped on the butt of her gun. She couldn't possibly use it without alerting the vampires in the Mission area. Victoria said vamps but for the disorderly sort stayed away from the Mission. For some ignorant, unforgivable reason, she had forgotten to bring her silencers. She'd have been surrounded and strung out.

She fiddled with her wrist knives and an amazingly sharp eight-inch knife she'd filched from Habib's kitchen.

"I can smell you, girl," said a youthful voice out of nowhere. Her mouth suddenly dry, Poe swallowed. *He could tell I'm a girl. Probably from the girly scream.*

"Best to come out now because we're too hungry to play," said another creature with a French-like accent. "Dirty custodian or not, we're going to eat you."

Poe blinked three times and stood up. "What's up, my man?" she said in a horrible accent that was a mix of '70s black inflection and Cheech Marin.

The vampires reached her and looked her up and down. They were both shaven and vicious looking. Iron cross rings and tattoos decorated their necks and arms. "A male custodian?" said the one with a youthful voice with a confused look on his face. "A runaway?"

"I'm not a runaway," insisted Poe. She was badly allergic to skinheads after watching *Romper Stomper* and *American History X*. "I have narcolepsy. Just like that I fall asleep wherever I go. The kitchens of the big boss know this, so they give me a pass."

"What a story," said Frenchie in disbelief. "And what kind of accent do you have? What the fuck race are you, little man?"

"Your accent bites, too, gator man. Where you from? The bayou?" said Poe with annoyance. "I'm Blaxicano if you must know. If you eat me or harm me in any way, the big boss will cut off your head."

"Big boss, eh? Ugly man, I wouldn't drink your tainted blood if it was the last drop on this earth," grumbled the younger looking of the two wearing a Metallica t-shirt. "Come, Blaxicano, follow us. We've got something to show you."

Poe had no choice for Cajun pushed her roughly on the back. "Alright, alright. Let me get my bag here." She slid the backpack on her shoulder and hoped that the moron twins would lead her to the underground. If they were evil, they would've attacked her neck already. But then again, she was a minority, and minorities were considered too dirty to eat.

Poe glanced at her watch. One more hour until sunrise. The black sky and foggy air didn't bode well for Poe who was starting to kick herself for not killing the two vampires right away. The three of them had been walking for 20 minutes before they reached a Methodist church with a substantial concrete and stone façade that obviously belonged in the '60s. Frenchie knocked on the wooden door and was let in right away to the sound of hollering and booing. The vampire exterminator's eyes widened as she was prodded inside the packed church. The church pews had been moved alongside the walls, leaving a gaping space in the middle of the main sanctuary.

Two tatted up vampires with Hitler square fuzz on their upper lips fought on the makeshift ring. With their shirts off, they sported Nazi body art. One skeletal vampire with "HH" inked on his back had one of his eyes gouged by his bigger opponent, a scarred dead who probably made his living fighting for bored bloodsuckers dying for entertainment. About 50 folks rooted for their chosen warrior and screamed profane encouragement. The surrounding faces etched of bloodlust, boredom, and evil gave her the willies. *Who would've thought I'd find myself in a bind like this?*

Poe thought the smaller one would eat it for sure, but when the scarred vamp leapt to punch him with a fist covered by sharp bones, Skinny moved out of the way. He kicked his opponent in the chest, sending him reeling on the altar decked with a black swastika-shaped candle.

Meanwhile her new friends pointed in her direction and spoke with a seedy-looking creature with a whale of a belly, thick gold rings, and fat chains. Hitler's ugly mug was embedded on his forehead. Suddenly her belly ached. If she could have kicked the shit out of anyone in history, it would have been Adolph Hitler. She was the only minority in a sea of bald skinhead vampires whom she suspected would torture her as a finale to the Thunderdome for morons. Perhaps the iron cross banners and a large picture of the Fuhrer where a cross should have been were obvious indicators. *That's just like you, Julia Poe! Getting yourself stuck in the lair of neo-Nazis!*

Again the crowd roared as they screamed, "Finish him! Finish him!" Skinny leapt on top of the warrior and began to pound his face with thin wrists that split the bigger vamp's face into ground beef. The ringside bell sounded out of nowhere to end the bout.

"Fuck that fight!" someone screamed.

"Give us something new for fuck's sake," said another spectator. "I'm tired of watching those two have at it every goddamn night!"

Similar angry voices shouted their unhappiness when the whale belly promoter turned on his microphone that resembled a silver ice cream cone. "Alright, cretins! We've got something for you. Lucky and Hooch just brought

in a dirty custodian." The promoter was known as
Ben. He had come up with the idea of MMA-style
vamp fighting and something extra besides. His
white skin, bald head, and distrustful eyes studied
Poe from foot to fro. "You know what this
means."

Every eye in the room turned toward Poe,
who stood out like a blueberry in a bowl of milky
yogurt. "We haven't seen a Revenent fight in
ages. What do you say?" asked the promoter,
yelling the last bit to rouse the crowd. The crowd
didn't seem too excited at the size and look of
Poe. "Every hit and kill this impure scum makes
will be marked and tallied. If he exceeds the total
of the last custodian, and if he doesn't die from the
Rev, one of you by raffle will get to torture
blackie here in front of all of us."

The crowd roared out of excitement more for
the torture than the gambling part, for torture
meant bleeding the custodian and having a healthy
meal, dirty blood be damned. The promoter's
assistant grabbed Poe by her backpack and flew
her down to the ringless arena. Poe blinked her
disbelief away as a dull machete was thrown at
her. She was going to have to fight something,
and she hoped to Xena she heard wrong. Revs?
At least she comforted herself that she was given a
weapon. She waved her machete in broad sweeps
to get used to the feel, and the audience roared
with laughter. Fuming, she swiped the black
candle shaped swastika to the floor. She stomped
on it, eliciting angry curses.

Poe flipped off the crowd for belittling her non-warrior pimp look. Immediately angry shouts laced with racist epithets filled the church. She adjusted her wig, smoothed down her mustache, and spat on the floor. "Bring them on, you fat prick," she yelled at the promoter. "Then I'm coming after you!"

"How dare you speak to me like an equal, you son of a bitch bean snatcher!"

"Fuck you, lard gasket!" screamed Poe. "Get this Thunderdome going, or I'm gonna cut you down myself like Mad Max."

The promoter blew into a whistle, and the doors behind the altar opened. Poe shook her head in disbelief. "Fucking Revenents. For crying out loud."

"Eat the wetblack!" yelled someone in the crowd.

Five creatures were pushed out the door, landing heavily on the ground. Poe could hear bones breaking from the starved humans who had each been turned accidentally into something ravenous and dead known as a Revenent. They were unthinking skin-and-bone beings that could repair their bones and click back to their disconcerting selves. Most were naked for their clothes had fallen off their skeletal bodies. Poe shivered. She hated Revs and their fishy smell but abhorred racist pieces of shit more.

Before the two Revenents that fell could repair themselves, Poe swung at their heads, halving the skulls. The growls from the crowd of baldness were good signs as she could hear the promoter's voice screaming, "Let them all out."

Suddenly the church was bursting with Revenents. The skinheads began to kick the clicking beings onto the floor when they tried to join the vampires on the benches. *Calm down and lob off their heads. Do it.*

Poe's heartbeat calmed, and she started hacking at heads, limbs, and necks. Whatever tried to grab her, she kicked sideways. Her instincts told her which creature was getting closer and when to leave her back unprotected. A tall near-skeleton took hold of her jacket, and she had no choice but to crouch low and swing at his lower legs. When he fell twitching on the ground, Poe swung the machete to his skull.

Poe was methodical and fierce. She'd dealt with such aberrations before, and they were easy to down as long as she locked fear out of her head. When their fishy skin brushed her hand, she seethed with revulsion. In fact just a glimpse of their withered hands with yellowing nails filled with dirt and blood disgusted her like nothing else. She swung, hacked, and maimed as gracefully and calmly as she could. Within 10 minutes a pile of headless bones lay convulsing on the church floor, finally reaching peace.

The guest stood in the middle of the carnage of over 20 dead Revenents. Poe's chest heaved from giving such profound entertainment to a bunch of delusional dumbasses. "Who's next?" she asked vociferously. "Take me on, you shinehead motherfuckers!"

A vampire who looked 18 got to his feet and rushed Poe with super speed. It was a good thing Poe stepped out of the way or she would've suffered internal bleeding as he bunted his head toward her midsection. She lunged at the dazed vampire who hit a pillar of concrete, stabbed him in the throat, and severed his neck. Three other vamps jumped toward her, careful to step over the fallen Revenents which could trip them up and make them lose face in front of their comrades.

"You fucking blemish," a high-pitched dead said.

Poe merely smiled, reached inside her jacket, and took out her .45s. She shot him in the head and continued with shots at his two racists friends just because. Before long every vampire was flying or jumping at Poe, but her bullets tagged them before anyone could harm her. *You've got 28 bullets, Poe. There are two clips in your pocket. Good luck trying to replace the magazine,* said an unidentifiable sarcastic voice in her head.

Some vampires moved so swiftly that she missed them altogether. One even shoved her with enough force to send her five feet in the air and down upon a pew. She groaned as her spine hit wood. Thankfully she kept her hold on her guns and shot the opponents that came for her first. By her count she only had four bullets left. The thought of dying in the hands of fucking Nazis nauseated her.

"Stop, everyone!" she ordered. "I've killed a lot of you already. Who wants to be next?" She quickly took a head count. *About 19 left. I don't think they'll let me replace my clips.*

"You're out of bullets, 8 ball!" accused a chisel-faced vampire. She answered him with a bullet in the forehead. As his muscular body slumped on the ground, Poe hissed. "I've got 20 bullets in each clip, you Hitler-loving fuckfaces," she lied. "I can shoot mosquitoes from a mile away, so think twice about crossing me. And keep this in mind – Hitler was part fucking Persian, you assholes and he was Austrian to boot!"

Poe hoped they would buy her bluff, but anger at a brown man who could either be black or Mexican and dared insult the white race took the fear out of their bigoted hearts. They nodded at each other for confirmation. They were going to attack all at once. "Help me, Xena and Bruce," she whispered as she shot her last two bullets at the most violent looking dead. She crouched on the floor and covered her head.

"Enough!" a gruff familiar voice ordered. The 15 or so vampires paused in their tracks. They sensed the vampire's power without even looking at him. They studied the handsome vampire, disfigured by rage that floated in the air. He blared his fierce eyes at the skinheads with bloodlust in their hearts.

"Hello, brother," one of them said, mistaking Sainvire for a compatriot.

Sainvire landed next to Poe and said in an even tone, "Stand up." He stared at the vampire who called him brother. "I'm not your brother. You're lower than garbage, you pond scum."

He put his arm around Poe and kissed her deeply and passionately to the disgust of the skinheads that surrounded them. Poe's eyes remained open in confusion. The vampire should have realized how inappropriate a kiss was at that juncture.

"Race traitor!"

"Forget race traitor, he's a fucking fag!"

Sainvire ended their kiss, and he stared at the angry shaven vampires before him. He smiled at the disgust and hatred on their faces. "You ought to try kissing a man this gorgeous," he said and slapped Poe's rump with a leer. Before Poe could utter a protest, his lethal nails shot out of his fingers. With the speed of a master vampire with true-to-life powers, Sainvire darted around the room, slashing heads and bodies until the neo-Nazis became horrid vestiges of history.

Poe was busy picking up the microphone from the floor and tackled the hefty promoter trying to escape. They both rolled to the next pew, and as quick as a cowgirl roping cattle, Poe shoved the microphone into the vampire's mouth. The church echoed the sound of teeth breaking like fine porcelain. The man tried to get up, but Poe tied the cord around his fat neck. Satisfied that the sick promoter was done for, Poe rose to her feet and landed her boot on the back of his neck.

"White power's dead, you asshole," said Poe short of breath. "Hitler lost and committed suicide with his girlfriend. Get over it."

CHAPTER 11

"You're such a hard-headed woman!" roared Sainvire irately as he lit the church on fire. "If I hadn't heard gunshots, I wouldn't have been able to find you in the fog. You would've been tortured by ignorant bastards who worship a moron with a postage stamp for a mustache!"

Poe was never one to take criticism. She walked away from the vampire, and before any daywalkers investigated the burning church, she retraced her steps to the tortilla factory where she'd stashed her bicycle.

"I don't like you bald. You look evil. Especially with the fault line on your lip," said Poe to annoy Sainvire. He'd offended her by accusing her of being a raging lunatic that ran into trouble before calmly checking the waters. In Poe's mind, however, it was the rat's fault for stepping on her foot and making her scream like a girl.

The vampire clamped his mouth shut and followed Poe in her one hell of an ugly disguise. He couldn't believe he'd kissed such a creature with a fake itchy mustache for the benefit of the Aryans. But he couldn't stop himself. "You look frightening yourself, you know. From your wig down, you look the absolute picture of a seedy minority. We're all trying to humanize each other, and you wear something insulting like that."

Heaving with anger, she stopped walking and turned around with a smile. She took the vampire by surprise and punched him in the jaw. Her fist hurt like a mother, but she swallowed the pain. "You always lecture me, Kaleb Sainvire. I won't listen to you anymore. For your information, I was going for an Isaac Hayes mixed with Cheech look, so fuck off!"

Sainvire massaged his jaw and kept quiet. There was nothing worse than a pissed off Julia Poe.

The Mission District seemed deserted, only used by some vamps for gaming and sporting purposes. Sainvire didn't detect any movement or hear any voices, so he followed the girl inside the tortilla factory to retrieve her Huffy bike. Rufus had stuffed the tremendous frame in the Cessna with much hardship. Poe pulled out a map from her coat pocket and pointed to the square that marked the Civic Center. "This is where we're going. Victoria said the armory might be in City Hall, but maybe we should destroy it last in case we run out of explosives for ships and stuff," said Poe more to herself.

"All the Hummers and vehicles are in the Tenderloin north of us. We could start there."

Poe finally looked up at Sainvire and squinted. She groomed her mustache and nodded. Sainvire was eternally disturbed by the act. She hopped on the bike, adjusted her backpack, and said, "Get on."

"I'll walk, thanks," he said as he stared oddly at his girl.

"Master vamp too good for a bicycle? There're pegs on the back. Stand on them so we can go."

Because the girl sounded so abrupt and off-kilter, he shook his head and stepped on the protruding metal pegs. He rested his large hands on Poe's shoulders. The initial push was hell for Poe for they hardly budged, but after Sainvire said, "You can't possibly carry me. I'm too big for you and this bicycle," Poe gritted her teeth and pedaled harder. *Fuck, he's heavy*, she thought. *My ligaments are going to snap!*

Exertion cleanses the soul, her old friend Goss used to tell her. She was most definitely exerting and sweating away her tan. She huffed and puffed up steep hills until she thought her lungs were going to burst and her thighs disintegrate. Out of sheer mulishness she biked for what seemed like 15 miles without complaint. Poe had the urge to tell the vamp not to push too hard on her poor shoulders but bit her lower lip instead. They encountered a few custodians and plenty of scalawag leeches just waking up to look after the blood cattle and perhaps pester them.

The odd sight of a hooded day vamp looming over a tiny cyclist generated more than a few curious looks. But then again, they weren't far from the Castro District. Relations between custodians and vamps weren't such an improbability.

The Tenderloin was one of the least attractive neighborhoods in glorious San Francisco, and the apocalypse hadn't changed the neighborhood much. The place had been turned into an open-air junk yard for car parts and a storage area for a fleet of heavy-duty vehicles like Hummers and construction trucks. Sainvire jumped off the bicycle before Poe could even clutch the brakes. Poe let the bike fall to the ground and reached for her water bottle. Like a lost soul in the desert, she sucked on the water bottle until droplets fell on her chin. Forcing herself to stop drinking and save some for later, she placed the bottle in the outside pocket of her pack.

"Go do some damage with your nails, mister," she said, sitting on the ground. She extended her left leg and stretched. "Destroy the engines, and let's move on."

Sainvire nodded and gazed at the odd looking man stretching on the road. "Yes, boss." He shuddered and moved to the first vehicle, a Hummer, and lifted the hood. He did a Zorro with his powerful nails and damaged the engine for life. The homes along the streets were empty so no soul could watch the ruin.

"You have about a hundred more to go," said Poe the smartass. "So hurry up!"

He threw his girl a look of horror and once again shuddered. "Yes, sir! Will do."

The Blaxican watched the vampire methodically slash engine after engine, and she was glad Sainvire was with her. She would've been dead if the vamp hadn't appeared at the skin church in the nick of time. But then again he habitually had arrived when her life was at the most perilous. And here he was serving humanity by destroying trucks that might have been used to invade Los Angeles in the holiday season.

The mustached girl lay on her back in the middle of the road and slept. She hadn't caught some zzz's the night before because of the bored skinheads, but she tried her best to compensate. Sainvire shook her awake, and she instinctively reached for her gun. Sainvire captured her hand and said, "It's okay, my love. It's me. I've killed all the engines, so we can go."

Breathing heavily, Poe tugged her wig down and combed her mustache which disgusted Sainvire to no end. "Thanks. How long did I sleep?"

"About an hour," he said with a smidgeon of conceit in his voice. He took a hit of Plasmacore from his flask and pushed the container into the back of his pants. "I'll drive this time, okay?"

Not about to argue, Poe nodded. Her legs were leaden. The renowned Kaleb Sainvire pedaled a bicycle up hills with a funny looking man riding behind him. "It's a good thing the dead are asleep in San Francisco," he said in a low voice. "Otherwise I would never live this down."

Poe giggled. "Someone should've videotaped you kissing me in front of all the weirdos. That would make movie night at home."

Sainvire pedaled as fast as the bicycle could handle and got off when the tire hit a nail and nearly crashed them into a ditch full of broken stained toilets. The vampire did a quick swing and caught Poe before she hit ground. The girl ended up on top of him with a smirk on her face, and it scared him. When wiggy kissed him, he shuddered again.

"We better go now. These buildings have eyes," he said so he wouldn't have to kiss Poe again.

Poe took out the map once more and said, "It says here we have to take Octavia Street all the way then we'll hit Lafayette Park. That's where they stash their air support." She shoved the map in her back pocket and shook her head. "It's so beautiful here. I can see myself living here with all these nice buildings and the water surrounding the city. Too bad that asshole Nesbitt owns this town. Fifteen hundred vamps and humans. That's a big population to lord over."

"They're rebelling, Poe. His reign will end. Humans are dying off, and no one's here to replace them. Custodian blood is still taboo because these bastards are bigoted idiots. There are only two alternatives – steal our people or use Plasmacore. They would resort to feeding on custodians as the last option. Without custodians to keep the human cattle alive, chaos will rule."

Only three brightly painted Victorian homes remained standing on a part of Gough Street. The rest of the neighborhood had been razed. The infiltrators paused when they heard screaming from two of the homes across the street from each other. Poe and Sainvire couldn't walk away without investigating.

"I'll take the pink house," said Sainvire.

"The purple's mine."

"Be careful, Poe," he said, squeezing her arm.

"You, too, buddy ol' pal."

Poe didn't bother to knock and walked inside the three-story Queen Anne Victorian. The living room had on cots five blood slaves, their eyes staring at nothing. They were dead. *Poor people*, thought Poe.

A female voice screamed bloody murder from upstairs, and with one of her guns at the ready, Poe climbed the stairs two at a time. The second floor contained six cots, and she muttered curses under her breath. The third floor where the screaming emanated from chilled Poe to the bones. The scene reminded her of Quillon Trench and the horrid acts he had inflicted on her. Two custodians, an Asian and a Latina, were strapped facedown to the bed. Razor blades had ripped their naked backs as vampires hungry for fresh blood scooped and fed. No scars marred their backs. This was their first experience of severe torture. Hunger was driving vampires into blood thieves. She was sure these dead sucked dry the cattle downstairs.

Three vampires ladled and ate while four human leeches smoked pot and laughed at the jokes of one the vampires. Poe cleared her throat and called attention to herself. "Hola, amigos," she said. "What's happening?"

"Who the hell are you?" asked the greediest of the three vampires for he never stopped slashing and scooping.

"Help us," begged the Asian girl.

"Don't worry. I'll get you out of here," promised Poe.

"How you gonna do that, shit stain?" asked a leech with piss-yellow teeth.

Poe asked the women, "Do you want me to shoot their heads, girls?"

Both cried, "Yes."

Poe pulled the gun from her jacket pocket and said, "Okidoke!" In two seconds she managed to shoot three vampire heads and conjure up a bad trip for the leeches. Poe slid out her knife and cut the women's wrists and legs free from hemp rope. "Get dressed. As for you, corn teeth, pick a friend and pull out his tongue. All the way out. Sever it. And I'll take care of your buddies." The leech complied, but the last two leeches whimpered and kept sticking their tongues back inside their mouths.

"Look. Either I cut your tongues or I shoot your pricks off, yeah?"

With the memory executing leeches at the assembly still fresh, she wasn't going to kill any more leeches. However, she wasn't above leaving them a permanent reminder. Lucky for them, Sainvire appeared on the floor. The women screamed again.

"Sir!" cried a leech, overjoyed at seeing a vampire. "This man crippled my friends so they won't be able to talk. He killed three vampires, too. Sick. It's so sick!" The man was expecting help, but Sainvire grabbed at his collar instead. With a flick of his thumb he broke the man's neck.

"Hey! I thought you'd be proud of me for not killing randomly. What's the big idea?"

"New city, new rules," he said. "Ladies, set fire to this house and hide out. I've already torched the house across the street."

"What about the cattle?" asked Poe.

"They've been drained dead. They might become Revenents, so let's fire it up. Can you do that, ladies?"

"Yes," said the Latina. "Thank you."

"Who are you? From the underground?"

"No. But we're looking for them," said Sainvire. "Any idea where we can find the fighters?"

The women shook their heads in the negative. "Burn these guys alive if you want," said Poe. "Or torture them or whatever. Your street is deserted anyway. If some folks are still alive, take care of them."

The Asian and Latina thanked them both profusely and told them of a safer route to Lafayette Park.

A hearse with open windows drove by the burning houses as Poe and Sainvire rounded the street. It transported stacked dead human bodies, and one leg in particular protruded from the rear window.

"The hearse guy saw us."

"I know. He must be a custodian. Let's just hope he won't talk."

Once the hearse was out of sight, Sainvire picked up Poe and flew them parallel to the thick Acacia and Eucalyptus trees that concealed the street. They had work to do yet. With the help of flight, the two reached Lafayette Park which was no longer a park in the normal sense of the word. An expanse of concrete had transformed the lawn into an aircraft landing station.

Poe kissed Sainvire's cheek as he lowered her to the ground. The look he gave her made her pause. She combed her mustache and he quickly looked away. "Are you mad at me, Kaleb?"

"No, sweets. I'm not. Just anxious to destroy engines. That's all," he said. He left her to slash engines to smithereens. Poe had planned to release grenades to blow up the air power of San Francisco, but Sainvire's way was quieter. Her pack was heavy with small explosives and she couldn't wait to use them. She counted twenty-eight choppers and three small airplanes and hoped Sainvire would be done soon. She was hungry.

Out of the corner of her eye, Poe saw the same hearse pass Octavia and Sacramento Street. Right away she hid behind a green chopper and took out her gun. It wasn't a good idea to make a racket so early in the morning, but left with no choice she would use her firepower.

A prickly feeling stabbed the back of her neck 20 minutes later. She turned around quickly and found a day vamp waving a gun in her face. "What are you looking for, Poncho? Where's your friend?" he asked. Three other vamps appeared from nowhere and surrounded her. The one who called her out was holding a .38 Special. Her secret voice told her that there were no bullets in the six cylinder gun. *You better not be wrong*, grumbled Poe. Leeches used to spend their time shooting at cats and dogs on the street to ward off boredom, but their stores were depleted, and no vampire condescended to hand them much needed ammo. As a child of eight, the glue-drunk leeches had scared the life out of her.

His friends carried nothing but knives. Smiling, Poe said, "Hello, you ugly mugs. What's happening?" Her accent took a turn, sounding more like Yosemite Sam than anything.

"Where's your friend, pal?" a vampire in yellow pants asked.

"He's right behind you," said Poe, and sure enough, Sainvire magically appeared, snapping the vamp's neck in a blur. Poe took out her seven-inch knife greased with garlic oil and stabbed the vamp closest to her in the heart. Before she could get to the other two, Sainvire had already downed them.

"Hey. Those two were supposed to be mine! You're a selfish boss hog, Kaleb," reprimanded Poe.

Sainvire frowned. God help him, but he couldn't stand looking at a flirtatious Poe wearing a mustache and a fluffy wig. "We should go. That hearse has been driving around and spying on us."

"Did you kill all the engines?"

"Yes, except for one. That will be our way out of here in case we don't make it to the Mission District to meet Rufus," he said as he took her hand.

"You know how to fly?"

"Barely. And you?"

"Nope. My brother and sister were into video games, but not me. So I blew off Rufus' offer to give me lessons."

"I guess we're going to have to find a pilot somewhere in this town. Or else I'll try my hand."

"Scary thought," said Poe while twitching her mustache.

They avoided Nob Hill where the most important undead lived, according to Sainvire. Poe pulled out her map and suggested, "If we go north on Franklin Street and hang a right on Pacific Avenue, we'll hit Chinatown. I don't know if the streets are safe, though."

"Why don't you walk on the other side of the street? It seems conspicuous for a day vamp like me to hang around a Superfly troll like you."

Poe shook her head, a little hurt by his callousness at her specially selected outfit and disguise. She crossed the street in annoyance. She reached for the scar concealer and looked at herself in the reflection of an old toy store window. She dabbed at her trademark scar and stuffed the bottle back in her pocket. The girl was offended and hungry. Her food was buried in her pack along with grenades and bullets. She wasn't about to stick her hand in there and search for a sandwich.

She glanced at Sainvire, who walked a little ahead of her, and cursed his rudeness. Her musings ended when a battered avocado-green Vespa driven by a forlorn-looking custodian parked not too far from Poe. Four years ago she had the exact same color and model of Vespa. Her instincts told her to let it be, but once the human picked up her basket of cooked food and entered what seemed like a blood farm, Poe couldn't help herself. She adjusted the familiar seat and let the Vespa, engine still on, zoom away. She left a bewildered Sainvire behind.

From her rear view mirror she could see a blur of movement and smiled. Sainvire was running behind her like a pet dog. "That's what you get, you jerk," she said aloud knowing full well that Sainvire's ultra-sensitive ears would hear.

In the middle of her gloating, Poe's right profile was hit by a spinning football. She lost control of the Vespa and slammed her elbow on the asphalt street. Dazed, Poe ran her tongue over her teeth and said thanks upon finding they were unchipped. The girl had a rabid obsession with flossing, brushing, and keeping her teeth intact through many a fight.

Sainvire helped her to her feet. He was angry with himself for failing to reach the girl in time. Poe straightened her brown-tinged Ray-Ban sunglasses that survived the fall. "Ouch," she cried when he touched her injured elbow.

"Sorry, sweets. I should've watched out for you," he apologized, looking around for the person who kicked the ball at Poe. A bulked up Asian man of about 50 picked up the ball in the gutter. He threw Poe and Sainvire dirty looks.

"What's your problem, man?" asked Sainvire. He wanted to choke the air out of the human's throat for purposely hurting his woman.

"It was an accident," said the overconfident man with a Golden State Warriors jersey. "And she's riding my girlfriend's scooter."

Stretching her right arm and checking for breakage, Poe groaned and looked at the man. "Was this hers? Sorry about that."

"You should be. If she's late with her duties, the leeches flog her and feed her blood to vampires. They cut custodians whenever they can get away with it these days." He looked directly at the large bald vampire that could easily be a sinister opponent from a kung fu movie.

"She was just borrowing your girlfriend's ride, okay?" said Sainvire moodily. Glancing at Sainvire's mean face scared even her.

"There's no such thing as borrowing in this town. You should know that by now," the man quipped and walked away.

"Let's go, P...Superfly," said Sainvire. They walked miserably for half an hour until Poe couldn't take it anymore. She'd biked San Francisco hills and walked for miles, all without sleep. She was injured, hungry, and highly embarrassed for stealing somebody's bread and butter. "I gotta eat, mister, or I'm going to faint. My blood sugar is super low right now."

"I'm sorry. You haven't eaten since last night." They selected Great China Herb Company for a temporary HQ. Sainvire wiped the dust off the red padded bench for Poe. All the herbs had been snorted or smoked long ago. The vampire peeled the pack off Poe's back and unzipped it. He reached for one of the crushed peanut butter sandwiches among the grenades and handed it to Poe. He placed the bottle of water by her leg. "Take off your jacket so I can check on your arm."

Poe bit into the dry sandwich and extended her right jacket sleeve for Sainvire to pull. Her paisley shirt had blood stains around the elbow area. The blood had seeped through two layers of thermals and a cheesy shirt. "Just a scratch. Nothing's broken," said Poe with a mouthful of food.

"Humor me and let me inspect up close. That's an awful lot of blood," insisted the vampire.

"I'm not removing my clothes, Kaleb, so forget about it. I'm not undressing in front of you so you can get titillated."

Sainvire nearly saw spots. The thought of Poe naked with her awful hair, gigolo glasses, and mustache reserved for porn stars made him want to fly away and escape the hideous thought. "Yes. Wouldn't want to do that. We're working here." He helped Poe slip her arm inside the leather sleeve.

"Listen, I'm awfully tired. I've only slept an hour. We don't really have an itinerary, and we don't know how to contact the underground. You mind if I get in a couple hours shuteye? Then we can blow things up."

"Sounds good. You sleep. I'll canvas around, maybe get you some more water."

"Don't you wanna cuddle?" asked Poe as she sneezed while resting on a pile of dusty curtains.

"No!" cried Sainvire a little too succinctly. "I mean, I've got to see if Chinatown is clear of bad vamps. Their racism is off the charts, even for vampires."

"Good idea," said Poe. She stretched out on the ground using her pack full of explosives as a pillow and was asleep before Sainvire left the herb shop.

CHAPTER 12

EXCEPT FOR A FEW street lights illuminating the store window, Poe woke up to complete darkness. She sneezed five in a row from the dust she disturbed when she sat up. Disoriented but alert, Poe picked up her pack and slung it over her shoulders. The digital watch on her right wrist shone 8:30 p.m. *Where are you, Kaleb?* she wondered with mounting fear. *I shouldn't have let him walk around without me.*

"What kind of princess are you to take naps during a sabotage mission?" she whispered to the darkness. Now the dead owned the night, and she was stuck in the herb shop. She walked toward the display window and nearly shrieked when she saw a pickled mandrake that looked like the Stay Puft Marshmallow Man. Commotion on the streets snapped Poe to attention. Dead were running and herding custodians in front of the Buddha Universal Temple.

"If we find out there's more of you hiding in these buildings, we'll kill you on the spot," somebody yelled. "Custodians, this is your last chance. We have sniffers on their way, so come out, come out, or we're coming after you!"

Poe's nostrils flared as she made up her mind. *I'm a goner if a bloodhound vamp finds me hiding. Nesbitt's men must've discovered the sabotage.* Calmly, Poe walked outside and joined the twenty-some cowering humans surrounded by eight fuming vampires.

More than a third of the crowd was Asian, there were two blacks, and the rest were Latino. *I should be nervous, but I'm not*, thought the girl. *There's only eight of them versus my big guns.*

"That's it, Bradley," said the vampire wearing Bono shades. "Question them already. I have ceramics class tonight."

"Fuck your ceramics class, dumbass! Four Councilmen have been found with their heads missing. Three more kills and we'll have a dictatorship on our hands. Personally I can't stand that stiff-ass Nesbitt. Fuck how he wants us to us to call him 'Master' like he's fucking Dracula or something."

"Who do you think did it?" asked a vampire with a Michael Jackson voice.

"Who knows? L.A. people? Maybe Nesbitt himself? We should question these sorry fucks so they can go back to sleep. They've been working since dawn to feed our pathetic blood-makers."

Poe couldn't believe her ears at the way the vampires bandied their hate for Nesbitt and sympathy for the plight of the blood slaves and custodians.

Bradley, basically a fluffy guy with strategic muscles here and there like Russell Crowe, clapped his hands to get the custodians' attention.

"I know this is your rest time, but somebody's committed some heinous crimes against the Council. We've also learned that the choppers have been ambushed. Now we'd like to know if you can help us out. Witness anything strange? Anyone you've never seen before?"

Kind motherfuckers, thought Poe. *Vampires at home are a bunch of assholes. And could that guy really be into ceramics?* A bulky Asian man Poe recognized as the one who kicked a football in her face raised his head. Poe groaned inwardly.

"I did see something strange today," he said looking at Poe straight in the eye. "Two gay guys I'd never seen before were walking down the street. One is an ugly human and the other a vampire."

"What's so strange about that? You think this is ass-crack Nebraska? Folks hook up with other folks."

Poe narrowed her eyes.

The muscular Asian turned his head toward Poe once more. The girl readied herself for a fight. "No. I'm just speculating. They looked pretty suspicious."

Bradley took out a tiny notebook and a pencil. "Okay, what did they look like?"

"Oh, the vamp was tall and extremely plump, wearing a Mickey Mouse t-shirt. The human was tall. I think he was Indian."

"Dot or feathers?"

"Dot."

"Okay. Thanks for the information. I still think those guys are finding love where it counts, but we'll look out for them. Any other observations?" Bradley asked patiently.

The custodians shook their heads while Poe expelled a deep breath. The asshole was playing with her, and she wanted to choke his neck until his eyes popped out.

"We're tired, Bradley. Give us a break, huh?" said one of the black humans.

"Alright. Go on home everyone. Have a good night."

Poe narrowed her eyes at the Asian man and had the urge to flip him off double. She walked away and took to the streets of Chinatown. She imagined barbecued ducks with their heads bowed in humiliation showcased in window displays like the good old days. Now only empty hooks that brought torture to mind were displayed. She stared in front of Dim Sum Palace and salivated. Her parents would take Poe and her brother and sister to many ethnic restaurants, but Poe loved dim sum the best, especially dumplings dipped in soy sauce with vinegar.

Fresh out of things to do, Poe sat on the curb and waited for Sainvire. If he was close enough he would recognize her scent. The four dead Council members chilled her. She would've done exactly the same thing had she known where they lived. *Heck, I'd skewer Peter Nesbitt himself if I could.* But that wasn't the plan. She didn't want to create chaos in San Francisco until an interim government was prepared to take over. Without at least a temporary framework in place, blood slaves and custodians would be on their own.

There was nothing for it. She had to find the underground so they could ramp up for a takeover. In Poe's estimation, San Francisco was disorganized. Groups clustered, and vampires tolerated their leaders. Some were humane enough to acknowledge the hard work of custodians.

They had three more days to instigate havoc, and they had to make their way back to the Mission District to meet Rufus. Though she was loath to admit it, having Sainvire with her was an ego boost. His powers made her plans easier to execute. She would have unleashed incendiaries on those helicopters and Hummers and caused all sorts of noise. But Sainvire's quiet savage nails saved her from blowback and allowed her to nap for an hour. She was getting spoiled, and she liked it.

From the corner of her eye she noticed a black hearse round the curb and drive slowly down her street. Poe's feeler alert sounded, and she stood up and continued her walk down a dim street. She patted her guns and felt a modicum of safety. The car slowed enough to pace Poe's walking speed.

Either keep going and get followed, or face the music, thought Poe. She decided to stop and stare into the darkly tinted car window. Poe's scalp suddenly itched like a legion of lice attacked. Her hair needed shampooing, and so did her wig.

When the window on the passenger side lowered, Poe said in her toughest Mr. T impression, "What the fuck do you want, fool?"

The face that greeted her was Bradley the vampire. Behind the wheel was the buff Asian dude she wanted to kill. "We want you to sit in the back and take a ride with us."

"Fuck that shit. I'm walking home."

"And where is home?" asked the Asian man.

"The Squid Ink Eyeball Tentacle Restaurant in Kimchee Wonton Land. None of your business, goddamn collaborator. Now why don't you ride on out of here before I cap your ass."

Bradley smiled a kindly smile. "Listen. We know you and your friend burnt a bunch of skinheads in a church, destroyed Hummers, slashed our air power, and we don't have a clue who you are."

"Don't know what you're talking about, fool. But you best get out my face."

"Did Sainvire send you?" Bradley persisted.

"Who's that?"

"Oh c'mon. Now I know you're full of shit. Everybody knows who Kaleb Sainvire is."

"Well I don't," said Poe, combing her mustache. "You go away now."

Suddenly, Sainvire was next to her, shoving her away from the car. "What are you doing harassing my custodian?"

"Not harassing but inviting," said Bradley, the heavily lined driver. "You really are a skinhead."

"I'm not a skinhead. Just bald." corrected Sainvire. "I don't go for that Aryan bullshit."

"We know you're behind all the fireworks," said the Asian. He rolled his eyes. "Listen, I'm sick of this roundabout nonsense, so why don't you two just get in?"

"You've been following us all day," said Sainvire. "What the hell do you want? Kill us?"

"Hell no," said the Asian man. "We want to invite you to our headquarters. We're the underground."

———————

The pine scented flavor of the hearse was the smell of death. Poe kept as far away from the leather back car seat and cracked the window open despite Li's order to keep it shut. "You close the window there, my man, and I'll blow your head back to Nosferatu," threatened Poe. She'd seen the hearse carry corpses all day, and she was sickened.

Sainvire reached for her hand and squeezed. Though far from comforted, Poe nevertheless clutched tight.

"Where are you taking us?" asked Sainvire.

"To City Lights Bookstore. We built an underground hotel close by. It looks shitty on the outside, but it's state of the art inside," explained Bradley.

"How many people are in your network?" asked Poe.

"Over 500. Minus the custodians and the blood slaves, Nesbitt is left with about the same headcount on his side. And for those 500, most are ambivalent or they don't care enough to rescue cattle."

Poe changed the subject. "Are we almost there? I might throw up in your car."

"Almost there, dear one. We just have to make a right here then we're set."

Poe opened the door before the car braked to a complete stop at the crossroads of Chinatown and the Italian neighborhood of North Beach. She inhaled fresh San Francisco air to clear her lungs from the foulness of death. "We better go," urged Bradley who led them inside the pitch dark bookstore. Li drove the car far away.

The City Lights door opened and shut quickly once the three of them were safely inside. The lights were turned on and Poe frowned. As she expected, the bookstore windows were tarred to keep the lights out. Only a few books were arranged on the bookshelves, but a hell of a lot of vampires and humans lounged on couches as they took in the newcomers. The bookstore looked more like a multileveled series of living rooms.

"Famous and not-so-famous writers from the Beat Generation graced this bookstore," said Bradley. "This was an institution for great books."

Poe nodded and thought, *so this is what a hippie pad looks like*. They followed Bradley up steep stairs and into a less crowded room with three women and five men waiting for them. A lovely 40-year-old human with hazel eyes and fine bone structure stepped forward and introduced herself as Jane.

"I'm James Maclemar," said Sainvire.

"I'm Superfly," said Poe.

One of the black vampires rolled his eyes. "You're demeaning us by using such a foul name and wearing caricature clothes, my brother."

Poe reddened but stuck out her chin. "Superfly had pride and wasn't afraid," defended Poe. "Besides, I'm Blaxican. If you don't like my fashion, I don't like your motherfucking vest outfit and red headband with a feather sticking out, either. What are you, some kind of black Tonto? Stripper?"

Everywhere she went it seemed that she got lectured by politically correct dingbats. "Alright, people, cool off. We're in the same fight," said Jane.

Sainvire pushed back his hood and surveyed the place. Before he could say anything, Jane pulled out a Beretta with a silencer and plugged Sainvire four times before Poe could dislodge the gun and viciously snap back her wrist. Bone shards resembling icicles protruded from her arm. The woman screamed her hurt, and Poe was immediately surrounded.

Poe went after the Black Indian and let fly a wrist knife, tagging him on the shoulder. The humans backed away, and Bradley put up his hands in surrender. "Superfly! This wasn't supposed to be. Believe me, I don't know why Jane shot him. Put away your gun, please!"

"You shit!" she threatened the woman. "If you hit him in the heart, I'll kill you!"

Sainvire was slumped on the floor as Bradley and Poe pulled off his shirt and sweatshirt over his head. Poe always thought Sainvire had a worker's body. There was nothing soft about him. His crooked shoulder was glaring under the fluorescent lights.

The woman had fired at closed range, hitting Sainvire's liver, kidney, shoulder, and his heart. Poe bashed the wall behind Sainvire's head with her fist and screamed. "You fucking killed him, lady, and I'm gonna get you for this." But Poe didn't budge from where she was kneeling. She took Sainvire's head and laid it gently on her lap.

"Why would you do such a thing?" asked Poe quietly. "We came to help, that's all."

The woman bit her lower lip. "I'm sorry. I thought he was a skinhead trying to take us down."

"He's no skinhead! He's Kaleb Sainvire. You have no idea how many people he's saved. And he's my—"

The intake of breath in the room was palpable. "Oh my gosh!" said one of the female humans that looked like Daphne from Scooby Doo. "I noticed his gray eyes before. And there. He has a cleft lip and a broken shoulder."

Poe sniffed and corrected the girl. "He injured his face fighting Franco in Spain. That's from shrapnel." Her heart was bleeding out and her head sped ahead to a life without Kaleb Sainvire. She bit her lip to keep from crying.

Bradley covered his hands with his face. "What have we done? I'm so sorry, Superfly."

Her heart thudded in misery, and for some reason she didn't like being called Superfly anymore. She peeled off her itchy mustache and even itchier wig and let her greasy hair fall about her face. "My name's Julia Poe. I'm incognito and miserable right now."

A collective breath escaped. The great phenomenon that was Julia Poe was sitting on the floor looking dazed as she hugged Kaleb Sainvire's head to her. "We've put up Christmas trees, lights, and a skate rink for the kids, you see. They haven't experienced holiday festivities before. We have more kids now than ever since we rescued most of them from San Diego," said Poe, blabbering to keep her heart from pounding painfully.

"And then Nesbitt was going to send in his people to go to L.A. and destroy Christmas for everyone. We just want the children to live happy lives. I want to live a happy life and have Christmas all year long. I just want to love this man until I die of old age."

Sainvire's hand twitched and the four bullets on his body began to pop out. "But he was shot in the chest with garlic bullet!" said one of the people in the room.

"Kaleb!" cried Poe. "I love you so much!"

The vampire sat up like he'd just woken up and calmly looked around the room. He noticed the woman named Jane crying and clutching at her wrist. "Bradley, get someone to tend to that woman." Bradley nodded and had her escorted out by Daphne. *Always thinking of others to the last*, thought Poe proudly.

"How the hell did you do that?" asked Bradley. "Vampires die of garlic poisoning!""I was a guinea pig for a garlic study over 10 years ago. Long story, but I'm pretty much immune."

"But your heart. You were shot in the heart," said Poe.

"I can only thank Plasmacore for that, love. It's made me a stronger force to deal with."

"You shit! You didn't wear Kevlar again!"

"Sorry. Percy dressed me," apologized Sainvire. Poe shook her head for she couldn't talk. She had forgotten to bring a vest herself.

The black vampire Poe knifed in the shoulder sputtered, tossing over the wrist knife to Poe who caught it with her left hand. With a horribly gasping voice he asked, "If we drink enough Plasmacore, we can become like you?" His shoulder was burning from the garlic oil residue from Poe's knife.

Sainvire reached for his flask, uncapped it and drank the substance for a long time. He stood up and placed the empty flask back in his pocket. "I would say so," he answered, reaching out a hand to Poe. The girl took his hand in a daze and stood up. Everyone was drawn to the holes that had been extinguished and shook their heads in disbelief.

"You beheaded those Council people?" asked Bradley.

"Yes."

"Are you going to get Nesbitt, too?"

"If I can," he said. "But I think your people should handle that problem. You don't want outsiders to free your city."

"Believe me, we have a plan. We have people working within the Council chambers just waiting for the right moment to strike. And once the pieces are in place, we have teams to liberate humans and take care of them until they wake."

Bradley was getting too excited disclosing the underground's plan. Sainvire raised his hand. "I'm glad you've thought things through. I look forward to having friends and allies in this city. But now I'd like to go to the hotel for a short rest. We can talk around 3 a.m. if you wish. I heard there are ships Nesbitt's trying to outfit that Poe and I will need to blow up."

Fear could mess with the mind. Poe's hands quivered as she remembered the bullet lodged in Sainvire's heart. By all accounts, the vampire should have been permanently dead. She thought she'd lost him, and it hurt like hell, like she wanted to die, too. His regimen over a decade ago of small doses of garlic oil injected in his system had made him violently ill. It took years for his body to finally accept the bite of the pungent allium sativum and its poisonous properties. To her knowledge, Sainvire and Joseph were the only ones who'd ever participated in the study. *Thank goodness for Perla and her experiments.*

The vampire didn't have a clue that Poe suffered from his near death. He didn't understand when she wouldn't speak to him after Bradley showed them to their large bohemian room. Different colored sarongs from Indonesia decorated the walls, and hand-braided rugs covered the floor. Bradley handed them a stack of towels.

"Three in the morning. We'll all be upstairs. I really can't believe you guys are here," he said as he shut the door behind him. "Legends."

Poe had disappeared into the bathroom with two towels. She preferred two towels always for her hair and body. She had never liked the way water coursed down from her wet hair onto her drying body. She turned on the water as her teeth were clattering and shed her clothes as quickly as she could. When she was a kid, her mother had to bribe her to take baths after an afternoon in the dirt. She hated being clean. A tomboy to the last. Ever since the vamps ruled the earth, however, she couldn't loofah her skin enough.

"You okay there, Poe?" asked Sainvire as he knocked on the door.

"Yeah."

"Can I join you?"

"No way. Please leave me alone," she said with desperation. Poe walked into the tub and shut the vinyl shower curtain behind her. *This is a first*, she said to herself. *Panic attack. I didn't even have this when Trench fucked around with my body and mind. Or when Maclemar died.*

She poured shampoo on her palm and lathered her hair. Her hands were those of a crack addict. Poe reached for the newly opened bar of Irish Spring soap, her very favorite, and dropped it on the floor of the tub. The soap slipped from her unsteady hands five more times until she completed her task. She wiped her skin with a face cloth, and the brown tanning chemicals stained the white towel brown. The sight of her skin losing its nice tanned color undid her. The tint was supposed to last eight days but was fading quickly. *Must be the age of the lotion.*

Poe slipped on the tub and hugged her knees. She covered her mouth so Sainvire's superhearing wouldn't be able to detect she was crying. The reality of bad things bound to happen to everyone she loved chipped at her courage. *One day Percy and Piper will die along with Joseph and Morales if Nesbitt gets his way. Hell, Christmas could be cancelled anytime because of bitter old vampires clinging onto their glorious past.*

The vampire hunter cried quietly and urgently as if she herself was dying from the heavy weight of the world. She didn't see him kneeling next to her until she opened her eyes to let some more tears escape and blend in with the shower water. She sputtered, nearly screaming at Sainvire's bald head staring at her. Julia Poe had never been a cry freak, and she held herself in check. She tried so hard that her face turned livid red. Her hands covered her face.

"Poe, my love. Please don't cry. I'm never going to die on you. I promise."

The girl couldn't speak. She turned her face away from his and hugged her knees to her chest. Sainvire's eyes rested on the girl's slick back. Suddenly his incisors elongated. The lash scars on her back boiled Sainvire's already virulent mood.

Trench had succeeded in marking Poe's back during her humiliating time in his lair.

When he had learned that Poe was still alive, a rescue mission was carried out. He found three vampires scooping blood from her freshly whipped wounds. Julia Poe's usually fearless face was lifeless as if her soul was broken. Staring at Poe in the tub looking so fragile and wretched, he wished Trench was still alive so he could gut the son of a bitch and present his head to Julia.

Sainvire turned off the water and carried Poe, wet and shivering, to the bed. He dried her hair and body as much as he could and covered the girl. He'd never seen so many scars on a human body, and they made him love the girl's courage even more. He slipped inside the bed with Poe and hugged her as tightly as he dared without hurting her.

"Poe, I love you. I've always loved you, and I'm saddened to see you like this. I'm alive for a dead man. I have strength unmatched by any vampire, and I'm surrounded by dedicated and loyal friends. I'm not going anywhere." Poe had stopped crying, blowing her nose into the towels.

When she spoke, her voice was weak. "I thought you were dead. And you can't be dead while I'm still alive."

"And you have to live past the ripe old age of 90, my dear."

Poe blew air into her face. "C'mon. I won't live that long, and you know it."

"Don't say such a thing, Julia."

"I've gone through hell and back. My body's gross, marked by enemies already dead. I'm only 26 years old, and I don't think I can keep doing what I'm doing."

"You're still here because the world needs you. Whoever's looking out for you has made you into one hell of a fighting machine, though pint-sized." Poe pinched his thigh. "As for your body, I'm not lying when I say that most everyone, human and vampire, at home gives you once-overs when you're in their line of sight. I know this because I watch and make myself crazy."

Poe turned to look at the vampire for the first time since her breakdown. Sainvire's dead heart thudded in appreciation, or so he imagined. Her expressive brown eyes were puffy, her nose red, and her generous lips swollen from repeated biting. He'd never loved anyone so in his life. "I love you, Kaleb. And thank you for being here with me. I would've died without you."

"I can never be away from you again. You're my top priority now. Everything else can go to hell." His light gray eyes glinted in the one-lamp room.

"You know you don't mean that. Downtown means a lot to you. And to me. We've got to protect it together."

Sainvire kissed her lips and groaned as he slipped his cold tongue into her mouth. When he let the girl have a momentary breather, he asked rather embarrassingly, "Are you up to sleeping with me before our meeting in the middle of the night?"

"Geez," laughed Poe. "Yes. A roll in the hay in the City by the Bay, even though you're scary bald, arctic, and you smell of garlic."

"Pardon me," said Sainvire who smothered her next words with a deep crushing kiss that tickled Poe's knees down to her very toes. His cold body was forgotten. He pulled the wet blanket off of her and undressed himself in a span of seconds. "I've wanted to kiss your beautiful breasts again. It's been years," he said more to himself and swallowed a nipple. He spent minutes ministering to Poe's sensitive bosom until the girl squirmed her discomfort.

Poe pushed his head away and said, "No more!"

Sainvire agreed to give her breasts a rest and left a trail of cold tongue and kisses on her flat belly. Poe draped an arm over her face. She knew what was next, and she remembered Sainvire's skill at pleasuring her. As predicted, Sainvire's hard-working tongue explored her pleasure points, sucking and pulling at her clitoris. When Poe couldn't take it anymore, she cried, "Now! Please, Kaleb."

And so he entered her as requested and made her forget that he'd nearly died moments before. She was his life now. He knew she ought to be treated like royalty.

Poe washed herself while squatting under the tub faucet as was her way after sexual intercourse.

She hadn't had her menses in years, but she was careful to wash herself clean anyhow in a display of her sexual ignorance. *I can't even take care of Penny for Pete's sake. I couldn't stop that damn Tunic from kicking the old pup in the ribs. Imagine a child, a vampire child.* She wiped herself dry and walked to the bedroom.

Sainvire was staring at the ceiling with his arms behind his head. He was naked as a plucked duck. Poe had to cork her lust. She slipped into her Superfly outfit and jumped into bed with him. "You never sleep, right?"

"Nope. Too afraid I'll never wake up." Sleeping vampires were grueling to wake and easily killed. Poe remembered the days of cattle rustling with her gurus Sister Ann and Goss and the easy kills in the basements of sleeping vampires. Sister Ann staked hearts while Goss cut off heads with electric carving knives.

"What does sleeplessness do to you?"

"Nothing much. Just makes me think." He reached behind Poe's neck and brought her mouth to his. They kissed softly. "I hope I don't have to wait another four years to make love to you, Julia Poe."

"You won't. Just agree to my terms. Stay alive."

Poe played with the tufts of hair on his chest. The vampire hardly had chest hair unlike Maclemar. "So what do you think of Shandra?"

Sainvire blinked several times before answering. "She has overly enormous breasts, and she would be perfect to run a club."

"You attracted to her?"

"Nope. She'd smother me to death," he said, bringing a smile to Poe's face. "You're the only woman I want, Julia Poe."

Before Poe could reply, Cold War-era sirens blared all over the city. *I knew it! I knew fixing up the sirens in Los Angeles was a good idea!* Poe jumped to her feet and zipped up her boots. By the time she finished, Sainvire was already dressed with the sweatshirt hood over his head.

Poe slung her holsters on her shoulders and picked up her pack. "Let's go." It was barely midnight.

They went upstairs where vampires and humans had already begun to congregate. The third floor, devoid of rooms, was just open space with rugs and throw pillows and some battered couches. Poe was already getting irritated by hippie décor, and she'd only been in San Francisco two days.

"Shh! He's going to speak now," said Li who opened the window to let the alarm blare even louder.

Sainvire and Poe looked at each other and stood by the doorway. Many eyes were on them as their arrival at the hotel had been broadcasted loudly after the skirmish.

Nesbitt's voice broadcasted on the loudspeakers. The sound was like a knife twisting in Poe's kidney. How many times had he advised his protégé Trench to dispose of her? How many times did he share her with other master vampires? She tightly laced her fingers with Sainvire's. "I told you we should have something like this installed at home for emergencies."

"Yeah, but it's too Big Brother." He put his finger on his lip. He, Joseph, Morales, and Maple had memorized George Orwell's classic novel *1984* to remind them of the path from unchecked rule to totalitarianism.

"To you, San Franciscans, I speak tonight. Intruders have breached our security. Our air strips have been disabled. Four of our beloved Council members have been beheaded. Many of you must take a stand tonight because our enemies from Los Angeles have infiltrated. I've been told they stole 100 cattle yesterday and murdered the children in our orphanage."

Poe and Sainvire looked at each other in disbelief. "Propaganda, Julia. He's raising fear and insecurity to get what he wants."

"Imagine harming innocent little children, your children, for selfish gain. Sainvire and his partners claim they want to free humans. Don't be taken in. They stole those precious children to use their blood to make Plasmacore for themselves and to fatten up their stores. Are you going to let this happen? Are you going to allow Los Angeles marauders steal from your precious city? Decide. Anyone working against the Council is working against you. Root out the so-called revolutionaries. Expose them. As we speak they are helping our enemies. You will be rewarded by an extra ration of blood. Kaleb Sainvire is here wreaking havoc. I promise

anyone who captures him the title of master with all the benefits of the realm."

"He just reinstated the California Lottery. Mega Millions is on," said Poe mostly to herself. She looked up at a pensive Sainvire and said, "You're a wanted man again, Kaleb."

"I know," he said and gently kissed her forehead.

Moments after the voice from the blaring loudspeakers had faded, the hundred or so revolutionaries burrowing in the famous Beat bookstore remained quiet. They merely stared at Poe and Kaleb for guidance. Bradley, though full of heart, couldn't explain himself appropriately enough, so Kaleb came to his rescue.

"They want San Franciscans to believe we're here to steal your humans. Nesbitt said that we've stolen your blood source, including children, which you know isn't true. He knows what he's doing. Most vampires are starving from drinking anemic blood. The thought of them going hungry from what I supposedly did is meant to create panic." He looked around him, his intelligent gray eyes sharp. "Your revolution is in peril. People will point fingers for that extra tumbler of blood. I suggest that you disperse and hide out and let this pass."

"Are you going to get Nesbitt?" an ex-blood slave asked. Her face was sallow and wrinkled beyond her years.

"I'm not ruling that out, but I want to know if you have a takeover plan to carry through after Nesbitt's deposed."

"We have people in every sector of this city. They will organize and prepare for a fight. We also have friends in the government who will let us in when the time is right."

"Who's going to take Nesbitt's place?"

"I will," said Jane. Her wrist was bandaged up. "I'm not a vampire, but this city is open-minded enough. We've been making Plasmacore for the past few years, and we have stockpiles for distribution to quell any fears of starvation. And I'm truly sorry for shooting you, Mr. Kaleb."

Kaleb waved away the apology. "I'd have done the same thing. Every time I look in the mirror, I want to hang myself." His skinhead look humiliated him.

She smiled at Kaleb and gazed at Poe. "I apologize to you, too."

Poe nodded, but she couldn't be as forgiving as Sainvire. She turned to business. "We're gonna need explosives that can raze a ship the size of two tremendous yachts, 90-footers perhaps. We need them now. Can you supply them?"

"We have C4 in the basement of the bookstore. We also have some dynamite. I don't know if they're still good."

"Are they moist?" asked Poe. "Wet?"

"They're kept pretty dry. They've never been wet for safety reasons." Poe didn't want unpredictable highly charged explosives.

"Alright. We need to have them placed in duffle bags. And I suggest you all get out of here. This place is obviously suspect because of the history of the bookstore." She watched some of the team get up to leave. "Bradley, can we talk to you for a minute?"

"Sure, Poe," said the fluffy vampire wearing a cutoff shirt.

"We need someone to drive us around, and your hearse seems like a good enough cover."

Bradley motioned for Li to join them and explained the situation. "Sure thing. After you kingdom come the ships in the harbor, Chinese take-out is on me."

"So funny I forgot to laugh," said Poe in annoyance. She still hadn't forgiven the man for kicking a ball in her face. She had a burgeoning bruise on her cheek.

"That's Pee Wee Herman you just quoted there. And look. I can see the big ol' scar on your face. You look better than your wanted picture, let me tell you that. By the way, your spray-on tan is coming off."

Poe had a hard time with jokes. She felt the man who was ribbing her badly needed a punch in the nose. Despite Sainvire's stilling hand on her shoulder, Poe said, "Hey, asshole. Why don't you go gobble up some glass noodles? Just make sure they're made out of real glass!"

"Poe!" thundered Sainvire. "Be quiet! Sorry, Li. She's not usually racist. Believe it or not, she's part Japanese, Filipino, White, and Mexican."

"Goodness, all that flavor for this bitter stew? Maybe she should be sporting the shaved head, Sainvire."

Poe had gone too far, and she knew it. Swallowing her pride or what was left of it, she looked Li in the eyes and said, "Sorry, Li. You kicked the ball in face and made fun of my ugly scar. I couldn't take it. Please give me a pass this time for my crassness."

Li nodded sagely and said, "Sure, you dog eating, wasabi sniffing, hill of beans." Having jabbed the last insult, Li shook Poe's hand.

Like Sainvire had predicted, the bookstore was one of the first places checked by Nesbitt's security detail who all wore blue suits with blue berets. Ten minutes after Sainvire picked up the two duffel bags filled with bomb-making equipment, the blues swarmed with their nightsticks and semi-automatic weapons. By then Poe, the vampire, and Li had driven off to Pier 39 at San Francisco Bay. They took a meandering route to avoid detection and parked under a tree where there were no obvious homes within several blocks.

"We're gonna have to wait until daylight. Very few of them can walk in the day. The underground has more, of course, because of Plasmacore," said Li. "Is it true you can fly, slash, and all that because you've been drinking Plasmacore?"

"No," answered Poe with a wry smile. "Besides being able to walk in the sun and being immune to garlic, Kaleb's all natural."

"Nesbitt's been careless. His army is almost nonexistent, just a bunch of overfed bodyguards in berets," said Sainvire, changing the subject. "Besides handing out rations, his people are on their own."

"That's why he loves to torture anyone against him. He's been torturing and mangling anyone that demands basic human rights. Heads roll and he props them on spears to incite fear. Last month he stuck the decapitated head of a vampire known to distribute Plasmacore in front of City Hall. The whole production is ridiculous," said Li.

"Could he really be planning an attack on Los Angeles?" asked Poe, laying a hand on Sainvire's knee she'd shot so many times before.

"Oh, I wouldn't doubt it. SF needs a pick-me-up. Victory over your city would've impressed some, but not all. The old man's losing his grip as vampires starve and humans die. Nesbitt lives in this old world fantasy where he's royalty and his subjects question nothing. I drive around everyday picking up dead bodies, and let me tell you, it's not looking good for humans. Nesbitt needs to stop harvesting their blood. They're dropping like starving wasps."

"What can we really do? We're here to squash your city's fighting capabilities. If we do get Nesbitt, you'll be on your own. You've got to map out tasks for your captains to take care of. You have to keep a lid on chaos and protect human slaves, and there's a lot of ground to cover. For a compact city, everyone seems spread out."

"Believe it or not, Poe, we have plans to protect humans and take command. We also have plenty of Plasmacore. That will be the rallying point. We just need the opportunity, and Sainvire here is just the opportunity."

Poe felt miffed. Granted she had mostly slept while Sainvire did all the work, but the mission was hers, and people like Li thought she was useless.

As if Sainvire read her mind, he explained, "Poe is the reason we're here, Li. She is the tactician for this mission. She also killed over 30 Revenents in the Mission and nearly destroyed all 50 skinheads by herself."

Li nodded his head as if to say, "Yeah right!" and turned to face the windshield away from Poe's expectant face. "Okay, then. I'm taking a nap. Wake me up when the sun's out," said the bitter man.

I hate that guy, she thought.

Sainvire squeezed her shoulder and kissed her nose. His mirthful eyes conveyed that she should let the matter rest. She pinched his nonexistent love handle then insinuated herself in his arms. If the jerk was going to sleep, then so was she.

Poe woke up on the opposite end of the back seat of the hearse. With one eye open, she watched Sainvire as he assembled the C4 attached to timers and a stick of dynamite. Morales had held a seminar about bomb making, and even Sainvire was required to attend. "So you're finally awake," he said without looking up from his dangerous work. He could read her heartbeat.

"You almost done with that?" she asked while stretching. "Where's the moron?"

"He's sniffing around to see what's up." Poe looked out the window and realized they were at a different neighborhood. She saw a hardscaped open plaza with a jumble of stepped concrete slabs in the center.

"Boy, I'm taking on the sleep habits of a vampire. Where are we?"

"By the Art Institute. Li has some friends here. Lookouts." He finally picked his eyes up and took in the girl's sleepy appearance. Julia Poe with her lovely plump lips and expressive brown eyes suddenly made him forget that he was holding volatile explosives. Framing her face, her hair fell to her shoulders. Without the mustache and the hideous wig, Poe looked gorgeous in a tan. "I love you, Julia."

Poe smiled. "Love you, too, you crazy vampire."

Their flirtations were cut short when Li got in the car with his friend, a hairy-looking beast with a beard that swallowed his face except for his eyes.

"This is Joel. He's a day vamp."

Joel seemed giddy to be in the company of two of the most famous rustlers post-Armageddon. "I can't believe I'm in a hearse with the two of you! Julia Poe, you're a goddess! Didn't expect you to be such a beauty."

Li sighed his annoyance. "Look, Joel. This is basically Sainvire's operation. Julia Poe will sit in the car with us while he does all the work."

Poe calmed herself, even smiling up at Sainvire who looked alarmed.

"So what's the news?" asked Sainvire. He had thought Li was only funning, but the man was becoming insufferable. He didn't know whether Poe could keep her hands off the rude Chinese man when he left to carry out his business.

"As far as we know, the ships in the bay are empty. You can bomb them to smithereens. But we've seen about 20 blue suits this morning patrolling the streets. I think they're the last of Nesbitt's day vamps. Should've put them on Plasmacore regimen. Look at me. I'm walking in the sun after 40 years of moon watch," explained Joel.

"So here's the plan. You destroy those ships, and Julia Poe and I will stay in the car and take a nap. When it's over just fly over to us people with nothing important to do."

Poe's mouth became a line. *Keep riding me, asshole, and I'll feed your pecker to the birds.*

Sainvire took Poe's face in his hands and kissed her deliberately slow. He brushed his lips to her eyes and nose then kissed her again on the mouth. "I'll be back in a tick of the clock, you wonderful woman you."

"You better," she whispered in his ear. "Or else I'll be your replacement driver when you get back."

Joel was all grins. He didn't turn away when the couple had their private moment but stared excitedly like a peeping tom. "Love after the apocalypse. Hella nice."

"You stay here, Joel, until I get back," ordered Sainvire.

"Yes, sir. You're so awesome, Kaleb Sainvire! Good luck."

Carrying the duffel bags filled with explosives, Sainvire glanced one more time at Poe and stepped out of the car. Poe's heart thudded. She didn't know whether it was from complete love for the vampire or nervousness about his assignment.

While Li chatted incessantly about Sainvire's greatness to Joel, Poe decided it was time to relieve herself. The damn driver was a Sainvire fanboy. She leaned over and pulled some tissue from the box next to Li. "I gotta pee. Is that good with you?"

Li gave her a TMI look and waved her away. *Fucking dick! Just because you have some muscles on you, you think you can take me.*

Poe cracked her neck muscles and stretched as soon as she got out of the car. She hopped around like Muhammad Ali himself and started air boxing. She noticed Li's eyes roll toward the heavens from the driver side mirror. Disgusted with the man bent on spitting on her worth, Poe walked half a block until she was satisfied with a wild, untrimmed rosemary bush to urinate behind. She hid the used tissue in the thicket and poured in her hands some travel antibacterial gel she had filched from the hotel.

San Francisco was a wonderful place to live. Her parents had brought the family up when she was five or six, and she only remembered the

Botanical Garden and the magnificent Golden Gate Bridge. They'd walked part of the bridge until her sister Sirena's vertigo kicked in and had to go back to the Presidio.

The smell was quite different from Los Angeles in those days. The air, though colder, was cleaner because the bay winds swept pollutants away. Poe's musings ended after ducking behind sidewalk foliage as 20 blue suits that had been sniffing around the Art Institute ordered Li and Joel out of the car.

"I'm meeting Joel here because he's my boyfriend," said Li, smiling conspiratorially.

"It's true. He's my love," confirmed Joel.

The boss suit was immovable. "You're in a suspect area, a hotbed for deviants and miscreants, and you say you just happened to meet up here. If I'm suspicious it's because you have a bullshit story. What are you doing using city property for a liaison when you're supposed to be picking up bodies? And you, why aren't you registered as a day vamp?"

"I just woke up one day, and the sun embraced me."

The bulky, hard-nosed suit punched Joel in the nose. "You've been dabbling with Plasmacore, you asshole. That's a serious offense right there."

Joel held his broken nose and blinked away the pain.

"As for you, custodian, your driving privileges are hereby revoked. I'll make sure to reassign you to shoveling shit and wiping ass."

Poe had 28 bullets between the two Blackhawk Colts. There were 24 blue suits. She had a limited amount of time to kill most of them before they could train their own weapons on her. Changing the magazine was going to be tricky, so she put one on the pocket of her paisley shirt. *Just walk away from the hearse. We're gonna need it unscathed to move around town*, she thought. *I don't mind shooting your SUVs though.*

She unsheathed her guns and whistled the you're-so-sexy cat-call. The suits faced her way. *All in the forehead, Poe. They're wearing vests*, she whispered to herself. She shot the bastard in charge right over the eyes. The three surrounding the dead leader were shot consecutively. Guns were pulled off holsters, but Poe shot five more of the enemy between the eyes before they could return fire. From the corner of her eyes, she saw Li and Joel scramble to the ground behind the hearse.

"Surround her," somebody yelled, but Poe hardly budged. Her left hand took care of five heads while her right hand decimated six. She ran behind one of the SUVs as a volley of bullets followed her lithe form. She closed her eyes for a second and instinctively knew somebody was approaching from her right. Without even looking at him, she fired a shot. The blue beret fell permanently dead on the ground.

The atmosphere turned dire as explosions shook the ground. "Sainvire," said Poe. She was enervated.

"Four more dead," shouted Li.

Poe inhaled a breath and ran out into the open. She looked straight ahead at an oak tree and allowed the instructive voice to guide her. Muhammad Ali, Xena, her parents, Bruce Lee, Sister Ann, and Goss spoke as one. She shot two vamps on her left. One bullet hit the trees and another one struck a blue beret hiding behind an SUV. Another explosion reverberated around the marina.

She let her empty clips fall and replaced them with full ones. Poe looked for the minute chance that one of them survived or a new crew was coming. But like Joel had said, Nesbitt was short of day vamps, so it was unlikely more were on the way to give her hell.

Li and Joel surveyed the carnage. Vamps in uniform were splayed on the asphalt. "Fuck me," said Li. "You shot them all in the head."

"They're wearing vests," said Poe matter-of-factly.

"I've never seen such a thing. You're like a superhero Wonder Woman goddess!" said Joel excitedly as another explosion rocked the stillness of the morning. "That fucking shit broke my nose, and he was the first one you offed! Thanks."

"Yeah. That was dedicated to you. Now let's pick up their guns and get out of here." The three of them confiscated handguns, shotguns, knives, bullets, and other weapons they could lay their hands on. They placed the loot in the back of one of the intact SUVs. The other three vehicles they destroyed by scrambling internal components.

Joel was a weak vampire. His only power was the ability to lift items up to 200 pounds.

"Joel, get rid of those things quick. And hide the SUV. Might be useful in the future."

"You and me had better find a cleaner street, Li," she said to the shell-shocked driver. "Sainvire would know where I am. He has a great sense of smell, and he can hear my heartbeat."

Joel the hairy beast hugged her a little too enthusiastically and took the liberty of kissing her on the mouth. "You're my hero, Julia Poe! If ever it doesn't work out between you and Sainvire, consider me."

Poe wiped her mouth with the back of her hand. "Sure, man. I really think you should get out of here, though." She was disgusted by the hairy creature but tried hard not to show it.

He got in the SUV and grinned at Poe. "I love you!" he screamed and drove away.

"Let's go, Li," said Poe, getting in the back of the hearse. Poe heard the fourth explosion and felt relief. Sainvire was done. *Hope there's no more surprises*, she thought. "Go to the next block, okay? His hearing might be off with all the explosions. I don't want him to miss us."

"You're incredible," said Li, breaking his silence as he drove. "I can see how vampires can do what they can do, but a human? You didn't even look at some of them, and you got them smack in the forehead anyway. No wonder master vampires and Council members fear you. You're a human with the ways and means to kill them."

Poe swallowed spit. "Everyone has the power to kill. Even you."

"I thought Sainvire did all the work, and I was a real jerk to you. But now I know never to judge a book by its tiny, scarred cover."

"If the part about tiny and scarred is your idea of an apology, then save it. You're a dick."

"I know. I apologize till the day I die," he said dramatically but sincerely.

"Don't worry about it, bub. Just have our back, and we'll get this city cleaned up for you."

CHAPTER 13

"I CAN'T BELIEVE HOW easy it is to play bad in this city," said Poe, bouncing a small rubber ball on Sainvire's naked abdomen. "Everything seems unguarded. Everything! Nesbitt is all talk. He's unorganized, and he's scarred to bits. I wonder the craziness we can do before we leave. We have a day and a half left until Rufus picks us up, and we've finished our homework. Can't we sightsee? Let's walk the Golden Gate Bridge."

Sainvire glanced at Poe. She wore nothing and was completely comfortable in his presence for the first time. Her black wavy hair was untied, and he couldn't believe what he was seeing. Julia Poe was a stickler when it came to her hair. She left it in a ponytail most of the time. Watching the soft curls framing the girl's face was a privilege, and he adored her even more.

"Nesbitt lost a lot of people and vehicles tracking our group two years ago. Many fled because they feared clashing with our forces. Plus they didn't like Nesbitt all that much anyway, so they deserted with the formula for Plasmacore." He reached over to touch a curl and continued. "Nesbitt, according to Bradley, is pretending to have more help than he's got. This may be true. But in any case, we're not going to be tourists. I'm not going to risk it."

"But the bridge is so close," Poe said, frowning. Her naked breasts hypnotized him as she leaned on one elbow to speak to him. The ball kept bouncing up and down like the vampire's stomach was a table top. "I think we should try to kill him. You know where he lives, right?"

"I'll take you to the bridge some other time when democracy returns to this city. As for killing Nesbitt, I'm all for it, but I don't want to risk our lives to do it. The underground needs to organize itself and devise their own plan of attack. This isn't our town. We don't want to leave the city in shambles."

Poe bounced the ball on Sainvire's forehead, and he suddenly flipped her onto her back. "You're too damn cerebral, Kaleb. How am I supposed to have fun living with you?"

He exposed her belly and lightly bit her skin as a punishment. Then he kissed her hairless sex. "So you've decided to live with me, eh?" he said, peeking at her face.

"Only on Tuesdays, Wednesdays and Thursdays, baldy."

Looking glum, he turned over on his back. "I wouldn't mind moving in your place, you know. I'd love to help raise Percy."

Poe sighed. "I know, but our apartment is full of memories of Maclemar. I think it would weird me and Percy out."

Sainvire looked downcast, his light gray eyes flashing. "Then we can find a new place. There are plenty of lofts Downtown. You know that."

Poe pulled down on her open sleeping bag to cover her nakedness. She tugged the sleeping bag flap over herself and controlled her breathing. Their accommodations had been moved from a subversively hip hotel to a broken down motel in the Castro. The hosts provided two well used sleeping bags because the dusty mattress was stripped of sheets. *Don't you dare cry*, she told herself and burrowed deeper in the bag.

Why she was so emotional she didn't know. Perhaps she felt guilt about getting together with Kaleb Sainvire so soon when James Maclemar had passed only weeks before. Loving Sainvire more than Maclemar tore at her.

"We'll see, Kaleb. We can discuss this when we get back home."

He tried to peel off the flannel sleeping bag covering so he could see her face, but Poe's grip was strong. She wouldn't budge.

"I'm sorry, dear Poe, for pressuring you."

"I've only recently discovered you again, Kaleb. But I can never forget that you left me alone all these years. Maclemar was always there for me. He came to visit me when nobody else did. I'll never forget his goodness. And I can't gallivant around town with you so quickly after his death. I hear people are already calling me a hussy. You're the one that ought to kiss my feet and agree to everything I want." Poe paused. "And I wouldn't have stopped searching for you if you'd been taken by Trench. I would've looked until I found a body to confirm you were dead."

Old hurt surfaced. She had waited three months to be rescued while Trench tortured her. Granted, she thought Sainvire was dead at the time. The pregnant pause after her declaration heated her ears. She had no idea why she rehashed such a dark time in the history of their relationship.

Caught off guard by Poe's angry accusations about his past choices, Sainvire stared at the cottage cheese ceiling. "I should've searched for you, I agree. I'll never forgive myself for that. I'll never forget the sight of you tied to a bed, whipped and bleeding." He turned his back to face the window. He could almost see a sliver of the moon but for the blinds. "I hope you'll forgive me someday."

Poe remained silent. She spent the first 20 minutes fighting tears, and then thankfully she fell asleep.

She woke up alone. Kaleb was gone along with his gear bag of explosives. The only remnant left of her lover was his shirt that Poe was wearing. With a leaden heart, she washed herself with cold water and flossed her teeth. She brushed slowly so she wouldn't ruin her gums like her dentist Dr. Theodore had advised. *No cavity or rotten tooth yet. And my teeth will stay that way until I die*, she thought.

She put on another '70s-type shirt, this time in purple and orange, and dressed in her Superfly outfit. Her incomplete getup filled her with shame. The wig she'd forgotten at the bookstore, and she was left with the funny-looking mustache. She looked at herself in the mirror and saw George Harrison with a quickly fading tan during the *Abbey Road* period. Her hair could have been androgynous, but as she'd since shed her breast flattener a couple of days before she couldn't quite pass for a man. She tore the mustache off her face and threw it on the ground.

They'd holed up in the Castro because it was close to the Mission. Rufus was supposed to pick them up at dawn the following day. She left the motel wearing her pack full of unused incendiaries and walked the empty streets. Her words to Sainvire haunted her and wrung her accusing heart devastatingly. Trench was the one to blame, not the vampire she loved.

Occasional dogs trying to figure out what type of creature she was would pass her by. She didn't know herself since her mind was imagining all sorts of breakup scenarios with the man she'd basically blamed for her incarceration and torture at Trench's headquarters. Thinking back now, she'd been unfair to Sainvire. Knowing his resources were spread thin, she wanted too much from him. He had no time between saving humans and fighting corrupt vampires and ridiculous politics besides. All she ever wanted was to run away, ignore the problem, and live a fulfilling, selfish life with her lovers. And

Maclemar had paid the ultimate price. He was knifed in an island far away from the city because of Poe's selfishness.

The sound of a kitten mewling or a baby crying interrupted her train of thoughts. Poe followed the sound that piqued her ears. Something was off about the noise, and it burgeoned curiosity. She stopped in front of a well preserved Queen Ann-style Victorian mansion and listened intently for the mewling that seemed to be coming from the house itself.

Poe climbed the steps two at a time to the porch. She tried the knob, and the door was unlocked. As was her habit, Poe let herself in. On the first floor, four cots bearing human slaves made the girl wince, but the banging on the floor from above distracted her. She scaled the stairs as stealthily as she could with all the creaks and peeked at the row of cots of drugged cattle. She vigorously bit her lower lip when she noticed someone's ass bobbing up and down in the middle cot.

Too busy to notice Poe, the man rutting on a whimpering woman grunted his pleasure. Poe's eyes narrowed as she met the woman's terrified eyes. She was awake from the vampire stupor, and she was at least seven months pregnant.

"Jesus, Mary, and Joseph!" cried Poe. She unsheathed her knife, walked behind the man with a hairy ass and grabbed him by his unwashed hair. "Leech, I'm here to slice your throat." Before she finished her statement, blood coursed out from the man's deep wound, spraying the pregnant woman.

Poe pulled him from the terrified woman of about 30 years of age whose head of hair had turned white from her degrading ordeal as a blood slave.

"Don't be afraid, miss. I'm on your side," said Poe. She yanked the leech off the bed and hurled him to the floor. "Are you alright?" The woman must have been turned as a slave at a very young age.

The victim nodded and pointed upstairs. "I'll get them, too. Don't worry."

"Come back," said the woman weakly, hiding her undressed state with a stained hospital gown.

"I will. I promise," said Poe. She felt a lump in her throat but decided to ignore it. She had more filthy fiends to kill. *No wonder Michelle and the Tunics wanted to murder turncoats who worked for vampires while they slumbered. They raped Michelle. They plundered the helpless. I don't need a gun for this,* she said to herself as she wiped the bloody blade on the lacy curtains.

Three of them reposed on red, white, and blue bean bags and passed around bambalacha. Their eyes were halfway closed as they savored the high. All three men looked similar – thin, bearded, long oily hair, scuffed clothes. They were living the life, eating four meals a day, smoking out, and raping when boredom set in. Poe walked right up to them, sat on the coffee table, and waited for one of the rats to notice her. She put the knife away.

Too stoned to be startled, the man of about 50 reclining on the red bean bag with half-lidded eyes said, "Hey there, pretty girl."

His companions opened their stoned eyes with difficulty and grinned. "Are you a present from Santa?" White Bean Bag asked.

"I sure am," answered Poe sweetly. "Since you've been such naughty boys, Santa has sent Julia Poe herself to take care of you."

Blue Bean Bag fluttered his eyes then recognized Poe's five-inch scar. He sat up like he instantly developed goiter of the rear end and exclaimed, "Shit! The scar! It's her!"

Poe felt like a celebrity and smiled at the recognition. Surprisingly the marijuana haze didn't seem so hunky-dory anymore. Poe rose to her feet and clapped both hands on Red Bean Bag's ears to pummel his equilibrium. Next she stuck her middle finger in his left eye. While he screamed, Poe worked on White Bean Bag and slapped him five times in hard succession. She kicked Blue Bean Bag in the nuts when he stood and tried to capture her from behind.

White Bean Bag's nose bled, and Poe punched him with knuckles callused from slamming trees for practice. The blood flowed as his eyes, nose, and mouth bled like a squished ketchup packet. Tired of the game, Poe grabbed his ear and yanked down savagely until she heard a crack. White Bean Bag was no more.

"I heard she can't shoot straight anymore," one of the remaining men declared. "We mustn't be scared of her." *Even leeches know my business*, thought Poe.

"Too right, stoner man," said Poe with a smile. She slid a wrist knife from her arm and flung it at the greasy-hair leech. The knife landed in his inner thigh.

Caught by surprise the man cursed but kept to his gun as he pulled the small blade from his leg. "See what I mean? The bitch can't shoot straight."

Poe nodded in assent. "You'll be dead in 30 seconds," she said as her eyes surveyed the man's thigh that was oozing blood like a faucet. "Femoral artery, my man." She ignored his screams and focused on the last leech.

Poe concentrated her attention on Blue Bean Bag, who was clutching his nuts and calling her the vilest names in leech speak. She pushed the coffee table out of the way with her foot to give her speed leverage. From the opposite end of the room she sprinted, landing her knee in the potty mouth's chest and collapsing his lungs Muay Thai-style. The unstable bean bag nearly downed her but she rolled off before her head hit the hardwood floor.

And there was Red Beard who'd just entered the scene holding a skinning knife he'd pulled out of his tacky alligator boots with pointy toes. "Get away from me, bitch!" he said, nearly crying from fear. The man's equilibrium was off, and his left eye was blind. He swung the knife left to right.

"Wow. Manly knife you have there," Poe said with a laugh. "If only you knew how to use it, eh?" With a round kick, she dislodged the knife from his hand. It flew in the air, and the vampire killer easily caught it by clapping her hand together like a praying Buddhist monk. She kicked herself mentally for the dangerous and flashy move. "Oops! Looky here, I got your knife now."

Poe contemplated making the man take off his pants so she could cut off his ding dong, but the thought gave her the chills. She didn't want to catch disease, so she generously buried the knife in his last good eye.

She would feel guilty later she knew, but at the moment Poe felt satisfied with her methods. When she made it to the second floor, the pregnant woman was sitting up talking to a curly-hair Latina who looked like an emaciated J-Lo. By the stairs was a pushcart filled with blended and mashed meals that resembled vomit.

"Hi!" said Poe stupidly. "Problem's been taken care of upstairs."

The custodian's eyes widened in fear. "They'll think I did it, Julia Poe. I'll be killed!" The scar gave her away.

Poe shook her head. "Believe me, they won't because you can't do what I've done to those men upstairs. They'll come after me."

"Take me with you, please!" she said. The custodian was in her early 30s, meaning she'd been a slave since she was a little over 10 years old. And the pregnant woman must've been allowed to grow up as a child then turned into a blood cow.

"Me, too," said the pregnant woman. Her voice was unsteady like she'd just started learning how to speak. Most blood slaves unhooked from the system had the same initial problems including learning how to walk again and chew.

"I can't. I'm sorry, ladies."

"Please. Take us away from here," said the Latina. "We've suffered so much already."

"Listen. Any day now the vampire government will topple and the underground will take over. In the meantime you both have to look after your friends."

"Others will come to take care of them. Please," begged the pregnant woman. "Isn't that right, Jimena?"

"Lucy is right. We rotate every meal time," said Jimena. "These people will be fed. Besides, Lucy's having a bad pregnancy, possibly a breach birth, and she needs a real doctor. I can't handle this myself."

Poe had no choice. "Listen. My ride isn't going to be here until dawn tomorrow." She gave the location where she would be meeting Rufus. "If you guys can make it there, then I'll take you both. You're gonna have to find your own transportation. And please don't invite anyone else. My friend has a very small plane."

"Skinheads live there," said Jimena nervously. "And they don't answer to anyone."

Poe waved at the air. "Oh, don't worry about them. They're all dead. I killed them my first day here."

The weather was chilly, too cold for her tacky brown leather jacket to handle. The sun shone elegantly in Poe's mind as she inhaled fresh air to purge her lungs of the smell of blood and killing. The thickening fog upset her stomach. As surely as she breathed there were rows of Victorians that housed leeches who abused their own kind without sanctions from the vampire order. *I can't possibly go through each house*, she said despondently. "Who'll take care of the people until the full-blown revolution?"

Sainvire had left her. She was surrounded by suffering humans she couldn't even hope to save. Her damn outfit was embarrassing and reminded her of her crassness and ignorance. She missed Maclemar. He always had the knack for making her see the shiny side of things. "At least there's Christmas," she muttered. She still needed to track down Percy's presents and give Penny the attention she deserved. Poe had been too busy killing to pay attention to her loyal companion.

Poe's self-pity ended when a battered pickup truck nearly careened as it made a sharp turn from Castro Street onto States Street. Poe quickly moved from the street to the sidewalk. She walked as if she belonged. *Perhaps a custodian on an errand*, she told herself.

The truck slowed when the driver spotted Poe and followed her pace. From the corner of her eye, she could see a goateed driver waving at her. She was about to hide out in one of the houses when the man said, "Psst! Hey!"

Poe had no choice but to turn around and face the driver who was transporting in the flatbed five passengers wearing fatigues. The back of her neck prickled. Something wasn't right. The men in the back from what she could see carried no guns or weapons of any kind. The driver had a look of ex-cattle or drug-addicted leech. *Take your pick*, thought Poe.

"Sí," she said, sounding racially bugged up as she conjured her quarter blood line.

"You're Julia Poe, ain't ya?" said the driver. *He's definitely a leech.*

"No entiendo, señor. I am custodian, okay?"

Three of the soldier wannabes jumped out of the truck. The two remaining would've made Poe's mouth water for they looked too handsome to be believed. One in particular sat on the roof of the trunk with his hands crossed across his chest. The blue-eyed looker with light brown hair winked at Poe. His California blond friend, second place in the beauty contest, would've kicked any past blond actors in the ass.

The three shorter and burlier men bent on approaching Poe didn't worry her so much. "Your Spanish is as awful as your fake tan, Julia Poe," said a smallish man not much taller than Poe herself.

The girl was tired of pretending to speak a language she obviously didn't know so she shrugged her shoulders and began throwing darts from her eyes at the three men. "Okay. So you got me," she said. That was when her hands dug for her guns in her holsters and shot the three weaponless walking dead in the head before they could even blink. When she pointed her guns at the handsome devils in the back of the truck, she found that they'd disappeared.

The leech driver flattened himself on the seat but Poe, without looking, stuck her hand through the window and fired two shots. Her worried eyes roamed the street. The two day vamps had disappeared. *The runaways must have more power than the three I killed.*

Heads from windows along the street watched her as she tried to figure out what to do next. Some custodians waved at her. Leeches flipped her the bird and yelled profanities, disturbing her concentration.

"Shut the hell up!" shouted Poe. "Or I swear I'm going to bust into your houses and shoot your balls off!"

She felt wind on the back of her head, and she turned around to find a smiling cutie waving at her. "My name's Earl," said the handsomest tan halfdead she'd ever met. Surrender your guns, and no one else needs to get hurt."

The hell? She pointed the gun at the vamp and pulled the trigger. Without even moving, Earl caught the whizzing bullet in his hand like snagging a ping pong ball. "Oh, shit," said Poe out loud. Sure that he would miss at least one bullet, she emptied a full clip on the man, but she was wrong. He caught all of them with a wicked smile on his face.

Blondie landed in her blind spot. *Kill one of them at least,* she thought. Poe was chagrined that she didn't see the flying day vamp's look of surprise as her bullets hit him in the nose and heart for she had locked her gaze on Earl. He fell dead by her feet.

"I never liked him anyway," said her blue-eyed foe. "Too vain. Anyway, are you ready to give up?"

"Hell no," said Poe, pointing a gun that contained at least eight more bullets. "Just get away from me, you ugly son of a bitch."

His eyebrows rose. The vampire with neck-length hair obviously had never been called ugly before. "Wow. I like you, Julia Poe. You're spunky, pretty, and you killed every single bastard I work with. Thanks! No need to waste bullets on me. I'm on your side."

Poe shook her head disbelievingly. "Say again? I thought I heard a big fucking lie."

"I'm Earl. I work with the underground. We're supposed to take you to the Council chambers, but it seems you killed almost all of us." She looked him up and down, studying his uniform and blue beret, and scoffed.

"Do you think I was born 20 seconds ago? You're the enemy if I ever saw one."

He tucked his brown hair behind his ear. "You're prejudiced because I'm ugly. Well I'll tell you something. My sisters work for the Council, and they're in trouble. If I don't turn you in, it will confirm Nesbitt's suspicion that they're working with the underground because Sainvire forgot to decapitate them along with the other four Council members. I have no choice in this matter, cupcake. I'm sure Sainvire will turn up to get you. He's good like that."

"You want me as bait?"

"Not me, Julia. Nesbitt. He wants Sainvire, and he wants you. I'm hoping your boyfriend would get you and we can finally wrestle Nesbitt out of his damn golden throne. In the meantime he has lots of soldiers on his side, and we don't want humans or good vampires to get hurt. Bradley and Jane know of this plan because I spoke to them this morning. They're ready to take over tonight if, and only if Nesbitt thinks he's getting the two of you."

"That is the biggest bunk I've ever heard of! Sainvire's probably gone now. I don't know where the hell he is."

"Having a spat, eh?" he said, grinning. "Maybe you can consider going to the prom with me after this whole mess is over."

She was nearly hyperventilating. To believe Earl was to be utterly and irrevocably stupid. "I don't date canines, so forget about it." Her gut told her he was telling the truth. "Who are your sisters?"

"Sara and Mina. They're twins, and they're both part of the Council or what's left of it. They're powerful vampires where I'm only a halfdead. Sainvire didn't touch them when he went after the other three Council members because he knew they're with the underground. But like I said, Nesbitt is on to them, and I need to bring you in to show my sisters are nothing to be fussed over."

Poe handed her guns to Earl. Her face was stoic. If she was making a mistake, she could have Sainvire and herself killed. She pointed at the gun in his right palm. "If I come out without any of my limbs, I want you to shoot me in the head, alright?"

He nodded. "I promise."

"Pull the body out of the seat, will ya? I'm allergic to leech blood."

Earl tucked the guns in his military jacket and pulled the leech from the car. He found a spool of bubble wrap in the back of the truck and covered the front seat with it.

Poe went around the car to the passenger side and let herself inside. *Let me do the right thing, Sister Ann. If this vampire is lying, I'm gonna end up getting Kaleb and the underground killed.*

CHAPTER 14

THE HALFDEAD EARL DROVE through milky fog without hesitation. His half-vampire sight penetrated the thick fog San Francisco was known for. A smile lingered on his lips, and Poe had the urge to slap it off his face. Already she regretted agreeing to the word of a halfdead whose sisters were Nesbitt's Council members. When Kaleb had slaughtered four Council members, he didn't mention Sara and Mina. Perhaps the sisters hadn't been around when Sainvire went on a rampage. For all she knew, Earl's family was waiting for her arrival at City Hall. She glanced out the window and narrowed her eyes. Even in fog the city had class.

Like falling off a cliff, the truck lurched and flew, hitting the ground seconds later. While the chassis bounced Poe reached for her weapon but the gun wasn't there. Poe couldn't help it. She eked out a girly scream, and Earl whooped as he rammed his foot on the gas. "Fuck a duck!" cried Poe.

"This is Filbert Street, Julia Poe. The steepest street in San Francisco. Some say it's 22nd Street, but don't believe it. I thought we'd take the scenic route before going to the Civic Center."

Poe ought to have been annoyed, but the feeling of plummeting to her death invigorated her. Strangely enough, all fear and worry left her mind. "Let's try 22nd Street, why don't we?" she said, inhaling deeply and exhaling her chicken ways.

"Sure. Hopefully everything's coordinated. Bradley and Jane must've rallied their supporters and rehashed their plans with my sisters."

"Why is your entire family helping the underground oust Nesbit?" asked Poe.

"It's in our blood I suppose. Pardon the pun. Our parents were Bohemians from the 1920s who dabbled in vampirism when they learned about a cult called the Spring of Life. Mother turned all three of us and regretted it right away. We were just blooming into our adult lives, enjoying the perks of life, and were literally forced into the vampire club. Maybe I only half-turned because I was a kid. We've never forgiven her for cutting holes in our heads and spitting blood in our brains."

"What happened to your mother?"

"She's dead. Flung herself into the sun."

"Oh," said Poe awkwardly. She had nothing more to say about that topic. "Your sisters. Why the heck did they ever join the Council?"

"Mina and Sara are strong. They can fly and have the strength of a rhino. I'm the runt of the family. Because of the way we were raised, we tend to ask a lot of questions. My sisters hate being on the Council, but that's the only place they could make much of a difference." He turned toward Poe and smiled. "They've been working with the underground for 10 years now, and the time is right to destroy the old ways and begin again. Sainvire knows them very well."

Poe refrained from screaming again when Earl floored the gas, flew into the air on 22nd Street, and hit the ground with the shocks violently taking a beating. "How was that, Julia Poe?"

"Fucking great, Earl!" said Poe with a grin on her face. "And call me Poe. Let's go again." Questions left her. She wanted the thrill of dying because she knew death was a distinct possibility that night.

"No problema," he said. He made a u-turn and lugged the truck up the hill.

After four soaring adventures on 22nd Street, Earl parked on the sidewalk. "Time for you to show me the roadmap, Earl. My head isn't ready for the spike, so I won't go unless I hear a coherent plan."

"Fair enough," he said as he faced Poe's weary look. "Jane's people will replace the custodians on the building, and they'll be armed. There's about 20 guards around Nesbitt at all times, but they'll be called in for a meeting. Goodbye to them. Again they'll be replaced by our vamps."

"What about the vamps in the basement? Walking upstairs at sunset?"

"Our vamps will behead them until there are no more hindrances to the overthrow. You see, ex-cattle, reformed leeches, halfdead, and vamps for the cause have infiltrated the Council. My sisters will take care of Nesbitt if Sainvire doesn't get to him first since you're the bait."

"Where is he anyway?" asked Poe nonchalantly as she studied a bay house like a real estate agent.

"He's blowing up the last of Nesbitt's toys. Don't worry, he hasn't deserted you," said Earl, his ocean eyes twinkling.

"Of course he hasn't deserted me!" she cried. "He can't live without me."

Earl nodded seriously. "I can see that. You and Sainvire make quite a pair."

"Can't I have my guns with me for protection?" asked Poe to change the subject.

"Afraid not. We have to make your captivity authentic. We haven't seen Nesbitt use his powers because all he has to do is work his brain into a fever and order someone to carry out his plotting, but rumor is he's something to behold. We don't want to take the chance. But you're certainly welcome to your wrist knives. I don't want to leave you completely powerless."

"That'll do. Thanks," said Poe. She was silent the rest of the drive to the government campus. She thought of Sainvire and their conversation the night before. She had accused him of leaving her behind to be tortured by Quillon Trench. Her words hurt Kaleb, and worse, her blame was truly unfounded. Trench was the bad guy. He was the one who had tortured her and not Kaleb Sainvire who have sacrificed his life for her. Suddenly she wanted to weep, but it wasn't the proper place or time.

She cleared her throat and said to the halfdead, "If you pick up any signs that Nesbitt is going to torture me, have someone break it off. Otherwise I can't promise to be a good little prisoner. I won't be hurt again."

"I won't let that happen. I'll be at your side the entire time."

Poe nodded. "I think this is the beginning of a new friendship, Earl. I like you, so you better not turn against me."

"Not me. I like being half-alive," he said with a grin.

When Poe, Sainvire, and their allies stole most of the human cattle from Downtown Los Angeles, the world of the dead experienced an 8.0 earthquake within their pretentious world of old lord and master statuses. Fear gripped the master vampires that thought themselves unshakeable with a lifetime pass because of their age, strengths, and bloodlines.

Perla's Plasmacore planted seeds of hope for the troubled. Most didn't want to drink milked blood from emaciated, barely living humans. Though dead or halfdead, they still had their principles. And as the cattle weakened, the nutrition from their blood didn't satisfy vampires.

They were constantly hungry. So they turned to making Plasmacore in secret. The difference in satisfaction and power from a glass of Plasmacore was palpable.

Some could see far distances. Many developed strength they never could have imagined, and a lucky few could handle sunlight. The best and very rare gift, decided those who imbibed Plasmacore, was the gift of flight.

Poe determined that custodians were tired of looking after the dying, and sane vampires who had consciences wanted nothing to do with cattle. Leeches, the only contingent with something to gain for the perks of unlimited drug use and rape, were against the use of Plasmacore. Most were afraid that if the food source changed, they would have no role in the vampire realm. They would be shoveling shit and burying the dead like custodians.

As Earl drove, a sense of dread came upon Poe. She and Sainvire were alone in a hostile city. Her gut was telling her to trek to the Mission District to meet Rufus. Sainvire was strong with unmatched skills and attributes like flight, the ability to carry more than one passenger for long periods of time, rapid healing, and diamond-sharp talons that could split a vampire in half. He could withstand the sun and garlic thanks to Perla's painful experiments, and he retained other faculties that would scare off any dead.

They drove around the block to show Poe the white neo-classical building they would enter. About 20 heads had been lopped off and stuck on a spike, some so spoiled by insects and birds that they were grotesque like the melting gruesomeness of the funhouses that used to scare her as a child.

"There's more. Last time I was here there were four or five," Earl said somberly. "Nesbitt is shaking in his boots and using these heads to pump up the fear."

"Just make sure he doesn't axe my head. I don't want to be the main attraction on one of those sticks. I don't look good with plucked out eyes."

"Promise. I'll be with you the entire time." He turned his head and waited for Poe to look at him. His blue eyes were jewels like Maclemar's. For a couple seconds she hallucinated that her other love was pledging to protect her for life. She nodded and blinked away memories of the man who loved her so much he was willing to follow her to the ends of the world. And he died for it.

"Thanks, Earl. Tell me again how many of the Council are left," she changed the subject.

"Only my sisters and Nesbitt. And his guards, of course, which are to be replaced by Jane's people. His main collaborators are kaput like his beloved pupil, Trench. Your kill."

Poe's jaw began working. Indeed, she'd killed Trench herself after he had tortured her for over three months. Nesbitt had stopped by a few times to watch her whipping and her blood spooned for other vampires to partake. She detested the vampire. "Nesbitt can't fly. He can't handle the sun. What the hell can he do?"

"Rumor is he's as fierce as a lion and can conjure fire with his hands. Some have seen him with spikes twisting out of his arms," said Earl.

"Fucking A. I'm gonna have to beat him to it with my little wrist knives," said Poe with a half-smile. She was ridiculous without her firepower.

"Don't worry. Once the guards enter the room, we're set. My sisters will flank Nesbitt, and the guards will arrest him. You and Sainvire can do whatever you want with him while we look on. There's that. You can go back home, and we'll rebuild this city like you've done down south. Custodians and human cattle will be compensated and nursed back to life. Like your city, we'll have a new council represented by all the different types of folks from San Francisco. Life will be hard, but we're looking forward to starting over."

"You can see how things are run at home. You're welcome to visit," offered Poe.

"I'm there. Can't wait for a well deserved vacation."

They parked in silence. Poe couldn't shake the fluttering in her tummy. *Please Mom, Dad, Sister Ann, Goss, Bruce Lee, Xena, take care of Sainvire for me. I'm headed for Nesbitt's lair naked, and I'm not very happy about it. Let me just kill him and get this sham over with. Sainvire and I need to make it to our plane by dawn. Take care of him. Don't worry about me, although it would be nice to survive this, too.*

"Don't cuff me," said Poe when Earl brought out the handcuffs from the glove compartment. Her look of panic and anger took Earl aback.

Earl demonstrated by cuffing his own wrists then slipping out of the restraints. "These are gag cuffs. Here's the lever that gets you out quickly and without a hitch. I got it from the joke shop years ago. Once you feel you're in danger, just pop out of the cuffs and ready your knives. We gotta make this look like the real thing, Poe."

"Gotcha," said Poe as she cuffed herself and pressed the levers, releasing a sigh of relief when the cuffs fell to her lap. She secured them once more and nodded at Earl. "This is pretty cute. I hope you don't use them for kinky stuff, and if you do I hope you disinfected them. But thanks."

"No prob." He looked uncomfortable. "Just be ready to protect yourself. I'll toss you your guns as soon as everything's in place. Sanvire should be coming after you soon, so let's skedaddle." Earl, wearing a stodgy military uniform replete with blue beret, looked entirely the mercenary tough. Poe had no choice but to trust him and hope his tongue wasn't as smooth as a serpent's.

The vestibule of the building had more than 20 fierce-looking sentinels by Poe's count. In reality there were more than 50 wearing dark-blue military clothing and blue berets. Their professional mien reminded Poe of the Third

Reich. She despised Nazis and the morons that followed them. Earl shoved her harshly across the gauntlet where each guard threw shards with their eyes at her hippie-pimp look.

"They don't seem friendly to me," said Poe in a whisper. She didn't dare turn around to castigate Earl for the push. She nearly slammed into one of the guards.

"Hell if I know. Those are the regular guards Nesbitt employs plus the 20 in the chambers. Jane and Bradley are running a little late, I guess," he whispered, uncomfortable about speaking. Certain vampires had sharp ears.

"You guess? Shit. Nesbitt can have me tortured and maimed before the cavalry comes to the rescue," Poe gritted. "And believe me, I am over torture. I'd just as soon slit my throat than be Nesbitt's revenge doll."

"Don't worry. It'll turn out," Earl said almost enthusiastically. "Sara can fly. Mina is as fast as a tornado."

"And that will save me how exactly?" In her experience flying vampires were weak with their aim, and strength to carry a passenger was non-existent. As for tornado vamps like Joseph, they could whisk a person out of harm's way or inflict major damage by stabbing hearts or other weak spots in rat-a-tat succession. But for some reason Poe had no faith in the sisters' abilities or sense of solidarity with the underground movement. She was relying solely on the word of a half-vamp she had barely met. Poe admitted to herself that if

Earl had been repulsively ugly she wouldn't voluntarily be handcuffed.

Their conversation ended when two guards wearing black sweaters and black army pants complemented by red berets opened the chamber doors.

Poe exhaled with indecision upon seeing Sara, Mina, and 20 steely-eyed red beret guards that turned cautiously to her, ready to battle. Nesbitt wasn't in the room, and her fears abated somewhat. Mina, a short-cropped redhead, ordered her in a not-so-friendly voice to sit at the interrogation chair in the middle of the chamber floor. Sara, blonde and also sporting hair like a boy, asked if she wanted a beverage.

"No thanks. Someone will spit in it," said Poe grouchily.

"You're probably right about that," answered Sara with amusement. "These guards aren't your friends. They're under the command of me and the rest of the military force in this building, so be glad that no harm will come to you. Unless you put up your Julia Poe berserker act."

Poe's nostrils flared. Sara just about told her that the guards inside, red berets, were no friends of hers. The revolutionaries had screwed up. Underground friendlies hadn't replaced the guards. With only wrist knives for defense, she was surrounded by enemies.

"Where can I find some friends?" Poe asked testily.

"If you're lucky within the hour," answered Mina in her smoker voice. "For now try not to jump out the windows or go into the vestibule to your left leading to the lavatories."

"Will do," Poe said, clearing her throat. They were in the first floor of the building. Mina implied that she could jump out the window or go toward the lavatories where a window or an exit door might be waiting for her. *Good to know.* Nesbitt was a sun-sizzler, and darkness was fast approaching. The dictator was coming out of his cubby hole. Poe could feel it in her bones.

The vampire exterminator studied the guards with the red berets. They were smallish, even the men, but Poe had learned that size didn't matter in the game of dead politics. Halfdead her size could toss tanks and derail trains. But then again Nesbitt was a megalomaniac who was as tall as his guards. The lunatic didn't want to appear the dwarf in front of dignitaries because of his deranged pride. Poe wondered about the vampire's true power. No doubt about it, Nesbitt was intelligent, conniving, and one hell of a strategist. How many times had he advised Quillon Trench as to how to annihilate Sainvire and his people? He kept San Francisco under strict control and had time to dabble in the politics of San Diego and Los Angeles. The vampire was a busy bee. He was dangerous.

Poe turned her head to stare out the window. Fog and darkness had set forth. For the first time in a long time Julia Poe felt the pang of fear. Not since Trench's torture and Maclemar's death had she experienced the dread of mortality. The artily crafted terra cotta cupids on the chamber pillars gave her a stomachache when she leaned her head back to take a breath. Even if she were able to jump out an open window, her sight would have been limited. She'd memorized the San Francisco streets, but in the foggy night, she'd have been like an owl with cataracts.

The steady tap-tap of formal shoes pulled her from her murky thoughts. Poe turned to the small man with an immaculate tailored black suit with shiny leather patent shoes. Briefly she studied him, the master vampire that had been a bane in her life since he tutored Quillon Trench in his excessively barbarous ways. There was a smidgeon of charisma to the vampire, but far from the qualities of Trench or Sainvire. The dead's plain face, sour demeanor, and detachment destroyed any hope of complete love from his people.

Peter Nesbitt wore a plain gray tie. "Nice tie," Poe pointed out as the chamber door closed and the vampire headed her way. His shoes clanked down the marble floor. Poe itched.

The vampire ignored her and spoke to Sara and Mina out of earshot. Poe glanced at Earl who stood posted near a window that dripped with caulking or some type of epoxy. He looked away. *This better not be a set-up with Earl luring me into the enemy lair.* Even with the easily removable handcuffs, she was outnumbered and outgunned.

Peter Nesbitt turned to her and watched her with cool contempt. He walked behind the podium and adjusted the metal-tipped microphone like in the Sun Studio days of Elvis and spoke. He twisted his diamond-encrusted cufflinks and straightened his tie. The master vampire gazed intently at Poe as he readied to speak. His words reverberated throughout the chambers, the grounds, and most probably all corners of the Bay Area. The vampire made it a point to speak to the public once in a blue moon to spew out Big Brother doublespeak. He had installed broadcast towers all over San Francisco.

His smooth, confident voice filled the night, and Poe couldn't help but shudder.

"Julia Poe, Public Enemy Number Two, has infiltrated San Francisco to cause havoc, thievery, and death. Yes, thievery. She wants to steal your blood like she did in Los Angeles. She has murdered several of our esteemed Council members. She has destroyed most of our road vehicles, ferries, and air strips. She is scouting because she wants to take over San Francisco and its food supply and steal our custodians." The master vampire sent her a withering look full of loathing. She wondered if he knew that Sainvire was also in San Francisco and he had damaged most of Nesbitt's firepower.

"She will not succeed. Tonight we will eliminate her once and for all. I encourage everyone within the sound of my voice to make your way to City Hall. Witness the flogging and beheading of the so-called superwoman who is nothing more than a greedy little child," Nesbitt proclaimed in an old-fashioned staccato voice.

Poe quit listening after the word "flogging." She had heard his bullshit already while at the

City Lights. Memories of her torture flooded back, and she became weak to the stomach. She glanced at Earl and found his jaw was working despite his nonchalant air. If they succeeded in torturing her, the entire population of San Francisco would witness. She would be Hester Prynne to be judged. If blows came to blows she would've gladly welcomed a beheading. But never torture.

The vampire continued his monologue about the greed of Los Angelinos and their viciousness. He mentioned Poe murdering Quillon Trench, their fateful ally. He once again recalled her balls at stealing over 300 blood cattle four years ago and the murder of the entire Council in Los Angeles.

In his rather laborious speech, not once did he mention Sainvire as he had days before. *Please, Xena and Bruce, let Sainvire be alright. I need to apologize for my rude behavior. Please, Mom and Dad.* Poe hoped Mina and Sara omitted the information in their report to Nesbitt.

"Yes, her head will roll, ladies and gentlemen." His voice dramatically upticked a few notches, bringing her back to reality. "We have a special place for her head above the building entrance, and her body will be hung upside down on the flagpole. But first you will see the mighty Julia Poe stripped of her clothing and flogged. A lucky few will share her sweet, untapped blood. This will be my Christmas present to you all."

Poe felt like vomiting. Nesbitt knew her fear of humiliation in the state of undress, and yet that topped the entertainment list. She made up her mind. She would stab her heart with a garlic-marinated wrist knife before she would be publicly exposed.

When Nesbitt stopped speaking, no one in the room, not even Earl, dared look at her. Sharp feedback from the microphone invaded the ears of those still thinking about the sinister speech – and lingering on the detailed descriptions of the vampire killer's torture. Poe had stopped listening. The vampire killer decided then not to allow Nesbitt to mess with her mind.

"Nice one," Poe said in her husky tone. "Too bad I will be the one to string you up on the flagpole buck naked and gut you like a snared badger, you miserable son of a bitch."

Nesbitt's expensive shoes clicked on the marble floor once more as he slowly approached Poe who was fuming on the chair. She itched to free herself of her gag handcuffs and slug the vampire, but she knew it would be premature. The underground fighters hadn't arrived yet, and she didn't know the extent of Peter Nesbitt's powers.

The master vampire, one of three left in San Francisco, stopped short of Julia Poe and raised his small, manicured hand. With no expression on his face, his hand landed with a thwack on Poe's left cheek, nearly cracking her jaw. She slid from her chair.

Poe shook her head and rotated her jaw. She slowly stood but was promptly pushed down by a hand on her shoulder. Earl kept her from making trouble. He squeezed her shoulder twice as if to convey the postponement of the fight. Earl kept her seated as Nesbitt walked away.

Her cheek stung as she ran a tongue inside her mouth, making sure her teeth were all in place. *At least there's no blood to tempt the guards*, she thought.

When she was six an older kid in the Sawtelle neighborhood of West L.A. had slapped her just to practice his sociopathic tendencies. She cried. Later she realized it wasn't the pain she was tearing for like a Sicilian mother whose son was killed by the Mafia. He hadn't slapped her that hard. The slap was meant to cause abject shame much like rape or torture. But this time Poe didn't cry. She thought. The vampire laid his best slapping shot, and the blow felt like a smack from Percy. The vampire whose powers took on mythical proportions was a fraud. He was weak. No powers to speak of besides having a conniving brain that kept himself and his city functioning for 20 years with a boost from an invented legend.

Poe smiled with elation. Nesbitt happened to glance at her at that moment as he sat rigidly in the chamber seat meant for the highest order of master vampires. Her face lit up and beamed even more. The dead fascist walked slowly and deliberately every time she saw him. He took his time for he didn't have the speed or powers of the weakest of his guards. At least that was her theory. She imagined kicking him to death Muay Thai-style and knifing his throat, ending the bullshit of old vampire privilege. This was America where everyone was equal under the law, or the law they were rewriting anyway.

———

Time ticked for Poe like a death row inmate waiting for the needle. She could hear the growing number of people whisper and laugh outside the City Hall lawn. After an hour a monstrous crowd of San Franciscans formed. They were leeches, vamps, halfdead, and custodians. Poe imagined herself naked and flayed in front of the crowd and banished the thought. Nude torture was out of the question. The mortification of being paraded and debased wasn't going to happen again. *Never.*

"Mina. Sara. It's time," said Peter Nesbitt, rising from his seat. The two sisters nodded at him and in turn gestured at the guards. The red beret guards, the cream of the crop, marched toward Poe, and the lead guard lifted her off her feet. With head held high, she allowed the guards to escort her through the white hallways and outside City Hall where about 400 beings waited curiously to see what was to happen to the most notorious vampire eliminator in history. They looked from her to the flagpole where the American flag used to fly proudly and whispered into each other's ears.

Fuck that. I'm no Joan of Arc, she thought belligerently.

Again she heard buzzing discussions of her height and how they couldn't believe a child could eviscerate so many. *Size doesn't matter*, she thought angrily. *I'll get you all, just watch!*

Peter Nesbitt spoke from the highest steps of City Hall while five red berets flanked Poe on the well manicured lawn. The blue berets stood in a C-pattern to act as a barrier to the awaiting spectators. An assistant handed the vampire a cordless microphone.

"Thank you for coming to the flaying of Julia Poe, a nuisance, a thief, and a murderer of the worst kind," he repeated. "You see, Miss Poe is a very shy person. She doesn't like to be seen in the nude. One of her outstanding weaknesses, really. But tonight you will glimpse the loveliness she is withholding from the world.

Poe's full mouth became a slit. *The underground isn't going to help me, and Sainvire is nowhere in sight. This isn't going to happen again!*

Adrenaline coursing through her veins, Poe pounced on the closest red hat. She wound her cuffed hand around his neck and like a monkey jumped on his back until the vampire dropped chest-first on the ground. Another small hop breeched his neck, loudly severing spine. Quickly she removed her cuffs and assumed a fighting stance with one foot behind the other and fists in front of her face. The other four guards raised guns, but Nesbitt sternly ordered them not to shoot. He wanted her to suffer an agonizing punishment. Poe smiled and kicked two vampires in the crotch. She'd tried the dirty trick before and found that vampires actually thought that their manhood was bruised when struck in the balls. But they were vampires and mended well. Mental fighting. Poe loved it.

Poe slipped the knives from her wrists and slashed the downed in the heart. She accurately threw the garlic-soaked knives dead center to the hearts of the remaining two guards. She retrieved her daggers and stared with feral hatred at Nesbitt and his guards.

"Nesbitt is a dictator!" Poe screamed. "You bastards have tortured cattle and milked their blood for so many years they have the nutritional value of cardboard, and you all know it. They're literally dying right now, and leeches are raping their children. How can you live with yourselves?"

Poe instinctively knew that somebody was behind her, and she turned around to find a red beret sneaking around with a rope. Before he could think twice, Poe high kicked him in the face then buried her knife in his eyeball. The vampire's yell was excruciating.

Poe resumed her talk like she had never been interrupted. "I know most of you use Plasmacore. You're more powerful because of it. You feel like a million bucks. It clears your conscience."

"Enough!" ordered Peter Nesbit. "What she says is propaganda meant to divide our city. Get her!" The vampire was visibly shaken, his usually aristocratic bearing wilting. When nobody made a move he barked, "Now!"

Half of the blues surrounded Poe but with their backs to her, keeping the red berets out like honed Roman soldiers. "What the hell is this?" asked a ruggedly handsome red beret vampire with missing teeth. "We're your superiors."

"Not anymore, you swine," answered a scarred woman in the blue regiment. "Your lording over our city is over. Either join us or be killed."

"Yeah, by you? You blue hats have less power than us."

The woman pointed at the crowd. "There's almost 500 out there. Most of them are ours, and they're armed." To prove her point, she raised a fist, and the crowd on the lawn imitated the gesture.

Poe tiptoed between two blue berets to search for Nesbitt, but he was gone from the City Hall steps. She tried to tear herself from the circle of powerful vampires and couldn't. "Let me out," she shouted, but no one was listening.

Sara picked the fallen microphone off the floor and raised it to her mouth. She spoke with composure, and her gray slacks and simple blue shirt made her accessible to the folks gathered around City Hall. "My sister Mina, my brother Earl, and I are part of the underground. We want to work with humans, halfdead, vampires, custodians, and whoever's willing to make a change. We will all be equal. No one above another. But there will be rules and regulations that to be voted on and parceled out by a council composed of different beings. This is the United States of America where freedom once reigned, and it will once more. We'll be a democracy again." She nodded to someone in the crowd, and up the concrete steps walked Jane, her arm in a sling, followed by Joel and a custodian.

Poe cursed and dropped down on her knees. She stuck her knife into two different shins. Two blue berets stumbled on the lawn. The hyper Julia Poe hurdled over the injured parties and avoided guards like Ms. Pac-Man outmaneuvering multicolored ghosts. She reached the steps where the fledgling seeds of a government broadcasted their plans to San Francisco residents. She noticed Li among the new dignitaries, grabbed him by the shirt, and made him follow her inside the building. "Where the hell is Sainvire?" she asked, praying that nothing had happened to him.

"He was destroying boats at the harbor and a bomb exploded prematurely. He was damaged badly, but he's healing quickly," said the annoying Asian man.

"Where is he?" Her heart twisted into a bed of nails. She should have known something was wrong. Sainvire wasn't one to hold a grudge or to avoid her for being rude and deranged.

"I don't know. He wasn't at HQ when we left." He patted her back. "Don't worry, Poe. I've never seen a vampire heal so fast. We fed him Plasmacore until he couldn't swallow another drop. I'm sure he's just taking in the clean air. I heard L.A. air stinks."

"Don't talk about my city like that, Li, or I'll gut you," Poe said seriously. Despite the bad memories, Los Angeles was her home, and her home was more than adequate. "When you see Sainvire, tell him I'm going after Nesbitt."

"But they want you to speak to the city residents. I believe some guards took him to the chamber room for safekeeping."

"Tell them hello for me." With that, Poe lit like a rabbit with a purpose. "This isn't my city. I won't be a poster girl for your makeover. I've done what I set to do, and Kaleb and I are going home."

"Fair enough," said Li. Earl walked toward them, but Poe didn't have time to chat.

Be alright, Kaleb. I can't lose you, too. You're my life, she thought as she sprinted to the chamber followed by Earl.

CHAPTER 15

THE MASTER VAMPIRE WAS a sure shot like herself. The carnage in the room was ghastly. Twelve blue berets and three underground resistance fighters died with bullets lodged perfectly centered on their foreheads. They looked stunned like they couldn't believe they were permanently dead. They lay askew on the chamber floor, and the eyes and mouths of some were still open. Poe felt ill. She'd killed roomfuls of enemies, and she'd never once bothered to examine the dead. A rush of coldness enveloped her.

Peter Nesbitt, her equal or possibly superior in shooting accuracy, sat on his high chair, taking in Poe's reaction. Her knives were mere rocks. The master vampire laid out the most expensive and accurate firepower she'd only read about in gun magazines. Four gold-dipped Purdey guns, Holland and Hollands, and a Perazzi used for Olympic shooting competition. Each weapon ran up to 30 grand each 20 years ago. Magazine clips carried 13 to 20 rounds. She was one dead fish.

"You've ruined what we stood for, Julia Poe. Because of you, this city will be overrun by vermin."

"Neat of me, hey," said Poe, trying to subordinate the fear in her voice. "No more master this, master that in the biggest cities in California. For all we know you could be pardoned and given a Victorian home, and you can garden to your heart's content."

"Your humor has never amused me, Julia Poe. Your disagreeable self will end tonight," he said, rising.

Poe jumped when Earl whispered in her ear. She'd forgotten about the halfdead. "Let's book, Poe. The guy's insanely accurate. We'll be Swiss cheese."

"You go," she said with her last dying courage. She pulled him behind her. Waiting for her brain to conjure up something interesting to say, Poe stared at Nesbitt. "So you're a waste," she said finally. "You have boring vampire powers. You're just a good shot."

Nesbitt's face darkened. "I am no such thing. I am one of the most powerful vampires."

Poe scratched her head, wishing she'd tied her hair back. "That's because they're all dead. I killed them. Besides, I bet I can kick your ass in hand-to-hand combat."

Like an angry kangaroo molested by cars and industry, Nesbitt leapt from the ground to the wooden chamber dais. From there he hopped and landed in front of Poe who instinctively jumped forward. She met his angry body and shoved her knife into his ear. She would've aimed for his heart, but the dead was wearing Kevlar, and his left arm had suddenly extended an extra two feet and encircled her upper body.

Nesbitt cursed like a barman at the blade still lodged in and burning his eardrums with garlic acid. His snake arm squeezed her torso slowly but vindictively. She heard two of her ribs crack. Earl shot at the vampire from behind so as not to injure Poe, but the master vampire unwound his hand from Poe's body and plugged him with his Perazzi. Poor Earl had no idea that the left-handed shooter was wearing a bulletproof vest. The halfdead that Poe considered a friend in the short time spent with him tumbled with a groan on the frosty marble floor.

Poe tried to cry out, but her broken ribs constricted her breathing. She staggered to one of the dead guards and unslung his Beretta. She ran as fast as she could to momentary safety behind a marble pillar. For the usual stupid reasons she'd neglected to wear protection herself. She'd always reprimanded Sainvire for not donning Kevlar, and there she was facing a foe that was most likely a better shot.

"Good. You've chosen a gun, Julia Poe. Now we can finally crown the superior shooter," said Nesbitt with a haughty voice laced with pain.

She breathed through her mouth, the pain on her side so excruciating that inhaling was like taking in shards of glass. "That's why you broke my ribs? So you can win? You're a lousy dime-a-dozen master vampire. So what that your arm grows like a dumbass Gumby cartoon? Your powers are embarrassing for your social grade. I killed this vamp once with a long-ass snake tongue, and he had more dignity and class than you'll ever muster. That's why you hide your embarrassing secret powers."

Nesbitt growled and fired at the column she was hiding behind, blasting down chunks of polished marble. One hunk of cheese-size marble clunked Poe on the head and cut her scalp. Blood seeped over her forehead. With annoyance she wiped at the blood before it reached her eyes. Nesbitt emptied his Perazzi before unsheathing a Purdey. Before he could fire once more, a commanding voice halted the bickering of the two hawk-eyed nemeses.

"Enough, Nesbitt!" said a bald Sainvire with a dangerous blaze in his eyes and a massacred hoodie riddled with holes. He looked as though he had been blown to bits and reformed into a less dignified master vampire. Truth be known, Sainvire preferred to dress down than dress in Armani suits like the master vampire she was fighting at the O.K. Corral of the vampire age.

"Ah, Kaleb, the master vampire traitor who's been a pain in my joints for a generation. You've come to rescue your princess?" he mocked.

"Certainly not. Julia can take care of herself. She's a superhero, haven't you heard? I've come to watch her kick the shit out of you," said Sainvire with a smile of steel.

Poe shook her head when Sainvire turned to her. She pointed at her ribs to convey that she was in a lot of pain and he should take care of Peter Nesbitt himself. Of course she couldn't have expected the vampire to understand the meaning of hand and eye gestures.

"Julia Poe is no more than a girl. I broke her, and she is no match for me. Can you smell her blood? She is injured. But you with your speed and powerful nails—" said Nesbitt. Before he could finish his thoughts, he raised his weapon and fired five shots at Kaleb Sainvire, hitting him three times in the forehead and twice in the heart. The Los Angeles master vampire fell backward with a loud thud by the column Poe was hiding against. His gray eyes remained open with the same stunned look of the blue hats lying dead on the municipal floor.

In shock, Poe didn't even scream. She wanted to hurl herself on the love of her life and protect him, but she knew that the bullets would pop out of his body after a few minutes. Sainvire was close to indestructible.

"There's your boyfriend, girl, finally erased from this god-awful world," chuckled Peter Nesbitt.

Poe took a deep painful breath and closed her eyes. *Mom, Dad, Xena, help me. Give me my old confidence back*, she prayed. *Let Sainvire be alive. Help me do this, Maclemar.* With her eyes still closed, she snuck her right hand around the pillar and concentrated. She visualized where Peter Nesbitt's voice originated from and calculated. She fired once and she heard a tumbling sound. Poe, with self-assurance, walked away from the pillar and approached Peter Nesbitt with halting, pain-filled steps. The dapper man who was sage to Quillon Trench writhed on the floor and clutched his throat.

Without smug words Poe stood over him and fired all 13 rounds into the despot's face until he resembled pulped pomegranates. *Nobody hurts my man*, thought Poe while ignoring the pain from her side. She dropped the gun only when the vampire's legs stopped twitching.

As quickly as her broken ribs would allow her, she walked to Sainvire and sat down on the floor. He hadn't moved since Nesbitt shot him. Poe examined his heart. The two bullets were ejected by Sainvire's garlic-immune body. She seethed that Kaleb again came to a gunfight without Kevlar. The three bullets to his forehead were burrowed in his brain. The vampire was unmoving. She stayed with her lover, holding his hand and praying to all her patron saints.

A swarm of people came and went to check on Sainvire's state of health. Sara and Mina examined him after picking up their brother's corpse and placed him on one of the wooden tables in the chamber.

"He's not responding to your voice or to any ministrations, said Mina. "You have to be brave and accept that Kaleb is gone just like my brother Earl."

Poe shook her head. "He's not dead. Garlic bullets can't touch him. See how these two bullets popped out of his chest?"

"But these bullets penetrated his brain. Brain injury is different from—"

"Thanks for your input, but Kaleb isn't dead! Bullets can take a while to leave his body, that's all," said Poe confidently. "I've shot him in the kneecaps so many times, and sometimes they took longer to pop out."

Mina shared a look with her sister. The girl was odd, but shooting Sainvire on purpose? Her own lover? Quietly they left Poe cradling Sainvire's bald head on her thighs and ignoring the pain at her ribs. *Déjà vu*, she thought as her lips trembled. *First Maclemar then Sainvire.* She ran her hands on his bald head and mentally slapped herself. "You're not dead, Sainvire. I know it, so wake the fuck up!" she ordered. Already she could feel and see black stubble on his head. Kaleb was alive, and she'd kick Xena herself if the warrior said any differently.

Hours passed until Li interrupted her prayers to Sister Ann, Goss, and Megan. "It's going to be dawn soon, Poe. You have a flight to catch. We'll take care of Sainvire here," said the usually callous man in a display of sincere humbleness.

"I'll take care of him," said Poe blisteringly. "He'll wake up. Don't worry about that. Have someone carry him to the car. Then we can go."

He's not dead. We're just starting our lives together. I don't believe life can be this cruel. First Maclemar then Kaleb. There's no way both of them would be taken away from me when the world is finally healing, she thought, biting down tears.

———————

Rufus' usual good humor left him as the body of Kaleb Sainvire was fastened securely in the back of the plane. Poe's unintelligible chanting which he'd guessed was praying buzzed uncomfortably. A bursting pregnant woman named Lucy and a 50-year-old custodian called Jimena sat behind him. They had been waiting with their meager possessions when he landed the plane at the Mission.

The two claimed that Poe had promised to take them to Los Angeles. Always the doubter, Rufus believed a bomb was hidden in the bulk of Lucy's stomach and Jimena was a collaborator. After a half-hour, however, Poe arrived with Mina, the short-hair blonde carrying the limp body of Kaleb Sainvire. He helped fasten him onto the back of the plane, and he thanked the pretty vampire. For the sake of assuaging his paranoia, Rufus laid a hand on Lucy's stomach and jumped when he felt a kick that was definitely no bomb.

"Kaleb, wake up," said Poe over and over while willing the bullets to leave her lover's brain. "You can't leave me. You just can't." And her words were drowned by the humming single-engine of the Cessna.

CHAPTER 16

THE MOOD IN THE city was one of mourning.
Kaleb Sainvire, their leader and friend to the
browbeaten, could enduringly die. Fear
reappeared in the residents' hearts. The vampire
was more appreciated now that he might be gone
from the world. Like Perla said to Maple, heroes
are only appreciated when they die.

The entry wounds on Sainvire's forehead had
closed, but no bullets exited. Joseph sat pensively
on a chair by his best friend's side and held
Kaleb's cold heavy hands. "I met him over 40
years ago," he said more to himself than Poe who
hugged her knees to her chest on the corner of the
room. She didn't deserve to sit on a chair when
she was the cause of Sainvire's death. Still
bandaged from the kick to the ribs, Penny curled
on the floor. Friends to the last bone, she and Poe
had similar injuries.

She wanted to give Kaleb's friends the chance
to visit him, but she refused to leave the room.
Her suspicion that one of them would take
Sainvire's body away and bury him kept her
vigilant. The vampire was alive she was sure.
Any day now and the bullets will leave his head.

The fact that Kaleb was intact and slumbering on his simple full-size bed proved he was still battling. Most vamps would have oozed into jelly and deteriorated by the third day. Kaleb had been reposing for 10 days.

"I met him in a movie theater. It was a Roger Corman flick, I think," continued Joseph whose signature smile was nowhere to be seen. "We were both shadowing a sadistic vampire who called himself Fulgar and wore a black cape with red silk lining. Total tool," he said as the top of his lip twitched at the memory. "It was painfully hard to concentrate on finding Fulgar the Disillusioned when a bevy of heavy-breasted beauties on screen distracted us both. Fulgar the Idiot believed himself to be a combination Vlad the Impaler and Jack the Ripper. He'd drain prostitutes and hang their mangled bodies on city landmarks for everyone to see."

Poe's haze lifted. Neither vampire had told her how they'd met. Too submerged in her own world, it never occurred to her to ask. "I spotted him, and so did Kaleb. We had to leave glorious breasts the size of melons behind. We followed the freak, and with my speed got to him before Kaleb. When my fellow vamp catcher flew down to corner the bastard, we had a fight on our hands. Then the dilemma of who was going to kill him. 'Since you already have him, you can kill him,' he said. I've always tried to avoid direct violence, so I insisted he do it. He had those fearsome nails, so why not use them?" Joseph shook his head slowly, and a true smile touched his lips.

"Then what happened?" Poe asked when Joseph didn't continue.

"We decided to kill Fulgar at the same time. A double homicide, you can say. I was to break his neck, and Kaleb was supposed to nail him in the chest. And so we did it and threw Fulgar's miserable body in Lake Michigan. We've been inseparable ever since."

"Sounds like a love story," said Poe with a tired smile.

"It was. I loved him as a brother and vice versa. I was willing to lay my life for him, and it was the same with him. Kaleb had a conscience, and I'd like to think I do, too. We were politically on the same page, and we both loved this country. And then there was Megan."

"I miss Megan. We all miss Megan," said Poe, scratching an old scar. She hadn't bathed since they arrived in Los Angeles, and she was disgusted by the grime under her fingernails, her oily hair, and her redolent scent. She didn't remove her shoes for fear of suffocating Kaleb and finally killing him off.

"Poe, let Kaleb rest. He's truly dead. I don't want to have to see him leaking and turn into a pool of sludge in a couple days," Joseph said forlornly. "He's done so much for this city and all of us. He deserves Peace. He can be buried at the cathedral next to Maclemar and Gregory Peck, your favorite men."

Poe wiped her runny nose on her sleeve. "No. I'm telling you he's still alive. I mean for a vampire."

"Morales declared him actually dead," insisted Joseph. The girl threatened to shoot her old friend and everyone who insisted that Sainvire was gone. Maple, Passionada, Perla, Habib, Rufus, Michelle, Danby, and even Percy tried to plead with her, but her heart knew the truth.

"No!" cried Poe with resentment. "You won't bury him. I won't let you."

"You haven't eaten in days, Poe. You won't even drink sodas. I don't want to say it, but you're obsessed. You even threaten your friends. And sister, you stink like a four-day-old rat."

"Shut the hell up," Poe said snidely. "I have a purpose, and I'm going through with it."

"Well eat and drink something. No one's drugged your food or water. Penny's the proof. That Fanta is still sealed for Pete's sake."

Poe wiped her nose on her sleeve once more. She was starving. The trays Habib had left for her contained the most delicious food that caused her stomach to rumble, but the voice inside her head warned her that the eggplant was laced with drugs. A bottled beverage wouldn't hurt. She needed the sugar for energy. She was about to pass out. Gingerly she reached for the Fanta and the bottle opener and popped the cap. She drank hastily and spilled orange syrup on her already stained pimp shirt.

"Feel better?"

"Lots."

"I love you, Poe. You're a sister to me."

"I love you, too. You've been a brother to me since the first," said Poe. Her voice was breaking.

"Kaleb loved you. I never saw him so happy than when he was with you. His dream was to abscond with you and travel the country backpacking. He was a rugged, earthy man, that Kaleb. But you know he spent too much of his time correcting the wrongs of society and saving cattle instead of pursuing a quiet life. You were the only one that could make him run away from his responsibilities. But he held on and regretted leaving you over and over to save a city and a few souls."

"Yeah. He left me many times and chose cattle over me. He even left me to go back home broken and beaten. But I don't care about that stuff anymore."

"Letting you go took a lot out of him, Poe. He didn't sleep these past years."

"Well he's still sleeping to compensate for the four years of civic duty. He'll wake up anytime. He can make it up to me then."

Joseph stood up and walked toward Poe who pointed a Beretta at him. Her hands shook. They felt like rubber, and her vision dizzied her. "He deserves to finally sleep, Poe. Morales needs to tend to your ribs. In five days it will be Christmas, and we're going to need you there."

"You drugged me," accused Poe. She dropped the gun. Her mouth was slack as if her gums had just been injected by Novocain. "I hate—" Penny growled at Joseph as he lifted Poe in his arms. The injured dog cried then followed the ponytailed vampire from Sainvire's room, her firecracker tail between her legs.

As she slept in a drug-induced state, Passionada bathed her thoroughly, changing the bath water three times. She manicured Poe's nails and brushed her friend's black hair until it shone in the light. Passionada's tears flowed for her friend. Her heart broke at the wrongs fate had dealt her little Poe.

The next day Poe allowed Morales in, and he bound her ribs tightly with cloth. T-Doc who was Poe's oldest living friend was far from perverse at seeing the girl unclothed. His throat constricted at the many scars on the small woman's body. Every single mangle, slash, stab, or burn was received while protecting her allies from harm. She deserved retirement. Happiness. But Sainvire was dead, and Maclemar was a memory. Poe was alone. Trying not to lose his composure, he inhaled deeply.

———

Kaleb Sainvire's body was placed in a crypt next to Maclemar and Gregory Peck as Joseph had promised Poe. The chamber was filled with all sorts of beings paying their respect to the vampire who had sided with humans against tyrannical master vampires. Even a contingent of Christian farmers who had worked with Sainvire to supply humans with fresh meat and vegetables attended the services. The farmers deeply respected Sainvire's tenacity in freeing human cattle.

"He was our friend, and a magnificent friend Kaleb was," said Habib, concluding his eulogy.

"We thank him for what he's done for us, and we will never allow his memory to fade. This good man will be remembered forever."

A small figure in a hooded coat rested her shoulder against the wall of another crypt. Her face was tired as if she had surrendered to the viciousness of life. Before Habib could finish, Poe moved as quickly as she could amidst the mourners and climbed the stairs to the cathedral above. The statues were miniscule inside the vast church sanctuary. Tiny bronze angels hung on the wall. The cross on the altar was small in scale for such a considerable cathedral as if humanizing the man that was nailed on the wood. Quietly she kneeled on one of the pews until her knees hurt. Her mind was silent, and she had nothing to pray for. She stood and left.

Under orders from Morales, Percy brought Poe in for a bandage check Christmas Eve. T-Doc seemed nervous. Poe was quiet and docile and would not speak unless prodded. "Here's some acetaminophen for pain. Take six every four hours. The amount is excessive because they expired 14 years ago."

Poe pushed the bottle of pills away. "I don't need it. Thanks." She stepped down with an impassive face as if she never had broken ribs.

"Don't be silly, Poe. Broken and bruised ribs hurt like hell. Nearly worse than knee surgery.

We'll have the tree lighting ceremony at midnight. I don't want you in pain."

"Don't worry about it, Morales. I'm good," she said, stumbling. Percy was there to catch her elbow.

"Damn it, Poe! I know it's a miserable time, but you have to take care of your health." Morales, handsome, bowlegged, and reeking of too much aftershave, cared enough to end her pain. But there was no medicine to take away the spike hammered in her soul.

When they left Morales' office, Poe asked, "Did you get it?"

"Yeah. Here," said Percy slyly while handing her a stethoscope. "Merry Christmas!"

Poe smirked. "Yeah. Thanks for your present to me. Best present ever." She parted ways with Percy and took Penny along with her. The two friends hobbled together in the cold like rickety old veterans. They headed for the cathedral and descended to the mausoleum. Poe located Sainvire's crypt and sat down carefully as she swallowed the pain on her side. With the stethoscope she listened to the marble slab. After half an hour of listening Poe put the stethoscope Percy filched under Morales' nose in her pocket and left for home.

The two visited Poe's old war bunker in Little Tokyo and sorted through her possessions. Maclemar had brought the good DVDs to Catalina. Still she found an unscratched copy of *The Iron Giant*, a duplicate *Harold and Maude*, and the cheesy '80s version of *Flash Gordon*. She also picked up a few Fellini and Bergman films. She left a sack of children's flicks behind because she couldn't lift them just yet. She remembered her box of trinkets with real jewelry she had snagged from the Jewelry District and stuffed them in her small pack. The rest of the films were dirty in nature, so she left them. She realized how ridiculous and ignorant she had been and how right everyone was in laughing at her for believing porn was just bad production.

Dirty movies, cuss mouth, stubborn jerk. If she hadn't insisted on flying to San Francisco, Sainvire wouldn't have followed her to score bullets in the head. Poe studied her posters of Bruce Lee and Jim Kelly. She loved those posters, but they were part of the past. The most recent years had changed her for better or worse. She needed to find her niche. She needed to stay away from politics and grow up. Now that Sainvire was supposedly dead she crossed her fingers that the city would be administered successfully and the ties with San Diego and San Francisco would be diplomatic.

That afternoon Poe handed Percy her Christmas presents. DVDs and jewelry. All unwrapped. "You're a good kid, Percy. Happy holidays." She kissed the top of the girl's head then went to her room and slept, lightly hugging Penny to her.

She missed Christmas. She slept through carols and the sound of children laughing. Percy spent Christmas with Joseph, Morales, and baby Piper. She was too entranced by the lights and excitement to worry about Poe. She kneeled in front of the fir tree in the middle of Pershing Square and patted her pig. "Let next year be a peaceful year even without Sainvire," she whispered to Chops. She'd prayed the sentiments of most Downtown inhabitants who were afraid their nice life would end in the absence of their protector.

CHAPTER 17

THEY LET HER ALONE to grieve so she could hopefully return to the old tree-kicking Poe who was afraid of nothing. The vampire hunter walked from her apartment to the crypts everyday as if she was floating in a fog of disbelief. She didn't hear the greetings of people or the sight of children kicking football in the streets, some merrily learning to ride scooters and skateboards. She'd been approached by the Council to become an ambassador for the City of Los Angeles but she merely shook her head and declined. She was obsolete. She didn't even wear guns anymore.

A lawn chair would be waiting for her at the tombs. Percy would prepare her lunch and pack her a book as she spent time with the two men she'd loved in her lifetime. Sometimes she'd read to them, mostly American literature since Maclemar was a huge fan, and sometimes she'd sing old songs with made-up lyrics to kill time. Poe figured her grating voice could wake even the dead.

On depressingly cold days, she would be extra maudlin as she snuggled a plush San Marcos blanket about her. She'd removed the ring

Maclemar had given her and placed it on top of his tomb. She'd chosen her man, and it was Sainvire.

"I'm sorry, James. I love you, but Sainvire is my life. I'll always be thankful for your attention and support. I wish you were here but in a selfish way. I wish you could comfort me, but here I go again using you," she spoke to the other man she loved lying next to Kaleb Sainvire's resting place. Poe often oscillated in conversation between Maclemar and Sainvire. "If you can just take me for a boat ride right now I'd be incredibly happy. Maybe I can teach Kaleb to drive a boat, and we can go fishing one of these days."

For three hours she sat in the wintry crypt with her cheek against Sainvire's tomb. She listened for any movement with the stolen stethoscope. This went on for over three months with no results. Surprisingly Poe was patient about Sainvire's reawakening.

Some days she would be peevish and angry. "C'mon, you bastard! I know you're alive. I know you're only sleeping because you're bushed from patching up the mess of the world," she said, her teeth rattling from the cold in late-March. "They've moved on without you. They've sent cattle by boats and trucks to San Francisco and San Diego to tide them over. Some farmers volunteered to start farms around those cities and teach folks willing to learn about animal husbandry and farming. Nice of them, yeah? This city is doing fine without you, so quit hiding out. Sometimes I hate you so much. I'm always last on your list. I bet you wouldn't even be so pathetic as me as to double-check if I was asleep or dead in a tomb."

Her friends approached her several times to join a panel or help out around Downtown, but she repeatedly turned them down. Michelle asked her to work with the police force, and Morales offered to teach her to be a physician's assistant and eventually a doctor. Desperate, Joseph even egged her to babysit Piper and the other babies in the nurseries. Law enforcement wasn't for her. She'd end up beating people. Working in the medical field was a no go as she was naturally clumsy. She was good at creating wounds, not patching them up. As for babysitting, forget about it. She knew she'd drop babies on the head, and everyone would hate her.

"I've paid my dues," Poe would answer. "Leave me be."

All in all she didn't want responsibility. She'd done her job, and she didn't know why people wouldn't respect her wishes. Even Percy took the initiative and walked the animals every morning and night. She fed them on a schedule and made sure their loft was clean. Though disheartened most by Poe's singular obsession with Kaleb's rising one day, Percy persevered and became Julia's connection to the outside world. She didn't mind taking care of the vampire killer who'd saved her life and treated her like a sister.

And then there were those who persisted in destroying her routine.

One evening John Danby, Maple, and Joseph visited her loft. Poe admonished herself for thinking ill of the situation without hearing the problem beforehand. The spacious and uncluttered loft had powder-blue Eames furniture and space-age orange plastic chairs as homage to Goss who loved '50s modern décor. The three visitors sat on the couch while Poe lounged on a pod armchair with Penny napping by her feet.

"What can I do you for?" she asked in a patient tone.

The three glanced at each other as if asking who was going to start. Joseph cleared his throat. He was the winner. "Just wondering how you are, Poe."

"I'm good."

"It's been a while since we've seen you at the meetings," said Danby with a wince. Poe had never attended any meetings since she returned from San Francisco. "It would be a privilege if you came out just to observe. The government is running more smoothly than we expected."

"I'm sure you guys are doing a swell job."

"Er, well we're thinking about asking you for help," began Maple uncomfortably.

"Shoot," said Poe monosyllabically. She reached down to pet Penny who'd completely healed from her broken ribs. "I can't promise anything. I've done what I can."

"Of course. Well Michelle can't make it tonight. She really wanted to because she can explain the problem more resolutely," said Danby. "Michelle's in San Diego helping rebuild and rewrite law enforcement policies with the adjunct police force there. Competent people were left in her stead, of course. But a gang of leeches who escaped Downtown after Trench died have been terrorizing people from the Westside, burning their crops and abusing the women. They figured that since our best fighters are down that they can get away with trouble. And they don't know that the people from West L.A. have been under Kaleb's protection since the inception."

Poe's interest was piqued. She had lived in the Westside as a child and again to hide out and retire a few years ago. Many folks who had escaped being cattle and wanted to remain independent from Downtown politics lived there, but they kept their ties and loyalties with Kaleb Sainvire. In fact they had helped provide her with food and protected her from Trench as a favor to the master vampire who'd always been fair to them. Maple as good as implied that not having Sainvire around to bother with little city outposts was a free-for-all.

"How many leeches?" asked Poe in a disinterested voice.

"A dozen or so. All miscreant escapees," said Maple.

Poe didn't want to admit it, but her heart raced at the thought of an assignment of this sort. Her throat was getting dry from talking to Maclemar and Sainvire. She needed a break, but she didn't want to jump at the opportunity lest they keep pestering her in the future. In truth she needed to kill, she was so frustrated.

"I'm retired."

Joseph raised an eyebrow. How many times had he heard such proclamations from Poe? "They've taken some women, Poe. You know what leeches do to women."

Poe's nostrils flared. The hell with being coy. "You want me to kill the leeches or save them for jail?"

"We prefer the leeches alive. We'll punish them with jail time," said John Danby.

"Any day vamps or vampires in the gang?"

"None as far as we know," said Joseph.

Poe pulled at her ponytail and sighed. "So you want me to be a cockroach exterminator?"

"For the people of the Westside," said Maple. "They've been good friends, and they've asked for our help. In fact they specifically asked for you."

Poe bit her plump bottom lip. That was a surprise. She remembered baseball batting the windshields of their emergency cars and stealing their chicken eggs. She shrugged. There was nothing for it. "Alright. I'll leave tomorrow. I think I can drive." She remembered driving the Welshman's truck by pressing on the gas and brake to get Maclemar to the hospital.

"I don't think that's a good idea," said Joseph, rubbing his tummy.

"Or I can ride a Vespa. I can maneuver it better but how am I going to bring the criminals back? I think I'll take a truck. I just follow the Santa Monica Freeway and exit Bundy. I can't get lost because it's my old neighborhood." Poe was speaking more to herself than her guests.

"Then you can take James' truck," offered Maple. "You can bring two or three day vamps with you."

Poe's train of thought was broken. "I always work by myself, Maple. I don't want to get anyone killed because most of the time I don't know what I'm doing."

Joseph smiled his signature grin. "That's true. She works from the gut. She might shoot our own men."

Danby cleared his throat. "We don't want you to get hurt."

Poe grinned. "Thanks for thinking of me, John. But I gotta tell you, nothing bad can happen to me because I'm already dead." She thought of the captives getting violated repeatedly, and she itched to leave then and there.

No one commented on her declaration professed nonchalantly. "Three days will be enough, do you think?" asked Maple to clear the air.

"I'll leave tomorrow morning and bring them back in time for dinner."

The three visitors nodded. Poe hardly exaggerated. If she said she was going to bring the criminals back in less than a day, then Julia Poe would.

———————

Driving was easier than she thought once she willed herself not to hit the brake and the gas too hard. Keeping the steering wheel steady was also a must. She attempted a three-point turn on the freeway but failed, slamming the right headlight on the concrete median. *I'll work on that later*, she thought philosophically.

Quillon Trench had started the freeway cleanup by stacking cars on the median and emergency lanes. Ed, the five-foot tall Latino with mad strength, finished the rest. He had cleared the road up to North Hollywood to give the farmers a wider route. Poe remembered a time when Sister Ann, Goss, Morales, and Megan moved one car at a time to transport human cattle to safety. *How much things have changed*, thought Poe. Downtown was the pits and the most dirty and dangerous rat-infested inferno Poe had grown up in. She shivered at the memory.

Now Downtown was clean, and the rats mostly pushed out of the city. There were beauty salons, tailor shops, dance classes, and karaoke contests. Shandra, the ample-breasted vampire, was even able to launch a dead/alive dance club that became a Downtown mainstay. She'd been promising the exotic dancer a visit, but she hadn't quite gotten around to it.

Driving on the freeway reminded her of her parents and brother and sister. It had been a while since she'd seen their faces clearly. By the time she exited on Bundy Drive she was actually excited. She made a couple turns, found Sawtelle Boulevard, and stopped in front of a burnt Spanish-style house that used to be her home. She shook her head. *Don't go in there. It'll kill you. Nothing to salvage anyway.*

They found her sitting in Maclemar's truck. Men and women in their sixties or older surrounded her vehicle. Some wore glasses, but they all squinted at her. Everyone looked healthy living 10 minutes from the beach and eating fresh produce. However, she didn't recall the West L.A. community being so old.

"Hello, Poe. The name's Rick. I don't know if you remember me?" said a balding man with wisps of hair.

"Sure. Of course," said Poe in a white lie. She opened the door and let herself out. She shook hands with the 10 prefects of the area. By the third introduction she gave up memorizing their names and got straight to the point.

"Thanks for letting me steal your chicken eggs," said Poe. "And your tomatoes."

"No biggie. Sainvire told us not to let you starve. He was a good man, and he cared dearly for you and humanity in general."

Poe cleared her throat. "That he does. So how many leeches do I get to hunt down?"

"Nine by our count," said a sturdy woman with white hair. Poe wondered if they had younger community members. Molesting them would have been a violent act of desperation. But then again, leeches raped the sleeping. They lacked compunction. And just like that, Poe was angry.

"When do they attack?"

"Anytime," said another oldie. "They stole a piglet and some vegetables. They trampled

Ginny's garden." Poe ran her gaze at the rows of cottages on the street and remembered her family.

"Where do they hole up?"

"The Rec Center at Stoner Park. They filled the pool with water and have been living the life eating our chicken and pigs and swimming all day."

"Sorry for being so blunt, but I was told some women were assaulted."

Rick ran his fingers through his balding head. "They took three of our women. One is my wife.

"Sorry about that. I know how traumatic it is to be taken against your will," said Poe. She startled herself for her little confession. "I'll get them back for you. But, um, I was wondering if you have any young people here?"

"Eight young ones in their forties, but that's about it. We're aging, and we just want to spend the last of our days in peace."

"We would've taken up arms," said a woman named Clare. "But we're all practically blind. Eat your carrots, Poe, to keep your eyes sharp."

Poe nodded. She would make it a priority. Without her eyesight she would be as helpless as these folks.

She knew Stoner Park. Her family used to walk there from their house. Her parents played tennis while she and her brother and sister played handball. She was supposed to take swimming lessons there, but it was cancelled because of the Gray Armageddon.

Memories hurt, so she shook them away. She parked the pickup as close as she could to the Rec

Center with the front right wheel on the sidewalk. *Gotta work on parking. Very important.*

Roasting meat permeated the fresh Westside air. They were 10 minutes from the ocean after all. Her mouth watered despite the fact that she was vegetarian. The fuckers were having luaus without realizing that the people they were inconveniencing were friends of Kaleb Sainvire. Her hand twitched. She wanted so badly to go psycho killer on these leeches. She had to remind herself that Danby, Maple, and Joseph wanted them alive. *They ought to go to prison for a long motherfucking time*, thought Poe. *Or I could gut them like the pig they're never going to eat.*

Poe had left her favorite guns in San Francisco, so she had to go to the armory for a refit. She chose her favorite combination of Glock 17 and Beretta with shoulder holsters. She filled her pockets with clips and carried her homemade machete in a hip sheathe. The item that most pleased her was an unused Rambo knife so similar to her birthday gift from Sister Ann that she got teary-eyed.

"Kill only when they annoy you," she whispered to the chilly air. She had an hour left until sunset, perfect in her opinion. Even leeches were afraid of rogue vamps, and they primarily stayed indoors for protection. She followed the scent of meat and saw the cook outside an indoor swimming pool, basting dinner like an Iron Chef. He had some fat on him like most leeches because drugs and food were their only happiness. But drugs had aged him and jerkied his skin.

Poe took a breath. She sprinted toward the leech as fast as she could, leapt, and landed her right elbow on top of his head. He never saw Poe who'd wanted to try the Muay Thai move since she saw the movie *Ong Bak*. The man fell with linguini legs, and Poe was there to capture his arms and bind him with plastic cuffs. The leech was out cold. "That was cool," said Poe to herself. *Don't be too cocky, chick. Dying is easy during peace time.*

The metal slab that served as a door to the pool building was ajar. A voice from within shouted, "The pig ready yet? I'm fucking hungry!"

Poe grunted an answer and entered. She swallowed and warned herself to stay away from the water. Swimming pools were her kryptonite. "Hello, fellas. Got the pool heated up and everything," she said brightly.

"Who the hell are you?" said the smallest of the eight, clocking in about Poe's height. The little worm was the leader. Poe chuckled at the men in neon hibiscus-patterned swimming trunks.

"Julia Poe at your service. I've come to take you Downtown. Now if you'd just cooperate and—"

"Watch out!" shouted one of the naked older women huddling on the floor to hide her breasts. Poe turned to her left to see a leech in a towel point a shotgun at her. Quick as Mercury, Poe dove to the ground and took out the Beretta. She shot at the towel leech. Her bullet traveled faster than his trigger finger, and it lodged in one of the shotgun muzzles. The gun exploded in his face, perpetually ruining his looks. *At least he's still alive. I'm not gonna get in trouble for that one.*

Poe scanned the pool area in search of more firepower. Except for the short leader who lifted his Smith and Wesson at Poe, the leeches were too shocked to even move. Again she aimed for the gun, and it exploded in his face. A heated shard punctured one of his eyes, and he screamed like a stuck pig.

"More, wiseass?" asked Poe. Two leeches were in the water holding onto the edge of the pool, and five leeches raised their hands in surrender. "Good boys." She looked down at the shocked women." I see your clothes over there, ladies. Get dressed."

The women tied yellow plastic cuffs on the wrists of the leeches and ignored the screaming of the two injured leeches. Three of the women looked as old as Poe remembered her grandmother while the other women were younger, perhaps in their forties. They yanked at the cuffs as hard as they could as they embraced their anger.

"You fucking shit!" said June with a shaking voice. The woman was beautiful with porcelain skin and dark eyes. Her entire body was trembling. "I hope you kill him, Miss Poe!"

The vampire killer shook her head. "I'm bringing them in, ladies. They'll face jail time." Poe knew how they felt for she herself had been violated and had wished death upon the perpetrator.

"How long will they will be jailed?"

"I don't know. A hundred years."

Poe handed her makeshift machete to a white-haired victim. "Chop off a limb if you want."

The renegade leeches cried and pleaded. "Can I?" asked the woman.

"Sure. But I have a better idea," said Poe. She conspiratorially handed her Beretta to the white-haired woman, and placed the Glock in the palm of June, the youngest of the three victims. "You can shoot their balls off, and I'll look away. Only the balls. They've got to make it back alive."

And so they accepted Julia Poe's offer, and as shots rang out and echoed in the pool room the hysterical screaming of leeches filled the air. For the first time Poe thought taking the assignment was the right thing to do.

By 6:30 p.m. the boys were loaded in the back of the truck by the Westsiders. They were decent enough to place a blanket on the nearly naked bodies of the freezing leeches, severely in shock for losing their dear friends in life. An hour later she parked the truck in front of the Biltmore Hotel where T-Doc was waiting with his staff to care for the wounded. She was a woman of her word. She delivered the leeches in less than a day alive.

"What the hell did you do, Poe?" asked Morales harshly. "This isn't the Middle East!"

"I shot the guns of those two leeches, and they exploded in their faces. The rest you can blame the victims. They took matters in their own hands. But luckily they're all alive like John Danby asked. Hope you know how to sew back pervert balls, my friend."

CHAPTER 18

SHE SHIFTED AND LAID her other cheek against the cold stone of Sainvire's tomb. "There's no more need for the likes of me, a violent beast. After two of those leeches died from infection, everyone looks down on me. Now they think I'm going to allow victims to cap their victimizers, which I probably would. Joseph suggested I plant spring crops in the Valley. Imagine me a farmer? It doesn't seem so bad really. I'm actually thinking about it. Four days at the field and three here. The train to North Hollywood is truly efficient now.

"Habib sends me the best foods, and no one demands anything of me anymore. Michelle is a top-rate law enforcer. I've only seen her twice since you died. She's fair, Percy tells me. And she can run in high heels. Killers are obsolete now, and I only know how to kill. Thank goodness for Passionada who cooks dinner for me every Friday. She's the only one who treats me like a normal person.

"And you know how clumsy I am at everything else. I'm useless. I don't think Morales appreciated what I did to those leeches.

Human rights he said. Yeah, whatever. Getting raped is no picnic. And to tell you the truth the catharsis I saw in those women's faces calmed me. So I'm obsolete, and our friends are pushing me to be Farmer Julia."

"On the contrary," echoed a voice in the empty house of the dead, startling Poe. It was Perla. "Your influence and skills are always needed. You rescued those women and brought those leeches in like we asked you to."

Poe straightened her spine. She felt embarrassed for talking to the dead. She removed the stethoscope from her ears and slowly placed it on the floor. "You've been eavesdropping."

"Just a little," said the mother of Plasmacore.

"Not nice," said Poe.

"I apologize. I haven't been nice for a while, but my mind is straight now, and I am doing my best to help Maple and the rest feed the people left behind."

"Glad for you."

"You can join us. Everyone respects you."

"F that. I'm incompetent at everything unrelated to shooting, gutting, and torturing. Besides, I'm waiting for Kaleb to wake up."

"He's dead, Poe. The bullet never dislodged from his head. You've got to move on."

Poe grimaced. "I'm not as changeable as you, Perla. First you want to kill leeches. Then you're planning to make their imprisonment sweet and cozy. I know Sainvire is alive. For a dead man, that is. No amount of dissuasion from my friends can change my mind."

"We all appreciate your faith in Sainvire, Poe, but most likely his body has turned to after-mash. He's gone."

Poe nodded instead of laughing off her friend's assessment. "Alright then. If Kaleb's turned into the Swamp Thing, I'll go to the Valley and plant spring harvest with the farmers and bring bushels of corn back for you all to consume. I can't do much damage there, can I? All you have to do is open the crypt. You're a vampire now. You're strong enough to slide the lid off."

Perla was aghast. "I can't do that. That would be desecration. Joseph would have my neck."

"This is between us," said Poe cunningly. "No one needs to know. If we see sludge, we close the lid, but if his body is intact, then he's alive and imprisoned. Either way, I'm out of the crypt."

The two debated until Perla's armor was chinked down to chalk. Her somewhat chubby face looked worried. The scientist didn't like to do things that didn't make sense. "Fine. We don't tell anyone about this. I need you to move on with your life. You're so young, and you have a long life ahead of you."

"Sure. I'll start dating and traveling to SF and San Diego as an ambassador or whatever. I promise. Just open his crypt."

Perla shook her head in defeat. She crossed herself and momentarily bowed her head at a beatific marble statue of Mary. With vampiric strength, she pulled the entire tomb out and placed it on the ground. Poe's heart was thudding like a pack of hyenas was in pursuit. Perla heaved the lid off effortlessly and gasped.

Sainvire lay in once piece like he'd just fallen asleep. No sunken cheeks, no smells of decay. Three bullets lay by his neck. His once bald head had grown down to his ears.

Poe backed away though her dreams had come true. She sat under the statue of Mary and hugged herself.

"My God, Poe. You're right! He might still be alive," Perla cried. "Go get Joseph and the boys. Tell them to get down here."

Poe buried her head in her knees. "You do it. I can't."

Perla nodded, ran up the stairs to the church, and sought their friends. As hopeful as she was, Poe didn't dare look at him in case his body was merely preserved. She'd waited months for this miracle to be revealed. She'd always known. They'd only have to wait for Sainvire to awaken, and all would be stunning again.

Morales, Joseph, Michelle, Perla, Maple, and Danby arrived within minutes. Joseph glanced at Poe who looked like a small child chided for misdeed. She was rocking back and forth. Morales studied Sainvire's body quickly then knelt next to Poe. He hugged her tightly and Poe wound her arms around T-Doc's neck. They watched Joseph examine the uncorrupted body of Sainvire. With excitement and disbelief in his voice, he said, "He's asleep. My pal must be alive."

"Let's take him up to the hospital," suggested Danby. "We wouldn't want him to wake up in the mausoleum."

"John's right," seconded Maple. "Let me carry him to the hospital.

Joseph nodded and watched Maple carry Sainvire's body like it was a pillow. Joseph picked up the stethoscope from the ground and walked over to Poe. With one knee he knelt in front of her. His brown eyes were shining. If vampires could weep, Joseph would have bawled his eyes out.

"Sis, you were right. I'm sorry. I didn't have your faith. Even I thought you lost it, so I ask your forgiveness."

Morales let go of Poe and sat farther away on the lawn chair. A Bukowski book lay by the chair.

Poe shook her head. "Nothing to forgive. Nothing at all. I have lost it. I stole Morales' stethoscope." Everyone stared at the device, and their tenseness lifted at the absurdity.

World spread about Kaleb Sainvire like butter on hot bread. A second wave of Christmas joy put a smile on those who'd known or been rescued by the selfless vampire.

Poe visited her slumbering love after showering. She wore her freshest clothes that added femininity to her usual dry outfit of black t-shirt and olive pants. The third day she chose a bright red blouse with gray slacks and red Adidas shoes, the brand Sainvire preferred. She stared at the bathroom mirror as a touch of red lipstick brightened her lips. Out of embarrassment for being so girly, Poe stopped at that. She combed her obsidian hair and debated with herself whether or not to hide her scar with a concealer. She decided against it, rationalizing that Kaleb might not recognize her without the centipede scar.

An excited Joseph knocked on the door of her loft. "Poe, Kaleb's alive! And you look good," he threw in. "Wanna hop on? I'll zip us over there."

"He's awake?" Her nerves were buzzing in every fingertip. Without protestation, she jumped on Joseph's back as he ran like a cheetah to the hospital. Poe was thinking of her hair when they reached Sainvire's room.

He was sitting up and sipping a glass of Plasmacore in his hospital bed. Laughing with him was a giddy crowd of 12 of his closest friends, including the pixie-haired Jenna who refilled his glass with a gleeful smile on her face.

"Remember when you pulled me out of the burning building outside of Santa Cruz? I owe you big for that one, Kaleb," said the jaunty voice of Jenna.

"Yeah, I remember. How can I forget? You were screaming like a banshee," said Sainvire in a voice a touch rough from disuse.

Jenna bending over Sainvire made Poe lose her composure. The tornado that was Joseph blowdried her hair, and she tried to straighten it. Everyone kept quiet as Sainvire looked at Poe with curiosity. He smiled kindly at her but turned toward Jenna again. Poe was crushed.

Joseph and the buddies in the cramped hospital room shared confused looks. Joseph put his arm around Poe's shoulder and brought her closer to Sainvire's bed. "Hey, Kaleb, here's Poe. She insisted you were still alive."

"Oh my. Forgive me, Poe. I thank you for rescuing me." He reached for her hand and squeezed it. "I'm Kaleb. Nice to meet you."

Poe's limp hand fell on the mattress. He didn't recognize her, yet he recognized everyone else in the room. Her stomach hurt. The bullets had erased her from his memory.

Joseph was as shocked as Poe. "No. You don't realize, Kaleb. Poe is—"

Poe slapped Joseph's back to shut him up. "I'm a big fan of yours. I'm glad you're alive and well. Nice to meet you, too." She flashed white teeth at the vampire she'd loved her entire adult life and turned to leave.

"Thanks again, Poe. Say, is that your first or last name?"

Poe swallowed hard and willed herself not to cry. "Julia's my first name. I'll see you around."

Morales intercepted her in the hallway. She shrugged. "That's just how it is, Morales. Besides living through torture, Revenents, and gunshot wounds, I'm really an unlucky girl. Don't feel sorry for me. At least I can move on with my life. Sorry about filching your stethoscope."

T-Doc stared at the back of Julia Poe. Her small body ramrod straight, she took the blow with great aplomb. His eyes turned misty for his friend. Fate had a way of knifing the already downed. If Poe wouldn't grieve for her ill fortune, then Morales would.

———

Kaleb Sainvire back again was good enough for Poe, so she told herself. She didn't weep that he no longer loved her. She was a stranger to him, and she was too tired. An asterisk in an outdated history book.

For the past month she avoided people she knew. With enthusiasm she worked with scholarly humans and vamps to restore the Central Library. She voluntarily scrubbed soot from the walls and restore books that survived the fire from Quillon Trench's bombardment of the sacred place of learning. Hardly anyone chit-chatted in the tradition of quiet in the library and fear that the librarian would shush their voices. She preferred it that way.

Downtown was small despite its dense development pattern, and she was bound to run into him. Passionada's well intended love match angered Poe so much that she didn't talk to the woman for weeks. She invited Poe for their usual Friday dinners where the voluptuous woman cooked gourmet food for the two of them and watched a movie or two. The shock she received when she found Sainvire on the couch sipping Plasmacore from a pink mug overwhelmed her.

She had no idea the vampire was going to stop by, and the experience proved awkward.

Passionada left them as often as she could with the usual excuses of putting a proper dinner together. Poe swore to give Passionada a piece of her mind as soon as the sham of a dinner was over. *Kaleb didn't even eat human food*, she thought angrily.

The master vampire was dressed in dark slacks, a white long-sleeved work shirt, and tie. Something he never would have worn. "I've been meaning to see you sooner, Julia, but you're a hard woman to find."

"Been working at the library," said Poe curtly. She felt uncomfortable wearing black Adidas running pants and an "Am I Chopped Liver?" t-shirt.

"Ah yes. That's what Passionada was saying," he said. His startling gray eyes twinkled. "How do you like it?"

"Pretty fun." She looked at the kitchen door and grunted. Passionada was being too obvious. "Listen. I'm not hungry, so I'll leave you to have supper with Passionada."

Sainvire's face darkened. "But everyone's been saying that we need to talk."

"Well that's their problem. I see no need to talk about the past, especially since you don't know anything about me. You're not the Kaleb I used to know."

"We were lovers? I loved you?"

Poe's throat constricted. "Was is the operative word. We're nothing to each other now.

I'm completely over you," she lied. "Feel free to live your life. You and I don't owe each other anything."

"But they said you listened to my crypt—"

"Fuck this shit," mumbled Poe while rising. "Tell Passionada to stuff her Tofurky where the sun don't shine, alright? And stay away from me, Kaleb Sainvire. I'm extremely allergic to you and your downsized personality."

She bolted out of the room and ran down the emergency stairs. By the time she reached the bottom level, Sainvire was waiting for her with a raised eyebrow. "You're the little hero that saved Downtown and the love of my life they say."

"Well they're exaggerating," said Poe, pushing him out of the way. She stepped out into the moonless night and inhaled the fresh air. There was no need to carry flashlights any longer since the streetlights had been restored. "They just want a soap opera. If I were you I'd shack up with Jenna and have vampire babies. The men of my life both died last year."

"So bitter," he said in a deep voice. "For a hero."

Poe turned to face the tall vampire with an imperfect face and said, "I'm no hero. I was a butcher that just happened to save a few people along the way. I don't love you, and I don't expect you to love me. You don't know me, and I sure as hell don't know you."

"Couldn't we at least try to get to know each other? They've been trying to get me to strategize how to safeguard our city and other cities. But really I have no mind for it anymore. Maybe the two of us can concoct something for problems like building cisterns to catch rainwater next winter."

Poe raised her hands and slapped them clean in the air. "Not my problem, Sainvire. I'm retired. In fact I'm going on the food train to the Valley tomorrow. I'll try my hand at farming. If you have no idea what to do, then you should retire too."

She was distracted by the sly smile on his lips. His dark lashed eyes bore into hers as if hypnotizing her. "Joseph said if I kissed you I'd get my memory back."

"Joseph has a low I.Q., and so do you if you think I'm going to kiss you."

"But I insist. I want all my memories back. You've made an impression on me, so may I kiss you?"

"I don't believe this," Poe muttered angrily as she walked away from the vampire. "I have Steve McQueen waiting for me." Suddenly Poe was lifted off her feet and was in the air. She could barely see for the darkness except the lights from certain buildings. Despite the spring season the night was chilly, and she shivered. Sainvire captured her mouth with his cold lips and kissed her deeply, startling the vampire hunter. Without knowing what she was doing, Poe kissed him back as she remembered the taste of him.

"Take me down," she said when their lips parted. She was mortified at her reaction and the nightmare that she was being used as an experiment. A memory charm.

"I believe I felt something," said Sainvire with lust in his voice.

"I said take me down, you son of a bitch!"

Sainvire sighed and flew her down in front of her loft apartment building. Poe narrowed her eyes for he knew where she lived. She shook her head as she recognized that Joseph told him.

"You don't know me anymore, and I don't want you messing with my head, Kaleb Sainvire. From now on don't even speak to me."

"I could easily love you," he said quietly. "But you're making it so hard."

"Life is an infernal bitch, and I'm tired of being its plaything. Good luck with the city. Everything will come back to you." She walked toward her building.

She didn't see his face, but Sainvire smiled as if he'd just understood an inside joke. He flew away only when Poe pulled the door closed behind her.

CHAPTER 19

THE FARMERS DIVERTED SOME of the Universal City land for agriculture. The once famous amusement park was surrounded by verdant farmland as far as the eye could see. Cattle grazed in the hills and pigs, chickens, turkey, and rabbit were fenced in clean and humane pens.

Poe didn't really know much about the farmers except that they were traditionally Christians and they had worked with the old master vampires to feed the human cattle. They hadn't approved of the treatment of humans, but they had no choice but feed them. When Sainvire, who supplied had them with Plasmacore, took back the city, the farmers rejoiced and eagerly helped in the restoration of Downtown. They were peaceful and did not want blood on their hands, but in the matter of the resistance the leadership lent Sainvire their support.

The farmers consisted of undead pastors, priests, nuns, monks, and their respective followers from a range of religious denominations that balked at violence. They reached out to each other to avoid killing after the Gray Armageddon.

They chose to drink animal blood and later Plasmacore instead of milking humans.

Menial work suited her. Scrubbing soot from walls, restoring books, feeding chickens and pigs, and planting seedlings soothed her soul. Poe experienced peace at the quiet, repetitive work. When the sun-worthy farmers did speak to her, they were encouraging. They never offered their names unless she asked but were warm for short talks and giving direction. Many ex-cattle who worked at the farm restored their health and started families. At the farm she wasn't Julia Poe but a fellow farmer. Penny seemed at home sunning herself wherever Poe went, especially laying on freshly tilled soil. Her porcupine fur was shinier than ever.

Leaving Percy behind was a hard decision that haunted her nightly. Poe needed time alone, and her adopted sister meekly shook her head at the prospect. "Do whatever you need to do, Poe. Life has been awful to you." Life had been outrageous to all of the Gray Armageddon survivors.

She spent two months at the farm learning about wind turbines, irrigation, and seasonal crops. Except for watching bison on Catalina Island, Poe had never been calmer. No boogeyman appeared, and she was just one of the farmers and not a psychotic vampire killer. Being around living things and inhaling the scent of newly picked crops healed her. The ducklings and chicks especially gave her a kick, and she was quite proud of Penny for not gorging on them.

The quiet meditation of planting into fertile soil gave her the courage to forget about what she couldn't have in life. Sainvire was alive, and she was glad. They could never recapture their past again, so in her heart she let him go.

A letter arrived in mid-July from Joseph. Piper was to turn three, and as the godmother, neglectful at that, Joseph and Morales expected her to show up. She'd done wrong by Piper. She had promised Megan to help raise her daughter, but she let tragedy and self-interest hinder their bond.

The leader of the farmers was named Seth. He and his wife Beth also received invitations. They were clearly instructed to bring Poe with them. Beth, a beautiful woman who resembled Bette Davis before she became a hag, gently insisted that she attend the party.

"I've nothing to wear," said Poe. She really didn't. She had a uniform in life, and it was fit for gas station attendants.

"Don't worry about that," said the vampire who led her to their farmhouse. Poe instructed Penny to stay on the porch.

"I know I should've thrown these garments away, but I still suffer from vanity," Beth said as she opened her closet. Stylish dresses and suits from the '30s and '40s lined her closet.

"Wow," said Poe in awe. "They're beautiful."

"I think you're a shy one. Would you like to wear a suit, or can you handle a dress?"

"No slacks?"

"No. I was a very feminine woman. Well what do you think? We're about the same size."

Poe examined the beautifully preserved clothes, and her eyes were drawn to a knee-length cranberry-red dress that was accessorized by a slim black belt and a black flower on the left shoulder. The dress had short, slightly puffed sleeves.

"Maybe this?"

"Good choice, my girl," the woman said. She removed the dress and placed it on Poe's arm. She reached to her collection of shoes and chose a black pair with straps. "These might be a little big, but that's better than pinching your feet."

The kind vampire handed her some hosiery with old-fashioned seams on the back.

"Thanks, Beth. I'll take good care of them," promised Poe.

"Honey, they're yours. I would be happy to see someone as pretty as you wear them.

Poe hung the dress on a wall hook in her cabin. She had a phobia of dresses and a fear of appearing half-decent. She hardly ever wore make-up or colorful clothing. But the red dress Beth had given her called out to her femininity. The vintage dress wasn't exactly sexy, but it was unique.

She imagined Sainvire falling in love with her when she appeared at the party but chided herself for her pathetic thoughts. Sainvire was probably back with Jenna. And really, she was tired of wanting someone who didn't even remember their past together.

"I'm crazy, Penny. Keep me sane," she said to her dog. Penny stared up at her with love in her eyes. "I love you, Penny Pen. You love me more than anyone."

A week later Poe donned the cranberry shade dress and cinched the black belt that showed off her trim figure. She slid the nude hose on her toned legs and put on the two-inch leather shoes with straps. She studied her face in the mirror but was disappointed. Her hair was ordinary, and she had no make-up on. That was when Beth entered her cabin without knocking. She brought a curling iron and a make-up kit with her.

"Not too much make-up, please," requested Poe.

Betty raised an eyebrow at the girl. "With your nice skin, you don't need a lot of make-up. You need to be more confident. There's nothing wrong with looking beautiful."

Poe nodded in silence. Within 20 minutes she had the hairdo of Gilda and light make-up accentuated by bright lipstick to match.

"You look beautiful, Julia," assured Beth when Poe fidgeted awkwardly. "You have nothing to be ashamed of. You're a hero, and you deserve to look like a goddess."

Poe nodded. *Yeah. I deserve to be a goddess. I killed enough for Downtown folks to fill up a train. And Sainvire, you fuck, eat your heart out!*

North Hollywood is one big meditation center for the broken, thought Poe. No wonder the farmers had very little need for speech. Each seed planted in the ground was prayer enough. Poe sat with Seth and Beth on the train loaded with chickens and vegetables. Penny curled down by Poe's feet and enjoyed the bumpy ride. Poe reached down to stroke the dog's soft ear. Her hand didn't shake. She was as calm as the Dalai Lama. *I'm never going to be frazzled again. I deserve respect.*

She ran a hand to the soft flowing dress and was truly glad she was wearing it. Her dislike for wearing dresses and high heels had been heightened by Quillon Trench. He had forced her to wear revealing gowns and spiky heels she had no skills to pull off. Her enemy insisted she bring out the woman in her, and he made her feel like a whore. Fear, insecurity, and the feeling of being desecrated snatched all her courage.

Beth's dress was different. Poe had chosen it herself and approved of the vintage design. She was aware of the flowing material clinging to her body that softened her usual cavewoman tendencies. For once she felt pretty, and she was grateful to Beth and the farmers for their grace. She wasn't a joiner, but she was impressed with the deeds of her hosts, their tenacity not to drink from humans, and their tendency not to proselytize.

The three walked from Pershing Square Station to the Biltmore Hotel unhurriedly as Seth, a handsome Gary Cooper look-alike, lent the two women his elbows to hold. Poe took in Pershing

Square and grinned. There were hardly any kids playing. Most likely they were attending their first birthday party. The tall buildings and clean streets constricted her chest. Despite living through the nightmare that was her childhood in the city, Poe was drawn to Downtown Los Angeles. She knew then that she was going to live there for the rest of her life. No more Catalina or the farm. She was going to be a sister to Percy and a doting goddaughter to Piper. She glanced at Penny whose tail was wagging at being home again.

She no longer had enemies. The L.A. underground and Kaleb had destroyed most of them. Poe exhaled in relief at the realization that she was free.

"You alright, Julia?" asked Beth.

"More than alright," said Poe. She couldn't wait to see her family.

Silent Seth patted her arms as they ascended the stairs of the Biltmore. "We'll be by your side, my dear." How the three of them must have appeared. They looked like a time warp back to the days of Bogey and Bacall with a straggly-hair dog that loyally in tow.

Rufus was carrying a wrapped present under his arm when he spotted Poe and blinked five times to clear his eyes. "Poe?"

"Hey, Rufus," said Poe. "Listen, could you open the door for us? We're kinda linked at the arms."

"Sure." He pushed the door wide open to the children's nursery. By the time they walked four steps inside, the large crowd quieted and left the squealing of children to triumph over the still adults.

Sainvire was holding Piper who wore all sorts of flowers in her head like a wood nymph. Joseph and Morales had encouraged the children to give flowers and shiny rocks to Piper instead of toys. Sainvire's smile faded when he saw the three farmers. Joseph grinned at her, and Morales winked lustily like his old self. Maple and Perla silently toasted her with Plasmacore. With poise she smiled at them and disengaged her arm from Seth's elbow. From behind someone grabbed her waist, nearly ruining her poise.

"Poe! You look so good!" cried Michelle. The top cop wore glittery tank tops that were cut to expose her belly ring. Her oh-so-short bleached denim skirt exposed her muscular legs. "You make me look like a slut!"

Beth raised an eyebrow and stirred Seth toward their friends. "We'll see you, Julia."

"Yes. Thanks, Beth." Her pillars had left her. She was alone to reacquaint herself with old friends.

The usually reserved John Danby came over and hugged Poe. Others did the same, even the vamps, halfdead, and people she hardly knew.

"Forgive me, Poe," said Passionada, her slick red lips trembling. "I drove you to the Valley!" Poe laughed. "You didn't do such a thing. I expect Friday dinners to be on." "Of course, my love," said the thankful six-foot woman.

Joseph hugged her good and hard. "You look gorgeous, sis. I'm very happy you're here."

"Me, too. I've been an awful godmother, and I swear I'm gonna remedy that."

Joseph grinned and rubbed his belly. "Thank you, Poe. Megan would've wanted that."

Morales kissed Poe on the mouth and chuckled when she punched him lightly in the stomach. "You coming back to live with us?"

"I think so, but I think I'll need to go to the Valley every once in a while to clear my head," said Poe with a smile.

"Whatever, Poe," said Morales. "As long as you come back to us. You don't know how much we missed you." Poe could tell that T-Doc was also referring to her supposed mental breakdown.

"You guys are my family," Poe said with surprise at her own words. "We sink and swim together. I'm good at protecting, and I'm going to protect everyone."

She noticed him approaching. He stared strangely at her as he handed Piper to Joseph. "Hello, Poe."

"Hey," Poe said and reached for Piper's chubby arms. "Hey, kid. Do you know me?"

Piper had her mother's red hair and father's brown eyes. "Uh huh. You Aunt Poe."

Extremely pleased, Poe smiled. "You like movies?"

"Cartoons," said the child. She traced a finger in Poe's dimple.

"I'll show you lots of cartoons at my place. Would you like that?" Poe was actually afraid of getting a no for an answer.

"Shue. I want Penny," the baby said, pointing at the dog sitting on her haunches.

"Shue means yes, sis," translated Joseph. Piper's fathers left Poe and Kaleb together. Like she understood, Penny followed the squealing toddler to give the ex-lovers some privacy.

Sainvire was back in his usual black shirt, blue Dickies, and Adidas. "Maybe I'll try the farm."

"You got lots of responsibility here," said Poe. "The new government will collapse without you."

Sainvire laughed, his gray eyes amused. "I'm like you. Muscle. I don't participate in politics anymore. I'm retired. You can see they're doing very well without me."

Poe's wavy Bacall hair kept obscuring her sight, and she constantly flipped her head to the left. Sainvire reached over and tucked her bangs behind her ears. The vampire hunter nearly lost her composure. "Don't do that."

"What?"

"Touch me," said Poe quietly.

Percy ended the awkward situation by running toward her. The girl had been helping with the food and missed Poe's entrance. "Poe!" The sisters hugged.

"Percy, I'm never leaving you again," said Poe, her voice breaking. "I'm sorry for neglecting you. I'll teach you everything I know, and we're

going to overdose on watching DVDs, alright?"
Percy's eyes watered, hugging Poe until tears
splotched the red dress.

The touching moment was curtailed when
Maple asked Poe to follow her to the corridor.
"Sorry for interrupting."

"That's alright. What can I do for you?"

"We have a situation," said the mallet-armed
vampire.

Poe nodded. She knew her place in the new
society. Like Sainvire said, she was muscle.
"Shoot."

"We have friends in Malibu. They've been in
contact with Sainvire since he rescued them from
vampire catchers nearly 20 years ago. The town is
quite large. Maybe 60 or 70, I believe, and that's
counting children."

"And?"

"Rogue vampires have been draining
members for three days now. The days of cattle
aren't over. The messenger only made it to us
several minutes ago."

Poe bit her lower lip. "I'll go home and get
dressed."

"Thank you, Poe. We estimate 14 vamps.
Two can fly, four are day vamps, and the rest we
don't know anything about. I assume you're
driving there?"

"Yeah. Maclemar's truck."

"The truck will only get you so far on the
Coast Highway. There's debris on the roads from
last winter's storms. You're going to need to ride

your Vespa, walk, and hike the rest of the way. You should leave at sunrise tomorrow."

Poe thought about Maple's suggestion and decided it was sound advice. She felt calmer, more level-headed. "Okay. Just draw me a map, and I'll take the scooter."

"Want some help?"

Poe shook her head. "I work alone, remember?" She thought of Sainvire whose memories were erased because he followed her to San Francisco. She needed to curb her impulsiveness.

"How many communities escaped the Vampire Council anyway? How many did Sainvire protect all those years?"

"About 12, Poe. Sainvire's frequent absences were from his visits to these holdout groups. He kept them from becoming cattle."

"Everybody knows this except me? That there's pockets of survivors who were lucky enough to keep their veins untouched?"

"Only a few of us know, Poe. We kept the information secret to safeguard their positions. Trench and the Council would've gone out of their way to steal those people for the food supply."

Poe nodded. Years ago in Koreatown she had met independent people who helped hide her after Quillon Trench bombed the Central Library. There were the West L.A. folks too. She wasn't the only one with a virgin neck after all. The extent of Sainvire's good works elevated him in her mind.

Maple laid her hand on the middle of Poe's back and led her back to the party. "Enjoy this day with your goddaughter, Poe. And if you haven't noticed, your friends have missed you." Poe heeded her friend's advice and shyly approached Piper who sat on a cushion, building a precarious house of Lego bricks.

"Can I play with you?" Poe asked. She was sitting cross-legged on the ground and realized her folly. She had exposed herself to the group of people surrounding her. Quickly she eased her position into a mermaid pose and pulled the dress material down to her knees. She cleared her voice to get the embarrassment out of it. "I'm a Lego expert. I can even make a dinosaur for you."

Piper looked up with awe on her face. "Really?"

"Sure. My brother and sister and I used to have competitions to see who can make the best figures. We had bins of this stuff."

"What's competition?" asked the child with Morales' eyes.

"That's when we try to outdo each other. Um. You know. Whoever builds the best building wins. Our mom and dad decided the winner."

"Okay. Make me dinoso," she ordered.

"Please," corrected Poe.

"Please," said the girl. Poe reached out to ruffle the girl's red hair. "Legos are supposed to make you smarter, you know, especially in math and logic."

"What's logic?"

"For crying out loud," Poe said under her breath and slapped her forehead. The kid wouldn't stop asking questions. Joseph leaned down and whispered in her ear, "Don't use big words you can't explain. You're doing fine so far. Good job."

Poe sighed as Morales, Joseph, Sainvire, and a few others hovered nearby. They were waiting to see if she was exaggerating about being able to put together a dinosaur. With deep concentration and a Buddha smile on her face, Poe chose appropriate blue and green tiles and assembled a Tyrannosaurus Rex. Within 20 minutes she handed a professionally made T-Rex to the smiling Piper.

"You awesome, Aunt Poe!" Piper exclaimed. She hugged Poe, and the vampire killer grinned.

"What else can you make, Poe?" asked Sainvire from a tiny toddler chair that looked ready to collapse.

"Yeah, Aunt Poe. What else?"

"Lots. Star Wars ships, boats, robots. Whatever you can think of. My mind figures out how to put them together."

"That's why you're so brilliant. You're a Lego nut," said a chuckling Joseph.

"I wouldn't discount it. That's why these kids should build Lego cities and learn how to read maps. We need geniuses."

"So you're saying you're a genius now?" asked Morales.

"Not a genius exactly," she said and met Sainvire's amused eyes. "Perhaps a prodigy." Poe's grin brought laughter in the circle.

"What's genius? What's pro-gidy?" asked Piper.

"I'll let you answer that, Sainvire," Poe said, rising to her feet. "You're good at explaining things. I've done my job here, dear friends. Time to knock out some chores."

The men watched as she left the room. "What bouncy hair she has. A real looker," said Morales, glancing at Sainvire.

"That she is," agreed Kaleb Sainvire. As if to himself, he said, "What I never knew about Poe was how shapely her legs are. She is a fine figure of a woman."

"Hell, you don't know anything about her," said Morales with a scowl. "Unless you're remembering?"

"No. I don't remember her at all." He glanced at Joseph. "I wish I did because she seems like a lovely woman."

Morales brushed an imaginary dandruff flake from his shoulder. "Funny how fate interferes so rudely in life. Poe was the woman you loved the most on this earth, and yet you don't remember a thing about her, and here you go talking about her legs. The saddest part is you remember monkeys like me and Joseph and whoever else you meet on the street. It's just too painful, man. I feel for Poe. Really I do."

At five in the morning a powder-blue Vespa was provided to her with a five-gallon emergency gas tank strapped to the back. Poe's pockets were bulging with clips for her two hand guns and a high-powered rifle was slung on her shoulder. A small pack containing more ammo, night vision goggles, dried food, and a half-gallon water jug was slung on her back. She felt so damn uncomfortable like she was bogged down by too many toys. *No choice. There are 14 of them.*

Joseph and Percy were the only ones to see her off. "I'll be there in no time. I just need to avoid landslides and rocks."

"Be careful, sis. We want you back by tomorrow," said Joseph. He gave her shoulders a squeeze.

"Yeah. Come back quickly," said Percy who reached out to pinch Poe's perky nose.

"Ouch!" she said. "I'll kill them all and be back for supper. You take care of Penny. She can hang out with Chops." Poe reached down and patted the balding liver-spotted head."

"Keep the speed between 20 to 30 miles an hour on the good roads. Otherwise stick to 10 miles an hour or less on the PCH. The cars and debris were never cleared up the coast."

Poe tried to be alert by sweeping her sights to points vulnerable to ambush, but her heart wasn't in it. How many humans were stupid enough to go on a solo hunt for 14 vampires? She wasn't infallible. She nearly died two years ago, and here she was, the same vacuum cleaner for Los Angeles.

Somehow this assignment bothered her. She knew she could die that day, and no one would even bother to find her remains. Everyone was busy with important tasks, and searching for her body would be a non-existent luxury.

Malibu was a beautiful seaside place with great ocean views. Her aunt had a mansion on top of a hill and often invited them to dinner and parties. Her husband was a pompous screenwriter who'd written nothing but nondescript rom-coms for springtime release.

Poe would watch surfers defy the waves keeping their footing despite devastating water surges. Movie stars dripped from the Malibu Colony area. During rainy seasons, landslides would block streets and teeter houses to the brink. In the summer brush fires would assault the beleaguered paradise and consume multimillion-dollar homes. Not even the water in custom swimming pools would help combat fire. But between the perilous seasons, the community of Malibu once thrived in its bikini-clad dreams of perfect living.

Poe remembered her brother and sister diving into the blue pool with mosaic tiles and feeling jealous. Her swimming classes were to start that summer, and she was peeved at her siblings who had better life skills than she. Clearly she could picture her mother wrapped in a sarong and comforting her, but Poe was stubborn and far from maudlin, of course. She harrumphed, jumped on her father's back, and tickled him. Her father was quite ticklish.

Riding on the scooter made her pensive from uncorking old memories. If it hadn't been for the Gray Armageddon, she would have graduated from college by then and spent every Christmas at home with her family. "What the hell are you?" she asked the wind. "Your poison ruined my life and the lives of the survivors. You let them reign, those bastard vampires."

Hours passed and Poe contemplated her life. The slow Vespa irked her, but she had no other choice. After exiting the Santa Monica Freeway, Poe made her way to the Pacific Coast Highway. Joseph had correctly assumed the highway that undulated along the Pacific Ocean was a mess. Mangled cars rusting on the road made the drive a challenge. Poe found herself driving five miles an hour because she had to zigzag around vehicles and avoid large rocks, metal shards, and mounds of dirt.

She had expected to arrive before noon, but the painful trek delayed her ETA. Twice she took a spill and scraped her elbow rather painfully. The third accident occurred when she wasn't vigilant enough to notice a sharp rock the size of a chicken blocking her way. The scooter slammed into a parked Cherokee and spun three times until it ejected Poe and cracked the drum of gasoline on the back of her Vespa.

"Fuck me!" Poe gritted and stood with difficulty. "Maybe I am going to die today." She straightened the Vespa, poured the rest of the petrol into the scooter into the fuel tank, and flung the container in anger. She studied her surroundings and inhaled fresh air tinged with gasoline. She was in over her head. One nail on the road would have left her stranded. "I'm so damn cocky, right, Sister Ann? I could've used some company, but I'm stupid enough to believe I can handle things on my own. Well I can't this time. I can't ever."

With her arm she wiped the tiny beads of sweat from her nose. "I never believed I was a superhero. I'm just a girl who's barely trying to make sense of the world. I can't even make sense of my own pathetic life."

Poe got on her Vespa and drove slowly through the debris with a promise to bring a team on future assignments. At 26 she was no spring chicken. She braked and turned to study the ocean. She blinked a couple times to double-check that a boat wasn't on the water like her peripheral vision had made her believe. The Chameleon, James Maclemar's ship, came to mind.

"I'm so sorry for getting you killed, James. I insisted on living away from Downtown, and you humored me. You were the nicest, most loyal person, and I'll never forget you. You're probably sick of hearing this, but forgive me for loving someone more than you. Thank you for your love and kindness. I'll always hold you dear in my heart," she whispered to the tides. She revved the Vespa and continued her journey.

The PCH mess set her back. She arrived at a forked road leading to the top of the hill where the community compound was supposed to be located. Apparently they lived on a 60-acre property. The California contemporary house built by the famous architect, D'Aury, was kept as a meeting hall while bungalows in chic designs surrounded the house. The ongoing threat of vampire visits kept them close-knit.

"Four day vamps, two flying vamps, and the rest standard issue vampires," Poe said under her breath. "Gotta get rid of them first then kill the sleeping vampires." She left her scooter behind a tree and hiked up the mountain. "Plenty of time. The sun sets later in the summer," she assured herself.

A blur of movement flashed by her. The creature wasn't as fast as Joseph because she could see the outline of his back. The creature was running away. Calmly Poe unsheathed her Rambo knife and hurled it at the back of the day vamp. The vampire dropped face-down. The knife pierced the golden-tanned creature in the heart. Poe walked over to him and pulled out her knife. She wiped the glop on the creature's faded jeans and resheathed the knife.

It's a nice 75 degrees out here, Poe thought randomly. *Why the hell was he running down the mountain like he was getting chased by the chupacabras? Only one way to find out.*

Poe ran up the steep hill and was glad to know she was still in shape. She reached the top where a driveway began and an eight-foot high silver gate blocked the entrance. The lock was open and she slid inside the gate with her Beretta in her grip. She was sweating but only on her nose.

She heard laughter and at least 30 voices. Her heart went cold. Maple said there were 14 rogue vampires, and now she was hearing more than double the number. *I should've brought a team.*

A boy of about 14 years came out from behind a 5,000-gallon above-ground propane tank and pointed a gun at her. Poe wanted to laugh at the absurdity of a kid threatening her life. He reminded her of herself. "Look, boy. I'm here to help."

"Put your guns on the ground. Walk straight ahead," said the squinty boy with an unbelievably dark putty tan that hid even his freckles.

"I'm Julia Poe, kid, sent by the Los Angeles Council, and I'm not giving up my weapons," she said with a tight smile. To be killed by a pre-pubescent little boy would have been fitting.

"I know your name. You have the scar. Follow me," he said.

And there they were, more than 70 of them sitting by the pool, sunning themselves and talking animatedly. Nine gurneys lining the pool area contained catatonic recently bitten humans. They were sleep tanning as well, it seemed to Poe. 13 bodies, killed cleanly, lay in a pile like old garbage as children swam in the tremendous Roman-style pool replete with Doric columns.

So that's what these privileged folks do while regular folks suffer. The rich keep their decadent lifestyle while everyone else fights rape, anemia, abuse, and what have you. She seethed but told herself that she would've wanted such a life if it had been presented to her rather than drinking rainwater and eating from expired cans of yams in an underground bunker.

"Oh there she is," said a woman that looked like Goldie Hawn riddled with wrinkles. She was as dark as a fresh turd. She must have been 40, but she easily looked like she was 60. She was wearing a tank top, shorts, and flip flops. "Hello there, Miss Poe!"

Poe looked around with alarm. Tribe of Too-Much-Sun confounded her, scared her. "What's going on?" she said, taking some effort to speak.

"All of them are dead, dear," said Goldie. "You missed the fun by an hour. A day vamp escaped, but that'll be taken care of later."

"Was he tan like a weatherman?"

"Why yes!"

"He's taken care of."

"Oh my. You're just like how he described you. Thank you. Thank you!"

Poe still had the Beretta in her hand, and her grip was wilting. "Who's he?"

Goldie pointed with her chin at a man lounging on a lawn chair and sipping white liquid decorated with a pink miniature umbrella. He was surrounded by teenage girls and adult women. "Jesus, Mary, and Joseph," said Poe under her breath. Suddenly their eyes met, his light gray eyes resonating with the reflection of the pool. Poe broke contact and slipped the Beretta in her sheath. Without saying goodbye to Goldie, she walked hastily away, slamming the gate and nearly running down the hill past the golden corpse along the way. The vampire waited by the Vespa with a culpable look on his face.

Poe ignored him and continued walking to the street until she crossed the highway and stepped onto the sandy beach. She stopped when the water was nearly touching her boots. She unslung the backpack and procured a water bottle. She took a long draught and capped the lid. Only then did she turn to Kaleb Sainvire, the man who knew nothing about her.

"I'm glad you handled things, Sainvire," she said matter-of-factly. She saw him sit beside her from the corner of her left eye. "I was out of my league. Next time I'm bringing backup."

Sainvire was surprised. Everyone mentioned the fury Julia Poe could unleash when annoyed. Instead the woman sat straight back and gazed calmly at the blue ocean. "I'll be your backup," he said, laying his thick hands on his knee.

"Because you're muscle, too?"

"That and because I love you." He stared into her brown eyes when she turned to look at him.

Poe laughed a powerful belly laugh that shook her shoulders. "You don't have to say that because everyone keeps telling you that you used to love me. Seriously, I'm over you."

Sainvire rubbed his temple as if he had a headache. "I hope that's not the case because I've never been over you."

Poe's laughing eyes flickered and became serious once more. "You remember?"

"I never forgot."

"What do you mean?"

"I willed those bullets not to leave my temple, Poe. I pretended I was dead. You nearly ruined my grand plan by delaying a burial. It was damn hard to keep those bullets from popping out for the 11 days you kept me above."

The old Poe would've become furious, but the new Poe forced herself to listen. She studied the scar on his upper lip and felt a pang of hope. "Why?"

"Because of you," said Sainvire simply. "Time and time again, I made you my last priority because of circumstances that forced me to choose between one person and many. I told myself that you will never get hurt again and I will never abandon you.

"People and other beings have become too reliant on me. They think I can save them all. They think I can solve everything instead of taking care of problems themselves. Many had reservations that they wouldn't be able to run a government without me. They wanted me to be president, head council, or what have you. I never liked politics, yet I was always thrust in the middle."

"When you were gone our lives ran smoothly with very few bumps," said Poe, understanding. "You wanted to show them that they can lead a democracy without your help."

Sainvire took Poe's small hand and massaged it lightly. "You visited me everyday. You read to me. You talked to me about your childhood and your parents and sang Pixies songs to me. And you told me how good Maclemar was. Each day you reminded me that you loved me and that you knew I was alive. Lying in a tomb is no picnic, especially because I was biding my time. Many times I was so sick of the dark and the cramped space that I wanted to punch a hole through the marble. But then I'd hear your voice, unfailingly, for three hours a day. Sometimes you'd nap on your lawn chair and I would listen to your breathing."

Poe bit her lip then said snidely. "I knew you weren't dead. Julia Poe is almost always right, you see."

"I see," said Sainvire. He wrapped an arm about her shoulders. "I told Joseph about my plan a couple of months ago. And now you. My secret will remain. I will be the dodgy, perhaps incompetent master vampire returned from the dead. I'll take muscle jobs with you as my partner. We'll protect each other. And most of all we'll always be together."

Poe reached for his neck and brought his mouth down to hers. They kissed softly then with passion. When their lips parted, Kaleb said, "I promise never to leave you again, Julia Poe. I promise you will be first in everything."

The vampire killer couldn't help but cry, and she covered her face with her hands. It had been a long road, and the world had changed before her eyes. She could not deny that she had a big hand in the changes, and so did Kaleb Sainvire. But they'd given every ounce of their spirit, and it was time for the two underground resistance fighters to live their lives.

The lovers held hands like they were holding onto dear life, waiting for the infamous Southern California sun to set.

The End